DL Havlin

Turtle Point

In The Iron Lady
Mystery/Suspense Series
Book 1

Palm Pe

Palm Pen Press
ISBN: 978-1-933678-16-0

Turtle Point
Copyright © 2018 DL Havlin
Library of Congress Catalogue
Fiction, novel – United States, Bokeelia, FL
Mystery/Suspense, Mainstream, Literary

Front Cover artwork and/or photography produced
by Palm Pen Press.

Dedication

Dedicated to the scientists who actually do their best to preserve our world, not the ones who use ecology as a weapon for advancing extremist political ideologies.

AND

Dedicated to the hard working humans who actually do something to preserve our world, the ones who patrol beaches to protect sea turtle nests and all the rest that do similar deeds to protect wildlife. This definitely does NOT include rectal apertures that fly their private jets to Audubon & Sierra Club meetings and exterminate any natural thing that causes them the slightest inconvenience in their personal lives.

DL Havlin

Acknowledgments

For years I read acknowledgments in books with little or no appreciation of what they represented. After over twenty years of writing, I read them with understanding and reverence. Anyone who writes has had others make contributions to their successes and mitigate their failures. I've benefitted greatly from *many* peoples' assistance in *many* different ways.

I owe a continuing debt of gratitude to my mentor/editors, Robert Fulton, Ph.D., Who forged some raw material into a writer, and Babs Brown who has been, and continues to be my writings watch-dog, barking loud and long when my work lacks in any area. Authors Bev Browning and Robert B. Parker, agents Mary Sue Seymour and Anne Hawkins provided me with encouragement when my confidence was waning and kept me at the keyboard.

Special thanks to Taylor & Seale, who publishes many of my books and to its Editor-in-chief, Mary Custureri, Ph.D. Mary's stellar resume in support of the written word is unparalleled. Her belief in my work and encouragement is supremely appreciated. V.H. Hart, patient editor, and muse has positively impacted my work as have true publishing professionals Bob Zaslow and Jan Kardys. I'd like to express my thanks to Rebecca Melvin, my editor for previous publications who staunchly supported my writing.

I've been blessed with many excellent "test pilot readers" during my career. The list has grown too long to mention them all, but there are several that have been with me for a long time: Chet Collins, Linda Kay Solinger, Paul Owens, Carol Robb, Nancy

Rogge, Gloria Andrews, Linda Hilliard, and Pat Cole who don't spare criticism or praise...if it's earned.

Finally, I reserve my largest, most heartfelt thank you for my loving wife, partner and do all assistant— Jeanelle. Without her support, encouragement, understanding, and tolerance I'd have abandoned writing long ago.

Preface

A word about sea turtles and their place in this novel...

Sea turtles have seniority. Some species have been swimming the oceans for 150 million years...that's 85 million years before the dinosaurs became extinct. Humans, from antiquity until the present, have harbored fascination for these creatures. Our species interest in these inoffensive creatures varies from curiosity, to worship, to use as a food source. Like characters in this novel, many humans love them. We see this fascination manifested in curios on shelves, jewelry, wall ornaments, paintings, even on tee shirts. Maybe this fascination comes from the fact that we can see them; they're hard to miss...the smallest species weighs a hundred pounds. Maybe it is because we know so little about sea turtles with one exception and that is nesting. Ironically the portion of their lives sea turtles go to the most pains to keep secret, a mystery from the rest of nature, is the part we humans know most about. It is equally ironic that humans and sea turtles share a trait...they bury things they wish to remain undiscovered.

This common "burying" instinct allows me to introduce my mystery novel, *Turtle Point*, and add a kernel of knowledge for my readers, in this case about sea turtles. I believe readers are thinkers, they're folks who have knowledge, are always looking to obtain more, they use it, and they provide leadership and rationale for those who don't. By passing along a few ecological facts, it helps frame my novel and provides you, who read *Turtle Point,* information to fill a few brain cells with info you may not have known...even if the information's best use is in a trivia contest.

Sea turtles colors vary from black and dark green to

brown and yellow. Depending on the species, adults weigh from 100 (Kemps Ridley) to over a 1,000 pounds (Leatherback). Most live in elliptical or heart-shaped shells two to four feet in length. They are solitary animals, spending most of their lives drifting the oceans. These creatures are harmless to all, except beach developers who wish to destroy their nesting grounds and are prohibited from doing so by law. This member of the reptile family eats seagrasses, jellyfish, mollusks, and crabs to survive. They aren't anyone's environmental competitor. They gather for mating and nesting...that's all.

The sea turtle that provides the starting point for this novel is the most commonly seen in Southwest Florida waters: The Loggerhead. Like other sea turtles, we know little about this creature because the animals live almost all of their adulthood at sea. We do know *some* things about them. They migrate over large distances from feeding to nesting grounds. Some Loggerheads travel from Japan to Baja, California. The males rarely, if ever, return to land after their births. Sea turtles may live to over a hundred years, but don't reach sexual maturity until they're from fifteen to fifty. Despite their awkward appearance, sea turtles are graceful swimmers. They live in tropical and subtropical waters. Turtles can stay submerged for long periods; Green Turtles stay down as long as five hours and can control their heartbeat, so it only contracts once in nine minutes. We know little about their behavior past this, with the exception of their nesting.

Most nesting takes place at night on sandy beaches where humans can observe them. That's why we know more about this portion of sea turtle behavior than any other. People like the central characters in this novel study and protect these creatures.

The beaches that serve as the setting for this mystery are located on Southwest Florida's coast. The warm, white barrier islands' sands of Cayo Costa and North Captiva are perfect incubators for eggs the turtles will lay. Females frequently return to the place they were born, often coming ashore within yards of their birthplace. Scientists marvel at this navigational ability. Some turtles travel 3,000 miles before returning to nest. Researchers believe that sea turtles can "read" magnetic signals emitted from the earth. A good way to describe this return home and nesting is to accompany a mother Loggerhead turtle as she follows her instincts on a night like the one when our story begins.

This turtle is returning to her ancestor's beach. She serenely paddles through the Gulf of Mexico's warm, moon-lit water toward the sound of gentle waves that push against Cayo Costa's white sands. This beach has remained unspoiled by human intrusion and exploitation. Her kind has visited this beach for millions of years. It is her time to perpetuate her species. Cayo Costa and Florida's southwest coastal barrier islands are premier nesting grounds for Loggerhead turtles. The tiny spit of sand she approaches derives its name from the visitations of her species.

She'd been born on the same small point where she will drag her 250-pound body from the water. Encased in its three-foot, brown-yellow, heart-shaped shell, the turtle will require all its strength to complete its reproductive ritual. Unlike her land-living brethren who can retreat into their hard casing, a sea turtle's shell doesn't provide defense for her head and flippers. Scars on her back and rear flippers had been inflicted by a predator like a tiger shark. Still, she was the lucky one-in-a-thousand hatchlings that survived to reproduce. Loggerhead sea turtles don't mature sexually until they reach seventeen and only lay eggs every two or three years. This is her third trip "home." She'd returned to the beach two weeks before to lay a hundred eggs. She'll make this trip up the beach and two more in two-week intervals before she leaves.

Her life at sea is perilous, but the dangerous excursion she's on now is worse for she is practically immobile and defenseless once she leaves the water. Hogs, raccoons, coyotes, dogs and many other animals might attack her including her biggest enemy, man. Laboriously, she digs her flippers into the beach sand and propels her shell, sliding it up to, and above, the high-tide line. She finds a spot in the sand she likes and digs a hole the size of a very large bucket to serve as an incubator and a safe-haven for her young until they hatch. When the hole is complete, she starts laying her eggs.

Droplets of moisture appear in her eyes. Many people believe turtles cry as they give birth. They aren't aware the turtle's lachrymal glands, located next to the eyes, maintain the animal's osmotic balance by removing excess salt from the creature's system and releasing it in droplets of water. Her tears are biologically induced. Instinct and body chemistry, not emotion, govern her.

Because of instinct, the Loggerhead mother, goes into a trance-like state, taking no notice of events around her. This includes humans if they are present. Humans should trigger a response. Humans destroy places where turtles nest, kill thousands as a by-product of their fishing practices, and, in many places, humans hunt their eggs and turtles to eat. The sea turtle remains oblivious of distractions. She concentrates on her imperative: she *must* lay her eggs.

The Loggerhead concentrates on her rhythmic effort to fill her nest. Each egg is dropped carefully into the pit with enough time between each "birth" for the eggs to settle into a safe position. The eggs are soft when dropped and soon solidify. She will not be hurried. If necessary, she will die in the act.

When the turtle finishes, she carefully covers the nest with sand. She hides it to foil numerous predators who try to solve the mystery: Where are her eggs buried? Raccoons, foxes, hogs, crabs, snakes, rats, birds, coyotes, and more will feast on the delicacy if they find them. If the eggs survive their incubation, the hatchlings will face all those and a new list of predators when they leave the nest and reach the Gulf. The mother turtle will be powerless to help. She must quickly return to the ocean for her own survival. The Loggerhead leaves the nest, trusting nature's cruel rules to select the offspring that will survive.

Nature normally does what it can to help the turtles conceal their secrets. Rains wash away the turtle's scent and that of the buried eggs. Despite the summer's cooling rain, the temperature of the sand remains warm and favorable for good hatching. Eighty-five-degree temperatures mean an equal number of the baby turtles will be male and female. Warmer, more eggs will become females; cooler, more males. Nature occasionally sends a storm and high tides to destroy a whole generation before the first embryo emerges or an insect infestation that can burrow beneath the ground to eat all the eggs.

If the turtle's secret is successfully cloaked, in sixty days over a hundred hatchlings will scurry to the beckoning sea. Mother Loggerhead's impact on the future is contained in the lives of those hatchlings.

The cycle of life continues.

Human ambivalence toward these simple, harmless creatures furnishes the match that ignites this novel's plot. Flames are formed by a clash of those who wish to exploit sea turtles and those who wish to protect them. The turtle's reproductive process, previously described, provides the incentives that place the humans harboring these different objectives in the same location at the same time. Brief interaction between these humans is the match that lights two fuses. One explodes immediately with lethal results. The other smolders on into an unknown future.

Unlike the turtle whose actions are guided by instinct, human actions are conscious decisions, rational or rash. A moment's rash action can be a stern compass guiding a life into an endless future of regret. What happens on the sands of Turtle Point produces this effect and, in addition, it impacts the lives of people thousands of miles away who will see the results thirty years in the future. A secret is born and needs protecting. And, the sea turtles continuing presence and eternal need to reproduce at this spot hides the secret.

Chapter 1
Cayo Costa Island
June 27, 1980

"How do you know they are gone, Señor Cole?" The man speaking carried a large double bladed ax. He was short, stockily built and was heavily muscled. He swatted at the mosquitoes buzzing around his perspiring body.

"They're gone." Lifting a bottle of liquor to his lips, the tall, thin, unshaven man took a gulp and then extended the tequila to his partner as they walked down the dark beach. Moonlight illuminated their footprints before the waves rushed over and erased them.

"You are sure?" The first man took the bottle from his companion. "I no want to go to jail."

"The bitch is gone back to Miami. She told me she was leavin' today when I was still bringin' her out here ... before that boy started doing it. Ain't no reason for her boyfriend to come out here if'n she ain't." Swinging at the bugs swarming around his face, the second man said, "We've done lost a month of the season. I got restaurants wanting turtle meat. We need to kill and butcher three tonight to catch up with orders. You can hunt eggs while I'm finishing the cutting. We need to get after it if we're gonna get that done."

"Is a lot of work."

The thin man stopped and peered down the beach. He pointed at something in front of them. "There's one heading back for the water. She's laid her eggs, and they'll be easy to find. Run down there and kill her and I'll find her nest."

The two men sprinted down the beach, intent on killing the turtle and stealing her eggs.

Chapter 2
Cayo Costa Island, Florida
June 27, 1980

"I was afraid of this." The girl knelt at the side of a hole the size of a small wash tub dug in the sand. The moonlight was bright enough to disclose a number of broken egg shells discarded around the excavated nest and to reveal the very feminine curves of the lady examining the hole. "Do you have a flashlight?"

"No, they're in the boat."

"I hate to ask, but I have to see how much damage they did." The girl was choked up as she spoke.

"I don't know. I don't like leaving you here. We don't know if these people are still around." The young man was concerned about his companion's safety. He relented. "You stay away if they show up, okay?"

"Yes, but I don't believe there's anyone around. The fluid from the broken eggs is dry. This was probably done last night." The girl gently lifted a mashed egg and put it back in the robbed nest.

"You shouldn't be here alone. Whoever did this might be dangerous. Go back with me; it won't take but a half hour." The young man wasn't convinced; he didn't want to leave her.

"It's a half hour we don't have. Remember, I have to catch a bus. I'll be perfectly safe. You haven't seen anyone, have you?"

"No."

"So, there's nothing to worry about. Besides, I think I know who did this. I can scare him off if he shows up."

"Hell, no! I won't—"

"Okay. You win. I'll hide if anybody shows. Now, will you run?" The urgency in her voice made him acquiesce.

"I'll be back as quick as I can." The boy raced toward his boat.

The woman rose. Her feminine outline painted in a dull gray suggestion against the white beach sand; she began examining nearby nests. Inaudible mumblings of shock and disgust came from her as she viewed the carnage inflicted by others. Her examination of nests brought her closer to two men who were objects of her anger.

Chapter 3
Cayo Costa Island, Florida
June 27, 1980

"There's another one," said the man's unshaven shadow. The two predators struggled through the beach surf, dragging the heavy corpse of a turtle, using the water to ease the effort required to move their load. He looked at a Loggerhead turtle who had drug her body up the beach to a point above the high tide line. She continued to lay her eggs undeterred by their intrusion. "We'll get her after we start getting' this one butchered. She's just started laying eggs. We got time. After we get the shell off the one we already killed, you put the ax to her and get her eggs. Let's drag this one up in the bushes right here." They were less than ten strides from the Loggerhead.

The man's companion muttered "Si," and groaned as they dragged the dead turtle up the beach's incline. That man was there to gather the eggs his culture believed was an aphrodisiac. He'd sell them at an inflated price so he could purchase tequila to replace the almost empty bottle he held in his other hand.

The two men alternately huffed and cursed as they hauled their bloody load past the large sand dune that crested the gentle bulge in the shoreline local residents called, "Turtle Point." They disappeared into the island's dark interior. As they made their way into the underbrush, the woman who had been examining nests followed them.

A minute later, the faint light of a lantern came from a low line of cabbage palms, sea-grapes, and scrub oaks behind the beach. While the mother turtle performed her duty, the men worked in silence as they prepared to dismember one of her sisters. Suddenly, the sound of a vitriolic confrontation rose. It intensified rapidly. Accusations and warnings were followed by the sound of a shovel repeatedly smashing flesh with a faint, quick, feminine scream interspersed. A panicked discussion between the two men shrouded behind the dimly lit underbrush and night's curtain was followed by the sound of shovels digging in the sand. Curses and grunts punctuated the grave-diggers chorus. It grew quiet again.

The sounds of combat renewed. A scream of fury was followed by the sounds of blows delivered by an instrument of death. The victims uttered sounds of pain and terror. There was begging, but no quarter. The assailant completed his deadly work. After mere moments the grave digging resumed, at a more frantic rate, but this time all sounds came from a single shovel. A shovel propelled by panic, desperation, and fear. Both the unseen human and the mother turtle completed their tasks of covering the night's work simultaneously. Both the turtle and human wished to create an unsolvable mystery to protect their secrets. When the Loggerhead struggled back down the beach to the Gulf's warm waters and relative safety, the turtle's concerns ended. Simultaneously, a human's concerns began with no vision or hope of their termination.

The turtle buried its secret to preserve her species. The human buried a secret that was to hide new death, not new life. Unlike the turtle, which would leave with a clear conscience, the person who would throw shovels and other evidence into Pine Island Sound, would not. In fact, the "guilty" person only knew part of the "secrets" buried during the night's dark happenings.

Nature favored the human. Rains washed away blood and its scent. A lightning strike burnt the burial area masking the smell of decay with heavy wood-smoke. Wildcats took up residence near the fire site, discouraging the appearance of raccoons, pigs, possums, and other creatures which might dig deep enough to unearth the victims. The rainy season increased the population of "swamp angels," the voracious salt marsh mosquitoes, which kept humans far away.

A hundred yards away from where the Loggerhead struggled back down to the Gulf's warm waters, the surviving human pushed a frail plywood boat from the shore as far as he could wade and shoved it seaward. Eyeing coming storms, the human fervently hoped the small craft would make a voyage to oblivion. Both mysteries were secure for a time. The turtle's secret remained cloaked as long as needed...until its eggs hatched. The human's secret would have to last a lifetime and ....

Chapter 4
Columbia University's Library,
New York City,
June 27, 1980

.... survive another human's scrutiny. Such scrutiny would come as a by-product of a man's search to learn another secret, a secret that literally held the key to unimaginable wealth. In fact, it was the wealth of a nation. A young assistant professor sat in Columbia University's library, the table in front of him stacked with books, records, articles, microfiche cases, old newspapers, and old magazines. All the records and media were focused on his area of expertise: European history immediately before, during, between, and after the two World Wars.

Most professors supplemented their incomes by using their knowledge to write a book, lecture, or offer their services to those who needed their specialized knowledge. Arthur Heller had acquired the reputation of being a genius when it involved locating "lost people and possessions" that disappeared in the chaos surrounding World War II and its aftermath. This reputation proved to be very lucrative, both in locating persons and things and remaining quiet about some individuals who did not wish to be found. Ex-Nazis and fascists paid handsome "fees" not to be unearthed. It was while doing work for a family rumored to have mafia connections that Heller made a discovery he would pursue for the rest of his life. Arthur Heller was excited; he'd narrowed his search.

He rubbed his hand over an old newspaper

article at the precise time, 1,000 miles South, the Loggerhead mother deposited the final egg in her nest. The UPI article, dated April 1945, was written by a war correspondent named James L. Roper and related the details of Mussolini, his mistress, and sixteen of his close associates executions by Italian partisans. "It is probably in Mezzegra or Dongo, but I'm sure it never made it to Switzerland." Heller pondered for a minute. "It could be stashed anywhere from Rome to those towns on the Swiss border." Heller's research had discovered *what* Mussolini had stolen and claimed for his personal treasure. It was an immense sum. None of the famous artifacts that were stolen had surfaced after their disappearance in 1943. They hadn't to the present time, thirty-seven years later. Surely, one of the famous missing Monet's would have appeared on some museum's wall or at an auction if the treasure had been discovered. In all, it was worth *billions*.

It would be difficult to find the last pieces to the puzzle. He knew what and who he needed to find. Finding them might take half a lifetime. It would be worth every second. He spoke to the old newspaper article, "I know you left it for me somewhere, sitting in a dark corner, hiding—"

"Damn, Arty, most of your students think you're crazy already. You start talking to your research, and they'll call you the nutty professor for sure." One of Heller's peers had walked up behind Heller and teased him good-naturedly.

Heller smiled and said, "That's alright, Fred. You can officially declare me insane on..." he looked at the calendar, "June 27, 1980..........."

Chapter 5
Subic Bay Naval Station, Philippines
June 27, 1980

..............."June 27, 1980." That was the first scribble Harper Sturgis put on the letter she addressed to her father. It was her second "after-action" report written about her first combat. Harper considered it more important than the one she'd prepared for her intelligence unit's CO. Her father, Sterling Sturgis, began training her for what transpired the previous seventy-two hours when he'd put an M-1 Garand in her hand at the age of ten and explained that it was a rifle, not a gun. Her note was addressed to the Paris Island Marine Depot where her father was still a DI turning the raw material the Corps furnished him into rugged and proud Marines.

She tried to isolate herself in the corner of the bar where her Marine brethren were celebrating their mission's completion. More correctly, they rejoiced surviving combat that could have taken their lives. Harper's preference would have been to be sacked out in her bunk at the base. The reason she was in that bar wasn't to let off steam, get drunk, or to chase the opposite sex as was the objectives of most of the Marines who'd accompanied her on the mission. Harper was there because, as an officer, she saw the importance of taking every opportunity to increase *esprit de corps* within her unit. This was a chance to do that. In Harper's mind, that included maintaining a closer than "normal" relationship to enlistees. She didn't fear her actions would bring negative responses. Harper simply didn't fear.

Her gender made her an exception and a bug under the microscope. She was an experiment, a product of General Margaret Brewer's thoughts on how to best use women Marines. A first. Pulled from the Embassy guard program, her aptitude for intelligence, Marine Corp pedigree, toughness, and NFL linebacker temperament made her a natural Guinea Pig. Harper's attitude was to shoot a bird at those who looked through the lens to find a failure. She'd be the model Marine, a true credit to the Corps, and she'd do it her way.

"Hi, Miss Jar Head." The hulking form of a naval ensign stood next to her table. His crooked smile, watery eyes, and slight sway were tell-tale signs the man had liquor in him. Harper looked up at him with a poker-faced expression she was cultivating. She stared into his pupils for several seconds trying to communicate her disdain and rejection before returning her focus on her letter. The man chose to ignore her message. Several of her fellow Marines became silent spectators.

"You aren't a friendly sort, are you?" The ensign wasn't about to give up on what he saw as a potential bed partner. "What'll make you friendlier?"

"Shove off, Swabbie." Harper didn't look up.

"Come on, sugar. Must be something. God didn't give you those big boobs and them long legs you got hid under your fatigues for nothing."

"You're drunk. Go back to your bunk and have a date with Mary Five-fingers." Harper dropped the pen from her hand, and the shape of her fist changed slightly.

"Why should I do that? I got me a pussy sitting here with legs long enough to wrap around me with enough left over to tie a bow knot." Then the ensign made one of the big mistakes he'd ever make. He reached out and rubbed Harper's shoulder.

The pussy instantly changed into a very large jungle cat that attacked with the dispassionate expression of an animal selecting a meal. Her table crashed over as Harper rose into a crouch. In the same series of motions, she drove her fist into his solar-plexus, grabbed his arm, twisted and thrust it up behind him, placed her other hand behind his head and drove his face down into the table next to hers. Blood from his nose and mouth colored in the white checkered spaces on the tablecloth under the sailor's head. As she held him bent over the table, Harper swung her other hand up under his crotch, grasped, crushed, and twisted his testicles. The ensign wretched twice before adding a mixture of vomited beer and pizza on the tablecloth. The bar patrons hooted and hollered their cheers.

Harper maintained her grips on the unfortunate "squid" as she pointed him to the bar's door and shoved him stumbling and groaning to the exit. The poker face remained as she bent over and whispered calmly in the man's ear, "If you ever come near me again, I'll tear your balls off, and I'll feed them to you, understand?" She shoved him through the door, held open by a Marine comrade, onto the sidewalk outside.

Harper walked slowly back to her table, set it upright, retrieved her pen and paper, then looked around the bar for additional challenges. There were none, only salutes from her friends. Harper straightened her fatigues, sat down and began to write.

~ ~ ~ ~ ~

Dad,

The first one is over. My report to you is your favorite para-phrase of Caesar's bromide. "We came, we saw, we kicked ass." I'm thankful that you prepared me for what

I'd be confronted with when the shooting started. The education I received at the academy and the training at Quantico all were important, but the things you told me about how I, and those around me, might react under fire were indispensable. Major MacPhee, who ran the show, would benefit from a heart-to-heart with you.

I ran into the problem you said I'd probably encounter, the woman thing. MacPhee told me not to go on the attack; to do my assessment after the fighting. I told him I couldn't do what my CO assigned me if I sat until it was over. Part of my responsibility was assessing guerilla reaction under fire. I told him I could handle combat as well as anyone in the group; I was a Marine and that was my job. Since I'd beaten the shit out of most of my mates on the judo mats, with a pugil stick, at bayonet drills, and on the range, they supported me. I took your advice and told him I'd relocate his balls if he didn't let me go, but in a slightly less insubordinate manner. It's a good thing I went. I knew and understood the op plans a hell of a lot better than he did.
The Philippine jungle isn't that different than the thicker swamps around Camp Lejeune, so I felt right at home. When we approached the communist weapons dump, everything was close to what our intel and maps showed. MacPhee was going to march right up to a few hundred clicks then send out flanking positions. The maps had "unmanned" bunkers and MG emplacements marked along the trails and the orders called to send recon teams out as an option. The Philippine government intelligence sources said to expect around twenty guerillas defending the weapons.

Everything I'd ever seen on this enemy said we'd walk into a beehive, they aren't that careless. I suggested we outflank the trail we were going to use and send a small point group up the path, but let it lag behind the flankers.

MacPhee didn't think it was necessary. Twenty guerillas were easy to over-power. He said he didn't want to lose morale by making everybody crawl through jungle and get bitten up by insects. I asked him if they'd lose more moral if they got bitten up by mosquitoes or stitched with machine gun fire. He didn't like that coming from a 2ⁿᵈ Luey.

I said it in front of Captain Waldron and Waldron said he'd prefer the mosquito bites. It pissed MacPhee off, but we sent out the recon teams and it was a hell of a good thing we did. Most of the bunkers and machine gun nests were occupied. The twenty enemy turned out to be right at a hundred. We didn't stay around to get an accurate body count. We thought we'd have a four to one numerical superiority. We ended up being the smaller force. No problem. The Marines were superb as always.

Above all else, I fully understand your sermons on emotional decisions being bad ones. I saw three examples. Worrying about the men's discomfort with bug bites was one. That could have killed a third of us.

One of the platoon leaders decided to attack a couple bunkers that had supporting fields of fire. We could have by-passed them and simply pinned them in place until we finished. It was a mess. Of the nine troops we lost, seven were killed there. Stupid. We ended up by-passing the positions anyway.

MacPhee insisted we give the guerrillas an opportunity to surrender even after two groups faked giving up and then tried to kill us with grenades and pistol fire. Waldron said, "Yes, sir," and told his men to toss a few grenades in the bunkers and emplacements then ask for surrendering troops. We didn't lose another Marine.

*I should be state-side in three or four weeks. I know you
don't like long letters so I'll save the rest. I hope to see
you then.*

Semper Fi
Harper

~ ~ ~ ~ ~

Harper folded the letter and stuck it in an
envelope. She looked at her hand. Many of her
buddies who had been in combat told her there was
an after-effect you experienced following your first
firefight. Shaking hands, guilt, nervousness,
insecurity, and other symptoms they'd described
didn't afflict her. Even killing the enemy for the first
time didn't bother her as she supposed it should.
They were trying to kill her, so it wasn't difficult to
level her M-16 at a guerilla's head and squeeze off a
couple of shots.

Harper was a Marine. They excelled at man's art-
form—killing. It was her job. She'd do it to the best
of her ability. She wouldn't allow herself to lose or
even consider that possibility. Her mother, Colleen,
would have been repulsed by her daughter's
thoughts. Colleen, a Ph.D. and medical researcher at
Duke, died of radiation poisoning when Harper was
still in her early teens. Harper inherited her
mother's high IQ. Colleen named her daughter for
her favorite author and told Harper that Atticus
Finch was a person to emulate. To a degree, Harper
did. She adopted the *To Kill A Mockingbird*
character's devotion to emotional control, logic,
detail, principle, and duty. The rest of her was pure
Patton. Feelings inherited from her mother were in
her, but Harper refused to acknowledge them.

When she stretched her six-foot-three-inch body
into bed that night, her thoughts would not be on

the two men she killed. Or, the bar fight that already exited her mind. It would be on how to improve on her next assignment and what she could do to prepare to be a lawyer, the profession she'd chosen to pursue after she retired from the Corps. Harper always thought ahead, way ahead.

Chapter 6
Thirty years later, Pine Island, Florida
May 2010

"You going out there tonight?" Mac asked.

"Yes." Benny looked at his friend. They'd had the same conversation a hundred times, maybe even a thousand. He saved his friend the effort. "You can't."

"That's a hell of a way to treat a friend." Mock anger and disappointment clouded Billy MacCardle's face.

It was a ritual. Mac asked, Benny refused. They both smiled. The walls in MacCardle's office had heard the instant replay too many times to show interest. The two friends eyed each other mischievously. The redundancy was a clue to a common trait, stubbornness.

Mac knew and accepted his ecologically minded friend's eccentricity. The Green and Loggerhead turtles that climbed the Florida West Coast beaches on summer nights were sacred to the man who sat across the desk from him. His friend, Benedict "Benny" Barron Dupree, was a logical, reasonable, and intelligent man in all matters except for his slavish devotion to the preservation of one of nature's most benign creations. He protected them and their nesting place, a strip of beach property he'd purchased at great cost to himself. Benny Dupree defended both fiercely.

That nesting ground, Turtle Point, is located on Cayo Costa, an isolated island a few strips of palm encrusted sand above Sanibel on Florida maps. The thirty acres belonging to Dupree were one of the few land parcels not owned by the State of Florida. State holdings were part of Cayo Costa Park. Only a half-dozen strips of land remained in private hands. Most of those had agreements that sold the property to the state government after the owner's death. Cayo Costa was nature's oasis in the desert of human development created on southwest Florida's coastline.

The island remained pristine because it was only accessible by boat. No private vehicles were on the island. It remained much as it was when the Spanish "discovered it" and when the Calusa Indians, who ruled it as part of their domain for two thousand years before the conquistadors arrived, lived there. Dupree's land was far from the park's developed portion. If you called erecting chain link fencing to keep other humans away from Turtle Point's sands an intrusion on nature, Benny was the island's main despoiler.

Houses were built on private lands on Cayo Costa's southern tip. One of many wars fought by Benny to protect the property, and his beloved turtles involved his building the fence. Neither the state nor the few south end island residents viewed his barbed wire topped, six foot high, chain-link "monstrosity" as a good thing. But, he declared all thirty acres a wildlife sanctuary and vowed to never develop the ground. Benny challenged others to do the same. Both adversaries collapsed and, as usual, Benny Dupree had his way. The fence was one of many extremes Benny employed to keep people away from the property.

Benny knew Mac's interest in Turtle Point was fish, not eggs. He also knew Mac. His friend wouldn't be able to resist bragging about the huge Snook that swam in the gently breaking waves a few feet from Turtle Point's beach in summer months. Letting Mac fish there would be like issuing a pass to all local anglers. That was the last thing he wanted!

Benny cultivated the reputation of being unreasonable and potentially violent when it came to protecting the nesting zone. For that reason, guides and local fishermen avoided Turtle Point. Many other places along the island's shoreline provided plenty of sport without the accompanying conflict. However, those knowing him on a more than a casual basis scoffed at the suggestion he was "violent."

"Catch a big old, fat snook for me." Mac grinned. "Don't tell me you don't fish when you go out there. I know you do. And, I know that's the hottest spot to catch them."

"Yeh? How do you know that?"

"Goodun. He told me that's the best spot for snook and Goodun doesn't lie." Mac cocked his head to the side.

Benny didn't smile. "I don't fish this time of year, Mac. I really don't. I'm too busy running folks away. If people saw me or you it would be an invitation. It's the middle of nesting season. People don't realize how easy it is to spook the turtles."

"Think it's really necessary to be out there every night? You have the fence and who knows what else on the property. Landmines? No locals would dare go out there. They know about you. Benny, admit it, there isn't one out of twenty nights that somebody shows."

"Landmines are too dangerous for the turtles." Benny turned from jovial to serious. "One of fifty is one too many."

"How is Goodun doing? I haven't seen him in a long time." Mac tired of goading his friend, so he changed the subject.

"Good, I guess. I don't see him often. I usually have to hunt him down if I want to talk. He'd never tell you if he wasn't okay. Anytime I ask him, he says, 'Same as last time.' Hell, Mac, he lives out there because he doesn't want to bother with people or want people bothering him."

Mac nodded. "I can't get him to warm up to me."

"I've known him since I was a kid. Ten years longer than I've known you. But, we're not touchy-feely. No one except my dad ever really knew him. My father and Goodun liked each other. They'd both spent time in combat. I guess that was their bond. Dad told me Goodun saw horrible fighting in Vietnam and not to talk to him about it." Benny paused and eyed Mac. "I stayed with him a few times when Dad left on business. Goodun taught me to gig. Showed me, is more like it. Flounder, mullet, anything that showed in the light back then. Mac, he's never said a hundred words anytime I've been with him. I think he likes me, but...." Benny tossed his hands up and checked the time. "I've got to get going. I want to eat before I go and I need boat gas. Want to ride over to Townson's and get a bite?"

"You want to get me skinned? Remember, I'm married. Ellen would peel me and dry my hide on the front door if I missed supper."

"Good reason to stay single," Benny said.

"Better reason is that no sane woman will have you." Mac laughed and said, "How many women have you dated in the past two years? Two...three?"

"More than that." Benny rose from his chair across the desk from MacCardle. "Know a really beautiful, sexy, tall, smart, wealthy woman that needs a man to guide her."

"Tall? Beautiful? Very smart and rich. Matter of fact, I do, but with one exception. She doesn't need *anyone* to guide her. She's a close friend from my Marine days. Harper Sturgis. She opened a law office in Tampa. Owns a PI firm there, too. I bet she has an IQ of 160 and she definitely has a body temperature to match, once you....." He grinned and his face flushed. "She isn't the type woman you'd want to disappoint."

"Doesn't sound right for me, Mac. My ex-wife provided me with all the experience on boss type females I'll ever need."

Mac laughed, "You're probably right. Harper *is* the commanding officer type. You two have personalities that would mix as well as sulfuric acid and water." He waved to the door and faked a scowl. "Get your ass out so I can close the office. I'll get the Feldman sale contract to you on Monday. It's Friday, and I've got a weekend fever."

"You'll have weekend fever when you show up here on Monday. You never lose it."

"Ahhhh...go...go...kiss a turtle." Mac wadded up a piece of paper and threw it at his friend as Benny exited the office.

"Kiss this." Benny patted his rump as he passed through the doorway.

They were both laughing as the door closed.

Chapter 7
Cayo Costa Island, Florida
May 2010

Benny took off his polarized sunglasses to remove salt-spray from them so he could see the bottom better. Not that he needed to, he could navigate his boat from his Pine Island home to the old closed pass located a mile behind Cabbage Key in the worst weather conditions, day or night. He'd done it too many times to count. Even the extremely low, seasonal tide wasn't a problem. Since his father first allowed him to steer the family Chris Craft up the channel curves forty plus years ago, it had become his private passage to an unspoiled beach and the Gulf of Mexico's languid waters. The old mangrove lined pass cut a deep slash into Cayo Costa's narrow profile. A hurricane or some other cataclysmic natural event closed the pass at its mouth leaving a three to four-hundred-yard dam of sand where, eons ago, water flowed back and forth from the Gulf to Pine Island Sound.

His hands robotically turned the steering wheel, guiding his Carolina Skiff on a gradual curve as the channel swept from one shore to its opposite. He completed the "S" required to stay in deep water, glancing at the roof of Goodun's cabin that protruded above the mangroves. The gleaming tin shone in the late afternoon sun, framed by many coconut palms that provided the old man part of his food supply. Benny always expected to see the thin, old black man in his boat fishing the waters near his home. Today, his friend wasn't to be seen, and Goodun's boat was tied to the dock.

Returning his attention to the final quarter-mile of his trip, Benny was surprised to see larger than expected quantities of redfish around the mangrove roots and swimming off the shallow grass flats. It was early to see large numbers of that species in the old pass. The presence of more fish was a good thing, but he wondered what that meant. He'd ask Goodun. The old man knew the waters and islands within a ten-mile radius better than any man or woman alive.

Benny pulled the throttle back, slowing the boat to idle speed. The wake rolling off the bow disappeared; the hull barely disturbed the surface. Swerving back and forth, he avoided old submerged trees and stumps that discouraged others from sharing his private port. He aimed his boat at the spot where he'd cut the mangroves back so he could tie up and get on and off the island. When he shifted the motor into neutral, the distraction of guiding the boat disappeared, and the bitter-sweet history of the spot haunted him. That history was as much a part of him as a Siamese twin would have been. It was the imperative that imprisoned him with bars made of sea oats, cabbage palms, scrub oaks, and sea grapes.

Benny slipped off his backpack before unlocking the imposing gate that provided the only access to his island property. Flashlights, bug repellent, water, and a few other items he'd need to make his "beach time" more comfortable and safe, were tucked into its confines. He looped one of its straps over a bracket supporting three strands of barbed-wire that topped the gate and fence enclosing his land. The sun hovered close above the Gulf, increasing his effort to get to the shore. Benny liked to sit on the beach and catch the "green flash" just as the sun disappeared on the western horizon. It fascinated him every time.

Removing keys from his pocket and unlocking the padlock, never provoked conscious thought. He just did it. Picking up an old beach chair and a battered bucket in which he smoldered "punk" to drive away mosquitoes, never reached his mind's surface. Benny's focus was on maintaining his vigil.

Then, everything changed. A loud grunt and noise made from something thrashing about in the bushes or in one of his pit traps sent his hand into the back-pack. His hand found his .38 caliber revolver and a box of bullets. Someone was inside the fence. No one had entered since he'd posted signs reading "No Trespassing! Wildlife Sanctuary for Protected Species. Violators will be prosecuted!" The warnings were placed every twenty-five feet around the fence's perimeter. That was eleven years ago. After loading his gun and carefully leaving the firing chamber full, Benny searched, listening for the noise to repeat.

Chapter 8
Cayo Costa Island, Florida
May 2010

"Shit!" Benny said aloud. The sun had dropped out of sight, and darkness was closing in. He'd left his flashlight in his backpack, and he'd walked halfway around the property. It wasn't a good idea to confront someone or something in the heavy underbrush without seeing what you were facing.

The sound of his curse brought a reaction. Guttural grunts and noises made from steel grating steel were close to him. His heart rate accelerated, his senses heightened, and perspiration flowed even heavier than the hot, humid night had already produced. Benny immediately knew where the culprit was. It had been a lot of hard work, work he hoped would never be used, but...... The trespasser had fallen into one of the pits he'd dug, lined with old oil drums, and mounted coils of barbed-wire inside. Covered with palm fronds, an unsuspecting interloper would end up in an eight-foot-deep prison if he stepped on them. Pits, like the one he was approaching, were excavated on every trail crossing the property inside his fence. The chain link and barbed wire protected the area that he wanted to be sure no one bothered, one he very seldom visited.

When he was forty feet from the trap, he stopped, chambered a bullet, and aimed at the path in front of him. In the fading twilight's dingy gray, he could see the fronds were caved-in. The hole created by the buried fifty-five-gallon drums looked like a cave entrance. Benny could hear labored breathing and random metallic clinks. He cocked the revolver's hammer before he cautiously completed the last five steps to the hole's edge. Still one step away, he leaned forward and peered into the darkness beneath him. He could barely make out something's shape crouched on the pit's bottom. The silence and stillness added to the oppressive tension.

Benny spoke, "Who's down th...."

A large black form leaped up and at him, triggered by his voice. Loud squeals and groans mingled with noises made by barbed wire scraping the steel drums as the form dropped back into the chasm. Benny relaxed. His trap had incarcerated a very big feral pig. He uncocked the pistol's hammer before returning to the gate. Benny mumbled to the surrounding underbrush, "I'll finish him up later. No use killing it now and having the meat spoil."

The apprehension generated by the thought that a human was snooping around his property, quickly disappeared. Pigs were notorious diggers; this one had dug to get inside the fence, not out. He'd find the hole and fill it tomorrow. Benny returned to the gate, picked up his chair, bucket, and backpack, and completed his trip to the beach.

How many hours had he sat in the same spot? Benny did the math. He was fifty-two. He'd met Nadine the summer of his junior year at the University of Florida. *Thirty-one years.* Before he bought the property and put up the fence, he'd spent more hours guarding the spot. That probably averaged over half the days in a year, say a couple hundred. That had been for twelve years, four or five hours a night. The calculator in his mind whirled.

Twelve thousand hours. He shook his head. That meant he'd served sentry duty in his chair and its predecessors for a year-and-a-half during that period. After Benny put up the fence and felt secure that he'd successfully restricted human access to the area, Benny cut his visits in half, except in turtle nesting season. Benny increased the number of visits and length of time he stayed when eggs were being laid. How many years... it wasn't important. "Who cares," he told the waves that lapped the beach sand.

Light from the full moon bathed the sea, shoreline, and island in enough light to make things visible, majestic, beautiful...an artist's portrait in gray tones. The spot he'd chosen as his command post was a sand dune on top a point that jutted into the Gulf a hundred feet or less. Coves on either side of the point were hollowed out by the tide's movement. Barely visible on the satellite pictures he'd seen, it was a tiny bump on Cayo Costa's shore when drawn by mapmakers. While the rest of the world saw Turtle Point that way, Benny Dupree saw it as a feature as colossal as Mt. Everest. It was where he'd first met Nadine.

The spot, the exact spot where he sat, was where he saw her for the first time. When he visited that dune, he was as close to her as he could ever be. Nadine's reason for being there the day he met her, was the turtles. She loved them. And, since he'd fallen in love with her, he developed her devotion to the inoffensive creatures who asked nothing of humans other than to be left alone. Today, she was a thirty-year-old dream; someone who only existed in his mind. Still, if he closed his eyes, he could see her, smell her, feel her.

Chapter 9
Cayo Costa Island, Florida
early June 1980

Benny's first glimpse of Nadine was her silhouette in the late afternoon sun. She'd faced the sea and stood on top of Turtle Point's sand dune...the one he frequented for years after that first meeting. Nadine's figure was electric and an immediate challenge to his macho, college boy ego. As he made his way toward the girl, her form disappeared temporarily when palms or bushes hid her from his view. Benny lamented that he'd left his Gator football game jersey in his boat. He decided it wasn't worth the half-mile walk back to the island's bay side to fetch it. His twenty-one-year-old mind was sure a "real" jersey was a chick magnet. Benny almost changed his mind when he caught another "framed" picture of the stranger's body.

The viewing angle changed. Benny neared the girl and the round firm curvature of her hips, long shapely legs, and tiny waist was increasingly sexually tantalizing. Hidden under a man's white shirt and a pair of white shorts, Benny's frustrated attempt to visualize what he couldn't see, made his heart race. Waves of dark auburn hair rested on the young lady's shoulders and fell six inches down her back. Rarely watching the path, Benny ducked his head around clumps of sea grapes, scrub oak bushes, and cabbage palm fronds to see her. The only thing breaking Benny's focus on the form in front him was his fishing pole's aggravating ability to find every branch extending into the trail. The tip caught in foliage once too often and became securely tangled. Benny freed it as he moved, but as it came loose, he tripped and fell forward. His free hand reached out to break his fall and landed on top of a prickly pear cactus. He remembered yelling, "Damn!"

The girl was forgotten in an instant. The fishing rod dropped to the sand; he needed the hand that had been carrying it to remove slender cactus spikes. Engrossed in removing the needle-like thorns from the pincushion his hand had become, Benny didn't see or hear the girl until she said, "I know that hurts. I sat on one of those." Nadine dropped down to her knees. "Let me see it," she said. She motioned for him to give her his hand. At the same time, Nadine extended her palm to grasp his. Nadine's hands were as tan as Benny's, her grip firm and gentle at the same time. Sea green irises focused on the "pins" protruding from his palm and fingers. Thick dark eyebrows arched over Nadine's wide-set eyes. A thin, perfectly shaped nose and full soft-looking lips combined to produce a face worthy of a magazine cover.

"You don't want to break the tips off in your hand. They can become infected. Believe me, you don't want that." The girl sounded like she had experience. "You already have one or two broken below skin level. I have a first aid kit on the beach with tweezers, needles, and a bottle of alcohol in it. I can get those out for you." Nadine didn't wait for an answer. She got back up on her feet and walked toward the dune, expecting him to follow. Benny did.

"Welcome to my office," she said as they crossed the small sand ridge that marked the storm created, high tide level. A lean-to shelter made from a piece of canvas and some pine saplings shaded a ten-foot square. Plastic fishing tackle boxes, a small cooler, and a duffle bag lay under the shelter. Several feet away, a folding chair patiently waited for a butt, its only current occupant being a notebook with the "University of Miami" lettering on its front cover. The word "Observations" was written in cursive beneath the printing.

"Go sit in the chair while I get what I need. Don't worry about the book. Just put it on the ground." Nadine ducked under the canvas, dropped to her hands and knees then opened one of the tackle boxes. Her rear pointed toward him. Benny swallowed a couple times and tried to politely look away. He couldn't. Benny's eyes were riveted on her ass. Besides, he knew there wasn't anything near as interesting to see anywhere else along the beach.

Thirty seconds later, she backed out from under the lean-to. She smiled as she walked to him. "This won't be bad."

"I appreciate you helping."

"Tell me that when we finish." Nadine knelt, taking his hand with the same soft, firm grip. Benny looked down at her, wishing the man's white shirt she wore revealed more of her breasts than it did. They thrust outward creating two bulges in the white linen. Concealed, they added to the girl's mystique and made her more fascinating.

With tweezers and needle, the girl removed the cactus thorns causing little more than an occasional complaint from his hand's nerves. Benny's male ego wouldn't have allowed him to move or show signs of discomfort if she'd been performing major surgery.

After ten minutes, the girl said, "I think that's all."

"Thanks, you really did that very well."

"I had a lot of practice. Besides, it's a lot easier when you can see what you're doing. When I removed them from my butt, I had to do it with a mirror and by feel."

Benny grinned. "You know, that's a straight line it's hard to resist jumping on."

"I'd advise against it." The girl saw no humor in Benny's attempt to start a suggestive conversation. Her face became guarded, clearly expressing that his words weren't appreciated.

He changed the subject. "I noticed your notebook. You go to Miami?"

"Yes," Nadine said, and a smile returned. "I'm a proud Hurricane."

"You're the enemy. I'm a Gator."

"Be prepared for our boys to beat your boys." She put her hands on her hips. "A Snellenberger team beats a Pell team every time. We'll have your whole football team begging for mercy by half-time."

"No, you won't."

"Oh, yes. You know some of the players? Better warn them to be prepared."

"I am one of the players." Benny grinned, "I can promise you *I won't* be doing any begging."

The girl remained silent for a few seconds, determining the voracity of Benny's statement. Nadine said, "You don't look big enough. What position do you play?"

"Strong safety."

"How much—'

"I weigh 207, I'm 6'1," and I'm fast."

"What's your number?" She said it fast, trying to see if she'd get hesitation.

Benny recited his number before the last syllable left her mouth, "Twenty-seven."

She looked at him shamelessly—as though he was a used car she was considering buying. "You've got big biceps and nice quads. I guess you might be telling the truth. What's your name, Gator man?"

"I'll tell you mine, if you'll tell me yours."

"I'm not trying to prove I'm something I may not be." She looked dubious.

Benny shrugged his shoulders. "That's the deal."

Nadine smiled. "I guess that's fair." Her bare foot

inscribed an arc in the sand as she waited.

"My given name is Benedict Barron Dupree, but everybody calls me Benny." He extended his right hand to shake.

"I'm Nadine." She reached her hand to grab his.

He pulled back a little. "All of it."

"Mary Nadine Bocelli." Her hand waited for his to return. It did.

"Glad to meet you, Mary Nadine."

"Just ... Nadine. I go by that."

"Okay, *Just Nadine*. What is an East Coast girl doing over here? You run out of sand on the Atlantic side?"

The girl picked up her notebook and waved it at him. "I know you were trying to be a smart-ass, but you're fairly close to right. I'm studying marine biology at Miami. I want to specialize...sea turtles, they fascinate me. Actually, I'll be starting on my masters next year. I'm a senior. Unfortunately, the area around Miami is so developed and the turtles are disturbed so much they don't..." Nadine shook her head. "I'm starting in the middle. What I'm observing are the turtles' nesting habits. This is a lot, lot better place to do it."

"This *is* a good place to do that. There are tractor-trailer loads of those things that come here every full moon this time of year." Benny looked up and down the beach. "Where's your boat?"

"I don't have one."

"How do you get over here?"

"I have a deal with a man to bring me over and pick me up."

"Who?"

"Walker Cole."

"Walker Cole?" Benny repeated the name as though its taste was from words removed from a restroom floor. "How did you get tied up with *him*?'

"I'm renting a little place on a canal in Bokeelia

on Pine Island. A man at the fish house down the street from where I'm staying suggested him because he'd pick me up at my cottage."

"You'd be a lot better off driving to the Marina. I can give you some names—"

"That's the problem. I don't have a car. I used a cab to go from the Greyhound Station in Ft. Myers to the place I have rented. Besides, most of my study and observations are at night. I don't think I could find someone else to come out at such weird times."

"Nadine, Walker Cole is a poor excuse for a human being. He's got a long criminal record and a reputation for mistreating women."

A twinkle of defiance shone in the young woman's eyes. "I can take care of myself."

"Sure. I believe you. But, can you outrun a bullet?"

Nadine became poker-faced and silent.

"If you can't," Benny said seriously, "Change how you get out here. The law knows about three people Cole's shot or knifed. One of those was a woman. I'd guess there are more."

"Do you have any suggestions?" Nadine's question was in complete earnest.

Benny hesitated as he thought about words drilled into him by his father. Never make a promise if you aren't willing to die keeping it. "I might learn a lot. Sounds like fun. If you don't mind getting a late start coming over, I have a boat, I'll bring you out, I'll take you back, and I'll stay with you occasionally if you want. I work for my dad's construction company. Depending on the rain we get in the afternoon, I could pick you up around six, most times before."

"What will your girlfriend say?"

"I'm between ladies right now." Benny saw disbelief slip into Nadine's countenance. "I broke up with my girl last semester. I'm not interested in a relationship until I go back this fall. I'll be a senior, too."

"What would you charge?"

Benny thought for a few seconds, "Put gas in the boat when I need it."

"Mr. Dupree, we have a deal. It's really not fair to you, but if you're satisfied..." Nadine hesitated and was stoic and serious when she said, "Please remember one thing; gas is the only thing I'm putting out."

Benny nodded, hoping that Nadine lied occasionally. The "deal" he made would change his life.

Chapter 10
Pine Island, Florida
early June 1980

"I can't, Dad," Benny said, "I committed myself to help someone in the evenings for the rest of June."

"Help someone?" Roulon Dupree was surprised. He knew his boy had been making the boat trip to Cayo Costa every evening for a week. Roulon could only think of one reason for that. "What you and Goodun working on?"

"It's not Goodun."

The big Cajun leaned back in his office chair. He looked at his boy critically. "What's *her* name?"

Benny cocked his head to the side hoping he wasn't always so transparent. He said, "Nadine."

"Nadine. Nadine? I don't know no Nadine on the island. She a local gal? From the Cape? Ft. Myers?"

"You don't know her." Benny tried to change the subject. "The days she doesn't want to go to the island, I could help."

Roulon had definite ideas about the wife Benedict should marry. The poverty he experienced in his youth, scraping out an existence around Pearl River, Mississippi, trying to fish for a living, left scars. He'd come to Southwest Florida with a new wife, an eighteen-foot mullet boat, and the determination to be successful. Dupree carved out a small construction empire that started with building piers and docks, eventually evolving to developing tracts of land and even small malls. Benny was his only son and heir—he'd be damned if his hard-won wealth would get squandered in a divorce like the one his twin brother Roubon suffered through. Dupree men's choice of women was often unlucky and unwise. Benny's mother, a saint for just living with Roulon, had only one failing, she was thin, frail, and not built for having babies. Incapable of producing the large brood her husband desired, they tried anyway. After several miscarriages, Annalene gave birth to Benedict. There were complications, and the doctor warned against more babies. After four years, Annalene decided she wanted one more child. It wasn't to be. Both mother and daughter died in childbirth.

Roulon squinted at his son. It wasn't like Benny to be closed-mouthed about girls he dated. In fact, it wasn't like Benny to be closed-mouthed about anything. This raised a caution flag. "You gonna bring her 'round?"

"She's just a friend. I don't have any interest in her."

Roulon knew his son. "Lie." He stood up and walked around his desk standing eye to eye with his boy. "She one of those co-eds from Gainesville?"

"No." Benny knew being evasive wasn't working. "She's studying to be a marine biologist. I met her on the beach. She's observing sea turtles. Nadine's not interested in men; she's all tied up in her education." He waited for his father's reaction; when none came, he added, "The turtles are really interesting. I'm learning a lot."

"Where's she from?"

"New Jersey, but she goes to school at Miami."

Roulon stuck his head forward a few inches. His expression was serious and intense. "You be real careful, now. Don't go poking 'round her. You don't want no babies until you're ready."

Benny laughed, "You don't have to worry about that. She doesn't like me. Or, she doesn't like me *in that way*. I'm not sure she likes men, period."

"She a lesbian?"

Benny shrugged his shoulders. "The subject of sex hasn't come up."

Roulon examined his son's face for subterfuge. None was there. "Keep it that way." He patted Benny on the shoulder. "Just be careful."

Chapter 11
Pine Island, Florida
early June 1980

Benny held the piling as Nadine stepped into his Crosby Sea Sled. The dull rumble of thunder reached their ears. The southeastern sky was black and filled with ominous clouds.

"What do you think?" Nadine asked.

Benny shook his head. "If we hadn't been rained out three times this week already, I wouldn't be here." He patted the gunwale of his open boat. "Old Betsy is a good little skiff, but an eighteen footer and forty horse kicker isn't a match for that." He pointed to the approaching storm.

"We shouldn't go then." Nadine looked worried. "I'm afraid I'll miss more hatchings. My records show I could have missed six already." She sighed. "I guess it's not worth dying over." She looked at the rapidly approaching storm clouds. "Will you be able to get home before that thing hits?"

"It will be close."

"Tie up and come inside until it passes."

Nadine and Benny sat across a table playing *Black Jack* as rain pounded the roof of Nadine's rental house. Lightning flashed followed by peals of thunder. The conversation topic was turtles, as always, until Benny broached a new subject. "Hey, what about going out to supper with my old man and me? He doesn't bite. It will get you out of this cracker box. Maybe meet some of the Pine Island folks. They're really nice."

Nadine frowned and remained silent for several seconds. Finally, she decided. "That's a sweet offer, but I can't. Benny, I know you won't understand this, but I don't want to meet the people here. Remember, I told you to promise not to tell anybody who I was or what I'm doing because I didn't want the turtles disturbed? That's true, but it isn't the only reason." When she finished speaking, it was apparent the subject was closed.

Chapter 12
Cayo Costa Island, Florida
May 2010

The robust breeze flowing in from over the Gulf was welcome. The wind was strong enough to decimate the swarms of mosquitoes and sand flies that were ever-present at night. A light spray of insect repellent would ensure his comfort for the hours he planned to spend on the beach. Behind him, the full moon rose above the island's trees and mangroves.

Benny expected the turtles would arrive in the surf soon and use their flippers to pull themselves up the sandy beach on their bellies. They'd dig holes fourteen to twenty inches deep and the diameter of a small wash tub using their rear flippers, then do what millions of years of instinct instructed their species to do; lay their eggs. After depositing over a hundred in their newly mined nest, the female would carefully cover her eggs and drag her 300-pound body back to the sea, trusting the warm sands to protect and incubate the next precious generation.

They'd come as they had since Benny started his self-imposed vigil-penitence thirty years ago. It was the height of the nesting season. The question was: would humans, both benign and malicious, come to destroy the females' dangerous work? Benny was successful in keeping his sacred strip of sand protected. Whether the humans were poachers bent on stealing the eggs and capturing the hatchlings to kill, stuff, and sell as curios, or "eco" guides who made a living with a flashlight and a boat charging tourists to get a glimpse of mother nature at work, or fishermen whose careless feet could crush half the eggs in a nest with one careless step, Dupree "ran them off." He did what it took to accomplish that, including *threatening* violence as a last resort. It never came to that. In thirty years, he'd been unsuccessful less than the number of fingers on his hand. His efforts paid dividends. Local guides and poachers avoided the area as if it contained the Ebola virus. He did little chasing and more observing over the last ten years. It was certainly easier since cell phones were available. Folks that considered tormenting the turtles knew Benny would be on the phone with the state Fish and Game officer in seconds. The risk far out-weighed the reward. There was always that one exception, however.

The first turtle arrived at the shore's edge after ten. Benny saw the creature make its first awkward thrusts up the beach through his night vision goggles. He could tell it was a Loggerhead by its large head and heart-shaped shell. Lady Loggerhead was a large adult, over three feet long and weighing 200 pounds. Though thirty yards away, he could make out the trail she left as she crawled toward the area where Mother Nature whispered, "Your eggs will be safe there." The tell-tale marking on the sand was a twenty-five-inch smooth patch with gashes in the beach on either side as the turtle dug her flippers in and wrestled her bulk to the nesting area.

Night vision made everything clear and easy to see. "Damn, I wish Nadine had been able to use these." No one was around to hear his words except the turtle, the sand, and a memory.

Chapter 13
Cabbage Key Cut,
Cayo Costa Island, Florida
May 2010

It was the same nightmare. The North Vietnamese soldier was running at him. His enemy had a bayonet fixed to the barrel of his AK-47. His M-16 lay at his feet, jammed and useless. The RNV private screamed when he was a few steps from Goodun, mistakenly believing that the Marine was unarmed. Night and the jungle's growth obscured the Kabar knife in the Marine's hand.

Sergeant Aaron Moses Warrington, or Goodun as his comrades knew him, stood his ground, prayed, and relied on his Corps training to give him a chance to survive. He saw anger and fear in the Vietnamese eyes.

Goodun made a football fake to his left, and the soldier thrust his bayonet in that direction. The Marine sprung back to his right and clubbed his left arm against the AK-47's barrel to parry the thrust as he slammed his sharp knife deep into the enemy's lower abdomen and slit the man's body from above his pubic bone to his breastplate. A primal scream came from the dying man's mouth. The soldier's momentum carried him onward, so their faces crashed together. Terror, from the knowledge he was dying, was the last emotion in the man's eyes as the last light of life disappeared. Goodun awoke thrashing around on his mattress as he'd done a thousand times before.

He swung his legs over the edge and sat up.

Both hands went to his face, first covering his closed eyes then rubbing outward pulling the skin on his cheeks toward his ears. Goodun opened his eyes, halfway expecting to see the green hell where he'd spent two tours of duty, but the familiar sight of his cabin's interior, bathed in moonlight that filtered through its windows, reassured him. Mosquitoes buzzing on the screens confirmed he was home. He looked at his thin legs and traced them down to the dark outline of his feet. Ticking from his alarm clock drew his attention. It was 12:35. He whistled. It was a long time before sunup.

"Yous mights well getta long, Aaron Moses," he addressed himself as his mother would have. "If yous has time, yous don't waste it." It was comforting to hear the words in his mother's accent. His parents were one of his good memories, memories that mixed in with way too many bad ones.

Going back to sleep wasn't possible. When the night started the way it had, he knew the nightmare's brothers and sisters waited to come from the recesses of his mind, just behind the thin curtain of sleep. Goodun had no desire to have them visit. No, he didn't want to see his friend John's intestines try to spill from his body as he carried him or view the mutilated corpses of two Vietnamese girls—their sin—having sex with GIs. The Viet Cong tied them to trees in the middle of their village, sliced off their breasts, and mutilated their genitals. That was after skewering their half-Caucasian babies with bamboo spears as the girls were forced to watch. Yes, there were many more visions he didn't want to see again.

He reached for his trousers and shirt that were draped over the chair beside his bed. The bright moonlight would make it easier to catch a few trout or reds for tomorrow's supper. No phosphorescence would light up the line and lure like on moonless nights that spooked the fish that made up a good part of his diet. He'd slip into his clothes, crank up his generator, and by the time he returned his small refrigerator would be cold, not cool.

Dressed, with fishing tackle in hand, he pushed through the screen door and walked out on the dock where his boat was tied. Goodun didn't bother to lock his house; he fastened a hook on the door through an eye on the jamb. It was to keep raccoons out, not people. People didn't come here, especially at night. As he placed his gear in the boat, the gentle roar of an outboard motor being started came from the end of the dead pass. Goodun, stood motionless, waiting to see if it was who he surmised. Within five minutes, a boat raced up the channel. Its captain was running without any lights. With the exception of Goodun, only one other person could do that and not crash into a piling or go aground on a bar. Benedict Dupree. Had to be.

Benny was another son as far as Warrington was concerned, just as dear to him as his flesh and blood. Barely visible as a shadow, Dupree's boat made the "S" curve as the channel crossed to the far bank. Goodun raised his hand and saluted his friend. "Good man," he murmured as he stepped into his boat. He knew Benny had good reasons for the vigil he kept...three of them. As he untied his boat and pushed off, he said, "Yes sir, he'd made a Marine." It was the highest compliment he could pay anyone.

Chapter 14
Cayo Costa Island, Florida
May 2010

He should have been on the island early in the morning, not at one-thirty in the afternoon. It would be brutally hot. June was mid-summer in tropical Southwest Florida. Benny readjusted the shovel to his other shoulder and switched the cooler to his other hand. He'd broil in the midday sun when he filled in the hole the pig had dug under his fence.

That damned hog! Killing it, getting it out of the pit, and carrying the hundred-pound plus carcass to the boat had been a lot bigger task than he'd bargained for. By the time Benny wrapped it and slid the partially cleaned hog in his freezer, it was three AM. Though he'd intended to be back on the island by nine the next morning, he hit the snooze button enough that his alarm gave up in disgust.

Benny reached the gate and rested. Still and silent, the humidity added to the oppressive heat. The sea breeze wouldn't give him relief for an hour or more. It didn't make sense to fight the heat. He decided to take his time, leave the shovel and cooler at the gate, and walk the fence's perimeter at a leisurely pace. Benny hoped the afternoon winds would start blowing off the Gulf by the time he found the place the hog dug under the fence, and he moved his tools there.

Benny removed the broad-brimmed, floppy hat he wore, held his shirt sleeve to his forehead, and wiped off the perspiration. The folding chair inside the gate whispered to him, "Come inside. Take me under a tree. Sit awhile. Relax." Its siren song tempted him, but the work ethic his father drilled into Benny won out. Though avoiding possible heat stroke made perfect sense, he knew he'd be uncomfortable and conscience-ridden within a few minutes. Benny sighed and began the slow walk around the fence.

He'd traveled a third of the way around the perimeter when he saw it. And, what he saw shook him. There was a large hole under the fence. But, it wasn't the rooting made by a hog— the dirt that had been removed was all neatly piled on one side. The "trench" was large enough for a man to lie down and slide under the chain link. Footprints around the excavation, old and crumbling, maintained enough of their shape to be unmistakably identifiable as human. Dupree's hair felt like an electric charge flooded through it. A mild panic seized him. The heat was forgotten as he ran back to the gate.

Nothing was disturbed. Nothing. He'd spent two hours scouring the most critical spots, but couldn't find one shred of evidence that someone had disturbed anything. It took another forty-five minutes to refill the hole and move one of his "no trespassing" signs right above the place someone had dug the trench. When Benny finished, he carried his chair to the sand dune on Turtle Point as the sun raced for the horizon. The sound of the surf rolling on the beach relaxed him, sweeping away his apprehensions. His eyelids were heavy, and it became impossible to keep them open.

Benny fell into a deep sleep. The turtles would be protected by a sleeping sentinel that evening.

Chapter 15
Pine Island, Florida
May 2010

"Hey, Benny." The voice on the telephone line's other end was Rollie Gates, head park ranger and manager of Cayo Costa State Park. The very fact he'd called had Benny Dupree's attention. Rollie never bothered anyone unless there was a problem.

"Hey, Rollie. How are things at the park today?"

"Ahhhhhhh, good enough, I guess. A couple of Yankee tourists got stung by rays, and Danielle happened upon a couple in the act on the beach, so for this place, we had a month's worth of excitement."

Benny laughed. The thought of Danielle, who turned red if the words "butt" or "boob" were mentioned, having to separate a couple "getting it on," was hilarious. "How did the park's number one flower do?" he asked.

"She did okay. Some parents complained to her. Their three girls got quite an education from what Danielle told me. Anyway, she got the couple back in their swimsuits and on to the shuttle ferry."

"What did she say...well...about *it*."

"She didn't want to talk about *it*, none, when I asked. The poor girl *was* embarrassed. Right before she up and walked away, she got this real serious look and said, 'Gosh, Rollie, I didn't know you could do it like that.' Poor girl turned red enough to light a cigarette off her face."

"You can bet one thing; she didn't have a course on that in college. We finally found a kind of wildlife Miss Biological Encyclopedia couldn't identify."

Rollie laughed then said, "There is one more thing. Some dude was asking a lot of questions about your property. Thought you'd want to know."

"Yes, thanks." Benny was glad Rollie couldn't see him stiffen and looked panicked. "What was he asking?"

"Crazy stuff, mostly. He asked Ken if that was the spot Ponce De Leon landed and if he could get inside. Then he asked if there was treasure buried inside. You know Ken, he filled the tourist up with a load of bull-shit and sent him on his way. But, the same guy tried to get a key from Danielle to get inside your fence. He claimed he was from the EPA and wanted to investigate something. Danielle insisted on seeing a badge or some papers. He said he left them in his car over to the mainland. She told him she couldn't let him in unless he had a court order. Danielle didn't like or trust him. She's right good at judging those things. That was yesterday. Today he came back. Wanted to talk to me. You know, there some people you just don't like when you meet them. Well, he's one of those. He's a sneaky looking, little rat-faced guy. He asked if I could let him in to see your property. Said he wanted to buy the land. I explained the set up you had with the state and how it would become part of the park if you decided to sell. He still wanted to get in. I told him he'd have to contact the owner. I asked, 'you know who it is?' He answered, 'Yes, it's Benedict Dupree's land.' I told him unless you personally told me he could get inside your fence, I didn't want him anywhere near your place. If I saw him sneaking around down there, I'd throw his ass in jail. Seemed to scare him and I reckon we've seen the last of the bastard, but I thought you should know."

"Did you get his name?" Benny asked.

"He told Ken it was Jim Jones. He told Danielle it was Jim Smith. I asked him if his name was Smith or Jones since he'd used both names with my rangers. He mumbled something, so I asked to see his driver's license. The name on that was Arthur Heller, New York, on Long Island. Heller is what it said; asshole is what it should have been."

"If he shows up again, will you let me know?"

"Sure." There were excited voices in the background. "Ahhhh, I gotta go. Ken's done stuck the tram in loose sand. He's never gonna learn. See you."

The call left Benny wondering who in the hell Arthur Heller was. He never recalled hearing the name before. Though he didn't know the man, he decided to find who the curious pest was as soon as possible. Benny knew one thing for sure; he didn't want anyone snooping around his property for any reason.

Chapter 16
Fort Myers, Florida
May 2010

Napoli Pizza was jammed with high school students hanging out on a Friday night. Sean and Devale sat watching girls parade from booth to table to booth. Their table was *not* one of the popular stops. The "babes" that did chat with the two boys weren't what Sean and Devale considered "prime pussy." Three girls walked by without acknowledging the boys' existence. Instead, they sat at Kyle McKensie's table; the boy's discontent bubbled over.

"Look at that. Lisa, L'trelle, and Jennifer, now that's some fine ass. They passed us up for that pimply faced shit-head. I'm not figuring that one." Sean mimicked a robot, moving his hands and arms stiffly and stared blankly straight ahead. "That does not compute. Bahp. Bahp. Bahp. That does not compute."

"Hey, man, the boy has coin. *We don't.* We definitely don't." Devale watched enviously as the girls giggled, wiggled, and displayed their breasts for the competition. "Sean, you see what he's driving? His father's Chrysler convertible. You think that serious pussy is gonna give a poor Afro and a poor Cracker a serious look? Seriously, do you."

After a few minutes, the three girls giggled and wiggled their way to the door in-route to the convertible, accompanied by McKenzie and another male specimen they considered, "A double useless mega nerd."

"See, Sean, we need to get some cool wheels. Man, we could crawl right into those saddles with a max-cool convertible."

"How bad do you want a convertible? Say, a shiny red Mustang with chrome wire wheels." The man who spoke to them stood next to their table and looked terribly out of place. He was short, thin, almost bald, dressed in a business suit, and had a "New Yorker's" accent.

What hair remained on the man's head and face was white blonde making him look perpetually scared. The man presented the appearance of an adult nerd. Devale's parents watched old TV shows, and the eavesdropper reminded him of a character named 'Mr. Peepers.' Dark rimmed glasses, pale blue eyes, a pointed nose, and a weak chin reminded Devale of a mouse.

"Me and my man aren't in the killing business, *old* dude," Devale said.

"Oh, you don't have to do anything like that." The man took his wallet from his pocket, removed a bill, tore it in half, and gave one portion to Devale. The boy looked at the bill and whistled. Benjamin Franklin's likeness was separated from the rest of the $100. "Come back tomorrow, and I'll give you the other half, *and I'll have that convertible parked in the lot outside.*"

"Man, we don't switch-hit. We are strictly into girls." Sean thought he'd guessed the man's motive.

"Same here. In fact, I've seen a few in this place I'd like to shaft." The man smiled, "But, this has nothing to do with sex."

"*What do you want?*" Devale asked.

"I believe I know where there's a treasure buried." The boys laughed.

"I know it sounds crazy, far out." The man paused for effect. "But, do you think I'd be giving away hundred dollar bills and cars if I didn't have strong evidence?"

The boys stopped laughing. Sean asked, "Why don't you just do it yourself? You ain't that old."

"Good question. The place it's located on is private land. I'm a college professor at Columbia— that's how I learned about the gold to start with."

"Gold!" the boys said in unison.

"Keep it down," the man dropped his voice to a loud whisper. "If I go trespassing on this property, I could get in trouble. I might lose my job. If it doesn't happen to be there.....Well, I have to make a living. The law sees you as 'kids.' You won't get into any serious trouble. Come back tomorrow. See if it's true. What do you have to lose? You have a car to gain. And, if we find the treasure, you two will get 33% of it. I'll have the title of the car with me. We'll do the same thing as with the hundred; we'll cut it in two, you get half. When we're done, you get the other half of the title, either way, find the gold or not."

"Deal!" Sean said.

"Mmmmm. Can you prove you're a college professor? Or are you just blowing smoke." Devale leaned forward. "I'm not into living in some dude's crack dreams."

The man silently removed his wallet from his pants, again. He opened it and showed the boys an I.D. Card with his picture on it. It read: *Columbia University Faculty Identification, Arthur Heller, Professor.*

Chapter 17
Pine Island, Florida
May 2010

"The Dupree Company, residential and commercial construction and development, how may we help you?" It was the standard phrase Corrine Foy used when she answered her boss's phone for the past sixteen years. Corrine joined Benny Dupree's business two years after he inherited it from his father.

The office door opened, Benny entered, smiled, waved, and walked past her desk. Corrine smiled and waved back. She spoke into her headset, "I'm sorry, Mr. Dupree isn't in, and I don't know when to expect him. Do you wish to leave a message?"

Benny stopped and looked at her, asking the question with his facial expression. Corrine answered by squinting her eyes and violently shaking her head. Benny resumed his journey to his office. When he saw his desk, he strongly considered leaving. A stack of invoices was waiting for his approval. Another pile was incoming correspondence to read. Next to that were outgoing letters to sign. Sticky notes littered his desktop with the most important stuck to the handset of his phone. Corrine was organized enough for both of them. Benny shook his head. It was going to be a hell of a way to start the week. He reached for the invoices when Corrine's voice came from the open doorway.

"Mr. B, I've got a couple things to let you know, before you get started. You've had six calls regarding that zone change on the Williams' property. People from both sides want your support. That was Tom Handley on the phone, just then. Do you want to take any calls regarding it?"

"No ... Oh, hell, Yes. I might as well. I don't care one way or the other, and I'll tell them that. I'm going to stay neutral, I think. Will that piss both sides off?"

Corrine seldom changed her facial expression from its perpetual smile. She simply nodded and said, "Yes."

"What do you think?"

His administrative assistant was silent for several seconds. "If you don't say anything, the zoning will probably get changed."

"So, that means there will be a strip mall where all houses have been built in the past." Benny Dupree sighed. "Okay. When is the zoning board meeting?"

"Wednesday. You want to talk to anybody about it."

"No. Just tell them I'm in the process of making my decision and I'll announce it at the meeting Wednesday." Benny looked at his desk. "Anything else need attention worse than any other?"

"Mr. Mac sent the Bill of Sale for you to sign for the property you sold to the Wynters Company." Corrine went to his desk and removed a group of papers clipped together from one of the stacks. She laid it in front of him and said, "Sign it, and I'll see it gets right to him."

"Okay," he said as he thumbed through the paperwork and scribbled his signature on the papers, "What else?" Benny handed the papers back to her.

"You have a request to speak to the Rotary Club about what you're doing to conserve the sea turtle population." Corrine hesitated. "It's a noon meeting. It's in three weeks. You don't have anything else scheduled. I said you would."

"Okay, Corrine. Anything *else*?"

"Your ex-wife called."

"What does she want, now?" Benny looked disgusted.

"Don't know, don't care. She wouldn't tell me when I asked." Corrine and Eva hated each other. "She wants you to call her. She sounded angry, but when isn't she?"

Chapter 18
Cape Coral, Florida
May 2010

"Hello," Eva barked rather than talked. Corrine was right; his ex-wife was mad as hell about something. "Now what are you trying to pull?" Eva didn't wait for Benny to say a word. She'd seen his number on her phone's LED screen.

"Hi, Eva. I'm fine, thank you. How are you?" Benny tried to remain and sound civil when he felt anything but being that way.

"Screw you!" Eva's voice rose an octave. "Why do you have that man snooping into our past? I want to keep that all behi—"

"Whoa, girl. I have no idea what you're talking about." Benny looked at his phone as though it were a snake. "What man?"

"Don't tell me you don't know about it."

"I really don't."

She remained silent for a few seconds. "Are you trying to get out of the pittance you pay me?"

"Hey, you didn't have any problem signing a prenuptial agreement." Benny was happy his father had insisted on getting one, even though at the time, he'd fought with his father, believing it wasn't necessary. It was one of those cases where father knew best.

"Up yours, you asshole!" Eva could make a football coach blush if she were mad enough.

"Hey! Remember? You'd have gotten a third of everything if you hadn't tried to bed every man in Lee County." Benny didn't mind reminding her of her numerous affairs during their six-year marriage.

"You know, I didn't have to pay you any alimony. Now, tell me what in the devil is going on?"

"You really didn't set this up?"

"No."

"And, you don't know the Foreman guy?"

"No, not at all. I don't know *anyone* named Foreman. What's he bugging you about?"

"The divorce settlement. He said he was investigating for the IRS. He wanted to know who got what property. Like, he wanted to know if I had a copy of the deed to the Cayo Costa property. He was very pushy. After he left, I asked June about the whole thing. She works for the IRS. She said they always do their *own* investigations. June said all that was fourteen years ago. There was something else fishy going on. She said you or somebody probably hired him."

"That sounds like June. Ever think of why I'd want to check on something I already know more about than anyone else?"

Eva sounded perplexed, as though she should have thought about the logic when talking to the man, but remained silent. She sputtered in disgust.

"What did he look like?" Benny asked.

"Scary! Big! He was at least 6'4" and more than 250 pounds. I think he was black because of his features and hair, but he had a light complexion. He spoke with a New England accent. The 'Rs' for 'As' kind of thing. Cuber instead of Cuba."

"Do you remember his full name?" Benny asked.

"I think it was Terrell Foreman. He showed me a badge and an ID card, but it was so fast, and I was so shook I don't remember anything for sure."

"If he calls or comes around again, have him contact me. And, don't tell him anything!

He sounds like a con man trying to pull some

kind of a scam."

Eva laughed bitterly. "I already tried that. When I told him to call you because you got everything, he said, 'I don't need to do that. I have what I need about him.' Then he took off."

Benny Dupree was shaken as he hung up his phone. The hole dug under the fence, one man inquiring about the property at the Park, and another nosing around his ex-wife and who knew where else. It had to be more than coincidence.

Chapter 19
Fort Myers, Florida
May 2010

Arthur Heller watched Foreman stop and talk to the hostess before strolling to Heller's table in the restaurant's most secluded corner. Foreman nodded to Heller and said "Hi" as he pulled out a chair and seated himself.

"You have a real thing about cloak and dagger stuff, don't you? How did you find this place?" Foreman's smile was an outward manifestation of the amusement and contempt he felt for the little man sitting across from him.

"Did you find out anything useful?" Heller ignored Foreman's questions as though he'd never asked them.

"Depends, on what you call useful."

Heller was upset. "Hey, I'm paying you—"

"Alright," Foreman was grudgingly apologetic, "You're the boss." He held his hand up asking for patience while he removed a small notebook from his shirt pocket. Thumbing back a few pages, he located what he wanted. "This is what I found at the courthouse." Foreman looked at Arthur as he said, "Most of this stuff isn't like you told me. First, Dupree's father never owned the property on the island. It was purchased by Benedict Dupree after his old man kicked off. The old man's been dead more than twenty years. Benedict actually purchased the property nineteen years ago. And, it's not a lie that Dupree declared it a wildlife sanctuary. Supposedly, there are two species, a burrowing owl and a gopher tortoise, that *could* have lived there. Evidently, they're on the mainland, but them being on the island is probably a crock. He *does* have an agreement to deed over the property to the state when he dies, and he signed a 'no development' pledge. That's probably why the county and state people support him so strongly."

Heller frowned, "You think they'll fight any attempt to gain access?"

"Oh, yeah. They'll fight like hell. They have a vested interest, and the Dupree guy is very well liked. He's got the reputation of being a loon over the sea turtles, but most of the local yokels around here, like that. Other than being considered eccentric because he protects the turtles and the land so adamantly, everybody I talked to think he's great. He probably could run for office and win."

"Anything, else?" Heller looked dejected.

"No. His taxes are up-to-date. Never had problems with the law. Worst thing I could find was a ticket for not coming to a complete stop at a stop sign. And, that was dismissed."

"Find anything out about the girl?"

"That was a shutout. There's nothing about her in any public records, taxes, licenses, criminal records, school rosters, hospital patient lists, nothing. Nothing in the newspaper archives about her. If she was ever here, it was for a visit. The Greyhound station's been closed for a while, so that's a dead end. You said you thought she might have stayed on Pine Island. I tried asking a few of the places that rented back then, but nothing. One of the motel owners told me he has a hard time remembering people that stayed with him three years ago, much less thirty. Credit card records were trashed years ago. My guess is you'll never know if she was here or not."

"She was." Heller scratched his chin. "How about getting on the property another way?" He asked.

"You mean trespass. Is it possible? Yes. I dug under the fence without being disturbed. That only took an hour. Are you going to be able to spend the time to do what you want? No, no, no. The Park people probably only get down there once a week Folks that live on the south end of the island don't go up to that area. Fisherman that go there are few and don't get off the shoreline. You might be able to work around them. But, Dupree spends a lot of time over there, and he shows up at odd times. The worst thing is a hermit that lives on the bay side of the island. The old shit has a shack a mile or so away. He snoops around the area like a shadow. I spotted him two or three times while I was scouting. He was watching me before I ever knew he was there. A cat couldn't work over there without him knowing about it in a day or two. Not and do what you're thinking of."

"What am I thinking?" Heller's tone was sarcastic.

"Well, you *say* you're looking for buried treasure. You *say* you don't know the exact spot. To me, that means a lot of hole digging. That's pretty hard to hide. That is if you're really looking for buried treasure." It was clear Foreman believed Heller was lying to him.

"Digging isn't the only way to find something buried under the ground." Heller removed a folded piece of paper from his sports coat pocket. He unfolded what proved to be a crude map. "X marks the spot."

"That doesn't look like anything on the island," Foreman said.

"It isn't. It's a map of an archeological research center on Pine Island. See the box with the X marked in it?"

"Uh-huh," Foreman was thoroughly confused.

"That's a maintenance shed. And, in that shed is a portable ground penetrating radar unit." Heller smiled at Foreman's surprised look. "It only gets used a few times a year. My sources tell me it won't be needed for three months. That's plenty of time to borrow it, use it to find what I'm looking for, and return it to the shed. So what do you think I want you to do next?"

"Borrow the unit."

"Correcto mundo!"

"When?"

"As soon as you can. It's just got a simple padlock on the shed and nothing on the cabinet it's stored in."

"That's no problem. It will cost you another thousand to get it out and ditto to return it."

Heller fished his wallet out of his pants pocket and removed five bills. "Here's half. You get the rest when I get the unit."

Foreman smiled, took the cash and nodded.

Heller looked at his watch and stood up. "Terrell, I have to go see a couple of boys and find out if they're enjoying their convertible."

Chapter 20
Pine Island Sound, Florida
May 2010

"Damn, Benny don't you feel guilty?" MacCardle sipped beer from a bottle while his buddy was fishing from the front of Billy's boat.

Benny was surprised and agitated. "What do you mean by that?"

"Don't you think we both should at least be a little ashamed? Our employees are working their butts off, while we're out doing the Benny and Billy show. The fish are biting, the weather's good, and the beer is cold. Back at the offices and construction sites, people are worrying about one problem after another, and the sun is baking everybody." Billy grinned. "I know you should. I know I should. Truth is, I know neither of us are gonna lose five minutes sleep." He tipped the bottle up and downed the remainder of his Coors.

Benny sighed and looked relieved. "We have it good on days like today. But, I can remember *whennnnnnnn*," He hesitated and added, "So can you."

"True."

"For a second, I thought you knew ... I'd forgotten to do something. I've gotten bad about that recently." Benny put his pole down, made his way to the cooler, and removed a beer. "I need a favor, Billy. A confidential one."

"No problem. What do you need?"

"You still keep in contact with your old buddy from the Marines. The one that's a lawyer and has a private investigation agency?"

"Harper Sturgis? Yes, I talk to her once a month or so. She's moved to Tampa from Mobile. We're close." Billy hesitated. "I hope you don't want me to fix you up with her. Love you like a brother. Love her like a sister. But the two of you...you're all emotion...she's no emotion. No way." Mac read Benny's critical look. "Not that she doesn't have a big heart. I've seen her run through machine gun fire to save a dog and cry like a baby when it died. Down deep she's warm she just doesn't want anyone to know it."

"I'm not looking for a lay, Mac. I've got a couple numbers in my book." Benny shook his head. "It's strictly business. Here's the deal, there have been two men asking a lot of questions about me. I don't know either one. I want to find out who they are, what they do, that kind of thing. I want to know why they are interested in me and my property. I want to do it without them or anyone knowing I'm checking on them."

"That's all?"

"Yes, nothing more."

"Give me their names. That will be a piece of cake for Harper. You can consider it done."

Chapter 21
Turtle Point, Cayo Costa, Florida
May 2010

"Benedict Barron Dupree you're one sorry son-of-a-bitch." Benny brought the bottle of Wild Turkey to his lips and took a swig. It burnt its way down his gullet, but he was already drunk enough not to be disturbed by the fire working its way to his stomach. He looked down the moonlit beach, but did not see its beauty. The turtles that would come, nest, and prolong their species existence because of his assistance weren't in his thoughts. His successes in business, in community activities, in charities were forgotten.

The only thing important was his one mistake. His failure. That failure froze time for him as though one hour had lasted over thirty years. He didn't need a shrink to tell him that his determination to be successful in protecting the sea turtles was his way of atoning for that failure. "Where are you?" Benny stood up. He swayed back and forth, lurched to one side, overcompensated, and fell face-first onto the beach. Trying to get his elbows under him to lift his head from the sand was difficult. White powder coated his face forming a gritty paste when it mixed with his sweat, sweat that covered his whole body. The world wanted to spin and trying to get up was hard work. "Screw it," he said as he rolled over on his back.

Benny looked at the sky. Stars glittered in a field illuminated by the bright moon. A few high clouds drifted toward the sea. Lightning from distant storms danced over the Gulf, but so far offshore the thunder rumbles seldom reached his ears. His eyelids weighed tons and sleep overtook him, but the irreverent, relentless rising tide drenched and awakened Benny. He cursed and struggled to a sitting position. Disoriented, he tried to remember where he was and why he was there. "Oh, yes ... Fucking turtles." Struggling to his feet, Benny tottered down the beach sloshing through ankle deep water.

"Come on in." Dupree tried running, but a few steps told him he wasn't in condition to manage a fifty-yard dash. He stopped, cupped his hands around his mouth and screamed, "Callin' all turtles. Callin' all turtles. Get your asses in here. It's time to get laid." Benny laughed at his humorless wit and sloshed through the water. The warm water. The very warm water. He screamed, "Damn, it's warm as piss. It's warm as piss. The Gulf of Mexico is as hot as piss." After a few difficult seconds attempting to reason, he concluded. "The Gulf of Mexico is piss!"

Why was he here? The thinking process was difficult. "Turtles. You Loggerheads. You big Green bitches. Come on in." He put his arms up and yelled, "Here, right here."

Benny took a few steps and shook his head violently. He thought he might feel better if he puked. So he did. Why was he there? "Turtles," he screamed. He decided he needed another drink. Yep, that would help. Then he'd sit and wait for the turtles. Maybe he'd sleep some. If he was lucky, he'd dream of Nadine. If not...

Goodun watched his friend's drunken moonlit struggle with demons neither of them could see, but both understood. He'd seen Benny confront these enemies before, but *never* this overtly. "You're one tortured soul," Goodun said to bushes that couldn't hear him. Though Benny was more tormented than Goodun had seen before, it would end the same. His friend would eventually find his way back to his chair, fall asleep and wake up hours later, a mosquito-bitten mess. Goodun shook his head. The past would be gone...for a while. There was nothing more he could do for the boy. He knew there were some battles that were so personal even friends couldn't help. After more wild shouts and staggering around, Benny Dupree slumped into his beach chair. Goodun was certain his friend was asleep and dreaming before his body completely relaxed in the seat.

Chapter 22
Turtle Point, Cayo Costa, Florida
June 1980

Nadine giggled.

"What's so funny?" Benny asked as he adjusted the straps from two duffle bags that rested on his shoulders and got a better grip on the cooler he was carrying.

"Nothing. Ahhhh, it's just you already have a creature to reincarnate as, if you believe in that sort of thing."

"Oh? What animal do you have in mind? A Lion? A porpoise?" Benny dodged branches that extended into the familiar trail that crossed Cayo Costa. The path they walked ended at Turtle Point. The transit back and forth from bay to beach took twenty minutes each way.

"No. What I had in mind was a burro. They can carry a load as big and heavy as they are." Nadine nodded toward the bags, the cooler, a radio, and beach chairs strapped, tied and carried by him.

"Like those animals that carry people in and out of the Grand Canyon? My father told me about them. He was there one time."

"Yes. They weren't the ones I was thinking about. My family is originally from Italy. When I was young, we went to the village where my grandparents used to live to visit relatives. It's northeast of Rome. The village is near Grosseto in the Province of Tuscany. The burros hauled the produce my family grew to the markets. That was in 1969. I often wonder if things have changed much there."

"Don't you stay in touch with your family?" Benny stopped to hike up the straps that kept sliding down his shoulder.

"Not since my parents died. They were killed in a car wreck a few years ago."

"Did your grandma come back to the US as a war-bride?"

Nadine looked toward the beach. When she spoke, it was softer than usual. "No. My whole family immigrated."

Benny did some quick math. It made sense. "I know things were bad over there during that time. Did your grandparents come to get away from all the destruction?"

"No. Benny, they came as political refugees." Nadine was agitated, but Benny missed the signs.

Bocelli wasn't a Jewish sounding name, nor did she look Semitic. Many of the political refugees entering the country were fleeing persecution that persisted even after World War II. "You don't look Jewish or even Italian."

Nadine spun around, stopping abruptly in front of him. She pulled open her shirt and pulled two chains out. Her hand found an ornately decorated cross, and she stretched the chain holding it out for him to see. The cross was obviously *not* custom jewelry. "I'm Catholic. I don't look Italian because my mother was Scotch-Irish." Nadine stuffed the cross and a key that hung from the other chain back under her shirt. There were tears in her eyes as she walked down the trail. "I don't want to talk about my family," she said, the anger clearly discernible in her voice. After four or five steps, Nadine whirled around and faced Benny, the tears now tracking down her cheeks.

Benny felt like a dog that had just eaten its

master's meal. He apologized saying, "I'm sorry. I didn't want to open any wounds."

"Oh Benny, I'm the one who is sorry. You couldn't know how I feel." She walked to him and extended one hand gently touching his cheek. "The last two-and-a-half weeks have been wonderful. I don't want to ruin or lose that. There are things about my family's history that are hurtful. Let's pretend we never discussed my family or my past. I want to savor the time we have left. It's only a little more than a week. Let's only make good memories. Okay?"

Benny's smile was sad and sincere. "I'm all for that."

Chapter 23
Turtle Point, Cayo Costa, Florida
June 1980

It had become a ritual. Camp Loggerhead, as Nadine had christened it, took form on each of their visits. The lean-to was erected, each item stored in its preassigned location, the chairs placed on the sand dune atop Turtle Point, cameras and flash equipment were checked, spare rolls of 35mm film placed where it would be quickly available in night's low light conditions, binoculars and flashlights placed next to the chairs, and the cooler went in whatever shade the lean-to could provide. After passing Nadine's final inspection, for she needed to be precise and in control, the radio-tape player filled the air with music. Music was the one thing that softened Nadine's focus on her scientific duties.

The next activity was a careful examination of each nesting site they'd cataloged and a search for new ones. Every site was marked with a numbered stake. Nadine recorded what Benny saw as even the most trivial information. The number of incubation days and similar facts made scientific sense. So did things like the distance above the high-tide line each nest was built. But, things like what kind of vegetation was close to the nest or what non-predatory animal tracks were near its sands, seemed irrelevant. That was until Nadine explained her reasoning for gathering the data. For example, she wanted to learn if the turtles selected a nesting spot with a particular type vegetation next to it because its root system would make it more difficult for predators to dig up the eggs or the plant's scent would disguise the eggs odor. She was smart and focused.

Their observatory ranged three-quarters of a mile on either side of Turtle Point. Most days, Benny was off work by three, being the boss' son helped, and he and Nadine were able to have Camp Loggerhead setup before five. It left them over two hours to peruse the nests. The afternoon sun was still at its hottest. Perspiration and sand coated their bodies by the time they finished. There was a simple remedy for that. They stripped down to their bathing suits and spent a half-hour relaxing in the tepid gulf waters.

For Benny, the evening swim was the best and worst of times. Benny was in love. Not in heat, in love. He was a perfect gentleman, scrupulously adhering to the girl's cautions when they started their relationship. He hoped, but that was all he could do.

Nadine wore two swimsuits, a black one-piece that was tempting enough, but the bikini she wore inflamed him. He didn't dare stand in shallow water because of the embarrassment that would accompany the unmasking of his arousal. The Bikini was two bits of bright orange cloth adorned with big brown Polka dots. It barely covered her rear and only covered half of her abdomen. Her flat stomach, tiny waist, and most tantalizing, her bubble shaped buttocks, were eye magnets with the power of attraction he couldn't over-power. The top was designed like a skimpy bra, made from the same material. Every movement she made suggested that her breasts were struggling to be free. That suit tortured him; it represented something he could never have.

The evening Benny made the mistake of asking about Nadine's family was one of those she wore her bikini. The cloud from her rebuke hung over Dupree. He was quiet, a condition not often observed in or connected to him. If Nadine noticed, she didn't say anything but paddled around in the clear water. She set the schedule, and it was evident she was in no hurry to leave the water on that evening. The sun was about to touch the sea when Nadine swam fifty-feet from Benny, paddled around for several seconds, then returned to the chest-deep water he stood in.

She cocked her head to the side, smiled and said, "You ready?"

"Sure." He started the walk to shore. Nadine moved very close to him. From the corner of his eye, he saw her lift something from the peaceful, calm water. Her bikini bottom rose above her like a flag over a monument. Her arm circled around his waist. Nadine's eyes closed and her lips elevated to reach his. They touched, and two deep, mutual fires exploded.

"Take my top off," she commanded. Her hands feverishly clawed at Benny's trunks pulling downward. Within seconds they were naked and in less time than that.

Benny realized it after they'd finished. He'd made love to a woman for the first time. It was not like the sex he'd had with a half-dozen girls. That had been largely a mechanical happening. Those co-eds performed dutifully, acting as they supposed they should to satisfy their partner. Sex with Nadine was nothing like that. She demanded, she commanded, she exerted. She'd have none of "one and done." By the time they'd finished, he'd done things for the first time and realized a level of satisfaction, and fear, he'd never come close to before. The satisfaction needs no explanation; the fear...the fear came from the realization that his relationship with the goddess lying on top and to the side of him would last a week.

He felt her stir, and he asked, "Are the bugs bothering you?"

"Yes."

"Shouldn't we get some clothes on?"

"No." Her leg arced across his stomach and her breasts rubbed over his chest as she kissed him and placed her body squarely over his. He felt her hands push against his chest and the soft moistness of her meet and demand the hardness of his.

Chapter 24
Pine Island, Florida
June 1980

Sunlight streamed through the window of Nadine's rental cottage. Benny woke in stages.

He vaguely knew it was morning, then realized he wasn't in his bed. Finally, the full sunlight meant it was late. He lifted himself onto one elbow. Sitting cross-legged on the bed, Nadine's naked body finished awakening him.

"You're going to be late to work." She smiled at him and lifted a cup of coffee from the nightstand. "Want a cup?"

"Yes."

"I have breakfast made. Depending on how fast you can shower and dress you should be to Cape Coral in an hour to an hour-and-a-quarter."

Benny calculated his time, "I'll do better than that," he said.

"No. I don't think so," Nadine said as she leaned toward him. "Remember, we only have a week to make a memory for a lifetime."

Chapter 25
Fort Myers, Florida
May 2010

"I'll take the rest of my thousand," Terrell Foreman said. He extended his hand.

Arthur Heller smiled and handed five-one-hundred-dollar bills to the man sitting across from him. "Have you found a place to train the boys?"

"Oh, yes." Foreman pocketed the cash. "It's up in the woods in Charlotte County." He hesitated. "Are the two boys smart enough to learn to use that thing in a reasonable time period?" The longer it takes them, the greater the probability we're all going to get caught."

"That won't be a problem. I knew the unit's make and model, so I went on the net and bought an instruction manual. They've been reading for a week and seem to understand it." Heller grinned. "Those two are more mercenary than you. Toss any kind of incentive at them and they go after it like a couple pit bulls go after a cat."

"They'd better. There's a lot of square footage to cover."

"Terrell, don't underestimate me. Check these out." Heller placed a flat map case on the restaurant table. He removed a large photo map and laid it in front of Foreman. "This is a recent aerial photo of the area. I've marked the locations that look like they could be the right spots. There are twenty-one in all, but I'm betting we find what I'm looking for in the first four." Heller pointed to the places marked on the map. "See how they look sunk?" Arthur leaned back, enjoying Foreman's surprised expression. "A friend who did military grave registration told me about using an aerial and what to look for. I'm guessing it will take three, four nights at the longest."

Arthur leaned toward Forman. He asked, "Have you figured how you're going to get the radar unit inside the fence and back out?"

"That's no problem. It's an old prison trick. All I need is three-step ladders and some heavy duty blankets. We get one of your boys inside by throwing the blankets over the razor wire. He takes a ladder in with him; we have two outside. We lift the radar machine up and over and reverse the process coming out. It will be a piece of cake." Foreman pointed to the map, "This is sure going to help. I have a boat rented for a month. It has a cabin and is big enough to store the unit on during the day. There's only one thing."

"What's that?"

"That guy that lives on the back side of the island. He stalks around the area, and you don't know where or when he'll show up. He's old and all that, but the bastard acts like he had experience walking point. We shouldn't underestimate him."

"We won't. I already know you always enjoy making more money so I won't ask. Find out if he has any relatives that live out of the area. Look for some reason to get him out of here. We need to see if we can arrange for him to make an unplanned trip."

Terrell nodded. "I have an idea or two on that. What about Dupree? We need to keep him away, too."

"Leave that to me." Heller smiled. "Those boys will come in handy for that, also."

Chapter 26
Chamblee, Georgia
May 2010

"IRS, Fraudulent Claims Division, this is Hector Sump." The man sitting behind the speakerphone put aside papers he was reviewing and frowned at the interruption. Subconsciously, he'd decided the person who'd intruded into his concentration would get a hard time.

"Hi, Hector, got a few minutes to chat?"

At the sound of Terrell Foreman's voice, Hector dropped his papers, snatched the phone's handset from its cradle and silenced the speaker. "Terrell, that you?" he asked.

"Yes."

"Aaaaa...Terrell, I'd appreciate if you wouldn't call me here." Sump's voice was as low as it could be and still be audible on the phone line's other end. He glanced at the desks and cubicles surrounding him. No one seemed to be paying attention. Hector took a deep breath. "You have my home phone."

"I heard the message that says calls may be recorded, Hector. I just want to do *you* a favor. It's come to my attention that a man I've come in contact with is cheating on his taxes. He's claiming false deductions. That's your area, isn't it?" There was a taunting lilt in Foreman's voice. "You always told me, you could arrange anything if it meant bringing a criminal to justice. You're still the man to do that, right?"

"Yes." Sump was tentative and apprehensive.

"Good. I knew I had the right man. I'd love to talk now, but I have a meeting, and I have to go."

Foreman emphasized his next sentence, "This has to do with business we had in the past, and *you know how important that was for you.*"

"Uh-huh," Hector said weakly.

"Give me your cell phone number and tell me when you go to lunch. I'll call back then." Foreman's words weren't a request; they were a demand. Hector Sump was well aware of that.

"I'll be leaving at 11:30, but—"

"Hector, Hector, there won't need to be any buts. We're old friends. I do something for you, and you get a chance to do something for me in the future. *Your cell number?*"

"It's 404-555-1331." Sump's face drooped. He knew the favor was going to be repaid ...now.

Chapter 27
Fort Myers, Florida
May 2010

Devale and Sean spied their new found benefactor seated in a rear booth of the Napoli Pizza Parlor. They'd responded to a text on Devale's cell phone. Heller was keeping them busy and staying in control. Though they had the keys and the car, "the old dude" retained the car's title. He warned if there was any lose talk or they divulged any information about the project, they'd lose the car. The professor kept them busy with small tasks, like learning how to use the ground penetrating radar unit. Liberal cash "tips" kept them happy.

Devale's mother had been very skeptical. "After all," she said, "It's perfectly normal for some old white guy to walk up to you and offer you a new car. That's as fishy as a week old mullet!" She had a friend at the Sheriff's Office discreetly check to see if the car was stolen. When it came back clean, she remained suspicious. But, after Devale retold a cover story furnished by Heller, and protestations that he wasn't doing anything illegal, she gave up exploring it further. She convinced herself that Devale's mystery employer was just that. Trying to take the car away, a teenager's treasure would have been impossible anyway.

Since Devale kept the car at his home, Sean's parents were unconcerned. Besides, since the two boys' good fortune, Sean's constant moaning about wanting a car of his own changed to blessed silence.

"Wonder what the shit he wants now?" Sean asked.

"Who cares," Devale answered. "I'm not bitching to someone who waived a wand and *gave us* some mega-cool wheels."

"Aren't you kind of concerned what he'll want us to do next?" Sean asked. "Honestly? Hell, no!"

Arthur Heller waved to them. His normal smile was frozen on his face. As they walked to his table, Sean muttered under his breath, "I'm keeping my hand over my hole. Sooner or later the shaft's coming."

"Shut up!" Devale cautioned. When they were a couple of steps from the table, Devale said, "Hey, Mr. Heller, you hangin' loose?"

"Hi, guys. I'm cool." Heller's attempt to sound mod and relevant was starched and reeked of being false. "Have a seat. I've got a pepperoni 'zza on the way."

Devale shot a quick look at Sean who was doing his best not to laugh. "That's cool," Devale said politely. "You're getting texting down. I understood what you meant this time."

"Good. I haven't allowed my students to text me in the past. I may reconsider that."

"It works," Sean said. "Why did you want to see us?"

"I wondered if you'd like to make some gas money for your 'Stang? I have an opportunity for you two to make a hundred apiece. And, it will make your lives a lot easier when it comes to completing the other part of our little deal."

"What do we have to do?" Sean asked suspiciously.

"Pull a dirty trick on someone." Heller's smile hadn't thawed.

"Like what?" Sean's tone wasn't friendly.

When Heller's smile disappeared, Devale quickly interjected, "Two hundred sounds real good, but we need to know what we're gonna have to do to score it. You know, some things sound too good to my bro here."

Heller's smile quickly returned. "That's wise." He leaned toward them and lowered his voice. "We've discussed the potential problem that the man who owns the property could cause. Well, I have a way to keep him from showing up over at Turtle Point for several days."

"How?" both boys asked.

"Mr. Dupree uses his boat to get over to his property. That's his only boat, and as far as I can tell, he never borrows one. If something were to happen to his outboard that would take a few days to fix ...."

"How do we make that happen?" Devale asked.

"Under the table, there's a five-pound bag of sugar. If that sugar were to get into Dupree's boat gas tank...well, he wouldn't be out to Cayo Costa for several days."

"That's fine, but sneaking around someone's home late at night can get you shot." Sean didn't like the sound of Heller's idea.

"You won't be sneaking around, and it won't be at night. In the same plastic bag with the sugar, there are two tee shirts with "Marine Detailing" printed on them. The two of you are in the boat cleaning business the moment you slip on those shirts. You're going to visit Mr. Dupree's house around 11:00 AM, while he's off at work. He lives alone. Mr. Foreman will loan you his rental truck so your car can't be identified. You do fifteen minutes of boat cleaning and leave the sugar where it will do what we want." He grinned heartily. "Mr. Dupree's boat won't run, he won't arrive at Turtle Point to interfere with your work, no one will know who did it, and you two will be $200 richer."

The boys looked at each other. Devale said, "It's an easy two," and Sean nodded to confirm.

"Good!" Heller extended his hand and shook theirs. "It should be simple. Dupree's boat is docked in the canal behind his house. Most of his neighbors are up North for the summer. Probably, no one will even see you, much less ask any questions. I'll let you know when."

Chapter 28
Pine Island, Florida
May 2010

"Mr. Warrington is here to see you." Corrine stood in Benny's office door. She was as surprised as Benny looked.

"Send him on in." Benny got out of his chair and stepped around his desk to meet his friend and very unexpected guest.

Corrine Foy led Goodun into the office much like she would lead a puppy into a new home. For his part, Warrington was obviously uncomfortable in his surroundings, nervous, and Benny guessed, mad about something. Goodun wore a plaid shirt, with a collar, that looked and smelled new, and jeans that didn't show a trace of fish slime or blood, an unusual condition for Warrington's trousers. For the first time, Dupree saw Goodun wear "real shoes," not flip-flops that got him admittance to local stores.

"Good to see you, Goodun. You look nice dressed up like that. What brings you in off the island?"

"This." Warrington removed a folded piece of paper from his pocket and handed it to Benny.

It was a letter printed on Internal Revenue Service letterhead. Benny read the letter.

When he finished, Benny said, "This is a mistake. The IRS thinks you're some type of a huge commercial fishing corporation." Benny found some of the phrases he'd read and quoted them aloud. "This office has received many documents confirming large sums tendered to your company for product sold that were not reported as income." He shook his head. "Your tax return was missing numerous required forms and information required ... blah, blah, blah. It sounds like they have you mixed up with Starkist Tuna."

Goodun shrugged his shoulders and pointed to the last paragraph. "I need to call him." Benny reread that part of the letter. "To resolve this matter call Hector Sump at ..."

Benny read the case number assigned and the phone number to himself. "This *has* to be a mistake. You want me to call and straighten this out?"

"No, I will. Need to use your phone, if I can."

"Sure, Goodun. You can use my office." Dupree started to leave.

Goodun shook his head, "You can stay." It was as close as Warrington could come to asking for help.

Benny watched his friend's face as Warrington's conversation with the IRS progressed. Since he was only able to hear one side of the discussion and given Goodun's paucity of expressing himself, Benny could only be sure of one thing; things hadn't gone well. When Goodun hung up the phone, he removed his hand very slowly, staring at the handset in disbelief.

Benny waited for his friend to say something...anything, so he could initiate a conversation and see if he could help. He'd never seen the look on Warrington's face in the forty years he'd known him. Helplessness.

The silence increased the tension. Benny couldn't stand it. "Did you talk to the guy the letter mentioned?" he asked.

"Yes."

"Did it go well?"

"No."

"Is there anything I can do to help?"

Warrington shrugged his shoulders, shook his head and said, "Nothing."

"What's next?"

"He said I gotta go up there."

"To Atlanta? That doesn't make sense. There are offices closer that you should be able to go to."

"He said no. Gotta bring records up there. I can't take what I don't have."

"That's shit. I heard you ask what would happen if you didn't go. What did he say?"

"They'd send a US Marshall to get me."

"This whole thing is crazy. When do you have to go?"

"Next week."

"How are you going to get up there?"

Goodun looked at Benny for a long time before answering, "I'll get there."

"I'll swap you the use of one of the company pick-ups for enough mullet to supply the church fish fry this fall. That's if you'd want to drive."

"Fair enough." He nodded to Benny, a gesture thanking Dupree for his help. Goodun left without saying goodbye.

Chapter 29
Pine Island, Florida
May 2010

"When are you going to tell me what's really going on?" Foreman asked. He twisted in his rented pick-up's front seat to stare down his partner. The engine idled and the AC hummed as he and Heller sat parked at the Jug Creek Marina docks. They were waiting for something.

Heller remained poker-faced. After several seconds, he answered, "Terrill, I can assure you there *is* a treasure." He frowned at the cigarette dangling from Foreman's mouth. "I really wish you wouldn't smoke those things when I'm in the truck with you."

Foreman returned Heller's frown, rolled his window down a few inches, and flicked the butt outside. "Sorry," Foreman said. But his tone and inflection made it as clear as possible; he wasn't. "You've made some big promises, Arthur. I don't want you to disappoint anyone." He left unsaid that it wouldn't be good for Heller's health.

"I've always kept my word to you. So far, everything has worked as I said it would, hasn't it? You're being well paid, aren't you?"

"Yes ... and no complaints about what you've paid me. But, sometimes crazy men do crazy things. You're spending a hell of a lot. I'd hate to see you go broke."

Heller smiled sarcastically. "Terrill, you surprise me. Your concern touches me. You can always cut your rates in half." He leaned forward to gain a better view of the waters in front of the marina. "Let me assure you I'm not crazy and the treasure I'm looking for would make a hundred times what I've spent so far, insignificant." Nothing was in view. Arthur leaned back in his seat. "Insignificant." His echo was more for his benefit than Foreman's.

"If the treasure's that large, how in the hell are we gonna dig it up and get it off the island? We'll need a backhoe, not two half-assed teenagers on shovel handles."

"I see what you mean. Maybe I should lease a barge, and a back-hoe, and maybe even a bulldozer." The smile left Heller's face. "Your vision is of huge wooden chests filled with Spanish gold coins, jewels, fabulous artifacts. When the word treasure is spoken, that's what flashes into most people's minds." He looked at Foreman. "That what you see?"

Foreman stared but said nothing. He thought about how much he'd enjoy strangling the arrogant son-of-a-bitch.

"With what I have in my motel room combined with what I'm sure we'll find on that island, I won't have to worry about what exotic place I want to vacation in. I'll just buy it instead." Heller leaned forward to gaze at the water. "And, we won't have long to wait. That's Warrington in his boat coming now. In three or four days, we'll have it."

Chapter 30
Pine Island, Florida
May 2010

He opened the three-ring binder that sat on his lap. In it were voluminous notes and many plastic sheet holders, each with a page that had been torn from a book, journal or magazine. Arthur Heller had pursued his dream of wealth for half his life. Not just wealth, fabulous riches incomprehensible to even the richest tycoons. In that binder and others were the products of his exhaustive studies, some gathered at the cost of human life. After reading several pages in the rear of the notebook, he smiled. He placed the binder on the mattress next to where he sat. The dream was within his reach. In mere weeks he would be one of the wealthiest men in the world. Heller picked up the cell phone from his motel room bed. He smiled when he recognized Terrill Foreman's number and turned on the speaker. His first words were, "Good news, I hope."

"Yeah. He tried going out about five. The sugar did its job. By six one of his neighbors had towed him back to his dock. He hitched up his trailer and jerked the boat. It's sitting in his side yard."

"That *is* good news. That's great news." Heller was exhilarated. "No use waiting. I'll call Devale and Sean. I'll have them meet you at the marina in a couple hours. Do you have the radar unit on the boat?"

"Yes." Foreman sounded unenthusiastic. "Arthur, there are lots of thunderstorms—"

"We don't have time to waste. Sump won't be able to hold Warrington up for very long, and you can believe Dupree will have his boat in the shop in the morning."

"Won't the boys' parents be suspicious?"

"The boys have that covered. They're telling their parents they're going on an all-night fishing trip." Heller took a deep breath. "I'll wait here. As soon as you find something, anything unusual at one of those sites, call me and tell me what it looks like. If it's the right thing, I'm going to want you to pick me up and go over right away. I'll be at the marina docks waiting."

Chapter 31
Pine Island, Florida
June 1980

For the first time in Benny Dupree's young life, he was faced with an inevitable situation. Nothing could change the fact that Nadine would leave within hours. Nothing could change the fact that Nadine wouldn't provide any information about how to reach her. Nothing could change the fact that she said the next few hours would be their last together...forever. Nothing could change the fact she admitted she had strong feelings for him, but that her mysterious past made a mutual future impossible. Most importantly, nothing could change the fact he'd fallen deeply in love with Nadine.

Benny loaded Nadine's suitcases and duffle bags in his Ford Granada, a three-year-old "hand-me-down" from his father. Benny was so concerned about creating a positive image in Nadine's mind, he regretted sharing that piece of innocuous information. He feared he wouldn't be seen as independent enough by this girl, who obviously was. Slamming the trunk lid was like slamming the door on part of his life. In fact, it was.

Inside her rental, Nadine made one final check to be sure she had all her personal belongings. He looked at the little house with longing. Was the last ten days he'd spent with Nadine what marriage was like? In his mind, he'd assumed ownership of the house, and it *now* belonged to Mr. and Mrs. Benedict Dupree. The memories would be so good! All except for one.

That memory happened one stormy afternoon when the winds and lightning made travel to Turtle Point too dangerous to attempt. During a lull in the storm's ferocity, a knock at the door sent Nadine into a panic. She jumped out of her chair, peeked out a window, and returned to Benny, terror covering her face. "Hide!" she said in a gassy whisper.

"What are you afraid of, Nadine?" Benny looked out the window.

Nadine's voice quivered as she said, "No!"

"It's only Andy Spurl, the newspaper man." Benny opened the door, carried on a brief conversation, and explained "thanks but no thanks," before the return of winds, lightning, and torrents disrupted the chat.

The fear was still fresh in Nadine's eyes when Benny sat down next to her. "Are you okay?" he asked.

Nadine stared at her folded hands that rested on her lap. "He looked like a man that's been following me. The people he represents, you won't believe this, I think they killed my parents and my little sister. The police said it was an automobile accident and fire. It might have been, but I'm sure they caused it."

"Why did they kill your parents?" Justified or not, Benny saw that Nadine's fear was real. "They wanted something from them. They tried to get it several times. My parents didn't have it, but they couldn't make them believe that."

Benny put his hand on her arm which was shaking, He asked, "Do you know who 'they' are?"

Nadine looked into his eyes, "The Mafia, I think."

He whistled softly and asked, "Do you know what they wanted?"

"Books, papers, records, and personal items that

were my grandparents. Things they brought with them from Italy."

"Do you have any of the stuff they're looking for?"

"No. Neither did mom and dad. They told me they didn't know where or what it was. But, I'm not sure—" She turned her head and looked at Benny. "It's the reason...let's not talk about this anymore."

No amount of Benny's prying could unseal her lips.

Chapter 32
Pine Island, Florida
June 1980

When Nadine emerged from the house, tears were crawling down her cheeks. She made no attempt to hide them. The girl arced around the car and slid into the Granada's front seat. The look on her face was defiant. "We'll never have a better time," she said.

"Never." Benny pursed his lips. He knew the words they wanted to form were futile.

"I'll never forget this place ... not if I live to be an old, old lady."

Benny's mouth blurted his thoughts before his brain could moderate, "It doesn't have to be that way. Stay here. Nothing or nobody will bother you as long as I'm alive." He knew they were terribly wrong as they left his tongue.

"Dear, sweet, Benny, you really mean those words, and that's why it can't be." Nadine closed her eyes and slowly shook her head. She deftly changed the subject. "My bus doesn't leave until 1:25. That's a lot of time." She sucked her lower lip in and bit it gently. "I know that we said we'd get a nice dinner." Nadine's pupils riveted to Benny's as she put her hand on his cheek. "Can you take me to Turtle Point one last time? Please? We can be back by midnight and make the bus okay."

"Your wish is my command, your majesty. May I assume there'll be no sand wrestling on this trip?"

Nadine smiled and blushed slightly. "No sand wrestling." She managed a weak smile. "Not that I won't want to, I will, but I can't travel like that ...

and ... I can't have that be the last thing we do. Do you understand?"

"Yes, I do," he said, but he really didn't.

Chapter 33
Turtle Point, Cayo Costa Island, Florida
June 1980

Benny eased his boat's bow into the mangroves. Nadine had become a practiced first mate. She hopped onto the sands of the ten-foot-wide mini beach and secured the boat's mooring line to the stilt-rooted, mangrove's gnarled trunk.

Benny said, "The sun is close to going down. If you want to catch the sunset, we need to hustle over there."

"I'm on my way. Don't forget the insect repellent; there isn't enough breeze to keep them away." She trotted up the trail hoping she wouldn't perspire too badly.

Benny snatched up the repellent and hesitated as his hand passed the flashlights. He didn't have a way to carry them. Even though it would be a practically moonless night, Benny knew the beach path so well he could walk it blindfolded. He'd done that once on a bet. He mumbled, "To hell with them," jumped off the bow, and sprinted to catch up with his lady.

Benny caught Nadine halfway to Turtle Point, and they finished the walk in silence. The sun clung to the horizon long enough for them to reach the sand dune on Turtle Point, get seated, and see the "Green Flash," the mystic puff of color that appears for a fleeting second at the exact time the sun disappears behind the horizon.

Several embraces and passionate kisses depleted the sun's last rays leaving them in the gray of twilight. Nadine abruptly rose to her feet and said, "I want to check a few of the nests that should be close to hatching." Both knew the inevitable result of continuing their necking.

"Let's go." Benny stood and fell in stride with Nadine. They walked along the high tide line, stopping to examine the various nests they knew about and new ones that had been dug during their absence from the beach. Though increasing darkness made it difficult to see, three nests bore the tell-tale signs of hatchings. Rumpled sand over the nest and tiny tracks that led to the Gulf's gently lapping wavelets meant the young had struggled to enter their brave new world. For these fledglings, it was a deadly one. Very few would survive long enough to return to Turtle Point to repeat the cycle.

They walked another two hundred yards when Nadine shouted, "No!" She ran ahead and dropped to her knees. "I was afraid of this." Piles of sand, some sprinkled with destroyed eggs, and empty excavated holes were evidence that poachers had done their deadly work. Large shoe prints covered the area around the destroyed nests. "Do you have a flashlight?" Nadine asked.

"No, they're in the boat."

"I hate to ask, but I have to see how much damage they did." Nadine was choked up, and Benny was sure there were tears, though it was too dark to see them.

"I don't know. I don't like leaving you here. We don't know if these people are still around." Benny knew how important Nadine's request was to her. He relented. "You stay away if they show up, okay?"

"Yes, but I don't believe there's anyone around. The fluid from the broken eggs is dry. This was probably done last night." The girl gently lifted a mashed egg and put it back in the robbed nest.

"I'll be back as quick as I can." Benny raced toward his boat.

Chapter 34
Turtle Point, Cayo Costa Island, Florida
June 1980

The run from the beach to his boat taught Benny a lesson he'd never forget: knowledge, skill, and effort can be trumped by tension, apprehension, and panic. Trying to race across the island in total darkness caused him to miss the trail's opening through the heaviest vegetation. Realizing he'd ventured into an area where his knowledge was limited, he tried to retrace his steps without success. Panic set in. Using the rising moon as a compass, he made his way eastward, fighting his way through the dense mangrove forest. Eventually, he broke through to the old pass and to his boat. Normally a fifteen-minute sprint, it had taken over forty.

As he climbed into the boat, he noticed a light go on in Goodun's cabin. He thought about the possibility of getting his friend to return to the beach with him, but the light went off as quickly as it went on. Benny abandoned the idea. He gathered up the flashlights and started back to the beach.

After winding through the heavily wooded area, he turned off his flashlight. Most people who have spent considerable time moving around in the dark know the flashlight's beam often is more of an impediment than assistance, particularly when the terrain is well known. A quick check of his watch told him he'd been gone almost an hour. He picked up his pace from a trot to a full-fledged sprint.

As Benny neared the beach, he froze when he heard a loud, "No!" come from behind clumps of sea grapes and cabbage palms to the trail's left. The voice was masculine and gruff; certainly not

Nadine's. Adrenalin shot through his system. His whole body responded transforming his senses to those of a hunting jungle cat. Benny stood like a statue, straining his ears to hear something, anything that would pinpoint the voice's location and tell him what was going on.

At first, he couldn't hear it—the sound of waves washing the beach only a couple hundred feet away concealed the grinding sound. But, as he remained immobile, he first heard, then separated one noise from the other. Benny identified it. The metallic scraping sound of a shovel against sand was one he heard on construction sites daily. It electrified him. At the same instant, another thunderbolt struck him full force. Where was Nadine?

Benny needed something to defend him and Nadine. He reached in his pockets as he took careful steps toward the sound. Benny didn't even have the pocket knife he normally carried; he was weaponless. Muffled speech came from behind the underbrush, but he couldn't make out the words or identify the speakers. Using the large clumps of densely foliated, sea grape bushes to cover his approach, Benny moved closer and closer to the noise and activity ahead. A faint light illuminated the brush. He stopped abruptly. The hiss from a Coleman lantern mixed with the shoveling sounds. Benny was close! He looked around hoping to see Nadine, knowing.........

Dropping onto his hands and knees, he crawled forward until he could see what was happening. Benny fervently hoped his fear was unfounded. Through the masking sea grape leaves, a horrible scene unfolded. Two men labored in a small clearing surrounded by a heavy growth of palms, scrub oaks, and sea grapes. Walker Cole and a man Benny didn't know were hunched over, busy covering something with shovels full of sand. Several buckets overflowing with turtle eggs sat to one side with a half-empty liquor bottle and the Coleman lantern next to them. Within twenty feet of Benny, partly obscured by the sea grapes, was the headless carcass of a large Green Sea Turtle. Leaning against it was the instrument of its demise—a double-bladed ax. It was the weapon he needed desperately.

Benny inched around the thick clumps of bushes, losing sight of the clearing until he was able to crawl within a couple yards of the dead turtle and the ax. From the changed angle, he could see into the hole the men were filling. The back of Nadine's head, her auburn hair, neck, and shoulders were visible in the shallow grave. Violent, uncontrollable emotion filled Benny.

As he rose to get the ax, he heard the second man say, "Este es muy mal."

"Shut-up Pablito," Cole said. They were his last words. Benny rushed forward, grabbing the ax and screaming as he attacked the men.

It was over in seconds, seconds that were like hours to Benny. They were seconds that placed him in the prison that was his life. He sat on the dead sea turtle's shell, looking at what he'd done. The two men who had killed Nadine were now dead. Their hacked bodies lay bleeding in the sand.

Walker Cole tried turning and swinging the shovel to defend himself, but his action was too late. Benny buried the ax blade in Cole's face up to the wood. Walker Cole was dead before he hit the sand. Benny felt a burning pain in his thigh. The man who Cole called Pablito stabbed him in the leg with a fishing fillet knife. Benny wrenched the ax from Cole's face. The man tried to roll away, get up and run, but Benny's next blow brought the ax down on the man's knee, almost severing the leg there. Pablito screamed in pain, but only for seconds. Benny swung the ax down on the man's back right below the neck. It buried into the body like it would have if driven into the soft earth under it. In the grip of rage, Benedict Barron Dupree rained five or six furious blows on each body.

Benny rushed to Nadine. With shaking fingers, he felt for a pulse in her neck. He could find none. Benny screamed, "Nooooooooo!"

Fear and remorse struck him as quickly as rage had. The enormity of what he'd done grasped him in a vice, and he shook in its crushing force. He staggered backward and half-sat and half-fell on the turtle. Though bewildered by what just transpired, the pain in his leg reminded him he'd been stabbed. He looked at his leg. Blood soaked his pants. He needed to disinfect the wound and stop the bleeding somehow. Benny looked at the cut. It was more a surface cut than a deep stab; he'd need stitches, but he'd been lucky. His body was in magnificent condition from staying in shape to play football; the leg wouldn't hamper him. Benny looked around for something to bandage his leg and to disinfect it. Panicked rationality returned to him as he used the liquor to cleanse his wound. The sight of the bodies, shovels, turtle, eggs, all whirled around in his head. All Benny could think of was that he had to make the whole thing go away. He had to do it quickly. Lightning illuminated thunderheads to the southeast. He had two hours, maybe three. It had to be done a lot faster than that! Benny rose from the turtle's corpse feverishly determined to dispose of everything around him. Quickly!

Chapter 35
Pine Island, Florida
May 2010

"What are you doing?" Billy MacCardle's voice squawked through the cell phone speaker Benny pressed to his ear. The din of nail guns assembling wall studs for one of his construction projects made it difficult to hear anything.

"I'm trying to get the Beckwith and Spaulding jobs back on schedule," Benny said.

"Okay, what are you doing at lunch?"

Benny left the half-built house and walked toward his truck as he spoke. "I'm taking my boat to the shop. My motor died on me, and I can't figure out why."

"Check the gas?" There was a hint of sarcasm in his friend's voice. Benny wasn't known for his mechanical genius.

"Yes. And, my battery and electrical were fine until I wore it down trying to get it started." Benny frowned. "Mac, you know me and fixing motors. Every time I try, I end up breaking something and making it worse. I'll just take into Harry's and let him worry about it."

"Mind if I ride along? I'll drive over to your house and meet you there. I'd like to talk to you about a couple things."

"Like what?" Benny was a little perturbed with his friend's persistence. "Just wanted to remind you that the zoning meeting regarding the Williams property is tonight."

"Shit! I forgot about that. I'll be there. I know what I'm going to say, so you're not going to change my mind."

"Oh, I know that. Nobody can do anything to change your mind after you get something into that concrete block you call a head. Besides, I'm 90% sure we feel the same on it. I just wanted to fill you in on some of what I heard Tom Handley is trying to pull."

"Tom has his ideas and I have mine."

Mac cleared his throat. "One other thing, Harper Sturgis is in town and would like to meet you. She's agreed to find info on the two men you asked about. Harper is unbelievably sharp, but she's one of those folks that...hell, Benny...she's just different."

"That's no problem; I don't mind meeting her."

"Okay. Just remember I met her in the Marines. And, remember about me warning you that she's different, *real different.*"

Chapter 36
Turtle Point, Cayo Costa Island, Florida
May 2010

"What about those storms?" Sean didn't like the idea of being stranded inside the razor wire topped, chain-link fence. He looked to the southeast and pointed at the flashes lighting the night sky.

"Get in, get the job done, and get out." Terrill Foreman growled at the boy. He didn't like him or Devale.

"We'll be cool," Devale said, trying to assure Sean, Foreman, and himself. "You say we won't have to worry about that old guy that hangs around here?"

"No. He's in Atlanta, and he'll be there for a couple of days. Get this done quick and we'll be out of here with what Heller wants before he ever leaves to come back." Foreman threw a heavy quilted furniture blanket over the razor wire. "Who wants to go in first?"

"I guess I will," Devale said. He climbed one of the ladders resting against the fence, tossed another over the chain-link, slid his body over the furniture pad, and dropped down to the ground on the inside. "No problems," he said as he grinned at Sean and Foreman.

Foreman was busy placing the third ladder against the fence and hoisting the radar unit into position to lift it over the razor wire. Devale was ready on the other side. Sean eyed the plastic case that held the unit. "How much does it weigh?" The question was to delay his trip inside the fence. Sean had lifted the unit several times. He knew it wouldn't be a hassle getting the unit in and out.

"Enough," Foreman snarled. "Get your ass inside; I can handle it by myself. Damn, boy you've trained with the unit several times. You ain't putting this off!"

"Okay, I'll help," Sean said.

"Get...your...ass...over the fence!" The look on Foreman's face told Sean procrastination was at an end. Sean mounted the ladder, rolled over the mat, and joined Devale on the inside. Foreman lifted the carrying case and handed it over the fence with such ease the boys realized he had the brute strength his size indicated he should have.

As they sat the radar unit on the ground, Devale asked, "Do you need any help getting across?"

Foreman laughed. "I'm not coming in. Not until you find something. You have your instructions and the maps. Get your asses in gear. Earn that Mustang."

"How do we know where we are on the map?" Sean whined.

Foreman did a quick count. "You're seven posts back from the beach corner on the north end."

Devale already had his flashlight on and the map case open. "We'll be cool," he said, reassuring Sean and himself.

Sean asked "What are you going to do?"

"Twiddle my thumbs mostly. And, just in case," Terrill hesitated then said, "Devale, shine your light on me." Devale swung the beam onto Foreman's huge body. "Just in case some nosey bastard happens along, I'm going to protect you two." He reached behind his back, lifted his shirt tail, and removed a gun from a hidden holster. "I'll put two 9mm slugs in between their eyes."

The boys' eyes widened as they stared at the Glock. Sean started to say, "Are you rea—"

Devale cut him off sharply. "Shut up! Help me

get this unit out of the case and running." Devale shone the flashlight on the carrying case. The boys eyed each other as they assembled the unit.

Foreman's voice came from the dark on the other side of the fence. "Sean, if you were going to ask if I'd really put some bullets in some slobs brain, the answer is, I would, 'bout as easily as I'd shoot a rat."

The intensity and speed with which the boys worked, doubled.

Chapter 37
Fort Myers, Florida
May 2010

The county conference room was packed when Benny arrived, just on time. He stood in the room's back corner as the county planning and zoning director called the meeting to order. Ignoring the official who read the lengthy zoning change request, Benny scanned the room looking for Mac MacCardle and his friend, Harper Sturgis. After a methodical visual transverse of the first couple rows, Benny located them on the far end of the third line of seats. Though he couldn't see their faces, he could recognize Mac's profile and body from any angle viewed. The black-haired woman sitting next to him had to be Sturgis. She was half a head taller than Mac and sat ramrod straight in her chair. She wore a gray jacket, but the rest of her, including her face, was hidden by the angle and the crowd.

The meeting's heated discussion failed to grasp his attention. He was curious and wanted to see if Sturgis' face might give him a clue to what Mac said, "made her different." When his turn came to speak, he approached the lectern purposefully avoiding snatching a peek at MacCardle and his friend. Benny didn't want to be distracted. Since he owned the most land in the affected area, he knew his opinion would carry weight. Benny stated that he understood Handley's desire to change the land use from single family residential to multi-family, light commercial and that the change would benefit Handley and him, financially. However, Benny said that he had sold a number of lots and homes to people currently living in the area, and though he'd not made any promises regarding zoning, Benny believed he'd given his implied word to keep it zoned as it was when he sold the property. Murmurs ran through the crowd; they knew his opinion would prevail.

His task being accomplished, Benny focused his attention on Mac and Sturgis as he walked to the room's rear. MacCardle said the woman was beautiful and he hadn't exaggerated. Her jet black hair was pulled back and held in place with barrettes. Black irises contrasted to her pale white skin making them very distinct and prominent features. He'd seen features like hers on TV or in a movie, but couldn't remember the star's name. Benny tried to read the woman's expression. The problem: there wasn't any. It was as devoid of any emotion as any face he'd ever seen.

After a few more speakers, some harsh comments between the communities "bunny huggers" and its "slash and burners," comments that really didn't have a place in the proceedings, the board voted four to one to keep the zoning as it was. A gavel banged, and the meeting was dismissed.

Benny chose to stand outside the conference room doors to wait for Mac and Harper Sturgis. The crowd filed out, Tom Handley glowered at him as he passed by, but that was offset by the thankful nods and winks extended to him by most area residents.

The last two people to exit were Mac and Harper. Billy MacCardle was nearly six foot tall. The woman walking next to him towered over him by *at least* eight inches. Yes, she was wearing a pair of stiletto heels, but still....... Her body was femininely shaped, her curves pronounced, but there was a masculine air to her look. Muscles in her arms and legs were defined enough to show under her clothes. There was no doubt in Benny's mind; she spent hours in the weight room. Her graceful movements had the strength of a lioness. Mac had told him a story about three drunken sailors who put their hands in places they shouldn't. Harper put all three in the hospital, one with a broken pelvis. Seeing her made the tale completely reasonable.

"Hey Benny," Mac said, "I want to introduce you to Harper Sturgis. Harper and I worked together at MCIA in Quantico. You'll never meet a better Marine or a prettier one. Harper, this is my friend, Benny Dupree."

"It's a pleasure to meet you, Benny" Harper extended her long-fingered feminine hand.

Benny felt that she restrained her grip. It was measured to *not* create an overbearing first impression. So was her voice's tone. Harper's face was inscrutable. There was no sign of approval or disapproval, smile or frown. Benny felt he was looking at a porcelain mask.

"Nice to meet you, Ms. Sturgis, or would you prefer, Harper?"

"Harper," She said. She wore a black dress that reached midway down her thighs. Her quadriceps were plainly visible even in a relaxed stance. The gray jacket she wore covered a white ruffled blouse. Her breasts were large but hardly seemed so. They didn't command the attention they would have in another female; Harper's presence was command enough. Her face hadn't varied in any way. She asked, "Is there a private place we can go talk? Mac asked me to do some investigative work for you. He told me what he knew. I did some preliminary looking. I want to know why. Curiosity isn't a strong enough motive to generate a request like you're making." Harper's eyes were as cold as those of the sharks he occasionally caught.

"We can go to a restaurant. There's a Durkin's I go to in Cape Coral that's usually deserted this time of evening." At that second, Benny was sorry he'd asked Mac to solicit Harper's help. "If there's some reason you'd rather not—"

"I wouldn't be here if I didn't want to be." Harper showed no emotional reaction.

"Let's go then," Mac said.

"You go home, MacCardle. I know you're best friends with him, but this is a professional relationship. Think about this: aren't there some things Benny here doesn't know about you and that you'd just as soon he never find out?"

"Aaaaa.......I can't think of any." Mac didn't look or sound firm in his conviction.

"Liar. Go home." Harper pointed to the building's exit.

Chapter 38
Cape Coral, Florida
May 2010

Harper led the way. She walked to a rear corner booth in Durkin's Pancake City's most secluded section. She waited for Benny to pick a side then sat across from him. The woman's countenance, bearing, and emotionless state hadn't varied since he first caught sight of her at the zoning meeting. Benny thought: *I'm sitting with a robot, some kind of android.*

"Hi. I'm Elise. What can I get for you?" A very young, apologetic sounding waitress stood next to their booth.

"I'd like a cup of coffee," Harper said. When she turned to look at Elise, a warm smile replaced her poker face.

"And you, sir?" The girl checked off coffee on her order pad.

"Make that two," Benny added.

As the girl started to turn, Harper stopped her. She reached into her purse and removed a twenty. "Elise, I'd like to pay for the coffees now." She handed Elise the bill, continued to smile and added, "No change. My friend and I would like some privacy. Could you see no one is seated close?"

"I sure can!" The girl beamed as she trotted off.

By the time Harper's head turned to face Benny, the poker mask had returned.

"You know, she probably thinks we're having an affair," Benny said.

"I hope so. When you make a request from someone, they lose their curiosity if they *think* they know the reason why."

Benny cocked his head to the side. "You have excellent emotional control. I'd hate to play poker against you, but why did you give the big smile to the girl?"

"Fair question. The girl, Elise, is the type person who wants to serve others. Elise feels for people like herself. She's threatened by aggressive individuals. I wanted her to do something for me, so I asked her in a manner she'd identify with, and I'll get what I want."

"Wow, that's cold.".

"So?"

Benny nodded, "How did you analyze her so fast?"

Harper raised one eyebrow. "Her dress, speech pattern, tone of voice, body language, facial expressions." She waved her hand. "This is a waste of time. Why don't you want the two individuals, Foreman and Heller, nosing around in your affairs? Don't tell me you're curious. There's something you don't want them to find out."

"You know who they are?"

"Yes."

Benny hesitated. Obviously, Harper was very good at what she did. But, did he really want this person to be involved? He stared at her, and she stared back. He became uncomfortable with the silence. "You said there are some things you don't even want your best friend to know."

"That's true. I'm not your friend. What we're trying to determine is if I'm going to be your lawyer and do investigative work for you."

"What do you have to know to represent me?" Benny asked.

"Nothing. I've already made that decision. You have the bank account to afford me." Harper's face was still a blank sheet.

"You're not concerned whether I'm a good guy or a low-life shit?" Benny looked dubious.

"No. I represent both based on what I assume your value system would be."

"Wow. That's honest. A little frightening, but honest." Benny leaned back against the padded booth seat.

Harper looked into the open room; her smile returned as she motioned for Elise to bring the coffee sitting on her tray. Elise had patiently held a position several yards from the table while waiting for some acknowledgment from her customers.

The girl smiled like the Cheshire Cat and said "It's fresh brewed," She put the cups in front of them, and giggled as she rushed off.

"You pegged her right," Benny said.

"People pay me to be right. Are you interested in my services? I know you need them ... I just don't know why, yet." Harper's smile had vanished again.

Benny took a deep breath. "Yes, I feel I should."

"Good. You should *know* it, not *feel* it, however. You look and act like a lost puppy. If I press you to find out what you're hiding now, I won't get the truth. I can start. Chances are I'll know before you tell me." She stopped talking and looked through him for several seconds. "Be very careful around Foreman. He's dangerous."

"Sounds like you've already done more than some light checking."

"I told you I decided I'd represent you already."

"You feel I'm okay, then?" Benny tried a weak smile.

Harper leaned toward him, "I don't *feel* any way. I *know* you're not a rectal aperture."

"You're not much on feelings are you?" Benny was trying to get some connection, an emotional response.

None came, "No, I'm not."

"You don't want feelings? They get in the way of making good decisions?"

"Good decisions make me good money. I'm a materialist. As far as feelings go, the only one I want is the one I get from a very strong, electrifying orgasm." Harper's face never varied.

Chapter 39
Cape Coral, Florida
May 2010

Benny fumbled for his cell phone as it played the first few bars of *Dixie* over and over again. Trying to extract it from his pants pocket, strapped under his seat belt, while driving, was a reoccurring problem. He swore it wouldn't happen again, each time it did. There were simple solutions—get a "hands-free" unit or simply lay the cell in the seat next to him before strapping into his car. He just couldn't seem to think ahead each time he slid into his vehicle.

"Hello," he grumbled into the microphone after the phone's liberation. "Hey, Benny. How'd it go?" Mac's voice was bursting with curiosity.

"You couldn't even wait for me to get home? You warned me she was different."

"Well?"

"Well, what?" Benny wasn't in the mood to talk.

"Are you two hooking up?"

"If you mean by *hooking up* is she going to check on Foreman and Heller, yes." He heard Mac chuckle in the background. "Different you said? Different doesn't tell the story. Not half of it. As far as hooking up with her any other way, I don't think so." Benny chuckled, "I don't think I could survive the frostbite."

"You couldn't," Mac said in a tone that conveyed knowledge, a warning, and regret.

Chapter 40
Turtle Point, Cayo Costa Island, Florida
May 2010

Foreman watched the boys' flashlight beams float around in the underbrush. The lights were only thirty yards away from the fence. Sean and Devale had completed looking at the first spot marked on Heller's aerial map. Devale reported there was nothing under the six foot by six foot patch of sand marked number one. They moved to number two and began slowly pushing the radar unit over the ground.

"I think we found something!" Devale's excited voice blasted through the night air.

"What do you mean, *something*?" Foreman asked and added, "Keep your voice down, asshole."

"Let me run the radar over the whole thing," Devale answered.

Foreman could hear excited comments being exchanged by Sean and Devale. "What the fuck is going on back there?" Foreman demanded.

"This thing is big. It could be a chest, except it's kind of oval shaped, not rectangular. It has four flaps sticking out, and there's a ball looking thing next to one side."

"Give me a size," Foreman said.

Sean answered, "It's about three-and-a-half feet by maybe two-and-a-half."

"Oh, shit!" Devale shouted, "That ball thing is a skull."

"A skull?" Foreman repeated.

"It's a skull, but I don't think it's a human one," Devale offered.

"Dig a small hole down. See if you can tell what it is." Foreman pulled out his gun and made sure it had a bullet in the chamber.

The mumbling of voices was followed by the sounds of shovels crunching sand. Several minutes later more mumbling began. "Did you find anything?" Foreman was getting impatient.

"Yes," Devale said.

"What is it?"

"It's an old turtle shell that's been buried," Sean said. His voice was muffled as though he might be lying on the ground, looking in the hole.

Foreman considered whether he should report their find to Heller and decided against it. "That's not what the professor is looking for. Leave the hole open for now. Go on to the next spot."

"Can we do spot number four next? Number three is way back in the bushes and four is just a few yards away?" Sean asked.

"Okay." Foreman added, "Just keep moving. You're taking too long."

There were grunts of acknowledgment and the murmurs of what Foreman was sure were complaints. The lights moved a few yards to the left. Slow, steady movement of the beams meant the radar unit was in use. Within minutes, Sean's excited voice said something, but Foreman couldn't understand it. Devale spoke, but Foreman couldn't hear what Devale said either.

Foreman yelled, "What's going on back there?"

"You might need to come look at this, Mr. Foreman," Devale said.

"Tell me what you think you see, then I'll decide." Foreman frowned. He wasn't going to crawl over the fence unless he had to.

"It's somebody's skeleton, except it doesn't look exactly right. I'm moving up from the feet toward the head." Devale became quiet as he very slowly moved the unit along the ground. One of the boys yelled, "Holy shit." After a few seconds of silence, Devale shouted, "Ahhhhhhh, Mr. Foreman, there are two skulls here. And, I'm pretty sure these are human."

The sound of crunching underbrush and a light flashing aimlessly meant someone was floundering through the sea-grapes and palms. Sean was to the ladder and had started up before Foreman saw his intent. "Freeze maggot!" he hissed. The boy continued to climb the ladder until he heard Foreman rack the slide to chamber a round on his Glock. Sean froze.

"Damn, man! There are two bodies back there!" The boy was frantic.

"Want to make it three?" Foreman fished his cell from his pocket. "Get your ass back to your buddy until after I speak to Heller."

"But—"

"But, what asshole. Get back there—" Foreman didn't have to finish. The terrified Sean was already racing back to his friend.

"Already?" Heller was surprised by the call. Foreman had transported the two boys, the radar unit, and himself to the Island less than four hours before.

"I don't know. Depends on what you're *really* looking for," Forman's voice had a bite in it as he spoke into the cell phone.

"Okay, so what did you find?"

"A dead turtle shell in one spot."

Heller snorted, "You called me for that?" Shit, I thou—"

"That's not all. A few yards from it we found skel—"

Heller cut off Foreman abruptly. "Get back over to the marina and pick me up. Now!"

Foreman was very sarcastic. "You been looking for skeletons all along? Where's the treasure? They have gold teeth?"

"You have no idea how valuable th...you said skeletons... as in plural?" Heller sounded shocked.

"Yes, as in two. You still want me to come get you?"

"Yes."

Heller heard some babbling. He asked, "What's going on? I hear talking in the background."

"Sean and Devale want me to take them back to the dock."

"No! Keep them there."

"You planning on doing some digging?"

"I'm not; they are."

"They're telling me they don't want to stay here. You don't have to say anything. I'll explain it to them so they have a clear picture."

Chapter 41
Turtle Point, Cayo Costa Island, Florida
May 2010

The fiberglass cut a groove in the sand a few feet from the shore. Heller looked into the darkness and the night-blackened waters in dismay. Terrill Foreman read his thoughts. "Arthur, you're going to get wet. If you don't want to ruin those fancy shoes and pants, you'd better strip 'em off and carry 'em ashore. I'm on the bottom now and tide's almost out. Why didn't you wear sneakers and jeans?"

"I don't own *that* kind of clothes. I have some shorts, but the mosquitoes..." Heller didn't finish his sentence as he removed his shoes, socks, and pants, rolled them into a packet he could carry ashore along with a bag containing a hand-sized trowel and rake. Arthur carefully eased over the side of the boat.

Foreman shook his head and leaped into the calf deep water.

They waded the twenty feet to the beach in silence. When the two reached sand dry enough for Heller to get back in his clothes, they stopped. The loose sand made it difficult for Heller to keep his balance as he tried to step back into his pants. He lost equilibrium and flopped into the sand. Foreman snorted, chuckled, and made other signs of his disdain for his comrade. He made no attempt to help Heller up. Heller was aware of Foreman's opinion, took as much as he cared to, finally saying, "Remember who *is* paying the bills."

"Heh, I'll keep that in mind." Foreman was in his element, Heller out of his, and both men knew it.

"Where did you choose to go over the fence?"

Heller asked.

"About seventy feet back the fence line from the beach. We're on the north side, and that's the closest to the first spots you had marked on the map."

A thought suddenly struck Arthur. He frantically asked, "Damn Foreman, those boys probably climbed the fence and are headed to the park rangers' residence."

"You told me not to underestimate you. Now, you do the same for me." Foreman stopped. "Before I left, I had them hand out the ladder they had inside, their flashlights, and I removed the furniture pads from the razor wire. I'm sure that would keep them from going anywhere, but just in case, I had St. Glock explain to them that if they did anything to louse up retrieving that treasure you *say* exists, St. Glock would scatter their brains all over the sand. But, if they were good little boys, the gold fairy would come to visit them."

"You idiot! They'll jump ship and go to the authorities at their first opportunity!" Heller was seething. "What are we going to do to stop that?"

"Arthur, you can't be that naïve. What we were going to have to do from the beginning."

"Kill them?"

"Yes, but you don't worry about that. Taking care of those problems is what you're paying me for. You just concentrate on making yourself the richest man in the world with me being a close second. That was your promise, remember. Still good, right?"

"If we find what I'm looking for." Heller knew if he didn't, St. Glock would come looking for him.

"I'd guess we'd better get moving. You wouldn't want not to be successful." Forman confirmed Heller's thoughts.

Heller looked at the images on the ground radar screen. He was expecting one skeleton, not two. The two sets of bones were intermingled. That meant they had to have been buried at the same time. One set of bones was smaller. It was probably the one. If it was, he was close. Heller still could find what he was looking for if it wasn't. The image showed items interred with the bodies, but not in the detail he needed to be sure he'd found what he wanted. They'd have to dig, but if this wasn't the right place, they couldn't afford to lose the time.

"This is what we'll do," Heller explained. "The only way I can tell if this is what I'm looking for is by digging up those bones." He pointed at the ground. "At least, the area close to the skulls. That will take most of the night. But, we can't lose that much time if this isn't what we want. Foreman, you take Sean and check as many spots on the map as you can. Devale and I will stay here and dig. We probably have this night and two more before Warrington is back from Atlanta and Dupree has his boat repaired. We need to find it in that time."

"We're looking for a single skeleton?" Foreman asked.

"Yes," Heller said.

"Do you know who they are?" Devale pointed at the ground.

"Hmmmmm. I guess I can tell all of you." Heller quickly concocted a tale. "If this is the body I'm looking for, it's a pirate captain. He hid the treasure. His crew was pissed when he didn't share it with them. They killed him and buried him here, somewhere. He had the way to find the gold with him when they buried him. That might be him and some other man in his crew. It might be something that has nothing to do with the treasure."

"Then, like you didn't have anything to do with

putting them here?"

"Oh, no."

"Mr. Foreman kind of—"

"I know, he scared you. He did it to be sure you didn't blow billions of dollars for us and millions for you two." Heller reassured them with the oily tongue of a snake oil salesman.

"Millions?" Sean echoed.

"Yes. Hey, I can swear to you that Foreman would never hurt you, would you Terrill?"

"Never."

The two boys nodded

"Okay, let's get this done." Foreman took the map case from Devale and said to Sean, "Get the radar and follow me."

"Start digging here Devale," Heller took a couple steps. "I need to look at the map with Terrill for a few seconds. I'll be back to help in a few minutes."

Sean struggled to keep up with Foreman and Heller; soon they were thirty feet ahead. When they were distant enough from both boys, Heller said, "Don't waste time on anything except another skeleton. Keep moving." He paused, then continued in a whisper, "I think what I said will calm them down. They'll be alright."

"You know how to spread the bullshit." Foreman agreed as they parted ways.

Chapter 42
Turtle Point, Cayo Costa Island, Florida
May 2010

"I hit something," Devale said. He backed away from the pit they'd dug and dropped the shovel as though electric shocked his hands. The terror in Devale's eyes told Heller he'd have to finish the job. *That is a good thing*, he told himself. *I don't want to damage what I'm looking for or have it overlooked because of its size.*

"I'll take over," Heller said as he dropped to his knees and opened the bag of garden tools he'd brought with him. "Just shine your light right where I'm working." Whatever Devale struck wasn't visible in the sand pit.

"Where did you hit something?" Heller asked.

Devale picked up the shovel and laid the handle's end on the spot saying, "There."

Heller carefully probed the sand in the area where Devale pointed. Within a few seconds, the trowel encountered resistance. It wasn't the hard contact Heller expected. He removed sand until the object was visible. It was cloth. More scoops of sand exposed more cloth and a bone extending from it. Devale gasped at his first sight of the skeleton the radar had promised was buried there. Heller looked at his find and nodded. It was a shirt. "Humerus," Heller said as he identified the bone.

"Man, that's too bad. Finding some dude's bones ain't funny." Devale's fright and apprehension lit his face.

"That's the bone's name, Devale. I'm not saying it's funny." Heller fought the urge to laugh at

Devale's statement. "Did you sleep through the human anatomy portion of biology?"

"I never took no biology."

"My error." Heller's profession wouldn't allow him to pass the teaching moment. "Knowing what bone I'm looking at tells me where I need to dig next. The humerus is the only bone of that configuration in the upper area of the body. The shirt tells me I need to dig here." Heller held the trowel on the opposite side from where the bone protruded from the fabric.

Devale mumbled, "Man, the radar screen kind of told you that."

Heller grinned, "That's true. However, it defines it better for us. You know what the radar did tell us?"

Devale shrugged his shoulders and said, "No."

"Whoever planted these two did us a favor. The skulls appeared to be within a couple feet of each other. If this is who I'm looking for, we won't have to expose much more of them. I'm only interested to see if one of them had things around their necks." Heller used the trowel to inscribe a circle five feet in diameter adjacent to the exposed bone. "Remove some of the sand from this area. If you hit anything, stop. It appears they're buried two to three feet deep so don't take out more than half that. I'll get the rest."

Devale stared at the circle but remained frozen.

"Something wrong?" Heller asked the frightened boy.

"Man, this is *not* cool." Devale's pupils kept switching from the yellow-white bone in the hole to Heller's face. "I'm not saying I believe in this shit, but if there ever was such things as ghosts they'd be hanging around here, and they aren't likely to want us busting up...well, what's left of them."

"Devale," Heller adopted a fatherly tone of voice,

"You don't have a thing to be concerned about. There aren't *such things* as ghosts. Do you think I'd be down here unearthing them if we were in any danger? What you fear is what Hollywood's planted in your mind. Think how good you'll feel when we finish this, and you know all that is fiction."

Devale looked unsure but repositioned his hands so the shovel was ready for use. However, he couldn't force his body to remove the first blade full of sand.

Heller stood and took the shovel from Devale's hands. "I'll take the first scoop," Heller said. Then he turned to the darkness and issued a challenge. "You ghosts, if you're there, I'm digging these bodies up. I'm making Devale do this, so be mad at me, not him." Heller removed three scoops of sand from inside the circle and tossed them. He stopped, waited for a reaction, none came. Then he handed the shovel to Devale. Heller said, "Go ahead."

The boy nodded and began to dig.

Both Arthur Heller and Devale sat on the pile of sand they'd removed from the grave. Heller's face showed the disappointment he was experiencing. The pit in front of him housed two skulls, and almost half of two human torsos were exposed. He was sure that neither was the one he was looking for. The remaining fragments of clothes and what he knew about skeletal sexual differences told him both were male. Not what he was expecting; not what he wanted. The discovery added all kinds of complications to the scenario he'd been so certain had transpired. Where was she? He was still convinced her body was hidden somewhere in the sand around Turtle Point. Heller was just as sure

Benedict Dupree knew what happened to her. Dupree's elaborate fence and protection of the turtles was a charade to cover her murder. But, how did these two bodies figure into the mystery? Were they witnesses to Nadine Bocelli's death? Was the mangled condition of the skeletons due to the actions of a desperate murderer? One of the skull's facial bones was crushed by a horrendous blow. Broken ribs, severed spinal columns, and smashed bones in the portions exhumed were evidence of the horrible destruction to their murdered bodies. Who knew what an examination of the area below the victim's midsections would disclose? Those parts were still undisturbed beneath the sand.

Devale's mind focused on one objective, one quite different from Heller's. Was there any way for he and Sean to extricate themselves from the mess they'd become involved in?

Snapping twigs, flashlight beams fluttering through the underbrush, and Foreman's inaudible growled instructions to Sean drew their attention. Foreman was the first to enter the clearing, glance at Arthur and Devale, and stare at the grizzly remains in the pit. The sight didn't affect Foreman. Sean, who followed several steps behind, was shocked. He gasped and dropped the radar unit.

"You dumb ass," Foreman said to Sean and shook his head violently. "Get over it. That's what you'll look like when you're dead." Foreman motioned to the radar unit. "Take care of that thing. We might need to use it again." He looked at Heller and asked, "Well, you find what we're looking for?"

"No. Neither of these is the right one. I do think they might have a connection to the...captain. They look like they've been here a long time, probably the right amount of time, but I don't know." Heller stood up. "Did you find anything?"

"No additional bones. Sean found a couple of pit

traps." Foreman nodded toward the sullen looking teenager. "Dupree or someone dug holes, sunk empty fifty-five-gallon drums in them, covered them with palm fronds, and sprinkled a little sand on top. See the scratches on Sean's arms. The bastard who dug the traps lined the sides with barbed wire. We'll have to paint a few scrapes on the radar unit, but Sean did a good job protecting it with his body." Foreman grinned, and Sean frowned. "Of the major spots you marked on this map, we were able to do seventeen. That leaves nine for tomorrow night. That's if you want to try this again." Foreman looked at the bodies in the pit. "You said you marked the most likely sites for us to do at first. What's that tell you about the last nine?"

"She's... What we're looking for is here somewhere, I know it!" Heller swung his arm around in a circle parallel to the ground. "It's a needle in a haystack; I know that! But, four to five billion...I'll look through a hundred haystacks and then go to the next hundred for that." The look of doubt decreased on Foreman's face, and the boys' enthusiasm returned. Heller underlined his last words, "Think of it. None of us will ever have to work. Never!"

Foreman was almost sold, but not quite. "You can't get that much gold in one place unless you have a dump truck. You were talking pirates; now you're talking skeletons that have been here less than say fifty years. I want to know what we're really looking for. Until I know that, you're on your own, sucker." The boys nodded to that logic.

Heller looked at his troops. He couldn't afford a revolt. His only option was to share enough of the information he possessed to keep everyone loyal, but hold out enough to force them to still be dependent on him. Heller had no illusions about Foreman. The man would enjoy killing them all if he believed he had clear access to the wealth. Heller knew that he'd have to face that problem in the future, but with enough money, a life like Foreman's was a minor annoyance that was easily eliminated.

"Okay. This is what I can tell you. Thirty-five years ago, I was still in college studying history. I wanted to teach. You know I'm a professor at Columbia. My specialty is Europe from 1900 to 1950 with emphasis on the two wars' impacts on civilians. To make some money, I did research jobs for companies and individuals who wanted information about those war years. I had a lot of success in finding out about obscure events, people, and ways to contact those who still knew about them. The contacts I had were mainly ex-Nazi's and Fascists. That meant I had great access to information about goings-on in Germany, Spain, and I had particularly strong ties to Italian sources. I knew how to trace people both in and out of the governments at that time. I had good luck in finding papers, even funds that disappeared during the chaos. That allowed me to develop a reputation as a miracle worker when it came to these matters. As a result, a family approached me about finding out what had happened to one of their relatives, a fascist, at the war's end in Italy. The money they offered was very good, and I took it, even though I had misgivings about the individuals I was dealing with."

Foreman asked, "The mafia?"

"La Cosa Nostra, the same difference. It's the mafia's Sicilian branch." Heller watched Foreman's face. The respect on Terrill's features told Heller he'd found a "poker chip" that would be valuable if he didn't overplay its use.

Foreman asked, "Which fam—"

"The Barrollios. Joe ran the show. That was part of Luciano's organization back when." Foreman's expression and silence told Heller his cohort was impressed. "He came looking for information on a woman from Tuscany. He believed she came to the US after the war but wasn't sure. I found out lots about her. The reason he couldn't find out about the woman was he was looking for her under her maiden name. She married a man named Cardone in a Tuscan town near Rome. Cardone had important connections to the Mussolini government, the most important one being that his sister was one of Clara Peticca's best friends."

"Who in the hell is that?" Foreman asked.

"Clara Peticca was Mussolini's mistress. Old Benito and Clara got caught when they tried to get out of Italy and into Switzerland. A bunch of partisans shot them at a little town named Mezzegra. Their bodies were taken to Milan and hung by the heels. I'm sure you've seen the famous picture."

"Can't say I have. All that's fine professor shit, but what does it have to do with five billion dollars." Foreman was becoming impatient.

"Clara was much younger than Mussolini ... and smarter. She figured they'd be caught and that her boyfriend and maybe she would be executed. Mussolini stashed a significant part of the Italian treasury in a safe place, along with many works of art and other valuable artifacts. Self-insurance of a sort. He insisted that Clara know the information on how to retrieve it. If he got murdered, she'd be taken care of. In 1945, when the war was close to the end, the Fascists formed a convoy to flee. The Cardones fled with them. When the communist guerilla group stopped the convoy, Clara gave the books with the information, a key, and an ornate cross to Illia Cardone for safe keeping. Clara probably guessed what was going to happen to her. The cross is the key to retrieving the hidden gold. When the convoy was stopped, and Clara and Mussolini were shot,

Illia Cardone was given the treatment that many Fascists sympathizers got. She was raped repeatedly, all the hair on her body was shaved off, then she was turned loose stark naked. However, her husband, he had the mafia connections, snuck away with their luggage, and they were able to reunite. That's the way the Cosa Nostra knew the story. In their luggage was the information on how to locate the treasure Mussolini had hidden."

"You found this out? You located the woman, right?" Foreman said.

"Yes. I traced her to the US and found that she had three daughters. One died of polio. Another was killed in a car accident. The third married a man named Bocelli. It's the third daughter's girl we're looking for. Illia Cardone gave the treasure information to her granddaughter, Mary Bocelli. It took years to find this out. Barrollio tried to get the information from the Bocelli's. Barrollio tortured them and ended up killing the family without knowing that the daughter, the only member of the family not present when they were abducted, had the secret and that she didn't know its value. Joe Barrollio lost interest and died."

"And?" Foreman asked impatiently.

"Mary kept the cross and a key around her neck. Her Grandmother Cardone made her swear never to take it off. The girl took the oath. Illia was planning to give her the rest of what she needed to find the treasure but died before she did. As far as I know, Mary never knew what the secret represented. To shorten the story, I found records of what items were missing from the treasury when Il Duce lost power. There were 890 tons of gold, that's over four billion; paintings, sculptures, and other materials that were worth another billion and a half."

"Even if you get the cross and that key, what good will it do you? You don't have the rest of the information to find it, anyway." Foreman said.

"Oh, but I do, Terrill. I most certainly do."

"Okay, you've convinced me. But we've got to button this up. It's 3:30 and it gets light early this time of year. We need to get out of here. We can hide some of this stuff in the bushes, the rest we'll take back to the boat. There'll be fisherman here at daylight or a little after."

"We'll finish tomorrow, right guys?" Heller was trying to cheerlead.

"Tomorrow," the boys chanted, unaware they weren't listening to Tom Sawyer; their benefactor was closer to Adolph Hitler.

"Tomorrow," Foreman repeated as he thought how he'd dispose of the other three.

Chapter 43
Cape Coral, Florida
May 2010

"Yeah, I thought you ought to see it." Harry Burrieter had two of three carburetors pulled off Benny's outboard. They sat amid a pile of motor parts and hardware from his Mercury.

"Harry, I'm sorry, but I don't know what I'm supposed to be seeing." Benny just saw parts.

"Some vicious S-O-B put a bunch of sugar in your gas tank," Harry said.

"Damn! Is that going to ruin my engine?"

Harry shook his head. "It doesn't screw up an engine near as bad as it's supposed to. It doesn't gum up near like people think. It ain't good, but ..." Harry held up one of the carburetors. "The impact is more like putting sand in there. That would actually be a lot worse. But, it is gonna foul you up for a week. I have to order some filters and carburetor parts, do a hell of a lot of cleaning, and Stan is on vacation. It'll be four days before I can get back on it."

"If I pay you some—"

"I won't have parts for three days. I can't do better than that, Benny. You're just gonna have to wait."

A week. He'd missed visiting the point for longer than a week many times, but not during nesting season. He sighed. Benny wouldn't have given it a second thought except for the snoopers the park rangers reported. It would just have to be okay. Turtles had laid their eggs there for thousands of years without his protection. They'd have to do it again.

Chapter 44
Chamblee, Georgia
May 2010

"I'm sorry I've had to delay seeing you for two days, Mr. Warrington. But, I will be able to see you tomorrow at three."

Goodun sat on the edge of the motel room bed and silently cursed the voice coming from the phone. He asked, "Mr. Sump, can I see someone else? Today? I'm running low on money."

"You did this to yourself, Mr. Warrington. It's your responsibility to be sure you file your income tax correctly and *honestly*." The sarcasm in the phone voice gnawed at Goodun's guts.

"I did."

"We don't see it that way."

Goodun seethed for several seconds. He hadn't done anything wrong; he knew that. "I filed my taxes the way I should. I did it honestly. I can't afford another day at this motel. I guess I'm going home."

"You do that and we'll be forced to take further action." Sump definitely was threatening him. "Believe me...you don't want us to do that."

"Told you, I don't have money to stay. Guess I'm coming over there and see your boss-man or whoever."

Sump was silent for several seconds then said, "You don't want to do that, it will make him mad."

"Sorry about that. You folks made me mad." Goodun picked up the pen and notepad from the nightstand. "What's his name?"

Nothing came from the phone for several

seconds.

"I guess I can find out when I get there. I got the letter you sent me to show whoever I need to. I'll eventually get to the right place."

More silence.

"Okay. I'll be sayin—" Goodun started to hang up the phone.

"Hold on; I'm looking through your records." Sump sounded panicked. After a long delay, Sump said, "There's some irregularity here. I'm going to put you on hold while I try to straighten this out." The phone clicked, and Goodun was suddenly listening to classical music. He'd spent so much time on hold he knew the Warsaw Concerto followed Claire de Lune.

After several moments, Sump's voice returned. "I need to verify a few things like your mailing address. Are you Aaron Morgan Warrington of Pine Island, Louisiana, or are you Aaron Moses Warrington of Pineland, Florida."

"Aaron Moses Warrington of Pineland, *Florida*."

"What's your Soc?"

Goodun was puzzled. "Soc? I don't know what you're meaning."

Sump sounded exasperated. "Your Social Security Number. You know what that is, right?"

Goodun bit his tongue so he wouldn't make an angry response and antagonize the man. He recited the number.

Sump said, "It'll take a few more minutes, but we might be able to straighten this out, now. I'm putting you back on hold."

The time period listening to music was longer during this hold. Warrington didn't count them, but he guessed he'd heard a half-dozen songs. Abruptly, Hector Sump returned to the line. "It seems we've mixed two peoples files together. The staff that did the work, hand wrote the information and combined data when they shouldn't, and incorrectly entered it on your info. Unfortunately, the data entry department didn't catch the error and entered the combined information as a single return under your name and Soc number. They'll be separated and properly recorded. It appears that we have no further need to see you or for you to stay. You can go. Since it appears we made an error, I'll personally process an expense reimbursement voucher for you. I'll send the check to your PO box in Pineland."

"That's it?" Goodun was shocked.

"Yes. You're free to go."

"What if I want to talk to somebody about this whole mess?" Goodun's voice cracked with emotion.

"You could. The person you'd see would be me. Do you think that would be productive?" Sump's tone implied a threat.

"Probably not."

"I'd suggest you go home. Right now. I'll be seeing you get a check, one I'll write because I think it's fair, but it's not one I *have to* write, understand. Of course, you can come over. We check your returns. Thoroughly. Say for the last seven years."

"Uh-huh. I do understand."

"Are you going home, Mr. Warrington?"

"Yes."

Chapter 45
Fort Myers, Florida
May 2010

Foreman entered Napoli Pizza, looked into the back corner, and saw Arthur Heller seated at his usual table. He waved to Foreman and smiled, something Foreman didn't expect. Their second trip to Cayo Costa Island and Turtle Point was far less successful than the first. All nine remaining spots were examined; the only things the radar unit "discovered" were a bag of buried trash, some rusting steel rebar, and an old kitchen sink. Besides the nine locations, they'd pre-identified, Heller picked seven additional likely spots. Their total finds were a couple of old boards and rusty pliers.

"You look happy," Foreman pulled a chair away from the table and sat in it 180 degrees from the way it was designed to work. "Enjoy the feeling; I've got some bad news. Actually, for you, double bad news."

"Oh, what's that?" Heller wasn't fazed by Foreman's promise of doom and gloom.

"My little prick in the IRS called to tell me he'd detained the hermit as long as he could with the bullshit he concocted. He got cold feet when old Warrington was going to show up at his office looking for his boss." Foreman tossed his head a little. "He promised he'd pay some money to the old guy for his expenses to keep him out of the IRS office. I said you would take care of it. After all, what's a thou to a 'bout-to-be multi-billionaire."

"When is he coming back?"

"I talked to Sump an hour ago. He could be on the road now." Foreman looked for signs of Heller's panic.

"That's fine. We'll have time to make a quick trip to the island to do one thing." Heller smiled, enjoying the surprise on Foreman's face. "We need to go get a bone to feed our dogs. I'm counting on what you said about being able to steal anything from anybody. You still stand by that?"

"Yes. Without any condition."

"Okay, let's get over to the island."

Foreman said, "What are you hatching now?"

"We're literally going to get a bone. Then we'll be sure we remove as many traces of evidence of us as being there that we can find. Our heavy lifting is done." Heller's smug smile goaded Foreman.

"We didn't find jack that's going to help us in three nights fighting the damn bugs. Don't we need more time? Why are you so damned cheerful about getting cut off from access to the place?"

"Terrill, why work hard when we can work smart? We're going to throw the bone to the dogs and let *them* find what we're looking for."

Chapter 46
Tampa, Florida
May 2010

"Tom." Harper Sturgis called to her associate as she entered their offices. There was no answer. His office door was open. She checked to be sure he wasn't behind his desk concentrating on a case or project, sleeping, reading, in a Zen-like trance, or just ignoring her. They were all equal possibilities. His office was vacant.

She tried the conference room and her office, shouting his name and getting silent echoes in return. Sturgis was about to call his cell phone when a blur of motion outside the window caught her attention. Tom Mooney was romping with a German Shepard in the yard outside their offices. Harper decided he'd be inside in a few minutes and to use the "waiting time." She looked at her desk. Neatly aligned sticky notes covered a portion of its top. The part that didn't have yellow squares attached, housed stacks of papers and documents. There were scribbled references to three different cases on which they were working.

The dog barking at her informed Harper that Mooney was inside the office. Mooney wore his perpetual smile and struggled to keep the leashed dog from pulling his arm out of its socket. He carried a stopwatch, some papers, and a plastic baggie that contained something that looked very much like poop. All were attached to a clipboard.

"Hey, Harper. How'd things go in court?" Tom asked.

"Better than they should have. We won and won

big. Quentin Poe was in rare form. He managed to wreck his own case. Quentin is an unending Christmas gift from the DA's office to all the state's defense attorneys. How in the hell that man passed the bar, I'll never know."

"Pass the bar? He seldom does. That's the reason he has tennis elbow so bad and never plays tennis. Ahhhh, I guess if your uncle is a state senator you get some corners cut for you." Tom continued to struggle with the dog. "Let me stick tricky Mickey in my office." He half-led and half-dragged the Shepard. Some fancy footwork and a slammed door later; he walked back to talk to Harper.

"And?" Tom asked.

"Acquittals on all five fraud charges. Guilty on the money laundering. Eighteen months." Harper folded her arms. "Sometimes I wish I wasn't so good. The courts didn't get him, but we can. Anything that's remotely billable...sock to him. My Mercedes needs replacing." She tilted her head toward Tom's office door. "What are you doing with Fido?"

"Proving there was another way for an individual besides Engels to get those diamond rings out of the jewelry store without setting off the metal detectors or showing up in the body search."

"How? I can guess, but—" She looked at the clipboard, and a flicker of emotion appeared and disappeared. "You check to see...that's revolting."

"Revolting...yes...reasonable doubt in the Engels case...yes. A number of people take their service dogs into the store. All you have to do is stuff rings into a treat, feed Fido, and wait. We have surveillance tapes of a woman and a man feeding their dog at the same time they had access to the rings. Dogs have remarkably dependable digestive tracts. Now we can prove there was someone beside Engels that *could* have stolen the rings."

Harper nodded and changed the subject. "Looks

like you got a lot done while I was in Court."

"I took the easiest case first, or what I thought would be easy."

"And that was?"

"MacCardle's buddy. I checked out those two that are stalking the Dupree guy. The more I check, the wackier the whole thing gets." He slouched down in the chair across from Harper's desk. Tom Mooney was a negative photo of the image Harper Sturgis presented. His expressive face, informal dress, and laid-back mannerisms said, 'I'm your friend,' without uttering a word. Mooney was unimpressive in stature and appearance; his *outstanding* visual trait was the bland nature of his features. Mooney was a man you wouldn't pick from a crowd. As soft and unconditioned as his body was, Tom's most strenuous activity was lifting a Sudoku magazine. No one who spoke to him could fail to see his mind was a polar opposite. Though one of his major duties was to serve as Harper's computer guru, he relied on pocket-sized notebooks to gather data. He pulled one from his bright colored Hawaiian shirt and asked, "You have time for this?"

"I've got plenty. I *am* interested in MacCardle's friend. He's in big trouble of some sort, knows it, but won't admit it ...even to himself." Harper held up a pen silently asking if she should take notes; Tom shook his head.

"This is strictly preliminary. A lot of it could change. Oh, you could be correct about him being in deep do-do. One of the men he's asking about is trouble spelled in all caps and the other one, he seems legitimate at first glance, has had some heavy duty mafia connections in past years." Tom smiled at Harper's poker face. "I guess we'll find out if leopards change their spots."

"Mafia, huh? That surprises me. I had a different read on Dupree and what I surmised his past would be like." Harper leaned back in her chair. "He didn't have the smell those underworld types have, even when they've tried to wash it all away."

"I'd say you surmised right. On the surface, I can't see any reason those two guys would have interest in Dupree. There isn't any connection that I've found." Mooney held his hand up and stretched his fingers out. "There's no geographical connection." He folded one finger down. "They've never lived anywhere close to each other. As far as I can tell, they probably never even vacationed in the same area." Mooney closed down a second finger. "There are no business ties. Dupree is a local builder and developer. Arthur Heller is a history professor at Columbia. Terrill Foreman is a soldier of fortune type, one very bad slimebag. His background is military, CIA, and private ops stuff." He folded the third finger. "No shared relationship at all. No ex-wife's brother-in-law involved or anything like that. No ex-girlfriend one of the parties is banging," He put his fourth finger down very slowly. "Finances. This one separates Dupree from the other two. There are definitely links between Heller and Forman. My guess is that Foreman's working for Heller. I found a lot of cash transfers from Heller's account going to Foreman's. Some were big. I told you a little about Foreman's enforcer skills already. He's the one I got the most info on."

"Go on." Harper's expression never changed. Though most folks observing her would have thought she was paying little attention, Mooney knew that Harper was recording each bit of info in her computer hard drive mind.

"Foreman spent eight years in the Rangers and eleven years in the Army overall. His reviews had high skills ratings, but character questions. He had a lot of little shit on his record...brig time for D & D, petty theft, two assaults, plus what got him a dishonorable discharge, he conspired to steal and sell weapons. After he got tossed, he did work for the CIA. So much for background checks. I'm not sure doing what, probably strong-arm stuff. Anyway, he hung in there for three years. The things he's been doing the last five or six years...they're scary. He weapon trained troops for a warlord who'd been part of Charles Taylor's force of thugs when he ran Liberia. After a year, he moved on but stayed in Africa. Foreman was reported to be involved in the genocide in the Congo, first for one side, then the other. Kabila hired him first. He was involved in training and rumored to field advise Hutu troops in that mess. Somehow he changed coats, and he ended up in the employment of a Tutsi group that was clandestinely sponsored by the Rwandan government. He was involved in training and arms procurement. There were unsubstantiated reports of him physically being involved in the actual fighting, the assassination of a local tribal leader, and the murder of his family. Get this, with a machete."

"He is scary." Harper held up her index finger indicating she wanted Mooney to be silent for a moment. "Tom, how in the hell do you find out all this stuff? And, so quickly?"

"You're an officer of the court, right? So, you don't want to know."

"You got this information through illegal means?" Harper showed no emotion or concern.

"You don't want to know," Tom repeated.

"No I don't," she said, "Just keep doing whatever you're doing." The mask remained. "Anything else on Foreman?"

"Not a whole lot. He left Africa in a hurry. When you play both sides, it tends to make you unpopular. He's lucky he got out with his skin intact. About four months ago, he got hooked up with Heller. As near as I can tell, Foreman's running errands for that guy. I can tell you he's being overpaid if that's all he's doing. I'm trying to find out more on that now."

"What about Heller?" Harper asked.

"He's what he claims to be, but there's more to his story, I'm sure of that. Heller teaches twentieth-century history at Columbia. He's been doing that for twenty-four years." Mooney turned a few pages in his notebook. "Writes a book on his subject every couple years, the old publish or perish thing, I imagine. Most of his books involve the period from the mid-thirties through 1950. He stays out of the spotlight. For the most part, he's an unremarkable figure. There are some really interesting exceptions. Arthur Heller is one rich college professor. He didn't inherit money. His family was dirt poor. Heller's salary is okay, but nothing exceptional. Even so, he's got over two mil stashed that I've learned of so far. He used to do a lot of research for companies and individuals. When he's finished some of these projects, he's added to his bankroll...significantly. What got him started was earning bucks for tuition. And, this is very interesting. Heller was involved with the Barrollio crime family back then. The Barrollio family was Cosa Nostra."

"That's the big time," Harper remarked.

"True. But Heller's association came a long time after its prominence. Years, in fact. Lucky Luciano and his people were long gone by then. The FBI investigated Heller, but came up empty. As far as they could tell, he was doing legitimate research, tracing refugees from Italy for Barrollio. I still have a lot of research to do on Heller. I have found out he travels to Europe once a year and visits the Miami area lots. As far as I can tell, he's never been to the Fort Myers area before six months ago. Now, it's like a second home to him. When I checked with Columbia, I found out he's taken a year's leave of absence to study the rebuilding of Italy after the

War. Interestingly, he made a couple visits to the
area north of Rome right before he took the leave,
but hasn't returned since. That's just the opposite of
what you'd think."

Harper nodded. "Any idea of what he's doing
here."

"Not the specific thing. I do know he's spending a
lot of money, both on Foreman and other things. He
bought a new convertible but doesn't seem to have
possession of it. That's weird because he continues to
rent a car and a truck. Heller spends a lot of time on
some of the barrier islands. Ones that aren't built up.
That's strange because he has a reputation for
disliking any sort of roughing it. The Plaza would be
his idea of slumming. As I said, there's a lot to do on
him."

"That leaves Dupree." Harper removed her high
heels and wiggled her toes as she placed her feet on
her desk. Modesty wasn't one of her concerns.
"Goody two shoes, goody two shoes, goody two
shoes." Tom Mooney flipped a few more pages in his
notebook. "He's lived in that area of Florida since he
was born. Dupree went to the University of Florida,
played football there, and inherited the development
and construction business he owns from his father.
He's active in the local community, and he's well-
liked. He's had zero brushes with the law. No
lawsuits and that's unusual when you're in the kind
of business he's in. Married once for a short period
of time then divorced. No kids. Doesn't appear to
have any domestic problems. No love interest, now.
He's one of those boring folks who just wakes up
each day to live. The only thing unusual I've found
about him is his obsession with protecting the sea
turtles. Bought some damned expensive property for
them to nest on. He runs off anybody who'd disturb
their laying eggs. Dupree's a village joke because of
that. The locals really like him, however." Mooney

shook his head. "There doesn't seem any way there's a connection between him and the other two."

Harper stretched her legs and removed her feet from her desk. "Keep looking. You'll find one. When you do, I bet it will be a shocker."

Chapter 47
Pine Island, Florida
May 2010

"Mrs. Foy," Goodun Warrington had approached silently, and Corrine was so engrossed in her work his words startled her. "Oh, Mr. Warrington, I didn't see you come up." Corrine smiled at the tall, lean man who looked uncomfortable in other humans' company. He conversed with pelicans, otters, manatees, hogs, raccoons, and great blue herons that shared the land where his cabin was built. Goodun trusted them. He didn't trust most humans. Corrine knew that.

"Mr. Dupree around?" he asked.

"Yes. I'm sure he'll want to see you." Corrine picked up her phone. She waited impatiently for her boss to answer. Finally, the exasperation left her face. She said, "Benny, Mr. Warrington is here to see you." She nodded to the unseeing phone. "Okay, I'll ask him to wait." She hung up the phone and told Goodun, "He's on his cell. As soon as he finishes, he'll be out."

Goodun nodded.

"Won't you have a seat, Mr. Warrington?" Corrine made a motion to her desk's side chair.

He shook his head, adding, "But, thanks."

Corrine asked, "Can I get you anything, Mr. Warrington?"

"Nope," He hesitated "Call me Goodun...I don't hardly recognize being called Mr. Warrington."

"Sure." Corrine hesitated but decided to ask a question she'd always been curious about. "Goodun, how did you come to be called that? I know it isn't your given name."

"My parents had seven kids. They always said I was the good one and started calling me that. It run together. The name just stuck."

"And, he is," Benny said as he came out of his office. He shook the old man's hand. "I see they didn't keep you. Is everything straightened out?"

"Yes. They had me mixed up with some other person with a name close to mine."

"Why in the world couldn't that have been done over the phone or at a local office?" Benny frowned and couldn't believe what the IRS had forced his friend to go through.

Goodun shrugged his shoulders.

"What kind of explanation did they give you when they met with you?"

"They didn't meet me but once, and that was just in the building's lobby. Just kept putting me off. Finally, they checked it out and said I was done."

"Checked it out? How did they let you know?" Benny was incredulous.

"On the phone."

"Unbelievable! How long were you there?"

"Three days a waiting."

Benny was angry. "That smells!"

"Like a three day old dead mullet lying in the bottom of your boat." Goodun wasn't being funny. "They said they'd pay some for my trip. I just don't want to have to go up there again."

"You okay?"

Goodun nodded, "Thanks, and you'll have all the mullet you want for the church fish fry."

"You been to the island, yet?" Benny asked.

"No."

"I was going to check on your place while you were gone, but my boat's been laid up. Some asshole put sugar in my gas tank. I won't get it out of the shop until tomorrow."

Goodun twisted his head to the side and looked quizzical. "So, you don't know if anything's going on out there." It was a statement, not a question. "That's about as strange as that IRS man." It was apparent that Warrington had something on his mind that bothered him, but he never volunteered his thoughts and was as unlikely to answer questions about them.

Benny interpreted the old man's comment as a concern that something bad might have happened in their absence. Warrington's concern quickly became Dupree's as he saw possible pieces of a puzzle fitting together. However, Benny believed their concerns were over far different possibilities.

Chapter 48
Fort Myers, Florida
May 2010

Franklin Forrest "Frog" Hilliard had been involved with law enforcement since he was old enough to hitch an occasional ride to kindergarten in his father's squad car. His father had been a deputy, his grandfather, sheriff of Transylvania County in North Carolina, and his mother worked as a dispatcher in the Sheriff's office. It was natural he should pursue a career in police work. When his father moved his family to Lee County in southwest Florida, Frank Hilliard was still in his high school years, but had already made up his mind he'd be Sheriff there, someday. While his peers were playing baseball and basketball, he spent his after-school hours volunteering at the Lee County Sheriff's Office doing all the little things the staff avoided. "Frog" relished his opportunity to help. By being the office "go-fer," he learned the department's inner workings. Coupled with the inherited knowledge from two previous generations, he became as knowledgeable of the ins and outs of running a law enforcement operation as the professors who taught college where he earned his degree in criminal justice.

Welcomed into the Sheriff's herd when he graduated, Frank rose rapidly within the department. His family connections, Sheriff "Brinny" Simmons personal endorsement, and an outstanding record let him ascend to captain in ten short years. In addition, Hilliard had a perfect blend of hardboiled discipline, "big-city" silver-tongued persuasiveness, a "good-old-boy" grasp of local politics... and an uncanny insight which told him what the proper combination of each of those gifts was called for in any situation.

The heir apparent to Brinny Simmons position, the only thing he lacked was a nick-name that his constituents could embrace. A tough sobriquet like his grandfather's "Iron Ass Hilliard," didn't fit. Franklin was an average sized man, reasonable and flexible in handling problems, one who would prefer to reach an amicable method of maintaining law and order, rather than the liberal use of a baton.

He had one feature that suggested his poetic nickname. Frank's large eyes were spaced wide apart. The whites of his eyes were more visible than most peoples. A flattened nose combined with his habit of rolling his pupils around suggested his resemblance to a frog. One of his partners started to call him that. Soon, more folks referred to him as "Frog" Hilliard than by his given name of Franklin. The acceptance and adoption of his nickname came in time for Brinny Simmons retirement. No runoff election was required in the five-man race; Franklin Forrest "Frog" Hilliard, won taking 57% of the vote. Within three months, he was running the department as though he'd had the job for twenty years...like his predecessor had. "Frog" had just been re-elected to his third, four-year term. He sat in his office, sipping his morning coffee, and reading local newspaper articles when one of his detectives sauntered to his door.

"Mornin' Frog." Lieutenant James McNeal leaned against the jam. He had a cardboard box tucked under his arm. It was wrapped in clear plastic. McNeal said, "I thought you'd want to take a look at this here before I turned it over to Maggie in the lab."

"What you got there?" Hilliard asked.

"Besides the box, a note addressed to the Lee County Sheriff's Department and a bone out of somebody's upper arm, according to Maggie. She said she thought it was a man's, but couldn't be sure until she examined it closer. She started yappin' about those egghead technical things she needed to do, so I tuned her out until she's gotten her shit together." James leaned forward waiting for the "word."

"Yeah, let me see it."

James crossed the room and rounded Hilliard's desk. Before he removed the box from the plastic, he said, "It's been gone over pretty good already. No prints on the box. The label on the top had a smudge of where one was. All but a sixteenth of it was wiped. Ain't no way we'll get an ID from it. I'll tell you what we know about the stuff inside when you're lookin' at it." He took the box out of the bag and opened the carton's flaps with a latex-gloved hand. Inside was a bone, twelve or so inches in length, completely devoid of any flesh. A folded piece of paper lay next to the bone.

"Looks like a humerus, alright. Maggie's probably guessed right—it's too heavy and big to be a child's or out of most women." Hilliard looked at McNeal and asked, "Did she venture a guess on how long it's been this way?"

"Maggie said she thought it had been buried for quite a spell. I asked her how long, and she said at least ten years. Made the mistake of askin' how she knew. Then she started into that scientific mumbo-jumbo." McNeal's face contorted as though someone close to him had just passed gas.

"What about the note?"

"That's the main reason I wanted you to see this stuff." McNeal carefully removed the letter sized paper and unfolded it disclosing a series of letters cut from magazines or newspapers and pasted together to read, "*Found on Cayo Costa inside a fence.*" The note was clean, and the lettering purposely contained the date as part of one of the letters cut from a newspaper.

"Whoever delivered this message, and that's what this is, wanted us to believe its current business." Hilliard's pupils focused on the paper like two lasers. "Business...somebody has a motive for doing this. Let's not rush. That's what whoever did this, wants. I have a feeling somebody will show their cards if we wait and let them stew a little."

"What about...well, this probably will end up being a murder investigation. You know they aren't but a couple fences over there and the only one—"

"You said Maggie wasn't sure what we have here, didn't you?"

"Yep."

"You know for sure where it came from?"

"Nope."

"She said that the bone's been buried, how'd you put it, quite a spell? I don't reckon they'll get any deader, do you?"

"Yep and no." McNeal smiled, the sheriff was suggesting they let the tipster help do part of their work.

"Tell the folks in the lab and anybody else that happens to learn about this to keep their mouths shut. That's shut real tight. No media! Tell them I could use another head to mount next to that ten point buck I shot in Georgia last year. I want the message out loud and clear, but I don't want to be the one delivering it. Can you see that gets done for me, James?" Hilliard's smile was jovial, but his eyes were intense.

"Yep. Everybody will make church mice sound loud by this afternoon."

"Good. I'll be doing a little nosing around while this thing is simmering."

Chapter 49
Fort Myers, Florida
May 2010

"Get it delivered?" Heller asked Foreman, who sat on Heller's motel room bed. There was little trust between the two and the tension in the room was palpable.

"Yes," Foreman answered.

"No one observed you?"

"No."

"You're sure?"

"Observed me?" Foreman echoed sarcastically. "No one saw me. Neither did the frigging TV cameras. Oh my, they had a power outage about then. I know my job."

"Keeping any information about us away from the authorities will safeguard what we're doing here." Heller was nervous.

"Look, you don't have to worry about what I'm doing. If we're gonna have a problem, it will be those teenagers. You can bet if one of them gets questioned he'll spill his guts faster than a bag without a bottom." Foreman's face and voice brimmed with hostility.

"Sean and Devale are a lot more afraid of you than they are of the sheriff." Heller knew he was.

"I won't be in the room when they're questioned...if they are. I'm telling you this; I'm not having a couple of snot-nosed, smart-assed teenagers screwing up me getting my hands on my part of the treasure."

"We agree, but Foreman, as long as no one is hurt by us, there won't be any reason for you and me to end up in jail."

Foreman remained silent for several seconds. He stared at his partner intently reading his resolve. "Heller, most times you have to break some eggs if you're gonna bake a cake. You just don't want to be one of the eggs."

Chapter 50
Tampa, Florida
May 2010

"I thought you might want to know this, Harper." Tom Mooney walked to Harper Sturgis desk, placed his hands on it, and said, "On the Benedict Dupree case. The way our college professor, that Arthur Heller guy has made money in the past is acting as a kind of history information hired gun. He got started researching backgrounds of people who immigrated to the US after the war. During the 70's, he found out what happened to family lands, estates, and wealth that the immigrants left behind in Europe thirty years before. He made good money on that. Then he hit a real bonanza."

Harper Sturgis looked up from the brief she was working on. "Okay, tell me?"

"I found where he did work for the Israelis. The CIA used him, also. He tracked down Nazis for them both. Heller checked some individuals to see if they had Soviet ties for the agency. Over the years, he opened two numbered Swiss bank accounts; one's grown to a balance with a high seven-figure amount in it. The way that account got that big wasn't only from the Israelis and the CIA paying off...it was also from Nazis he traced. Most were turned over, but some were very rich. He basically blackmailed them. They could pay him or die. On top of that, he's a sharp investor, and he's done well."

Sturgis nodded, and her eyes dropped back to her brief.

"One other thing. While doing this, he stumbled

across some tales about wealth that the Nazi and Fascists leaders stashed. He was able to run them down; one he verified was true. Huge. Tons of gold, paintings by the masters, all kinds of artifacts...priceless stuff. But, he wasn't able to retrieve it himself. At the time he verified its existence, he didn't have the resources and the connections. He enlisted the Barrollio family for whom he'd done work. They bankrolled him at the time, helped him meet the right folks in the mafia, and he promised to split the money. I checked with some of Heller's current associates. One, a professor he teaches with now, told me Heller bragged to him as a result of the work he'd done in the late 70's he knew that *"Eldorado was in the Italian countryside"* and that there is a girl walking around *"carrying the secret of how to get it, with her."* He said he'd been tracking her down for over ten years.

He'd lost her in Miami. Heller told him he was still searching for her. The professor told me he didn't put much credence in what Heller told him because of some of the wild stories Heller told about his research. Heller claimed the stash was worth billions, not millions."

"Billions?" Mooney had Harper's attention. Her face never changed, but her mind's focus certainly did. "And, you think this has to do with what's happening to Dupree?"

"I do. He either knows where the girl is or has the information Heller needs. Think about it; there's nothing else that provides any connection or reason for Heller to care if Dupree's alive."

"It doesn't make sense. If he knew the information—" Harper reconsidered. "He might not have believed what he learned. It's more likely they're looking for information he has on the girl. Do you know who she is?"

"No."

"Keep working on it. See if you can find if Heller is working for himself or someone else. When you do, I'm going to run down to Dupree and ask a few more questions."

Chapter 51
Turtle Point, Cayo Costa Island, Florida
May 2010

Benny hadn't felt as apprehensive about visiting Turtle Point since the years immediately following the event that still controlled most moments of his life. The calm morning waters of Pine Island Sound rolled aside as he guided his boat through the shallows behind Cabbage Key. Low tide forced him to enter through the north shore channel of what had been the pass eons ago. He didn't notice the abundance of redfish scooting in front of the boat's bow. Thirty years of dreading the discovery of the deed he'd done, hung on him like Jacob Marley's chain from Dicken's Christmas story.

Benny was so preoccupied he didn't glance at his friend's cabin as he flashed past. Had Benny looked, he'd have seen Goodun sitting on his dock, his feet dangling in the water. Benny gave little conscious thought to driving the skiff as it made the "S" curve when the channel changed shorelines. The motor chattered as it skirted a sandbar a few feet too close. The gentle jarring snapped his attention back to guiding his boat.

As Benny approached the cleared spot under the mangroves, he noticed that Goodun had already visited that morning. The unique shape and taper of the "V" mark left in the sand by Warrington's homemade boat and the still sharp imprint of the man's bare feet were as plain as a note left for him. That wasn't unusual...the man's ritual was an early morning walk on the beach if he wasn't fishing. Benny couldn't help wondering if his friend was there for the same reason he was anxious. Had someone been snooping? When Benny followed Goodun's footprints through the mangrove woods toward Turtle Point, his mind went back to a past walk to the beach.

Chapter 52
Turtle Point, Cayo Costa Island, Florida
June 1980

Young Benedict Barron Dupree stayed away as long as he could. The enormity of what he'd done finally overcame his fear of revisiting the scene. He'd murdered two human beings. What should he do? Benny fought that battle over, and over, and over in his mind for the last seventy-two hours. When Benny finished tying his boat to the mangroves in the old pass cul-de-sac, he hadn't reached a final decision.

Should he do the "right thing?" He supposed that was to go to the law, confess, stand trial, and in all probability, spend the rest of his life in jail. An alternative was to do nothing. Let the natural sequence of events determine if the bodies would be found and if he would be connected to them. He hated that thought for two reasons. First, there was no closure. Not for the families of the men he'd killed, justified or not. Not for his memory of Nadine. Not for his feelings of guilt and despair. Second, the uncertainty that he'd live under would linger like the sword of Damocles, hanging over him, ready to slice down and destroy his life. Should he destroy *all* the evidence? The ax, shovels, and other items he'd found scattered around the crime site were on Pine Island Sound's bottom. Destroying *all* the evidence meant exhuming the bodies from their shallow grave, hauling them to sea, weighting them, and then trusting to the sea and its creatures to destroy the remains. He'd abandoned the third option, though he recognized it offered the best potential to spare him harm. Benny knew he could handle the stench and the horribly objectionable task of removing the two men from their current resting place. What he knew he couldn't face was removing Nadine from the grave and, in his mind, desecrating her further. Benny knew leaving her body there, and its possible discovery would open a string of questions including whether he was the one guilty of killing her. A few people knew of their relationship, would report it, and it would be natural for suspicion to fall on him. Even so, sending Nadine's body to the bottom of the Gulf was unthinkable.

The walk through the mangroves, to the beach, seemed an eternity. Each step increased the length of time a second took to pass. Each step increased the dread of what he might find. Each step increased his guilt. He'd killed two men most egregiously. He'd failed Nadine. Benny wanted to turn and run back to the boat, but a cog in his moral compass wouldn't permit that. When he was a third of the way to Turtle Point, the smell drifted to him. It wasn't the one he'd expected.

The pungent odor of wood smoke surprised him. Heavy rains made the frequent lightning strikes that accompanied summer storms unlikely to start a brush fire. Benny stopped and scanned the trail ahead of him. Visible above the canopy of mangrove trees, smoke rose from the area behind Turtle Point. This unexpected complication electrified him. Benny sprinted down the path through the mangroves and emerged into the scattering of palms, sea grapes and scrub oak brush area between the beach and bay.

"Be careful where you step. There might still be hot spots a burning." Goodun Warrington's voice froze him. The man sat on the stump of an old scrub oak. His lean muscular body glistened with perspiration. He offered no further explanation. His silence made Benny uncomfortable. Did the man know? Panic set in. Benny picked his way through the underbrush eventually standing in front of Goodun. Benny hoped his face didn't betray him if the man didn't already know the truth.

"Lightning hit?" Benny asked.

Warrington shrugged. "Could be...don't think so." His stare bored through Benny.

"You were over here when it burned, weren't you?"

Warrington nodded. He said nothing and nothing in his expression provided any evidence as to what the man was thinking.

After several seconds, Benny couldn't refrain from asking, "Did you see anything unusual?"

"The fire."

"What did you do?" Benny asked a general question hoping Goodun's answer would give him a clue to his unanswered suspicion.

Warrington tilted his head to the side. "Not much. Pulled dead brush into piles and let them burn rather than spreading the fire. Ranger Gates came down with the tractor and tank, put water on it. Said it'd be okay and left."

"Did it do much damage?" Benny felt his first glimmer of relief.

"Burnt up some sea grapes, palmettos, weeds, and a couple cabbage palms."

"That's all?"

"Yes. Go look." Goodun stood. "I got someone over to the house. I gotta go. Anything else you need to say?"

"No."

Goodun smiled, turned, and walked away.

Benny's shoulders slumped when he saw where the fire was located. Part of the area burnt was over the spot where the bodies were buried. The surrounding brush was charred, and the clearing appeared to be one of several that Warrington had used to pile brush. The fire was localized. Benny guessed it was less than two acres. The thing Benny didn't expect and was pleasantly surprised by was he couldn't smell anything but smoke from the fire. Ash and a few burnt limbs covered the clearings sand. The expected decomposition smell was absent.

Had a sign been sent to him? Nothing could have been more fortuitous. The greatest potential for the bodies' discovery was the telltale smell from their putrefying flesh. Nature had afforded Benny with a great bit of good fortune.

Looking at the spot disturbed him. Benny wandered away, refusing to think as he walked. Ending up at the beach, he sat in the surf, ankle deep waves lapping over him and the sand indiscriminately. He built a scenario that his conscience needed to avoid what his morals told him was the correct course of action. His justification was that he hadn't been the first to murder. Benny would leave everything as it was. Do nothing. He told himself that if the bodies *were* discovered, he would accept the responsibility and the consequences. When Dupree rose from the water, deep in his heart, he knew he was lying to himself.

He walked back to the bay and his boat. Each step brought a new doubt; a new suspicion. Would the Rangers come back and investigate the fire? If they did, would they discover the remains? After a few rains, would the ashes dissipate and would the smell from rotting flesh lead someone to the graves? Did Goodun Warrington know more than he acknowledged? Did he know the bodies were there? Did he know Benny's connection to them? If he did, what would he do with that knowledge? Each doubt replayed itself in his mind like a student who repeated the scales on a piano.

A dark hump drew his attention near the grave site. It was forty yards away and hidden behind charred sea-grapes. The angle he'd viewed the area from when he spoke to Goodun hid the pile from his sight. Benny approached it cautiously. It was a wild pig the fire had evidently killed. "That's strange," he mumbled to the dead animal, "I'd have thought you'd been smart enough to run away." He looked at the animal closely. A charred rope was attached to one of its rear legs, the other rope end to a small oak. Benny nodded. Warrington frequently set snares for the hogs. They were part of the man's food supply. That was what he was checking. Relief flooded over Benny.

That pig would smell in a day or two. Anyone seeing it would assume that's where the additional smell was coming from. Yes, it seemed that fate was favoring him. Still, the thought of it tore at his insides.

Chapter 53
Pine Island, Florida
July 1980

Roulon Dupree watched his son pick at his breakfast. Something was dreadfully wrong with the boy for the last week. Benny liked eating. Second helpings were the young man's norm, thirds if they were available. But, the last seven days Benny actually left food on his plate. The boy was slumped over his ham and eggs, laboriously sawing on the slab of meat. Yes, something was definitely wrong. The only thing that had changed that Roulon knew about was the "turtle girl's" return to Miami. Roulon only met the girl once and then only for a few minutes. Even at that brief meeting, he could see how his son could have fallen in love with the young woman.

Roulon folded his arms and leaned away from the table. He smirked as he asked, "You trying to figure out what to do about the girl?"

Benny dropped his knife and straightened up as though a broomstick had been inserted in his spine. He looked shocked and turned pale. After a moment of silence, he said, "What do you mean?"

"It's apparent, boy. The girl up and disappears and your appetite with her."

"How do you know?" Benny hoped his father didn't see the slight trembling in his hands.

"Son! Your father was young once. I know what it's like to be in love."

Benny's stress and tension receded. He shrugged his shoulders, not being sure what, if anything, he should say.

"If you like the girl that much, go after her. Take a few days...drive over to Miami." Roulon bobbed his head from side to side. "Sometimes you can't let opportunities pass, boy."

Benny looked down at his plate. "It wouldn't do any good, dad."

"You won't know until you try."

"Believe me; it wouldn't do any good. I'm sure she didn't go back to Miami." Benny shook his head. "It's something I can't do anything about."

"You don't know where she is?"

Benny shrugged his shoulders as he resumed cutting up his ham.

Roulon sighed. He knew there were some trails a person had to follow to a conclusion whether the end was good or bad; failure to do so left a seed of restless discontent that would sprout in the future. "You do what you want," Roulon shook his finger gently at his son, "But, if you should hear from her, go! The 'I dids' cost you less sleep than the 'I wish I would haves.'" Roulon watched his son peck at his breakfast. "What are you going to do today?"

"I thought I'd go check on the turtle nests," Benny said.

"Those turtles aren't a substitute for what you really want."

Benny looked up from his breakfast. "They're as close as I'm going to get."

"Suit yourself." Roulon looked at his cold eggs and grunted. "I talked to Sheriff Simmons yesterday. He told me they found Walker Cole's skiff capsized out a couple miles in the Gulf. They think he was out at night and tried going through Boca Grande Pass when one of those squalls hit. Cole is supposed to have had some guy with him. Brinny's asking for everyone to look out for floaters. Keep your eyes open." Roulon shoveled up a forkful of eggs. "I doubt they ever find the bodies. This time of year, all those

tarpons in the pass and the shark feeding on them."
Roulon shook his head. "They'll be lucky to find any
big pieces."

Benny nodded as a piece of ham disappeared in
his mouth.

You be on the look-out, regardless, hear?"

"Sure, dad." Benny just wanted the conversation
to end.

Chapter 54
Turtle Point, Cayo Costa Island, Florida
May 2010

His past memories placed in his mind's storage cabinet. Benny walked through mangroves and emerged on higher ground that formed the "crest" of the barrier island, if a seven-foot elevation would qualify for that reference. Normally the walk was so routine, so common-place, it evoked little interest or mental response in Benny. That wasn't true today. He noticed the myriad of fiddler crabs, their bright oranges, reds, and violets disappearing as they scrambled for their holes. The mangroves' red stilt roots at the bay's edge seemed a deeper color than usual. Erratic gnarled shapes of tree trunks and limbs were models for some painter's surreal study.

When he neared the beach, the white sand beneath his shoes was softer. The gulls and pelicans gracefully floating on the air currents drew his attention when they normally wouldn't. Benny thought how most humans, he included, did not value or appreciate their life or surroundings until they were endangered. Benny's gut told him he was in real danger of losing the things he valued most. Increasing evidence led to the inescapable conclusion that someone was plowing up his past. That past lay buried behind the fence and gate he was approaching.

The first thing he observed was that the padlock that held the chain was undisturbed since his last visit eight days before. Benny examined the sand around the gate. There were no fresh footprints. The only depressions in the sand were old, rain misshapen holes without any definition. He sighed in relief. The only fresh tracks were of bare feet and were several yards away. Benny knew they belonged to Goodun. Those tracks paralleled the fence leading toward the beach.

Benny decided to follow them. The prints told their own story. Benny could see where his friend had hesitated a few times. On each occasion the toes pointed toward the fence; Warrington was looking for something. At the fourth stop, the tracks led to the fence. Benny's heart sank. Goodun's tracks were intermingled with many other prints. The shoeprints varied in size and sole patterns. Though degraded by recent rains, there were enough features visible to see several people had approached the fence in the last few days.

Benny traced the prints as he walked to the chain link. He saw *they were on the inside of the fence as well as outside.* Benny examined the area closely. Two tiny shreds of cloth were snared in the razor wire. It marked the point someone had crossed the fence. He looked at several deep rectangular depressions. After being puzzled for a minute, he realized he was looking at imprints made by ladders. His worst fear was being realized. Benny's only remaining questions were whether his visitors knew of the graves or if it was random trespassing. Benny wouldn't have made a bet that it was a coincidence.

Benny decided to follow Goodun's footprints as they resumed their trip to the beach. Those prints took him to the sand dune behind Turtle Point, made a ninety-degree turn south and followed the fence. Eventually, they circled the entire perimeter then disappeared back in the direction where his boat was tied. Benny decided to stop at Warrington's cabin on the way back to the mainland. If he worded his questions carefully, he might discover if the old man had observed something he hadn't without causing damning suspicions.

The Turtle Point sand dune called to him. He needed something to provide comfort and solace in his rapidly disintegrating world. That spot was where he'd found refuge at other times in his life when he needed his spirit assuaged. Benny ascended to its top and sat down. Leaning backward, he supported himself on his elbows and stared out at the Gulf's blue-green waters. It was clear forces beyond his control were after his secret. But, why? Who could know? Was it the families of the men he'd killed? At the time of his disappearance, Walker Cole's family didn't show any emotion except for relief. Of course, the theory was that Cole had been lost when his boat capsized. No foul play was envisaged. Why would anyone think otherwise after such a long time? The other man who he only knew as Pablito was never positively identified. People running the marina reported that Cole had a man with him when he left the dock, but did not know his name or anything about him. A local flower grower reported one of its workers missing, a Pablito Juarez, but when authorities investigated the worker's address the employer gave them, the location was a Cape Coral CPA's office. No one there ever heard of the man. No one inquired further about "Pablito" that Benny knew about.

Suddenly, Benny sat up straight as though a bolt of electricity passed through him. Maybe it had nothing to do with the men he killed. Maybe it was the mysterious and sinister people that Nadine feared. Benny remembered the rainy night the sight of a stranger panicked her and caused her to find a place to hide. Thirty years, though, that was a terribly long time to continue a search. What could create such an incentive and determination? If Nadine was the object of their quest, it simply heightened the danger he was in. Benny knew he'd be blamed for Nadine's death as surely as the turtles would return to the beach next year to lay their eggs. The fence he'd built to hide his shame would indict him for the death...for which he wasn't responsible.

The dread he'd lived with for several years immediately after the killings returned as though it never left. Each day he'd awakened, Benny wondered if that would be the day his crime was discovered. It would be that way again. Or would it? Benny stood, brushed the sand from his rear, and started the hike back to his boat. Determination gripped him. Thirty years of living in a world that had a trap door under it were enough. No more. He told himself he wouldn't volunteer his guilt, but he'd not deny the fact. He'd face whatever came.

Benny put his boat motor in neutral and let his skiff drift to Goodun Warrington's dock. Goodun's boat was gone, but Benny decided to stop anyway. He tied a clove hitch to a piling and scrambled up on the wooden platform. Benny looked at the cabin for life-signs; there were none. He called out, "Hello the house," and waited. No answer came, so he tried again. "Hey, Goodun, you inside?" After waiting a moment for a response, he walked to and looked through the screen door. Warrington normally left his doors open and unlocked. Years ago when Benny inquired if Goodun was concerned about someone stealing from him, the man answered, "I don't have much most others want." When pressed he shrugged his shoulders and added, "If they need it

bad enough to steal it, they're welcome to it."
Goodun Warrington had a unique way of looking at
life and what came with living it.

After straining his eyes in vain, looking for his
friend's boat on the inlet's waters, he knocked on the
screen and said, "Goodun, you there?" knowing he
wasn't. He pulled the door open and entered the
cabin. The cabin's one large room served as living
room, bedroom, and kitchen. Furnished utilizing
Warrington's Spartan philosophies, a bed, two chest
of drawers, a table, an old couch, and three chairs
was the total complement of his furnishings. The
only door in the cabin led to the man's one luxury, a
flush toilet fed by water captured from roof run-off
and stored in a 1200 gallon tank.

Benny looked around for something to write a
note. A paper tablet and several pencils sat on the
table. Benny intended to let his friend know he'd
stopped by. He wanted to remind Goodun to tell
Rollie at the Cayo Costa Park office if Goodun
needed anything from town. Rollie would call
Benny, that was their normal routine, and Benny
bring would bring whatever Warrington needed on
the next trip. When he picked up a pencil and
scooted the pad in front of him, he recognized
Goodun's neat cursive. One word was written on the
paper, "*Barlow.*"

That meant nothing to Benny. He turned the
first page back under the tablet and wrote his
message.

As Benny untied his boat and started away, he
was curious. Where was his friend? The old man
seldom left during the middle of the day. Benny
kicked the boat up on a plane and headed for Pine
Island.

Chapter 55
Fort Myers, Florida
May 2010

"Did you have any problems getting it back in the shed?" Heller asked.

"None," Foreman replied. "They'll never know the radar unit was ever gone."

"Did you wipe the—"

"Damn Heller, I do my job right. The unit and case were wiped clean with an alcohol rag. No prints. No DNA. I even sprinkled a little dust on it, so it looks like it hadn't moved since the folks put it up." Foreman scowled. "I just hope you know yours."

"Oh, I do." Heller kept a brave face. He hoped he did, too. Heller changed the subject. "Have you found out anything about the little present we left for the sheriff? Are they doing anything yet?"

"Not as far as I've been able to find out. I found a bar where one of the lab people and some of the deputies hang. Usually, it's relatively easy to buy some drinks and get flooded with more information than you can store on a mega-computer. These yokels are closed mouthed. Part of it is that I'm not a local."

"Is the fact you're black a problem? I could—"

Foreman laughed. "You could go and do what? Screw up bad enough we'd never get anything? Three of the people I'm cultivating are black, including Maggie the lab tech." Foreman snorted at the surprised expression on Heller's face. "You college liberal types are all the same. You preach equality, but are shocked as hell when we prove we are."

"What are we going to do?"

"*I'm* going to be patient. *You're* going to do nothing. Sooner or later, I'll get what we need."

"How long?"

Foreman shook his head. "I don't have a clue. I do know this; that sheriff has his people's confidence, and they like him. From my experience, they're a damn sight less likely to spill their guts when they like 'the man.' I wouldn't doubt he has them studying that bone now."

Chapter 56
Pine Island, Florida
May 2010

"Mrs. Foy."

Corrine looked up and was surprised to see Goodun Warrington standing in her office doorway. It was rare to see him anywhere except on Cayo Costa or during his monthly trip to the grocery. Goodun's visits to Benny Dupree's office twice in two weeks were kin to a shift in the universe. She said, "Hi, Mr. Warrington. Mr. Dupree isn't here. He's on a construction site or over at Turtle Point. You might have passed him coming over." She smiled, "Can I do something for you?"

Goodun nodded, "Need to make two calls. Long distance. I'll pay for them."

"Oh, you don't have to do that. We have unlimited calling here. You can use my phone." Corrine saw the uncomfortable look on Goodun's face and suggested, "Why don't you use Benny's office? I know he won't mind."

She nodded toward Benny's open office door. Goodun disappeared inside. Corrine watched the door close behind him. "I wonder what's up," she mumbled. "Forty years of shunning contact with other humans and all of sudden—" She was tempted to do something that her conscience would never allow. It would be easy to push the button on her phone, carefully lift the handset, and eavesdrop. She smiled, shook her head, and went back to work.

Warrington had been in Benny's office for such a long time, Corrine forgot he was there until he opened the door, poked his head out, and asked,

"Can someone leave a message for me here if there is an emergency?"

"Sure, Goodun. Have them call the 7788 number and ask for me." Corrine looked astonished. When the door closed, she shook her head. Maybe Goodun had more tax problems. Corrine reasoned that was probably it. What a pity the IRS was picking on a good, simple, and defenseless man like Warrington. Goodun emerged from Benny's office. He nodded and said, "Thank you," as he headed toward the office door.

"No more tax problems, I hope?" She pried.

"Nope." He said as he exited closing her door behind him.

Corrine went into Benny's office to be sure everything was okay. She'd have done that if the pope had been the one making the call. In fact, she wasn't sure if the pope was more honest than Goodun Warrington. Everything was arranged precisely as it had been before, except for a tiny detail. The only thing different was a small slip of paper with a phone number and the abbreviation "Dr." scrawled on it. She snatched it from the desk and ran, trying to catch Goodun. She went outside but was unsuccessful. It was as if the sidewalk had swallowed him.

As Corrine returned to her desk, she decided she'd keep the paper with the phone number written on it. She slipped it in her drawer in case Goodun should need it in the future. The 307 area code caught her attention. "Where in the hell is 307?" she mumbled. A quick telephone book check would tell her. Corrine flipped to the page identifying different area code locations. She straightened in her seat and said, "Who in the hell would he know there?" The area code was for the whole state of Wyoming.

Chapter 57
Fort Myers, Florida
May 2010

Frog Hilliard said, "Rerun that for me." He leaned forward against his deputy's desk. James McNeal pushed buttons on the DVD unit, and a grainy image appeared on his desk monitor. A large man wearing a pair of coveralls, a backpack, and a large black hat appeared in the camera's viewing range. Initially, his back was all that could be seen. The man made an obvious effort to keep the camera from getting a clear image of his face. What could be seen of his countenance was covered with a thick, bushy black beard. When the camera could have exposed more of his features, he walked in a crab-like motion. He disappeared around the side of building into the night's blackness.

"And, this was just before the power outage?" Frog asked.

"Yep," McNeal answered.

"Twenty-two minutes." Maggie Stevens, the senior and sharpest lab technician on the sheriff's criminology staff, added, "It wasn't an accident. I can't prove it because they threw the dead squirrel away, but I'd bet ten to one on that."

"Dead squirrel?" Frog said while McNeal grinned.

"I think I know how they made it look like it wasn't sabotage," Maggie said.

"And that is?" Frog asked.

"I checked with the power company's line crew that repaired the outage. They told me a squirrel had crawled into the transformer that serves our building and it shorted out. They also told me a couple other things. There aren't any trees around the pole the transformer is on; not for two hundred yards. The pole is concrete, not wood. I dated a lineman for a while. That's a very unusual place for a squirrel to be. I asked the line guys a few more questions. The guy who got into the transformer told me he pulled the animal out by the tail because it was stiff as a board. That tells me the squirrel was dead before it was ever put in there. Plus, I asked if there was anything else unusual about the fix. He told me two screws were missing from the box cover. So, I looked at the pole. I found some marks on the concrete that could have been made by a climbing belt. The power company used a hydraulic lift truck to fix it. Some gouges were on the surface that might have been made by climbing spikes. You only have to go up ten feet, and there's steel rungs cast in the pole for climbing. I think the dude we caught in the back door security camera footage, caused the power out. If I could prove the squirrel was dead before it fried, we'd know that."

Frog nodded. "Now, that's damned good work, Maggie." He turned to McNeal. "Let's look at that disc again."

McNeal nodded and replayed the sequence.

All three focused on the man's image strolling across the screen. Frog said, "Stop it." The frame the image froze on provided the best view of the man's face. There wasn't much to see. "We're gonna have to install a second camera at the back door, like we have up front. One ain't enough. And, I'll budget to replace the system with one that does color. That would help a heap. Well, that's about as good of a shot as we have on the whole sequence," Hilliard said. He tapped McNeal's shoulder. "You act as secretary, James. I know you don't have the legs for it, but....."

McNeal fished a pen and a piece of paper from his desk and got ready to write.

Hilliard scratched his head. "There's a lot we can't tell, but let's get down what we do know about our visitor." He asked Maggie, "What do you see?"

Maggie examined the image carefully. As she spoke, McNeal wrote. "Male definitely. Big. I'd guess he's six-three or taller. Two-forty to two-sixty. Even under the coveralls, you can see the dude works the weights. The hat, all that beard, plus the camera angle, it's hard to tell, but I'd say he's black. The facial hair is all wrong if I'm right about that. That's a white man's beard. We know he's trying to disguise himself as much as possible; the beard looks fake. He has high top work boots on that are distinctive. He might hang onto them. I imagine he's too smart to keep the coveralls and the backpack that we could use to identify him."

"How about you, James?" Frog asked.

"Maggie's right. I think he's black, too. He's a pro. See the gloves he's wearing? He doesn't want prints anywhere. That, or he doesn't want to make it easy for us to tell what color he is. That lump showing through his coveralls, at the small of his back, looks a lot like a pistol butt. At the beginning of the disc, I saw what looked like the outline of a big-assed knife strapped to his left calf. I'd say he's *definitely* a pro." McNeal rubbed his chin then added, "He moves confidently. The guy's real sure of himself."

"Anything else?" Frog asked.

"Nope."

"If he's so worried about leaving prints, it means they're on file somewhere. We'll start nosing around records of locals with priors and ex-military that fit the description we come up with. My turn." Hilliard gazed at the image on the screen for several seconds. "Wide range, but I'd say he's thirty-five to fifty." He paused studying the screen. "The disguise might help us. That hat looks like ones I've seen associated with some religions. Amish, maybe, Koresh an, Orthodox Jews. It's safe to assume he's not any of those. So, where he'd get it? Stole it? Rented it at a costume shop? Let's check recent robberies and local stores that rent or sell that kind of stuff. We might get lucky." He shook his head. "That's a long shot. One thing though, I think you're both right about him being a pro. And, I'd add to that. My guess is that he's ex-military. Check out his posture. Those habits don't go away. He did a decent job of covering up his body. See, he even turned up his coverall collar so you couldn't see the skin on his neck."

Maggie asked, "James, can you zoom in on the collar? It looks like there's something printed on it." McNeal worked on his keyboard and moved the mouse. A square formed around the collar and it suddenly became much smaller. He cursed and punched some different keys, and the image became larger.

"More," Maggie said.

McNeal punched more keys. The collar was twice life size on the screen. Maggie read the black inked printing. "Curt Smith 14778."

McNeal shook his head. "We couldn't be that lucky. I'll give you ten to one he ain't Curt Smith. That's something. Not much, but it is better than nothing. I wonder what the number's for?"

"Employee number, possibly an institution number like a prison uniform, could be a lot of things. It's one of those little bits that might add up to a big one in the end." Hilliard looked at Maggie. "Anything you missed?"

"He's got a nice bubble butt."

Both men laughed.

"Well, he does." Maggie looked indignant. "You

wouldn't think a thing about identifying some woman by pointing out her big boobs."

"Who knows Maggie, we might be able to make a positive ID from that. You an expert on bubble butts?" McNeal quipped.

"I've rubbed a few." She said in mock anger.

Frog Hilliard said, "I'd drop it there, James. If there is one person I've learned not to argue with, it's a qualified butt connoisseur."

Chapter 58
Tampa, Florida
May 2010

"Find anything more about those fellows hassling Benedict Dupree?" Harper Sturgis had time. If she was going to waste some, what better way than one which could lead to recovering *billions*?

Mooney leaned back in his chair, put his feet up on his desk, and smiled. He purposely took extra time for two reasons. He wanted his boss to focus on what he had to say, and the delay would let her flush out other issues from her multi-tasking mind. The second was that Mooney *knew* any delay aggravated her and that gave him great pleasure. "Yes." His answer wasn't what she wanted, and that would frustrate her more. From Tom's devilish point of view, that was a good thing.

"Okay, smart-ass, you've had your moment." Harper's voice had a little edge, but her face didn't betray any emotion. "You have anything important?"

"Yes." Mooney continued to play mouse to Harper's cat. Harper remained completely quiet and stoic.

The volcano inside Harper was building to an eruption. Tom Mooney knew when to quit. "Okay," he said as he opened his laptop. "I've got new stuff on both of them and a little about the woman they're looking for. Where do you want to start?"

"Your choice. Just get on with it."

Mooney switched his attention to his computer screen. After several seconds, he found the file he wanted. "I'll start with Foreman." Tom looked up, grinned, and said, "You know, Heller and Foreman are a lot like you and me. One's the muscle, and one's the brains."

"Go on," Harper said, blowing off Mooney's attempt to steam her further.

"I told you Foreman came back from Africa and was under the radar for a couple years. That was a period of thirty months. Seems he and an ex-Army buddy went in business. Moving and storage. They specialized in moving from Trenton, New Jersey to the Southwest: Texas, New Mexico, and Arizona. Border cities, mostly."

"Mary Jane?"

"That's what my sources think, but couldn't prove. This guy Foreman isn't a dunce. He's not the genius he thinks he is, but he's definitely not stupid. Anyway, he and his partner did what they did for two years. Then one day, the business goes up for sale. Foreman handles the whole thing. No one has seen the partner since. You fill in the blank."

"Who was his partner?" Harper asked making sure she committed the name to memory.

"Curtis Smith."

"Anything I should know about him?"

Mooney shook his head. "Other than he had dealings with Foreman and he's probably dead, now. He was a small-time hood, end of story."

"Any more?"

"Not on Foreman. Heller, yes." Tom stroked the keys on his laptop. "You know a trail that's thirty years old has a tendency to be covered rather deeply. You have to be a little lucky." Mooney paused and glanced up at his boss. "And ... we were." He put his hands behind his head. "I started out by looking at the public records in every locality where Heller lived since 1975. Mostly, pretty boring stuff, but, I caught a break. There was a request for copies of witness affidavits to an automobile accident involving three fatalities made by a law firm in Maryland. Heller was one of them, and it came up in my search under his name. I was going to pass on it until I saw an Italian name in papers filed by the insurance company. Cardone. I played baseball with an Italian kid by that name. I got to thinking and started nosing around a little more. One of the other witness' affidavits was from a Tony Barrollio."

"Oh, yes," Harper said. "That's no coincidence."

"Let me spare you the boring details. The Cardone family was claiming the insurance because one of the fatalities was their daughter. The only surviving family member was a girl who vanished shortly after the incident." He hit a couple of keys, smiled and said, "Her name is Bocelli. Mary Nadine Bocelli."

Harper nodded, "What else?"

"I traced that name to public schools in New Jersey. She lived with the Cardone family for a brief period. Near as I can tell, that's the grandparent's relatives. There was something going on there, she was enrolled as Nadine Cardone at first, but I think it had to do with the insurance money and nothing to do with Heller. There were a couple name changes—Mary Ryan, Mary O'Toole that accompanied changes in where she lived. It gets murky. Anyway, from New Jersey the trail goes to the University of Miami. I found records of her there. She completed her junior year but never registered as a senior. No requests for a transcript to transfer. Space aliens must have abducted her. There's no trace of Mary Bocelli after that. She was listed as living with two other girls in a Coral Gables apartment. I found one of them, but she moved out ten months before Bocelli disappeared. One of the things she knew was that Mary was studying to be a marine biologist. Get this; she was obsessed with sea turtles. You told me the Dupree guy is too. Want to take any bets on the connection?"

"You have any more information on her?" A flicker of emotion passed through Harper's face...and disappeared.

"I'll print out what part of the record I got from the university. It has her picture, verbal description, the works. They won't give me the part that would really help. *Yet.*"

"What about the other roommate?"

"I'm still running her down."

Harper nodded, "Keep after her. You're going to have the office for a few days. I'm heading to Fort Myers tomorrow." She lifted one long leg and used the six-inch spike of her stilettos to kick Mooney's feet from his desk.

"Damn, Harper that hurt!" Mooney whined.

"Tom, you've been around me long enough to know you weren't going to play that smart-assed game that you did when we started this conversation, without me evening things up."

Tom followed the curves of Harper's leg from her high heels far up under her dress. "I should have known better," he mumbled. Tom Mooney knew what those legs were capable of, both good and bad, and the pleasure and pain they could inflict.

Chapter 59
Fort Myers, Florida
May 2010

"I just want out of this thing." Sean sat in the Mustang's passenger side. The last rain from a passing thunderstorm pelted the convertible's cloth top. "I don't give a shit about this car; I don't give a shit about some pie-in-the-sky treasure, I just want to get away from this whole mess."

Devale's eyes widened, "Man, you can't be serious. Forget the car, forget the money, but don't forget that Foreman dude. He is a badass. You cross him and you'll end up like those two buried in the sand on Cayo Costa. What are you gonna do? Walk up to him and say, I quit. You might as well tell him you want to quit living."

Sean's face was sullen. He didn't know how, but he wanted out. "I wish I'd never been in the Napoli that day."

"I'm not going to get my black ass killed doing something stupid like bailing on Foreman. If you do, don't get me involved." Devale watched Sean swivel his head away from his gaze. Devale was sure if Sean tried to get out he knew what would happen to Sean and himself. "Man, you don't need to do something dumb."

"I already did that when I got involved."

"Sean, we're better off to just wait this thing out. I have a feeling Heller hasn't got a clue to where the treasure really is. I think he's just buying time trying to keep Foreman from pissing all over him. We haven't done anything serious, yet. Trespassing, screwing up the outboard, that's nothing."

"Yeah, and what if Terrill decides to slit Heller's throat? We're witnesses! Wherever Foreman puts Heller, you can be sure we'll be next to him."

"We won't be around." Devale was frantically trying to convince Sean not to commit suicide.

"How do you know?"

"Because that's heavy duty stuff and they don't want us anywhere around when they discuss that." Devale placed his hand on Sean's shoulder, and Sean promptly shrugged it off.

"Foreman will kill us like a sack full of kittens because if Heller disappears, we are the only ones knowing what shit has been going on. Devale, we're the only ones that connect Foreman to Heller."

"It isn't going to come to that. Haven't you been able to figure out Heller is paying Foreman real good to do what he's doing? Foreman's not going to kill the goose."

"I want out." Sean folded his arms and was defiant.

"Okay, okay, how? You gonna walk up to Foreman and say '*up yours, I'm quitting?*' Just be sure I'm not around. I don't want the blood spatter on me. You gonna snitch on him to the cops? He hasn't done nothing bad yet. And, what he's done, we've done. Think about what he'd do if we rat him out. No way! If we wait it out, we can always bail later."

"Okay," Sean said but thought at the first opportunity he'd find a way to protect himself and jump ship.

Chapter 60
Pine Island, Florida
May 2010

"One more thing, Benny," Corrine's voice halted him at his door. "Mr. Warrington was in yesterday. He said he needed to make some long distance calls, so I let him use our phones."

"Damn, I bet the IRS is bugging him again." Benny shook his head. He sighed. There was comfort in knowing someone besides himself had problems, though not near as severe.

"I asked him that, and he said not." Corrine was concerned. "Benny, do you think Mr. Warrington is sick or something?"

Benny came back to her desk. "No. Why would you think that?"

"Mr. Warrington never comes off the island. He's been over a few times in the last couple weeks; it's just not like him."

"Did he appear sick to you? Look bad? Not sound right?" Benny asked. His bet was on the IRS hounding Goodun.

"No. But...well...I let him use your office to make his call. I didn't think you'd mind. Anyway, I went in after he left to straighten up if I needed to. I found a little slip of paper on your desk. It had a phone number and "Dr." written on it."

"Mmmmm. That surprises me, though I guess it shouldn't. Goodun would have to be half-dead before he'd complain to anyone." Benny thought for a second then asked, "He say anything unusual or did you notice anything else strange?"

Corrine thought for a second. "The only—"

The phone rang interrupting the conversation. After a short give and take discussion with the handset, Corrine said, "It's the building construction inspector's office, Mr. Dupree. I think you need to talk to them."

"I'll take it in my office," Benny said and walked away. Corrine never got the chance to mention the unusual thing she noticed was that the phone number was in Wyoming.

Chapter 61
Pine Island, Florida
May 2010

"They tell me you're the man to see if I want some crab traps built." Foreman looked at the old cracker sitting on the steps of a house that was in need of paint and repairs. The old man spit a wad of tobacco juice on the ground. He eyed Foreman suspiciously. Roscoe Freed knew a "furner" when one stood in front of him. Foreman didn't belong on Pine Island. That made him a "furner." Roscoe didn't like strangers. He ignored Foreman and went back to repairing the cast net he was holding.

"Hey, old boy, you hear me?" Foreman reached toward Freed.

"I wouldn't do that. Not if'n you're wantin' that there hand to stay on your arm." Freed's hand disappeared inside his shirt and removed a large knife that gleamed silver in the morning sunlight. "Don't you go callin' me 'boy.' I don't cotton to bein' called that no more than you would."

Foreman's hand slowly withdrew. A smile crept onto Terrill's face and some respect. "I just want you to make some crab traps for me."

"Go to Walmart or some sporting goods place like West Marine. They sell them." The knife disappeared back under Roscoe's shirt, and he returned to his net repair.

"I don't want the wire mesh kind you buy at those places. I want to fish for stone crabs. They tell me you make the old wood slat style with weights in them." Foreman tried to be as pleasant as his temperament would allow.

"You gonna *fish* for crabs? If'n you're gonna be a crabber, shit lick, you gotta a bunch of learnin' to come by." Freed punctuated his comment by spitting tobacco juice a foot from Foreman's polished shoes.

Foreman guessed at where the old man's antagonism originated. "I'm not going in the business. I want to catch my own to eat. Some folks at the fish house told me you could fix me up right."

"Who'd you talk to? Henry?"

Foreman lied, "Yes, I think that was the guy."

Roscoe stopped working and looked up at Foreman. He sized up the man in front of him and shook his head. He said, "You know you're talkin' a bunch a money? You can't put out one trap and figure on catching anything regular."

"I figured that. I saw some you made that are stored up at the fish house. That the standard size you make?"

"Yeah. But they ain't *stone* crab traps. They'd be illegal."

Foreman ignored part of Freed's statement. "What is that about three feet by two feet by eighteen inches high?"

"That's what those are. Take's more an one man to jerk them off'n the bottom. Those boys use electric winches. I can make 'm smaller," Freed volunteered.

"No, those are just right. What would a dozen cost me?" Foreman asked.

Roscoe sat silently for a moment. A smile slowly twisted his lips. "Well, let me think. Slant wood. Nichol alloy wire. Angle iron. Lead. Fasteners and hardware. Labor." He lifted an eyebrow, looked skyward, and tried to think of a price that would be too high for the man to pay without sounding outlandish. "Three hundred-twenty-five per trap." Roscoe rounded up, "So's that's 'bout four thousand."

"When can you have them built by?"

Freed's jaw dropped, then he said suspiciously, "I don't do no work until I have my money up-front."

Foreman nodded, "I can understand you wanting that, but you have to understand I want to be sure I get my traps. I'll give you two thou up front, that's right now, and the other two when I pick them up. That good?"

Roscoe looked at Foreman to try to judge if the man was serious. "Let me see the color of your money."

Foreman removed his wallet from his pants. He counted out twenty, one hundred dollar bills, slowly, methodically, holding them within two feet of Roscoe's face. Foreman asked, "Deal?"

"Deal," Roscoe agreed. He reached out to take the cash, but Foreman moved the bills out of his reach.

"When can I get them?"

"Day after tomorrow."

"That's good but awful fast." It was Foreman's turn to be suspicious.

Freed grinned. "I got nine done built. Got everything I need except some of the hardware for the rest. Two days is fine." He extended his hand, palm up, and waved it a time or two. Foreman put the twenty bills in Roscoe's palm.

"I'll be back, day after tomorrow. Be sure they're done." Foreman turned to walk away.

"They'll be a sittin' right here, but if'n you *actually* want to crab, season don't open 'til October 15th." Roscoe looked at the money and then at Foreman. "What's your name?"

"Just call me 'The Four Thousand Dollar Man.'"

As Terrill strode away, he added, "That's all you need to know."

Chapter 62
Pine Island, Florida
May 2010

"Is Mr. Dupree in?"

Corrine looked up from her boss' expense reports which she was completing. At eye level across her desk was the bottom of a not quite mini-skirt. Her eyes traveled up the tall, shapely frame of Harper Sturgis to Harper's pale white-skinned face and coal-black hair. Corrine's mouth opened slightly. She'd only seen a couple of women that tall off the basketball court in all her forty-four years. The woman peered down at her like she was an ant. Corrine felt like she supposed a threatened insect would. She'd forgotten what the woman asked. Dupree's assistant babbled, "Oh, I'm sorry. I was concentrating on this paperwork. May I ask—"

"I'd like to speak to your boss. That's Benedict Barron Dupree, isn't it? I'm conducting some business for him." There wasn't any threat in the words or tone, but still, Corrine was thoroughly intimidated.

"He's in the field. I don't expect him back until after four." Corrine watched the lady's face for a reaction. There wasn't one.

"Fine. He has a cell, doesn't he?" Harper dropped a business card in front of Corrine. "Call him and tell him I'd like to speak to him, say, at super. There a decent restaurant around here?"

"Mr. Dupree's favorite place is good." Corrine read the lady's card. "Ms. Sturgis. Do you have a particular time in mind?"

"You said he normally gets here at four...say, six-thirty. That should give him time to shower before he comes. I don't like the smell of sweat mixed with...what do they serve at the restaurant?"

"Pancakes. It's Durkin's Pancake City." Corrine felt as unnecessary as a pimple. "But, they do have all kinds of things."

"Lord!" Harper took a deep breath. "Pancakes it is. Never mind instructions, I've been there before. If Mr. Dupree can't make it, will you have him call me at the cell number on that card?" Harper walked to the office door.

"Yes, Ms. Sturgis." Corrine looked at the card closer. *Harper Sturgis, Attorney at Law.* She remembered prior conversations and said, "Oh, aren't you *a friend* of Mr. MacCardle?" Corrine's comment carried a catty inference.

Harper froze in the doorway, turned and faced Corrine, then stepped back to Corrine's desk, hovering over it like a bird of prey. Her face maintained the same mask-like quality as when she entered. However, her eyes glowed with a smoldering inner fire. Corrine wished she could crawl under the desk.

Harper's voice was unstressed and calm as she said, "Mac and I go back for years. We're both Marines. The two of us have been through a lot together." Sturgis turned on her heel in a military fashion. As she left the office, her words were: "If you're curious...yes...and, he isn't that good." With her last visible step she added, "And, he knows that."

Chapter 63
Turtle Point, Cayo Costa Island, Florida
May 2010

He'd put off entering the sanctuary he'd built for the bodies that were buried behind Turtle Point as long as he could. Benny had to know. As much as he feared what he might see, he had to know. Though he entered the chain-link fenced property often, he very seldom went to the burial site. Each time it shook Benny to the core. He hated himself for several days afterward, until the futility of maligning the acts he'd done so long ago held sway in the logical portion of his thoughts.

Benny locked the fence gate behind him. Fearful of what someone might see if his worst concerns were true, he watched for any sign of human presence as he slipped through the underbrush. His steps slowed as he approached the clearing. Benny stopped thirty yards from the spot, purposely keeping heavy cover between the graves and his line of vision. It had been three years since he'd actually stood on the sand next to the bodies' hiding place. Eventually, the fear of discovery overcame the fear of what he might see.

Benny used the cabbage palms and other brush to continue to block his vision as he approached the site. He knew he might lose the last of his courage if faced with the reality for too long a period of time. When he got to the point where he could no longer shelter his eyes from what they might see, Benny stopped, closed his lids for several seconds, took a deep breath, then stepped around the palms to where he knew he'd only be a few strides from the graves.

Large piles of sand told him immediately his worst fears had been realized. Benny froze. He looked down into a trench four feet long, three feet wide, and two feet deep. Inside the hole, many bones were exposed including two skulls. "Ahhhhhh!" he screamed as he fell to his hands and knees. Benny closed his eyes, so the dreaded vision disappeared. His mind refused to cope, and he became an unthinking robot for a full hour. Using his hands as scoops, much like an animal burying something, he leveled the heaps of sand, shoveling it back onto the skeletons. When logic and reality returned to his tortured mind, his hands were bleeding from a myriad of small cuts created by bits of shell in the sand. He'd returned three-quarters of the sand piles back into the grave; he could no longer see the macabre spectacle. That only spared him the view. He knew his secret was discovered.

Benny used a palm frond to sweep the clearing, eliminating all foot-prints including his own. He brushed away the tracks that led to the fence where the trespassers had climbed inside. When he finished, he threw the frond down in disgust. Those individuals knew exactly where to find the graves; there was no hiding from them.

What should he do? He told himself he'd already made the decision to face the consequences, but he doubted his resolve. He thought about the possibility of exhuming all the remains and then what? Dump them in the Gulf? Bury them somewhere else on the island? He shook his head. Benny asked God to give him the character and the strength to... His cell phone vibrated in his pocket.

Shaking, he removed the phone and saw his office number on the screen. He took a second to compose himself before answering. "Benny Dupree, what do you need?"

Corrine's voice said, "Where are you? You okay? I've checked all the construction sites."

"I'm okay," he lied.

"You've had a visitor, and *she* wants to have supper with you."

"Who is it?" Benny's emotions calmed listening to Corrine's familiar voice.

"That lawyer friend of Mac's, Harper Sturgis. I told her you should be able to make it to Durkin's by six-thirty." Corrine repeated, "Where are you?"

"I'm looking at a piece of property I might be doing some work on." Benny walked toward the gate.

"Will you be able to get home, get bathed, and get to the restaurant in time? I can call her and make an excuse if you want. You could call her tomorrow." Corrine sounded as though she might enjoy delivering some negative news to Sturgis.

"I should be able to make it."

"Don't skip the bath. *That woman* made it very clear she didn't like eating with sweaty smelling men."

"I'll be sure to use plenty of deodorant and after-shave lotion."

"You be careful around her, Mr. Dupree. She looks like a vampire character from a movie or like used to be on TV. I know she isn't a real vampire, but she acts mean and nasty."

"I'll be fine. Corrine, I'm going to have to hurry to be on time. I'll go straight home. Can you take care of things there for me?" Benny asked, but knew she would.

Leaving the proximity of the graves gave him emotional relief. He hoped he could pursue the pleasures he enjoyed most for a few more weeks until his sins snared him and the law took them away. The dread of whether he would be discovered was lifted, only the uncertainty of when remained.

Chapter 64
University of Miami, Florida
May 2010

"You mean Professor Heller? Yes, he's been here several times and called many more. He inquired about the same three girls." The records clerk at the University of Miami returned Tom Mooney's big smile from across the counter. "His primary interest has always been the Bocelli girl. As you know, we don't have anything about her after June 1980. I've already given you everything I have on Amanda Hartwell. I gave the same information to Heller that I gave you. The last girl is Jane Smith. I gave you everything over the phone that I have on her. Sorry, I can't help you more."

Tom asked, "I don't suppose there's any chance I could see the Smith girl's records?"

"Oh, I'm sorry. Those are confidential records. I'd have to have Jane Smith's approval for you to get access to them. Since both you and Professor Heller have already attempted to find her and haven't...well, I'm very sorry."

Tom thought for a moment. "Could you look at it for me? I won't ask any questions you can't answer with a yes or no." He could see the girl wanted to help, but the rules weren't in his favor. "I promise it will be between you and me. I just want to find a way to contact her."

"What if she doesn't want to be contacted?"

"I won't bug her, and I certainly won't tell Smith how I found her." He smiled broader. "I promise. I won't create any grief for her."

"Just, yes or no answers?"

"Absolutely!"

The girl took a breath, looked at Tom critically. "I suppose you're trying to find her to give her a part of a fortune she's inherited, too."

Mooney shook his head, "I don't know anything about that. My employer is a lawyer, and I'm trying to find the Bocelli woman by finding Smith."

"That sounds a lot more honest than Heller. That man impresses me as a real dirtbag." She looked around the office before she leaned across the counter and whispered, "He offered me $200 to either look at it or get a copy."

"I can see you didn't." Mooney still smiled. "He's a poor judge of character."

The girl looked at Mooney for several seconds before adjusting her bra straps and saying, "Strictly yes or no, right?"

"Absolutely!"

She looked around to see if anyone was watching. "Give me a few minutes. Records this old are still paper. I'll have to find her file." The records clerk disappeared. When she returned, she was reading the file's contents as she approached the counter. "I don't see anything in here that would help you. I can tell you some things before we get to the cloak and dagger, yes and nos. Jane graduated in '81. She left the apartment that she had shared with Bocelli and Hartwell in July of '80." The girl wiggled her nose. "She and another girl rented an apartment right off campus, but they gave a PO Box number instead of a street address."

"Is there anything in there on her after she graduated?" Tom asked.

The girl flipped a few pages. "Yes."

Mooney asked the most logical question. "A transcript request?"

"Yes."

"From her."

After a quick check, the girl looked puzzled. "I'm not sure."

"Did it come from an employer?"

"Yes."

"Were her grades requested?"

"Yes."

"Is her name on the request?"

"Yes and no...I think."

"I don't understand?"

The girl leaned forward and whispered, "The authorizing signature is from a J.S. Burns, and the handwriting looks the same as you know who."

"I know you can't tell me any more information about Miss Smith. Could you tell me where J.S. Burns works?"

The girl smiled and said, "Craven and Crow Engineering in Marietta, Georgia."

Tom smiled. "You were most helpful. Thank you! Let me ask you something. Do you like lithographs?"

"I suppose I do," The clerk looked at Tom's hand which he extended as if to shake hers.

She felt him place something in her palm as they shook. "What's that?" she asked.

"A litho of Ben Franklin," Tom said as he dropped her hand and left

Tom Mooney whistled on the way to his car and half-way back to Tampa.

Chapter 65
Fort Myers, Florida
May 2010

"What is this shit!?" Heller looked at a handwritten bill for $4,000 from a Roscoe Freed. It said it was for "stone crab traps." He shook his head in disbelief. "How in the hell can we possibly use these?"

Foreman grinned at the irate professor. "They're insurance."

"Insurance?" Heller was angry and confused. "How? For what?"

"You never know when you might need it, or for what. Insurance isn't any good if you buy it after something bad happens. That's right, isn't it? I'm not teaching at Columbia, but I know that's correct." Foreman couldn't resist a dig at the man he disliked, distrusted, and increasingly disbelieved. As long as the money continued to flow, he'd put up with the nerd, but when that stopped...... "Remember, I'll do my job; you do yours. If I have to break any eggs, the ones we talked about or others, I need a place to put the shells." Foreman enjoyed watching Heller's face turn pale when the man comprehended the implied threat. Foreman asked, "Speaking of doing jobs, how are you coming along with yours?"

Heller relaxed. "Good. In fact, I have a little trip to make. I believe I've finally got a lead on the girl's other roommate. I'll need to make a trip to Georgia to question her, verify it is the woman, and see what she knows about Bocelli. I need you to make up some of those forged FBI documents for me like you said you could." The last part of his comment had a snarky retaliatory twang to it.

"Yeah, I could do it. Why? You won't be able to pull off imitating a Fed. You're a goody-two-shoes type. You don't look like it, walk like it, talk like it, hell you don't even smell like it. I have all the documents already set up for me. I've been there, done that. You tell me what info you want, and I'll come back with it."

"Pure and simple, I want to know if she knows what happened to Mary Bocelli and, dead or alive, where she is today."

"That won't be a problem."

Heller hesitated. He studied Foreman who had a superior look of disdain on his face. It scared Heller. He cautioned, "No rough stuff, okay. All the money in the world isn't any good to us if we can't spend it because we're sitting in prison."

"Rough stuff? Why would an officer of the law resort to such things? I don't break eggs unless I have to. You just don't worry your *little* head and *little* body about it. Like I said, you do your job; I'll do mine." Foreman tilted his head to the side, narrowed his eyes, and asked, "I'm curious. You've been screwing around, trying to find out where the roommate is for thirty years. All of a sudden, bam, you know. How'd that come about?"

"It took thirty years to find the right pair of hands to put two $100 bills in."

Chapter 66
Turtle Point, Cayo Costa Island, Florida
May 2010

As far as he knew, there were only two people who were aware of *everything* that happened on the sands behind Turtle Point, thirty years ago. Goodun was one of them. At sixty-five he was in good health and expected another ten years of active life. What he couldn't count on was what others might do to snuff out his life. If there was one thing he'd learned about other humans, it was there weren't many good ones. There were definitely some low-life men hatching dirty business to ensnare Benny Dupree. All the snooping and activity around the property, inside the fence, was proof enough. Goodun knew he was likely to become involved.

Warrington faced one of the biggest dilemmas he'd ever encountered. He'd made a promise. A solemn one. Breaking that promise was an unthinkable action within the code of honor Warrington lived by. Yet, if he didn't, he might destroy a friend. If he died, a truth that was bad enough as it was would be much worse with a lie added. With that in mind, he sat in lantern light in his cabin and began to write. He addressed an envelope – *Written by Aaron Moses Warrington, If I die, give this to the Sheriff.* Warrington sat silently for another ten minutes, continuing his internal battle, before beginning his story. He sighed, adjusted the pad in front of him, pulled the cap off of his ball-point pen, and began writing in his bold, legible cursive.

These are the facts of what happened on the night of June 27th, 1980 on the beach behind Turtle Point on Cayo Costa Island.

Chapter 67
Cape Coral, Florida
May 2010

"Hi Mr. Dupree, there's a lady waiting for you in the back corner. You want me to walk you back?" Elise was already working the tip she expected from someone who was one of her "regulars."

"No. I can find her."

"You want coffee?" Elise stared at Benny as he hesitated a few seconds before joining the woman. "Are you feeling okay, Mr. Dupree? You look a little flushed and—"

"The truth is I have been better, Elise. Maybe that cup of coffee will help." He smiled weakly and reluctantly made his way to the booth where Harper Sturgis sat. Benny glanced at his watch. He was twenty minutes late, mainly because he didn't want a meeting with her *until he could get a grip,* on the situation he faced *and* his psyche. Benny knew he needed her, but he walked to the table feeling like a man being wheeled into open heart surgery. Harper's face still had the corpse-like poker-faced expression that never varied. If she was perturbed by his tardiness, there was no sign. He said, "Sorry, I'm late." He tried to inject some humor, saying, "Corrine, warned me I needed to shower."

Harper said, "Good evening Benedict." She was wearing black slacks and a black shell that exposed biceps and triceps an individual only obtains through rigorous and continued training. Benny looked in Harper's eyes. He remembered when he first met her he'd thought her black eyes were like the sharks he caught. Cold. Heartless. Relentless.

That assessment was confirmed and underlined by looking into Harper's pupils. She was a shark.

"I hope it's good, Benny said, knowing that it wasn't.

"You hired me to do research into the individuals who are, let's call it, harassing you." Small talk was one of many things Harper had no time or use for. "I've made progress." She waited for Benny to answer. When he remained silent, she added, "We know why they're here, but I think you do, too."

Benny knew how a deer felt in a hunter's sights. "I don't ... I'm not sure. Why?"

"They're looking for a girl, Mary Bocelli, and they believe you know something about her. She disappeared in 1980. I know that's a long time ago, but do you remember her?"

Benny knew better than to try to lie. His face was expressive, and he had little control over what was written on it. "Yes, I remember her." He'd learned not to volunteer for anything, and that included providing information.

"So, tell me about her and your relationship." Sturgis examined him like he was a specimen under a microscope. She read every emotion that raced across his face.

"I only knew her for a month. She came to observe the sea turtle nesting season. That's how I became interested in them. I'm sure you know that. She went to Miami and was stu—"

"I know her background. How did you meet her? How well did you get to know her?" Harper leaned forward in an obvious effort to intimidate him. Though he knew her intent, it didn't help. Benny was intimidated.

"I went over to the beach at Cayo Costa to fish and met her there. She had a kind of observation camp set up. I ended up being her transportation back and forth from Turtle Point to the place she was renting. Marine biology and the sea turtles were her life. She taught me a lot about them. Nadine was—"

"Nadine?" Harper asked and waited for an explanation.

"That's what she *went* by. I know her first name *was* Mary, but she introduced herself as Nadine."

Harper noted the words went and was, both past tense, but said nothing. "Okay, go ahead."

"She stayed for the month then was going back to Miami." Benny hoped he'd given Harper enough to satisfy her. He hadn't.

"What else?" Harper persisted.

"What do you mean?" Benny tried being evasive.

A brief flash of disgust flowed on and off Harper's face. "You've been doing well until now. What else?"

Benny's head was swimming. He tried a half-truth. "Nadine was all business. She was interested in the turtles and serious about getting her degree. We were just good friends."

"That's a lie. Mr. Dupree, part of what makes a lawyer successful is to know when a person is lying to them. It's difficult sometimes, but in your case, it's not a challenge." Harper leaned forward. "Look, let's us dispense with the happy horse shit. I am a damned good lawyer. I'm sure you're going to need one. I can't help you unless you tell me the whole truth about Mary, or Nadine, or whatever she called herself. Fact one: she left Miami and came over here. Fact two: you appear to have been her primary human contact in this area. Fact three: As far as anyone knows, she never returned to Miami. You were probably the last person to see her alive and maybe dead. Now, what conclusion will most lawmen jump to, hmmm? The two men who are here want to get to the Bocelli woman. We're pretty sure why. She has information on where a huge amount of wealth is hidden. Bocelli may not have been aware that she had it. Evidently, they believe they can get it from her dead or alive. I don't have a clue how, but...my guess is the men could care less about you or any problems they cause you. You're just a means to an end."

"I knew she thought that someone was chasing her," Benny said.

"Yes, she was right. One of the two who has invaded your life is the man she was eluding. He's Heller. What he's up to and how he plans to use you in it, we don't know, but you can be sure that's their intent." Harper looked at him, fixing his pupils with hers. "You know what's next."

Benny stared back defiantly and nodded.

Harper leaned as close to Benny as she could and asked in a low voice, "Did you kill Bocelli?"

"No! I loved her. I did not kill her!" Benny's face reddened and emotion swelled in him.

Harper leaned away. She sat silently, as motionless as a mannequin, and was devoid of visible emotions. Finally, she said quietly, "I'm sure you didn't."

At her words, Benny broke completely. He folded his arms on the table and buried his head in them. Sobs he tried to stifle were muffled, but audible. His body heaved and shook under their strain. He suddenly straightened up, clawed at his face to remove tears that had turned from guilt to anger and shame. Benny stood up and said, "I know we have a long way to go to get to the end of this. I do need your help. I know that. But, I have to have time to think, at least overnight. Can we meet back here for a late breakfast? I have to go into the office first; I'll be here at nine. That okay?"

"If you need time...sure. But remember, time is damned important, too." Harper now knew there was much more involved than she had surmised in her wildest reconstruction of events. "I haven't checked into a motel, yet. Do you have a recommendation?"

"The Tarpon Inn. It's on Pine Island, very private and very nice. They have a good restaurant." Benny was still composing himself. "They know you?"

"Yes, very well. Why?"

Harper stated matter-of-factly, "I'll have them charge the room to you directly and call you if they have questions. It will save you the extra charge I'd put on if I pay and bill you. See you tomorrow."

Benny nodded and left the restaurant, his agitated emotions still plainly apparent.

"Is Mr. Dupree alright?" Elise asked Harper, Elise's concern visible in her face and voice. "He looks upset. The times I've seen him he's so happy. I've never seen him look like that before."

"I'm afraid I had some bad news for him," Harper said.

"Oh! Did a relative die or something?"

"Close."

Elise shook her head and said, "Mr. Dupree is so nice. I knew he had problems when he came in tonight. He looked bad. I hope he'll be okay."

"He will. I'm here to help him. Do you know Mr. Dupree well?" Harper asked.

"Yes! He's one of my regulars. Great tipper. He comes in at odd times, usually when we aren't very busy, so we talk a lot."

"Good. Tell me, what do you have besides pancakes and breakfasts?"

"All kind of good things."

"Recommend one. The best in the house, please." As Harper spoke, she removed a fifty dollar bill from her purse and placed it on the table's edge close to Elise. "Just so it doesn't go over this. You're going to get the change."

"The rib eye with fried okra, garlic smashed potatoes and the broccoli cheese soup." Elise's eyes were as wide as the plates she toted for a living. "But, it's not near—"

"We won't worry about that. I'd like iced tea, unsweetened. Oh, if you have time, come by and chat. I'll probably be spending quite a bit of time here. I'd like to know about shopping, how to get around the area, and I'd like to get to know you." Harper's words were accompanied by a warm smile.

"Sure. Let me get your order in and your drink. I'll be right back," Elise answered, returning Harper's smile. Elise knew she'd be pleased to have the stranger as a friend.

Chapter 68
Pine Island, Florida
May 2010

Harper Sturgis stretched out on the bed in her bra and panties. The hotel Dupree recommended was an unexpected pleasure. She guessed the building dated to the early 1900's, was furnished with antiques and provided service and ambiance not available in the concrete and glass accommodations built in recent years. Harper was scribbling notes from her conversation with Elise. She knew details she couldn't have gotten from mutual friend Billy MacCardle. They were things Dupree would have avoided; gossip that provided investigative strings to pick at and follow to where they might lead.

Her mobile phone rang. "Now what?" she said as she swung her legs out of bed. The screen on her cell identified the caller as Tom Mooney. She thought *he must have something important for him to call after nine.* "Hi, Tom. What do you have?" She flipped a page on her notepad.

"I found the information on where the second roommate is living. The one Mary Bocelli shared an apartment with right before she disappeared. She's in Georgia. She works for an engineering firm in Marietta."

Sturgis thought for a few seconds, "I don't know if that's important anymore. I asked Dupree *the* question about Bocelli. My guess is she's buried out on the island from his reaction."

There was momentary silence. Finally, Tom said, "I know you don't like to go off chasing intuition. I just think we'll miss something important if we don't follow this up."

"Okay, Tom. But, put it off until I get back." She thought for a second and changed her mind. "I think I'll be finished here tomorrow night or the following afternoon." She thought for a few additional seconds. "You know, if we're going to do it, let's do it right now. Make airline reservations for tomorrow morning. There shouldn't be a hurry, but if you have a feeling....."

Chapter 69
Fort Myers, Florida
May 2010

"What are you folks drinking, today?"

Maggie, James, and three other members of the sheriff's department sat at the bar in the Bourbon Barrel, the unofficial watering hole for Frog Hilliard's deputies and staff. Fred Wilson offered to buy his customary round. The big black man was affable, had a law enforcement background, a silver tongue, and a billfold stocked with a seemingly unending supply of cash.

A chorus of "Hi Fred's" came from the green-uniformed officers and from Maggie dressed in her "uniform," jeans and a tee shirt. He sat down on the stool next to Maggie.

Fred waved to the bartender and said, "Hey Alene, give my friends a round on me. I'll have a J & B on the rocks." He looked at the grinning officers and asked, "How are the Royal Green Knights of the Frog's Roundtable, today? Is there peace in the realm?"

"All is safe and serene, sire," James said as he fondled the full beer bottle Alene had just sat in front of him. Their conversations' opening had become routine two weeks after Wilson's first appearance in the bar. His visits coincided with theirs.

Fred claimed his daily visits to the Bourbon Barrel helped reduce his frustrations caused by his dealings with federal government officials. Wilson claimed to be working for an environmental lobbying group trying to change water flow release regulations from Lake Okeechobee. Anything past surface questions brought forth laughter from Wilson and a standard, "That's classified." He said the people behind his investigation didn't want to be identified. Wilson referred to them as, "The SS, the Stupidly Secretive."

"So, there's no bad guys to haul to the gallows today?" Wilson asked.

"My worst villain was a preacher who I issued a speeding ticket to for going fifty-five in a thirty zone," one officer volunteered.

Another said, "I was busy, but nothing heavy duty. Some teens selling grass, a vagrant I had to hassle, and one domestic disturbance. A chick poured boiling water on her live-ins tender parts while he was sleeping. She caught him playing hide-the-weenie with another gal." The officer took a drink from his beer bottle. "I hate doing the domestic calls. We'll end up back at that address with the coroner and a body bag." He shook his head.

"Well, while you were all having it easy, I was suffering." James McNeal raised his palms up even with his eyes and looked toward the ceiling as though imploring heaven for help. "I spent two-thirds of the day listening to Frog tell Brinny Simmons stories. I wish he'd number them so he could just say 'number 23,' I could laugh, and I'd save time listening to the same tale. I bet I've heard the hundredth replay on some of them." The group chuckled.

The third officer said, "I can understand boring. You know what Frog has me doing? I'm going over every missing person report since 1950, looking for ones where the body was never found. Seventy percent of them are runaway kids, runaway wives, runaway husbands, and runaway runaways. Most of the rest are drug or sex-related. They end up in an orange grove, a cane field, or a canal. There are some we never find, but you'd be surprised how low that percentage is. Way less than half. Still, it's boring as hell."

Fred asked, "Why does the sheriff have you doing that? Are things so slow he has to make work for you people?"

The deputy pointed to Maggie. "It's her doings. Her and her damned bone."

Maggie frowned. "Mark, I don't know what you're talking about, and *I don't think you do either*." The look in her eyes added, "Shut your mouth!" though not vocalized. The deputy looked at the foam on his beer and turned mute.

"Maggie you playing with someone's bone?" Fred Wilson got one of his *I'd like a pair of your panties as a souvenir,* smiles he'd shown her frequently over the past few days. Unlike her associates, Maggie wasn't "won over" by the outgoing "high-roller." When someone lacked authenticity, seemed too good to be true, or just plain gave her a bad gut feeling, Maggie's antennae raised. It was as high as she could elevate it.

"No, not...right...now." Maggie spaced and emphasized each word. "I don't know anyone whose bone is interesting enough to spend time playing with."

The deputies laughed, and McNeal said, "Whoa Fred! My man, you've just been cut down by a cold, cold knife."

Maggie maintained eye contact with Wilson. She sensed a deep evil there, hidden behind a broad smile. The man was dangerous. But, as much as her judgment warned against it, her hormones begged her to continue having her sexual fantasy about the big man sitting next to her.

"Maggie, do you want me to go away? I'll leave tomorrow." Wilson's question had a mocking quality embedded in his tone.

"Suit yourself." She picked up her Whiskey Sour, raised it to Wilson like she was toasting him, and took a sip.

"Don't let Maggie run you off," James said. "It must be her time of the month."

"No, no, no," Wilson said in feigned seriousness. "I'll depart the land of the Green Knights on the morrow."

"Shit, see what you did, Maggie? Who's gonna buy our beer now?" one officer remarked.

"Seriously, you going to leave us?" McNeal asked.

Fred Wilson asked, "Seriously?"

McNeal nodded and mumbled, "Yes."

"Just for a day or two. I have to fly out tomorrow, but I should be back within the week."

"Where you going?" one of the deputies asked.

"That's classified." Fred Wilson reached into his hip pocket and pulled out a hundred dollar bill. "Alene, can you get another round out of that?"

"Sure," the bartender answered.

"Good. I have to do my drinking quick tonight. My flight's early in the morning."

Wilson put his hand up, softly touching Maggie's shoulder. "Sorry, about the bone comment. Am I forgiven?"

Maggie tilted her head to the side, gave him a faint smile, and said, "I'll take it under advisement."

"You working on a case? Somebody find a body?" Wilson asked.

"Not exactly. Someone dropped off a bone at the office and—" Maggie realized she had violated Frog Hillard's directive and quickly covered. "And, the sheriff thinks the whole thing is a hoax."

"Oh, sounds to me he's not that sure. He has your buddy here, scouring the cold cases for something." Wilson paused and looked serious.

"Who knows, you might find out something that will let you write one of those forensics books. Get rich. Retire at, what, thirty?"

"Flattery won't get you in my undies," Maggie said, dropping her voice.

"That's too bad. Any hints for what might?" Wilson's voice was even lower.

"Nothing, *right now*."

"Good, that does let me leave with some hope." Wilson stood and announced in his now recovered voice. "Royal Green Knights of Frog's Roundtable, I take my leave of thee. My dragon flaps its wings at dawn. Till we doth drink again." Everyone laughed as he walked to the door.

Alene asked, "Your change, Fred?"

"Keep it. Sometimes Christmas comes in May."

Maggie watched Wilson leave the bar. He looked as good from the rear as he did from the front. Something triggered the neurons in her mind. There were dots she should connect, but what were they? "Damn, Maggie we'll have to buy all our own drinks for a couple days," McNeal said, interrupting her thoughts.

"You'll survive, James." Maggie took a sip from her Whiskey Sour and got back into the conversation with her workmates.

Chapter 70
Cape Coral, Florida
May 2010

"More coffee, Elise." Harper's patience was wearing thin. Dupree was a half hour late and didn't respond to his cell phone. She guessed it was turned off.

"Yes, Ms. Sturgis." Elise lingered at the table and finally said, "Are you waiting for Benny Dupree?"

"Yes."

"I thought you might be after last night." Elise pointed toward the restaurant's parking lot. "He drove up about fifteen minutes ago. He's just been sitting in his truck since then."

A wisp of a smile flitted across Harper's countenance. She whispered to herself, "And, the truth shall set you free."

"Please?" Elise asked, trying to respond to Harper's inaudible comment.

"Just talking to myself. Wait a second." Harper removed a small piece of paper and a pen from her bag, thought for a few seconds, wrote three words on the paper, folded it in half, and said, "Elise, would you do something for me?"

"Sure, Ms. Sturgis."

"Put another cup of coffee on my check, take it out to Mr. Dupree, and give him this note. Tell him it's from me." She handed the folded paper to Elise and grabbed the waitress' wrist.

Elise nodded and took the note. "Mr. Dupree's in really bad trouble, isn't he? Is it about that zoning mess?"

"I don't know anything about the zoning. As far

as whether Mr. Dupree is in serious trouble, I honestly don't know. That's what I'm hoping to find out." Harper paused getting Elise's emotional attention. "You like Mr. Dupree very much, don't you?"

"Oh, yes, very much."

"You'll help him a lot if you don't say anything about our conversations. Do you understand what I'm telling you?" Harper squeezed gently on Elise's wrist then released it.

Elise smiled broadly, "What conversations?"

Elise took the cup of coffee and the note to Benny's truck. He sat in the vehicle staring straight ahead and didn't notice her until she was within a few yards. His eyes opened wide as he put the window down. "Hi Elise," he stammered.

"Good morning, Mr. Dupree. Ms. Sturgis asked me to bring you the coffee and this note." She handed both to Benny and said, "See you in a little while?"

Benny looked at the note and answered, "I'll be right in." He glanced at the note a second time that said *when you're ready.*

"What happens if I tell you everything and you decide not to represent me?" Benny asked.

"That isn't going to happen," Harper answered.

Benny remained silent as he stared at the stone-faced woman sitting across from him. He hadn't had such a strong urge to run away since he'd walked up on his first rattlesnake as an eleven-year-old on his first quail hunting trip.

She prompted him. "You made up your mind to tell me the truth—whatever that may be—or you wouldn't have procrastinated coming in here. Don't change your mind."

He took a deep breath. "I'm not changing my mind. What I have to say is damned difficult. I thought all the shit was behind me, but..." Benny looked at the ceiling. He knew it would be hard to say the words, but not this devastating.

"Relax and take your time." Harper held up her index finger. "If I do that, stop talking. I'm assuming what you're going to tell me you don't want to be common knowledge. Elise said she'd try to keep people away from the tables close to us, but if she isn't able..."

Benny nodded.

"Start by telling me about Mary...Nadine...Bocelli," Harper said. "Tell me about the last time you saw her."

Benny nodded again and told Harper about Nadine's desire to make a last trip to Turtle Point to see the nesting sites, finding them disturbed, and his trip back to his boat to get flashlights to be able to see what damage had been done. Harper asked a minimum of questions and took few notes. Each time Benny slowed, Harper would say, "Then what happened?" When he reached the part where he was about to look into the clearing, he stopped and gazed at the table. Harper pushed again, repeating the same question.

"I saw two men, one that I knew and one that I didn't." Benny's voice began to tremble. "They were burying a body."

"Was it Mary Bocelli?"

Benny couldn't look at her, "Yes."

"Then what happened?"

"There was an ax laying there...I picked it up...I

picked it up...I... " Benny couldn't finish his sentence.

Harper's face remained frozen. She asked in a very low voice, "Did you kill them?"

"Yes."

"This will be hard, but there's information I have to know. I've got questions. Be sure you answer them truthfully and as completely as you can." Harper stretched and reached over the table and touched Benny's arm. "It's going to work out okay."

Benny nodded. He was surprised that Sturgis showed concern for his fears.

"Are you sure that Bocelli was dead?"

"All I could see was her back, neck, head, and her hair. They'd already buried the rest of her." Benny shook a little as he told Harper, "After I ..." He winced. "I removed some of the sand from her. It was all caked in blood. There was no life in her. I'm sure she was dead."

"Did you try to feel for a pulse?"

"Yes. At her neck" Benny shivered violently.

"Are you sure you killed the two men?"

"Yes."

"And how do you know that? Did you check for a pulse?"

Benny looked up at her for the first time; fire burned in his eyes. "I kept hitting them both with the ax until I knew they couldn't be alive."

Harper didn't react at all. "Then what happened?"

"Really, for a while I just did things. I don't remember much except swinging the ax and getting stabbed. And fin—"

Harper interrupted, "You were stabbed? So they fought you?"

"Kind of. I screamed at them, and they were turning to face me when I started hitting them with the ax. That's when one stabbed me in the leg."

"Do you have a scar?"

"Yes."

"Big and easily visible?"

"Pretty much so."

Harper nodded, scribbled a few notes on a pad then said, "Okay, you said you knew one of them. Who was it and how well did you know him?"

"His name was Walker Cole. I knew *of* him more than knew him. Walker had a reputation all over the county. He was fifteen to twenty years older than me. I met him once or twice when he worked for my father. That was only for three weeks. Dad caught him stealing gas from the company pump, so he fired him. He'd been in and out of jail for all kinds of things, assault, rape, robbery. The parole officer asked dad to give him a chance, that's how Cole ended up working for him. I probably hadn't seen him in over two years before..."

"How about the other man?"

Benny shook his head. "I never saw the man before. Walker called him Pablito. He's the one who stabbed me."

"Do you know of any connection between Bocelli and the men?"

"Yes, between Cole and her. She hired him to take her to the island and pick her up before I started doing that. I volunteered when she told me Cole was how she was getting to the beach."

"Miss Bocelli was attractive?"

"Very."

"You told me you loved her. She return the sentiment?"

"I believe she did."

"She ever tell you so?"

"Yes and no. The words, I love you, yes. But, Nadine said we could never have a future. She said it was because she was running from something and someone in her past. I guess it was the man you called Heller. She told me we had to make memories that had to last a lifetime. I don't think she believed she had long to live. Ironically, she was right, but not from whom she thought..." Benny pursed his lips while he fought his emotions.

"Anyone else know about the two of you, maybe saw the two of you together?"

"Not that's alive. My father is dead, and he's the only one I told. Nadine didn't want anyone to know about her being here. She made me promise not to mention her. As far as seeing us together, old Samuels who owned the marina did, but he's dead. The guy that ran the newspaper route saw me at her rental house. He moved away fifteen years ago. I doubt if he'd remember, even if we could find him." Benny paused and squinted. "It's possible that Moses Warrington did. He lives on the island and doesn't miss much that goes on. The old man's been there at least forty years. He's a hermit of sorts. I'm one of his best friends, but we probably only see each other once or twice a month. We've never talked about that, Nadine and me, so I don't know."

"If I wanted to talk to this Moses guy, can you give me a phone number?"

"He doesn't have a phone. I could take you to his place. It's very isolated. You'd have to take the state park ferry over to the island and walk through the mangroves to get to his cabin, otherwise. It would be tough."

"I had enough of that in the Marines."

Benny smiled. "You'll probably be able to get more out of him than most. He's an ex-Marine."

"There is no such thing as an ex-Marine." Harper's voice had the steely sound of a saber being withdrawn from its scabbard.

Benny nodded. "You two will get on well. Just remember, if you get fifty words out of him, that's a month's worth of discussion." He paused then added, "If you ask anyone about Moses, they won't know who you're talking about. Everyone around here calls him Goodun."

Harper scribbled a few words. "You built the fence for obvious reasons, right?"

Benny dropped his eyes to the table. "Yes. But if what happened, didn't, I would have built it to protect the turtles. That's what Nadine would want."

"You know anything about this fortune Heller's looking for?" Benny shook his head. "I never heard of it until you told me."

Harper sat silently for then said, "At this point, we do nothing. As long as no one knows the location—"

"Someone knows. I saw where the fence was crossed. When I checked inside, they'd gone directly to the spot and the bodies were partly uncovered. I covered them back up, but whoever was there, knows exactly where they are." Benny looked into Harper's prying eyes.

"Shit!" the first ping of emotion flowed across Harper's face, disappearing within seconds. "How would you find them? Unless you knew where to look. You've never told anyone?"

"Never!"

Harper's face returned to its emotionless mask state. She tapped her fingers on the desk. Her mind was grinding through the possibilities like a computer. "If it's Heller and Foreman one of two situations has occurred. First, he's found what he's looking for. In that case, we do nothing. Chances are he wants as little attention as possible, just like you. Second, is that he didn't. He'll try to get access to the property in some way. He'll probably do that by exposing what he knows and get the state to do part of his work. In that case, the authorities will be calling on you. If they ask for access, give it to them. Don't volunteer any information. Remember the words; *I don't remember.*" Harper hesitated then said, "Dupree, look me in the eyes while you answer my next questions."

Benny nodded and maintained eye contact with Sturgis.

"Are they going to find anything more than those three bodies inside that fence?"

"Yes."

Harper leaned back, the surprise showing in her body movement, but not in her face. "Another body?" she asked.

"No. Not exactly. I buried a turtle Cole and the other man must have killed. It's probably the reason why Nadine approached them. They also had buckets of eggs they'd dug up. Her emotions couldn't have handled seeing those two things. The turtle was too heavy for me to lift, so I buried it."

The first smile Benny saw on Harper's face appeared as she said, "That's the first lucky and good piece of info I have to use." She wrote notes. "Okay, I have enough for now. You go back to living your life exactly as you have. Change nothing. If the law approaches you, all your answers are?"

"I don't remember."

"If it gets specific, like are there bodies on your property, shut up and call me. Don't lie or try to be clever, understand?"

"Yes." Benny looked at the feminine Mount Rushmore seated across from him. "Do I have a prayer of getting out of jail before I die?"

"You have a prayer of never going."

Chapter 71
Turtle Point, Cayo Costa Island, Florida
May 2010

Benny called Corrine. He'd made the decision to take the day off. When he was stressed, he found relief by sitting in Turtle Point's sands. Benny had seldom been under such stress. His divorce. A financial business crisis. And, as a young man, that 1980 June event which created stress at its greatest.

He reacted to that June night's happening by making the decisions from which he'd never be free. Now, that old, young man came as frequently as he could to safeguard his secret and to honor Nadine's spirit in the only ways he could. Benny created his own mental shrine from the sands where he and Nadine built their lifetime memories...and... he fiercely defended the increasingly fragile ecological thread to which the creatures clung.

Waves of time and things he'd done to protect himself from others learning of his dark deed, lessened the fear, and with it, the stress in his daily existence. No one came to look for Nadine. No one connected Walker and Pablito's disappearance with the island's sands. Wildfires that were mysteriously common that summer helped hide tell-tale odors the event would have normally produced. In future years, he purchased the property. Then he fenced it. Those events transferred his interest and emphasis from evading discovery to aiding Nadine's beloved sea creatures.

The morning sun was at his back as he sat in the white powder on top the Turtle Point sand dune. Florida's broiling summer sun was heating air and water to the sweat-producing temperatures and humidity that were the southwest Gulf coast everyday reality. It took time for the realization to become apparent, but the act of sharing a secret so deeply guarded for so long was a release for Benny within itself. Maybe the heat baked that "realization cake" giving Benny some temporary peace.

The spasmodic offshore breeze flattened Gulf waters to pond smoothness. Light blue water spread to the horizon like a sheet covering the world. No wavelets reflected light back to him. The placid calm allowed the person who knew what and where to look to find signs of the myriad of life whose home lay beneath the surface. Benny watched the tiny ruffling of gin-clear waters as schools of white-bait made their endless journey along the sandbars that fronted the beach. Marauding game fish under the bait forced the tiny fish to erupt from the surface like rain. The flash and slash of the larger fish were apparent to his trained eyes. Far out in the Gulf, big splashes disrupted the calm. Most were too distant to see what created them, but Benny knew they'd be made by rays, tarpon, shark, or porpoise. As if to confirm his thoughts, a small pod of bottle-nosed dolphins, the proper name for porpoise, swam and played as they moved along the beach, fifty yards from shore. Occasionally, one would fire off to chase a mullet or other fish as a pre-lunch snack.

Life below the water's surface provided for life above. Gulls and terns circled the shoals of baitfish that frantically evaded death from under them, only to be captured from the sky. Pelicans flew in formations as they hunted fish schools to dive bomb. Osprey soared on the gentle wind currents, screaming for no apparent reason other than to announce their presence. Their sharp vision focused on individual fish close enough to the surface to drop on and lift in their talons.

Benny had a new appreciation of these mundane views nature offered. He knew the overwhelming probability was he would soon be denied the simple pleasure of watching them. Despite Harper Sturgis' calming words, Benny took little hope from their promise. The reality of what happened to individuals who did what he had was stark.

As he sat, squandering time and wondering if he should, he remembered his father's final months. Roulon had suffered a stroke, one that curtailed his movements, making him chair bound for most of his remaining life. For a man that had abhorred the thought of inactivity, Roulon made his peace with his condition so long as two things were available to him: Music from his past and his album of pictures taken from his youth to his present. Benny marveled at how his dad, a man renowned for his stubborn inflexibility, transitioned so smoothly and quickly. However, Benny was concerned that the transition was based on the possibility Roulon had decided it was time to die.

One day as his father listened to *Moonglow,* a song coming from a stereo playing a stack of old 33 RPM records, he looked at the old photos. Benny chose the moment to speak to Roulon about his fear.

"Would you like me to turn the TV on for you?"

His father shook his head and said, "There's nothing worthwhile on anymore."

"Come on dad; there's good shows on. You just have to find them." Benny took a couple steps toward the TV but knew better than to turn it on without being instructed to do so. He asked his question by looking at his father. Roulon shook his head, no. Benny squatted down next to the recliner his father occupied 80% of his waking hours.

"Dad, I'm worried that you're so immersed in the past, you'll forget you have a future."

Instead of the angry response, Benny expected,

Roulon grinned. "You're concerned I don't want to live anymore? Boy, you couldn't be more wrong. Do you know why?"

"No."

"Whether I had the stroke or not, it was time for me to realize that my days are past. When you're young, that's when you make the memories. Now, it's time for me to do two things with them. Use them to help others and to enjoy. In my memories, I'm young. See this picture." Roulon pointed to a yellowing photo of him holding a large tuna. "Every time I see this, I catch it again. I feel its pull, the thrill of lifting it in the boat, the joy, and envy of those fishing with me. I can live that again and again and again. My memories are here," he pointed to his head, "and here," he pointed to his heart, "I can play them like a tape on the VCR, anytime I wish. They keep me young and alive. I want to enjoy them the next day and the next day. Now, they help me, help you with the building business. They let me share things to do, and not to do, with friends. With you. Those photos and records are trails that take me where I want to go. Do you understand?"

Benny remembered answering that he did, though he only partially believed. How, he asked himself, could any man give up his relevancy? Now, sitting in the sand, reflecting on what might be his time remaining to make memories, he truly understood.

Chapter 72
Tampa, Florida
May 2010

Yes, I'm Jane Burns." The voice coming over the cell phone sounded very suspicious of her caller.

Tom Mooney expected that. He asked, "Was your maiden name, Jane Smith and did you attend the University of Miami during the year 1980."

There was silence then a click. Jane Burns evidently had hung up. Mooney tried redialing. The pleasant receptionist answered, "Craven and Crow Engineering, how can I direct your call?"

"May I speak to Jane Burns?"

"One moment, please." The operator repeated the same procedure as when Tom placed his first call. Instead of ringing through to Burns, the operator returned to the line. "May I ask who's calling?"

"I'm Tom Mooney, an investigator with the Sturgis Law Firm, from Tampa, Florida. I have a few questions I'd like to ask regarding a case we're handling."

"Just a moment, sir." After a few seconds, the receptionist returned. She said, "I'm sorry, Ms. Burns can't speak with you now."

"Tell Ms. Burns, I'm just trying to save her a trip to Tampa, and me, getting a subpoena."

After a few more minutes, the angry voice of Jane Burns said, "What do you want?"

"I won't take much of your time. I'm trying to locate a woman who I believe you knew at the University of Mi—"

"You're looking for Mary Nadine Bocelli, right?" Burns voice was sarcastic. "You're late. The FBI has already called. Like I told them, I don't know where she is, if she's alive or dead, I don't know anything. She never came back from wherever she went that summer. I got stuck paying the entire rent until I got out of there and got a new person to share a room with. If you find her, tell her she owes me rent money."

"You didn't see her after she returned from Cayo Costa?" Tom asked.

"She never came back from there."

"Okay, let me write a few more notes." Tom used the excuse to plan how to proceed. The fact that she acknowledged she knew *where* Bocelli had gone varied from the information Harper had given him. A personal visit was in order. "You said you hadn't seen her, have you ever heard from her?"

"No!"

"Alright. One last thing for my records, I need your home address, phone number, and email address." Mooney smiled as she complied. He looked at his watch. It said three-thirty. It was too late to plan a trip for later in the evening, and besides, giving her the night to cool off would help the conversation.

Chapter 73
Marietta, Georgia
May 2010

The doorbell rang. Jane opened her eyes and realized she'd dozed off watching TV. Who in the world was it? She snorted as she got off her sofa. It was probably a neighbor or salesman of some variety. She would miss Final Jeopardy, and that put her in a huff. Going to the door to address a stranger was the only time she missed having her "ex" around. This was particularly true since the economic downturn. Only two other tenants remained in their pricey eight-unit complex, and they were out-of-town more times than at home. She put her eye to the peephole glass to see who was outside her door. A large, well-dressed black man who carried a briefcase stood outside. She made sure her safety-chain was latched before she opened the door to the limit the chain would allow. She said, "Yes?"

"You're Jane Burns?"

"Yes."

"We spoke on the phone today, Mrs. Burns. I'm Fred Wilson with the FBI. I have a few more questions I'd like to ask. I'm not interrupting you and your husband, am I?" The man seemed pleasant, but Jane was not in the mood.

"I've already told you everything I know about Nadine." Jane was exasperated.

"This will not take long." The man who called himself Wilson moved close to the door. "We're looking for a picture of Nadine. You must have a snapshot around. I'll get in and out, quickly." He reached inside his suit coat. "I have an identification card and badge if you'd like to see them." Wilson pulled them out and held them to the crack between the jam and open door.

Jane leaned forward to look. His big palm rested against the latch chain as she examined them. While Jane was focused on the credentials, the man drove his palm forward ripping the chain bracket and screws from the door. He thrust the wooden panel into Jane knocking her down. Before she could react, his knee was on her chest, pinning her to the floor, and he'd shoved a gun muzzle in her mouth, muffling a partial scream. "Scream again and I'll blow the top of your head off." His eyes told her he was serious. She remained silent.

"That's better," he said as he retrieved his briefcase and pushed the door closed. "Get up," he commanded as he removed his knee from her body. "Go in there," he pointed to the living room where Jeopardy still played. "That's a good show," he said. "The two of us are going to play our own little game of questions and answers." He placed the badge and card in his briefcase and removed gloves and a roll of duct tape. "You can make this easy or very painful. I'd suggest easy because I'm very good at painful." He turned up the volume on the TV.

Chapter 74
Marietta, Georgia
May 2010

Mooney stared at a multitude of police vehicles parked outside the Marietta apartment complex. Crime scene tapes circled the lawn's perimeter. An ambulance, a crime scene truck, and over a half-dozen police cruisers told Tom there was a death involved. It didn't take a lot of intuition to realize it was a very good possibility that the victim was Jane Burns. Tom quickly realized that someone loitering in front of an active crime scene would draw attention. He pressed his rented car's accelerator and drove several blocks before parking and calling Sturgis.

"This is Harper," she answered.

"Hey, Harper, it's Tom. I've got a situation up here. I told you I was going to visit the Burns woman. I waited until today, so she'd cool off; it got a little heated on the phone. I'm afraid she might be really cold, now."

"Cold? Do you mean dead?" Harper's voice elevated.

"I'm afraid she might be. Her apartment building is blocked off with yellow tape, and it looks like half the Marietta police force is there. It could be someone else, but when I talked to her the other day, she said the FBI. My guess is the "F" in the FBI she talked to stands for Foreman. He beat us to her."

"You won't know until you verify," Harper answered. "Go back to her apartment. Speak to one of the officers and see if you can confirm that Burns is dead."

"If I tell them I'm looking for her, that's going to raise a lot of questions."

Harper hesitated for several seconds before instructing Tom. "We definitely don't want to get involved in a murder. Right now, we don't know that the Burns woman is dead. Even if she is the victim, we have no proof anyone we know was anywhere near. Anything we'd introduce now is conjecture." Harper was justifying her decision to herself as much as to Mooney. "When you approach one of the officers, do this: Ask what's going on, see what they volunteer, if you have to, tell them you're trying to verify a man you want to serve papers on is still living in the building. Wing it from there, but *don't associate us* with the Burns woman."

"Officer." Tom Mooney stood a step away from the crime scene tape, waved and called to a friendly looking policeman standing thirty feet on the lawn.

"Yes?" the officer walked to him.

"I'm trying to determine if someone lives in that building. Any chance I can get inside to check the mailboxes? The last address we have for the man is here. I need to serve him with some papers."

The cop smiled but looked skeptical. "Sorry, buddy. This is an active crime scene. There's no way."

"Do you have an idea when they'll finish?"

"None. I've been here six hours, but that doesn't mean anything. It could take a whole day. Or two."

"What is it, a robbery? What? It looks like it's serious with all the tape you have strung up." Tom fished gently.

"It's serious." The officer looked at him suspiciously. "You a reporter?"

"Oh, hell no! I work for a law firm. Do the dirty work, mostly. I despise those press people like you probably do." Mooney hoped he hit a sympathetic chord. The officer's smile told him he did.

"Someone die?" Tom asked.

The policeman nodded.

"Was it a man?"

The cop shook his head.

"Can you tell me the name? Just the first one?" Tom reached inside his sports coat and looked at some papers then quickly returned the car rental agreement to his pocket. "That will tell me if my case is involved. No wife, no divorce. Then, I'll get out of your hair."

"I believe its Jane, but I can't swear to that." The policeman motioned with his hand for Tom to move on.

"Thanks," Tom said as he smiled and returned to his car. When he opened the door, he cursed and removed his cell from his pocket. He autodialed the office, and when Harper answered, he told her, "I was too late. She's dead. Shit, Harper, if I'd gone last night, I might have stopped all this."

"Yes, you might have," Harper answered, "but you also might be lying on the floor in that woman's apartment, just as dead as her, if you had."

Chapter 75
Fort Myers, Florida
May 2010

"She isn't alive." Foreman sat on a chair in Heller's motel room. Heller sat on the edge of his bed and listened to Foreman recount his trip to Georgia. That was good and bad news. It meant Bocelli's body was probably buried on the island, they hadn't found it, and they had to figure a fool-proof way of getting the body "discovered." They also had to have a fool-proof way of recovering the cross and key that Heller was sure hung around Bocelli's neck.

"What did the roommate say to convince you of that?"

"She said they were very good friends, that Bocelli never contacted her after she left for the Gulf coast, never came back to get her clothes or any of her personal belongings, never got the money she had in the bank and lying around the apartment. The only good thing I got out of her was that Burns did know Bocelli was going to the Sanibel area. We knew that. Heller, face it, the bitch is dead. She's probably stuck in the ground inside that fence or maybe fed the fishes thirty years ago."

Heller thought for a couple of moments. "What we can gain if we find her body, is worth the effort, even if it turns out that it's not there. And, I fully believe it is. Well, at least, we have a way to get the law to help us. We can get the Burns woman to attest to the fact that the Bocelli girl was—" Heller stopped talking as he watched the frown grow on Foreman's face. "What happened? Did you rough the woman up?" Heller's voice elevated and his face reddened.

"She isn't going to help us." Foreman squinted at Heller. Heller ignored Foreman's visual message to, "drop it."

"You idiot!" Heller was shouting. "I couldn't get her to talk. How'd you do it? You blew it, you asshole! Now, I'll have to go up there, figure some way to separate my visit from yours, and pay her off."

"It won't do any good," a faint smile covered Foreman's face. "She can't."

Heller thought the unthinkable, dismissed it, and then the realization of what happened hit him full-force. "You didn't ... You did!!! You killed her, didn't you? You dumb son-of-a-bitch!" Heller was screaming.

"I had to break an egg," Foreman said. A vicious look formed on his countenance. "You want to be an egg, too?"

Heller's anger didn't fade, but his ability to mask it, improved. "Why?"

"She didn't buy the FBI credentials. She was going to call the cops. I had to make a decision. Did we want someone getting the authorities involved in this whole enterprise? Didn't think so. I tried to calm her down, but it just made her madder. Hey, I even told her all I wanted to know was whether Mary Bocelli was alive and if she knew where Bocelli was. Burns told me to get out when I didn't, she started screaming. I shut her up. Got her in condition to talk about Bocelli." Foreman raised an eyebrow and scowled. "I can be persuasive. She talked."

Heller looked at the animal in front of him. "You tortured her?"

Foreman nodded, "She told me she was sure Bocelli was dead. I already told you why. Look, no one will connect us to it. I made it look like a sex killing. The cops will be rousting every pervert in that part of Georgia. That's a long, long list."

"What if they find your DNA, or prints, or something?"

"I guarantee they won't. I know my job."

Heller wasn't sure of that anymore. A light knock at the door silenced the conversation. Foreman placed his index finger in front of his mouth and stealthily tip-toed to the door. His hand reached behind his back finding the gun butt. He jerked the door open. Wide-eyed and obviously shaken, Devale and Sean stood outside.

"Mr. Heller, we're here like you asked," Devale said.

"We didn't hear you. Been here long?"

"No sir, we just pulled up." Devale thought for a second and added. "Not more than a few seconds ago."

"Okay, boys. Terrill and I will finish up in a few minutes, and we'll be right out," Heller said. He nodded to Foreman, "It should only take a minute to finish. Terrill, will you close the door?"

After the door was shut, Heller asked in a voice barely above a whisper, "Do you think they heard?"

Foreman shrugged his shoulders and answered, "Probably not." He thought something entirely different, but there was no use spooking Heller. More eggs for him to break. As he thought about the complication, a solution to their other problem occurred to him. "Those boys might be the answer we need to get the authorities over to the island looking for Bocelli's body. Let me think about how we'll do it. If we explain things to Devale and Sean, get them to disappear for a couple weeks."

"What are you thinking about?"

"A wild idea. Let me flesh it out. I want to know it will work, before I present it to you, *boss*." Foreman marveled that Heller continued to believe

what he was told. He'd withheld important facts
from Heller on his visit to the Burns woman that
changed everything.

Chapter 76
Pine Island, Florida
May 2010

"Your boss in?" Corrine was startled by the Amazon-like woman standing in front of her desk. Harper Sturgis certainly could have been the embodiment of the Herculean ladies descending from the legend. The lady's marble mask was as cold and inscrutable as ever.

"Mr. Dupree is in the field. I don't expect him back in for an hour or two." Corrine enjoyed delivering the bad news to Sturgis. "I'd suggest you come back around 5:30."

"I'll wait for him here." Sturgis reached in her purse and removed her cell phone. "What's his number?"

"I can't give that out without Mr. Dupree's permission." Smug. Corrine was very smug.

"Uh-huh. Call and get it." Harper headed for Benny's open office door.

"I'm sorry, you can't go in there," Corrine said.

Harper stopped but didn't turn around. "Yes ... I can." She resumed her forceful march into Dupree's office as Corrine obediently called her boss.

"Close the door," Harper said to Benny Dupree as he entered his office. She was seated in his chair, looked perfectly at home behind his desk, and was as void of readable emotion.

As Benny closed his door, Harper said, "This thing has taken a turn for the worse."

"Worse?" Benny was even more uneasy than when he arrived and that had been with four tight cheeks.

"Prior to our conversation this morning, I sent my assistant to run down a lead to see if we could find information about Ms. Bocelli through her college roommate. My thought was that if we could find out the information Heller is looking for, or if it even still exists, we could use it as a bargaining chip. Maybe make him go away. We were able to find the girl through old records. Her name *was* Jane Burns. When my investigator, Tom Mooney, showed up at her apartment, the police were already carpeting the place. Someone killed her before he got there. I instructed Mooney to be sure not to get involved. We don't want any connection to that. Has that woman ever contacted you?"

"No, never."

"Know anybody by that name?"

"No."

"Did Miss Bocelli ever mention her?"

Benny concentrated for several seconds. "She mentioned her roommate. Nadine said they were a good match because they were both stubborn, competitive, and took foolish chances. She told me about her roommate starring down a bull shark on a trip to John Penne Kamp reef. The girl wouldn't leave and wouldn't use the shark stick she had for defense. But, I don't remember her name as being Burns."

"My mistake. She wouldn't have been married then. How about the name Jane Smith?"

"Yes, I think that might have been it because Nadine made a remark about Smith being such a common name." Benny shrugged his shoulders. "Past what I told you, I don't know anything about her."

Harper lifted one eyebrow. "I believe there's a very good possibility that Foreman killed her. What you just told me fits. She sounds like the type to resist giving up information. There was no way for her to know she was dealing with a psychopath. Foreman's answer to most problems he faces is violence." Harper hesitated for several seconds. "We can't be sure what Heller and Foreman were trying to find out from the Burns woman. With what they've been doing at your place on the island..." She shook her head slowly, reasoning as she made the motion. "It doesn't make sense if they're convinced Bocelli is dead and on the island. Unless," Harper hesitated, "they didn't find her skeleton. They may believe Nadine could still be alive." The eyebrow rose again. "How far are the men buried from Nadine?"

Benny was clearly distressed, but answered, "Three yards, maybe a little more."

"That's far enough for them to miss."

Benny shuddered but remained silent.

"Dupree, work on controlling those emotions," Harper said. "You may end up on the stand in a courtroom. I don't want you to piss away what I'm doing to get you free."

"I'll do my best."

"Okay, here's what logic tells me they'll do next. If they think that Bocelli is buried on your property, we know she is and I believe they still do, they're going to have to get access to it. How can they do that? They could trespass openly figuring you wouldn't be able to stop them. You wouldn't go to law enforcement, but the Park people probably would. Besides, there's too much ground to cover. They've tried clandestinely, that failed. How they located what they found so far is a mystery within itself. What does that leave? They could try to get the information from you. I believe that is a very good possibility."

"How would they do that?"

"One of two ways: Blackmail you by saying they'll expose you or beat it out of you."

Benny bristled. "Neither of those will work. I'll invite them to go ahead and tell the sheriff. Based on what you've said about their backgrounds, I don't think they'll want anything to do with law enforcement. If they decide to force me physically, I have a carry permit, and I'm a hell of a good shot. Shooting either of those two won't be a problem for me."

Harper starred at Benny for several seconds before saying; "Heller *could* go to the law. He isn't wanted, and I'd bet he doesn't care if Foreman landed under the jail. As far as extracting information from you, it won't be a problem for them either. Remember, the Foreman guy has been in violent confrontations one hell of a lot more times than you have. I'd say killing comes easily to him; he probably likes it." She analyzed him as she stood up, walked around his desk and grabbed his biceps with probing fingers. "You're not in terrible shape, but you'll lose any kind of fight with Foreman. He's a real pro." She returned to sit in Benny's chair. "Do you live alone?"

"Kind of. No humans, but I have three dogs."

"What kind?"

"They're all Labrador retrievers."

Harper nodded, "How are they as guard dogs?"

"They make a huge racket if anybody comes close to the house if that's what you mean. They aren't biters, and I don't think they'd attack."

"Okay. Remember, the place you'll be least safe is at home because that's where you'll be alone. You need to be with someone every second you're not in your house, except when you're in the crapper.

Arrange for that. Stay in your office as much as you can." Harper tilted her head to one side. "What kind of gun do you carry?"

"I have three, a Colt .45 automatic, a Smith & Wesson .38 revolver, and a little 25 automatic snub-nose. I know that last one is too light."

"Are you a better shot with the .45 or the .38?"

"The .38."

"Carry that. If you have to pull it, use it. Shoot to kill, not to wound. Put at least three slugs in them. We'll worry about the legal consequences later. I assume you have to go to your job sites. You have someone who can ride with you?"

"Tom Sickles, he runs my sites when I can't." Harper nodded. "Good. He a big man?"

"Yes. Six-two and two-forty." Benny asked, "Are you sure Foreman has returned here? After he killed that woman in Georgia—"

"Yes. Foreman's back. Why should he worry? He doesn't know about us. Right now we know more than the police, and we can't share without putting you in jeopardy. My man Mooney was able to track his flights. That's why I believe Heller and Foreman still think Bocelli's buried on the island. If they knew otherwise, they'd be gone." Harper stopped talking. Her face looked as though her mind had transported her far away. After several seconds she said, "There is another possibility. I'll look into that. For right now, do exactly as we discussed."

Chapter 77
Fort Myers, Florida
May 2010

Foreman watched Heller drive his rented Buick out of the motel parking lot. Felt his pocket, confirming the master keycard he'd stolen from the house maid's cart an hour ago was safely in place. He knew he'd have at least two hours to look through Heller's books, records, and other information he kept hidden in his room. Heller was a creature of habit, strictly adhering to routines and schedules. It took twenty minutes to drive through Fort Myers; Heller would eat at his favorite Italian restaurant, visit the bookstore to buy the Wall Street Journal, and sip coffee while perusing its pages, at a minimum it took that much time. It was a Tuesday ritual Heller never broke.

Foreman wasn't concerned about finding what Heller was hiding in his room. The man wasn't that smart, college professor or not. Foreman had a proletariat view of the educated class...he hated them. There weren't that many places to hide the items he was looking for. He didn't think Heller had them stashed in some other location. Arthur was too frightened that the info would somehow get taken away if he didn't have it under his personal control, all the time.

Whistling, he left his hiding spot behind a patch of the parking lot's decorative palms and shrubs. Foreman anticipated taking advantage of knowledge only he and one other *currently* living human being knew. He'd be the richest man in the frigging world, *not* Heller. Confident he'd be able to decipher the treasure's location clues when he seized Heller's research, his biggest concern was how long the yacht he'd buy would be?

Walking the hall toward Heller's room, Foreman reviewed his mental checklist of ends that needed tying. Four eggs to break after he'd finished with each. Then he'd do serious worrying about how to spend his money.

Foreman realized it wasn't going to be as easy as he thought the moment he opened the door to Heller's motel room. Heller hung the *do not disturb sign* on his doorknob and had placed a folded piece of paper between the jam and the door. The paper dropped to the floor as Foreman opened. The paper was designed to inform Heller if anybody entered his room. Foreman replaced it and hoped he put it close to where it was originally positioned.

Foreman knew Heller kept the three-ring binders, journal, and other records in a steel box, but Foreman hadn't seen a padlock on it before. It took time to pick the lock. When he did get in and started to look at the documents, he saw much of the information was in a foreign language and some in coded text. Trying to figure out the relevance of each entry would be impossible without the key.

Foreman spent time looking for a codebook or sheet but failed. He found a small leather-bound book in Heller's nightstand that looked promising. When he opened the book, a piece of paper with the words "Good Luck," written on it was the first thing he saw. Heller was sending a message to anyone trying to steal his secrets. There were pictures of flowers mounted on the pages... nothing else. Foreman said, "Shit!" He knew he was stuck with Heller for the foreseeable future as he carefully returned everything as he found it. He'd underestimated Heller. Most of his scheme would still work—he'd need the part using the boys as red herrings—the end game would be different. It was time for a plan "B."

Chapter 78
Fort Myers, Florida
May 2010

"Man, I want out of this. I want out, now." Sean sat in the Mustang's front seat, looking Devale square in the eyes. "That son-of-a-bitch will kill us without a second thought. You heard what he told Heller, and what Heller said. I wouldn't doubt he kills Heller, too, before it's all over." Sean slammed his fist on the Mustang's dashboard. "I wish I'd never seen this damned car."

"Shit Sean, we've had this conversation. Wanting out and getting out isn't the same," Devale said. "You're right about him killing us and not giving a damn. Think about that. If we do anything to set him off, to make him suspicious of us ratting on him, *we are dead*."

"He's going to kill us anyway after this thing is over." Sean put his hands over his face. "As soon as he can't use us anymore, we're dead."

"Then we have to stay useful to him until we can think of a fool-proof way out of this."

Sean shook his head. "I'm for just bugging out. Let's get the hell out of here."

"And go where? And live on what? Not only that, tracking people is what those two do. You think they won't find us? We have to get something provable on them and go to the law with it. Something big enough they won't be out of prison in two years and end up slitting our throats. If we don't have protection, we're toast. Until then, we smile, walk on egg-shells, and we say 'yes-sir' a lot."

Chapter 79
Fort Myers, Florida
May 2010

Heller read the copy of the Atlanta Journal-Constitution in disbelief. It wasn't a surprise. Foreman's claim he had killed the Burns woman was confirmed. The line that shocked him stated, '*A thirty-year veteran of homicide investigations would not describe the crime scene further than to state 'The victim was tortured and killed more brutally than any I'd witnessed in my career.'*

Heller laid the paper on the table and sipped bookstore coffee. Foreman was going to be *far* more dangerous than Heller anticipated and he'd already anticipated Foreman could not be trusted. The longer their association lasted, the more Heller could sense Foreman's dislike and loss of respect for him. Heller knew the man would seize any opportunity he could to betray him. And, kill him. As long as Heller controlled the secret to finding the treasure, he was safe. The moment Foreman believed he could recover Mussolini's stash on his own, Heller knew he'd be murdered. Foreman might think he could torture the information out of Heller. Heller muttered, "How do I keep that from happening?"

"Do you want more coffee?" The young Barnes and Noble waitress' words sent Heller spinning in his chair, so violently he almost fell to the floor.

The girl's face was panicked. "Mister, I didn't mean to scare you. I'm so sorry." She backed away two steps and said, "I won't disturb you again. Please don't complain to my boss. He's Italian and has a short temper. He'd fire me."

Heller smiled, "You don't have to worry about that." The girl had given him an idea, a way to protect him from Foreman.

Chapter 80
Pine Island, Florida
May 2010

"We're behind the curve, Harper. Everything we look at, they're one step ahead." Tom Mooney shook his head. "We know Heller is patient, that's a good thing. We know Foreman isn't, that's not."

"And?" Harper slowed their walk's pace to reduce Mooney's labored breathing.

"Think Harper. When they exhaust every way they can to locate where the girl's buried, what's the one alternative left to walk them to the body?"

Harper stopped and looked at the beautiful summer sunset painted over Pine Island Sound. She said nothing and purposely didn't look at her partner. The sound of an approaching car made her step off the asphalt road onto the sands that were just feet from the bay's water.

After it passed, Harper said, "He has a permit, and I've told him he should be carrying."

"Damn Harper! That's fine, depending on who Dupree ends up facing. You know it won't be the professor. You and I both know it will be the professional. You gonna stand there and tell me Dupree will come out okay in a confrontation? We both know that's just so much bull shit!"

Harper stared at the setting sun. She waved her hand in front of her face chasing a growing number of mosquitoes and sand flies buzzing around Tom and her. "I'd forgotten how aggravating these little bastards can be."

"Harper!"

She turned to Mooney, her face frozen in its

enigmatic mask. "If they were going to pursue that path, they'd have done so, and Dupree would be buried or feeding fish." She took one last swat at the insects and resumed her walk.

Mooney muttered, "It's not your life, you're rolling the dice for," and followed her.

Chapter 81
Turtle Point, Cayo Costa Island, Florida
May 2010

Five miles away, Benny Dupree sat on the sand dune atop Turtle Point, alone. It was the first day in weeks he'd kept his vigil to greet and protect the turtles. He knew Harper Sturgis would be angry if she knew he was doing such a stupid thing. Harper was trying to protect him, legally and otherwise. Benny didn't care. All that was important to him was that he could protect the turtle nesting site for as long as possible. He'd made his decision. One way or the other, he was toast. The sheriff would be visiting soon to haul him off to a cell, or his two stalkers would make the jump from observation to action. Sitting where he sat, he could feel Nadine's presence close by him, though he knew all that was left of her was buried in the sand less than a hundred yards away.

Benny grabbed the neck of the Wild Turkey bottle sitting in the sand. He made a half-hearted swat at the insects that buzzed around his deet-drenched face. "Little fuckers!" he shouted, as he put the bottle's opening to his lips. He tilted the bottle and took three swallows, sputtering as he lowered the liquid fire and coughed the amber fluid through his nose.

He wiped his face with his shirt sleeve. Benny's mind tried to retrieve his thoughts before the insects and bourbon interrupted. "Toast. I'm toast," Benny muttered as the cast-off thought was reclaimed. "Any day, old Frog Hilliard's gonna walk up and tap my shoulder. He'll say, 'you're goin' a jail, slimeball;

don't pass go, don't collect' ... " Benny's alcohol clouded brain rebelled a moment before finishing, "'Two hun'red frigging dollars.'"

"Jail!" The thought of molding in a cell for the rest of his life was unbearable, not to mention the disgrace. He thought of his father and cringed. It would be better if the two scavengers who were hounding him came. He'd fight it out with them. Die fighting like he should have done to protect Nadine all those years ago. Benny took another swig of bourbon...

Chapter 82
Fort Myers, Florida
May 2010

Napoli Pizza was practically deserted at two-thirty in the afternoon. Heller waited for Foreman to show up and wondered what the thug wanted. What was so important it couldn't wait until later when they were to meet with Sean and Devale. No matter, it would provide a better opportunity to introduce his "insurance policy" to his murderous accomplice. Heller fondled the prop in his pocket. Terrill wasn't dumb, but Heller believed his plan would work.

Within minutes, Terrill Foreman's truck eased into a parking place in the pizzeria's lot. The big man smiled at the waitress and clerk as he passed. Heller watched them return his greetings and wondered if they had any inkling they were addressing the devil in human form. Terrill folded his large frame into the booth and smiled at Heller with the same underpinnings of disrespect that always was manifested when Foreman was in Heller's presence. "How's it going professor?" he said disdainfully.

"I'll tell you after you tell me what was so vital that we needed to meet early, and," Heller paused for effect, "you answer a couple of questions for me."

Foreman eyed Heller quizzically. "I'll answer your questions first. What do you need to know?" He leaned forward and scowled, moves intended to intimidate Heller.

Heller *did not* react. Instead, he asked, "Have you ever been to Italy?" Foreman showed surprise and some confusion. "No, never been there."

"Have you ever been involved in an illegal action

involving an Italian citizen or the Italian government?"

Foreman thought for a few seconds before he lied. "No, not that I can remember. Why?" Heller said, "That treasure isn't going to get up and walk here after we find out where it is. We'll have to go get it. It means entering that country. If there is something that would keep you from entering Italy, I'd have to get it fixed." Heller tapped his fingers on the table impatiently and waited for his partner to speak up.

"You have friends in the government?" Terrill looked surprised.

Heller laughed. "Oh, no, not in the Italian government. My friends are Italians. More accurately, they're friends of my friends. They're eliminating any problems and guaranteeing our safety while we travel there." Heller paused, letting Foreman think about what he'd just said. He added, "And mine, when I return," when he believed Foreman comprehended.

Foreman's face went from surprise to shock. "Mafia?"

Heller smiled but didn't answer. He removed an envelope from his pocket. "This contains some papers that need to be filled out. Use Thomas Thurman as your name. That ID doesn't have any gun running dealings with an Italian firm connected to it. You need to get a picture of yourself for me. I'll send them to my friends, friends of the Borrollios, and we'll get back everything we need to go in and get out with the treasure."

Foreman gathered his composure. "They do this for free? That's definitely not their style."

"No."

"Well, I need—"

"Terrill, you don't need to know anything more. What they're asking for won't be a serious deduction from what we'll recover. I've done numerous favors for them. That and my agreeing to give them some famous art items that would be hard to dispose of, make us even." Heller held up his hand wanting Foreman to remain quiet. "Now, the most important question: Do you have any, let's say, negative history with my friends ... or their friends?"

Foreman relaxed, "None."

"Okay. I don't want complications like them sending you to sleep with the trout. Now, why did you want to see me before meeting with the kids?" Though Foreman displayed a less arrogant air, Heller watched his partner closely for signs of fear. If Foreman harbored those feelings, they weren't readily apparent.

"I think I know a way to get the sheriff interested in going onto Dupree's property without connecting us to it," Foreman said.

"Okay. How?"

"First we relocate. Make it look like we've given up and moved on. Leave a paper trail to prove it. We buy plane tickets, fly out. Then we come back and stay in Punta Gorda."

"Why do that? Who cares if we're here? No one knows." Heller saw no point.

"You can bet Devale's and Sean's parents do."

Heller looked at Foreman but said nothing.

"Look, you know teenagers. They can't keep a secret for shit. I'm sure they've talked about what we're doing to some of their buddies. Let's say we encouraged them to tell their friends they're going to go back to find the treasure after we leave. Then, we pay them to disappear for a couple weeks. Once it gets out what they're doing and they end up missing, the law will have to suspect Dupree. Hell, I'll leave their boat on the beach in front of his property. The sheriff will be out there tearing that fence down, so quick Dupree won't be able to do a damn thing about it. They'll dig up every square inch of his property. Particularly, when they find those skeletons." Foreman leaned forward. "If they find the girl's bones and the stuff is around her neck, they'll bring it back as evidence. Then, I'll get it."

"I won't ask how, because it won't get that far. Those boys will never agree to run off and hide for two weeks."

"Oh, they will. We offer them $2,500 each when they go and $2,500 when they come back *if* they do exactly as we tell them. I've picked out a place for them to stay and a couple of girls who'll keep them company. They'll go." Foreman grinned.

Heller frowned, "That's ten grand."

"More like fourteen when you throw in the motel, meals, and the whores. But, like you've told me before, that's just changed." Foreman watched as Heller removed his checkbook and began writing. Money commanded his respect.

"This is for seven. It will be enough to get it started." Heller tore out the check and placed it in Foreman's waiting hand. "Let's say you can get those boys to take us up on the offer, I don't think you will, but let's say you do. How are you going to get the necklace and key out?"

"I have someone on the inside of the sheriff's office I can get to help me."

"How much do I have to pay him?" Heller's voice was sarcastic.

"*Her*. Probably nothing," Foreman smiled and patted his pants front.

Chapter 83
Fort Myers, Florida
May 2010

"Sheriff Hilliard, got a minute?" Maggie Stevens stood in "Frog" Hilliard's office doorway. "I have some results back from FDLE's lab on the mystery bone."

He motioned to her. "Come on in."

She opened a file folder as she approached his desk. "We don't know a whole lot more than before. Confirmed it was male. Middle-aged. They were able to extract DNA from the bone section I sent them, but no matches ... or, at least, no *direct* matches."

Frog lifted his eyebrows.

"They believe they found a close relative in the military records. It belongs to a Marilyn Cole. She's forty-five. Grew up around here. She's a Tech Sergeant up at Fort Jackson. I'm running a check on her background now."

"Cole...Cole. There's something I should remember about that name." Hilliard shook his head. "Anything else?"

"One thing. They said the bones were briefly submerged in salt water. There were salt crystals in the pores. That gives us a minimum time for how long they've been buried. Last time the island was flooded was during hurricane Charley. That's six years ago, and Benson from the lab says all soft tissue was long since gone. Most of the island is five to seven feet above the tide level, so he thinks it wasn't intrusion if they'd been submerged for long periods of time, they'd be in a different condition. He thinks they've been there for at least fifteen years, probably a lot more."

"What do you think? Could they be from the Calusa? The Indians had settlements on all those islands." Hilliard trusted Maggie's judgment more than a faceless figure in far- off Tallahassee.

"I think Benson's right-on. And, that isn't a Calusa bone. That would make it 400 or more years old. Benson would have carbon-dated if he thought that was a possibility. *Benson is good.* Nope, no way." Maggie closed the folder and asked, "What do I do with this?"

Hilliard rubbed his chin, exhaled, and shook his head once. "Nothing...for now. We don't have enough to start digging up a six-mile-long island."

Chapter 84
Fort Myers, Florida
May 2010

"This is the third one of these, Devale. We sit around here, and they stare at us like we're animals in a zoo. That's all we do at these meetings. They want to keep tabs on us. Keep us under their thumb." Sean wanted to avoid Foreman and Heller's company.

Devale thought the meetings were unnecessary and creepy, but wouldn't admit that to his friend. Sean was spooked enough already. Devale pointed to the serving bar stocked liberally with pizza. "Maybe. Hey, that's fine with me. Nothing's going to happen to us sitting here in Napoli's. We've got a tab set up for us that Heller pays. So they give us the third degree about what we've told friends and family and lecture us to keep our mouths shut. We aren't *doing* anything except eating 'zzas." He stood pushing his chair backward. "Want more?"

"No."

"Suit yourself." Devale ambled to the serving counter. Foreman and Heller passed him as they came toward the table Sean and Devale were seated at. The smiles they wore were more pronounced than the masquerade masks their features normally were forced into.

As usual, Heller greeted them first. "Hey Sean, everything cool?"

Heller's pathetic attempts to be in sync with Sean's generation would have been funny if the source wasn't so dangerous. "I'm cool," Sean answered without any conviction.

Foreman and Heller sat at the table. Terrill remained silent. The smile on the man's face reminded Sean of his mother's cat's expression right before it killed a bird. A cold chill swept through the boy's body and he broke eye contact with the man. Foreman put two large envelopes on the table's Formica surface. They made a low "shish" as he pushed one in front of Sean and the other to where Devale was sitting. "Take a peek," Foreman said, raising his eyebrows as he spoke.

Sean glanced at Devale who was loading a plate with slices of pizza then at the envelope. "What's this?" he asked timidly.

"Something you can have if you're man enough." Foreman hinted at a challenge and a reward, something a teenage boy would find hard to resist. "And, be careful how you pull the pictures out. They're for your enjoyment only."

Foreman's words converted curiosity to action. Sean's fingers opened the flap and saw three, 8 x 10 photos, and a small, but bulging envelope, inside. Heeding Foreman's warning, he slid pictures from the large manila envelope so he was the only person who could see them. His eyes opened wide. It was a beautiful young woman's picture, completely nude. Tall and slim, her stunning black hair fell over her shoulders, and her curly black pubic hair made the pale whiteness of her skin an erotic poster. The next photo was of her on a bed, pictured from the rear in a kneeling position, with her head and shoulders pressed against the mattress. In the last photo, she was lying on her back, her eyes closed and head thrown back, as she enjoyed the last phase of masturbation. Sean was so captivated he never saw Devale return to the table and sit down. His friend had to say, "What you got, Bro?" twice before Sean emerged from the sexual fantasy he tumbled into.

When the speechless Sean made a motion to

hand the pictures to Devale, Foreman said, "Don't do that. He has his own." He turned to Devale and said, "Go ahead, open yours," as he pointed to the envelope.

Devale's inquiring features changed to surprise and smiles as he muttered, "Damn," and "Look at that!" as he thumbed through his photos. After examining and reexamining them, he asked, "That is one fine fox! But, man, what's this about?"

"You like that, Devale?" Foreman dangled the hook.

"What's not to like!"

"How would you like those ladies all to yourself for a couple weeks?" Foreman leaned forward looking at one boy first then the other. "Plus, look in the white envelope inside the big one."

Sean's hand beat Devale's, and when he looked inside the small envelope his breath gushed out, and he said, "Holy shit!"

"I'll save you the effort," Heller spoke for the first time. "There twenty-five one-hundred dollar bills in each envelope. They'll be yours, the money and the girls, if...if you do us a big favor." He watched the impact on the boys and finished with what he hoped would be the clincher. "And, there's another envelope with the same amount of cash when you finish."

The two boys reversed roles: Sean was sold; Devale suspicious.

"What do you want us to do?" Devale asked. He returned the photos to the large envelope and pushed it a couple feet away. "I'm not hurting nobody or nothing like that."

"You don't have to do anything to anybody." Foreman made a tossing motion with his hands like he was throwing confetti straight up. "You just have to tell your friends a story and disappear for a couple weeks, and Heller there, pays for the rooms and your food, too."

"What's the catch? What do we have to tell our friends?" Devale was far from sold as expressed by his uncomfortable, caution-filled voice. Sean, totally distracted, kept looking at the photos of "his" naked woman.

"Tell your friends what you might have told them already. You've been looking for treasure. Tell them Heller and I have given up, and we're leaving. Say you two are going back to find it."

Foreman looked at Sean. "You borrow your daddy's boat and leave it out by Turtle Point. I take you up to Tampa, and you use those girls for dick ornaments for two whole weeks. You get the rest of the cash. I guarantee you you'll never make an easier five thousand in your life and really enjoy doing it." Foreman winked at them both.

Sean nodded, "Hell yes!"

"Why? Why do you want us to do that?" Devale asked.

Heller said, "So the sheriff has a reason to find what we've been looking for, and he'll do it for us. He'll have to look for you two at Turtle point. That means going into Dupree's property and searching it."

"Can we tell our parents about what we're doing?" Devale asked.

"Absolutely not," Foreman said. "We can't take a chance they'd tell someone. That would ruin everything. Look boys; when you show up in two weeks, you can tell your parents anything you want. I can tell you they aren't going to be bad upset when you explain that your families are five thousand dollars richer."

Sean nodded, but Devale still had concerns. "I have to think on this some. When do you have to know?"

"You've got four days," Heller said.

"I need those envelopes back until you make up your mind." Foreman reached out and took Devale's package back and motioned for Sean to place the pictures in the envelope and to hand it to him. The boy did so, reluctantly.

"Call me as soon as you decide," Heller said. The two men rose to leave.

"Man, you're the one who wanted to get out of this thing. Now you want to get in twice as deep. I don't like it." Devale spoke so softly Sean could barely hear him.

"That was five thousand dollars and one hot chic ago." Sean leaned closer. "Look, Bro, once we get to the hotel and know everything is for real, we wait a few days, and we call our parents. If we tell them what kind of money we all stand to get, they aren't about to blow it.

Devale sat in silence, turning over his options in his mind. Finally, greed won. "I don't like it, but I'll do it. I'll call Heller tomorrow."

Chapter 85
Cabbage Key Cut,
Cayo Costa Island Florida
May 2010

Benny didn't remember walking back to his boat, getting in it, or driving it back to Goodun's cabin dock. Never-the-less, his boat was tied to a piling. He could see the clove hitch from the boat's bottom where he lay and had evidently spent the night. The sunlight blinded him and a pounding headache reminded him of the bourbon he'd downed last night. It was going to be a rough morning.

He tried to sit up, but the boat started spinning each time he tried. It took four attempts before he was successful. His friend's boat was missing; he'd hoped for breakfast before heading back to his house. Benny struggled to his feet, fighting vertigo, but dropped into one of the boat seats. His mind would take some time to stabilize. Something stuck him in the shoulder when he leaned against the backrest. A note was pinned to his shoulder. He pulled it loose and read Goodun's neat cursive, *"Coffee inside, take better care of yourself."*

The mystery of how he'd made it back to his boat was solved. Warrington didn't look like an angel, but he served the same purpose.

Chapter 86
Tampa, Florida
May 2010

Mooney focused on his computer monitor, blinked his eyes, and rechecked it. The airline passenger lists he'd hacked into displayed the names *Foreman, Terrill* and *Heller, Arthur*. Harper instructed him to watch for their departure. Mooney believed he knew why—to see if their adversaries had given up. He dialed her number on his speakerphone, slid it to the corner of his desk , and located a pad ready to write the questions he knew she'd ask. Harper always had questions. The phone rang, and Harper's voice came through the speaker, "Good morning, Tom."

"Looks like you were right. Heller and Foreman are flying out of Fort Myers this afternoon. They're hanging it up."

"What's their destination?"

"Atlanta."

"They're together on the same flight?"

"Yes."

"Do they connect with another flight from there?"

"No. The tickets are one-way. Atlanta is their final destination."

"They haven't given up. One of two things: Foreman got information out of the woman before he killed her and they are acting on that, or the other possibility is they *want* everyone to believe they left the area."

"Everybody? Who's everybody? Harper, as far as we know, the only people that they know they're here is Dupree and those two boys, and us. How would they know about us? How would anybody in law enforcement......" Mooney shook his head.

"Same way we know about them, at least, that is what might be possible. I believe it's a feint. Think, Tom. Neither of them lives in Atlanta. My best guess is that as soon as they hit Hartsfield, they'll head back here. Maybe, fly under false names or possibly come by car. They want an alibi. Remember, one option left to them is to extract the information they want from Dupree. Either that or they've picked up Bocelli's trail there. If so we're done.

"How are we going to know?" Mooney frowned at the phone on his desk.

"We aren't unless you can figure a way to pull another rabbit out of the technological hat you wear. The only thing we can do is plan for them to return and be happy if they don't."

Mooney shook his head. "And, how do we do that, Harper?"

"We plan for them to try to abduct Dupree or find a way to blackmail him."

"That's mission impossible or close to it. Plus, it will cost you a bunch just to try."

The speaker remained silent for a few seconds. Finally, Harper said, "It will be, but as you reminded me, it's not my life I'm rolling the dice for. Do it."

Chapter 87
Boca Grande Pass, Florida
May 2010

"Foreman said he'd be anchored at these GPS coordinates." Sean glanced at a paper on the clipboard next to him and waved his finger at it. "We're supposed to anchor a couple hundred yards away, fish, wait until right before it gets dark, then go over to him when he signals." When Sean reached the last channel marker on the Gulf of Mexico side of Boca Grande Pass, he turned the wheel and pointed his family's small boat to the southwest.

"Did he say how far out he'd be? I don't like to be out here this time of year." Devale scanned the surrounding skies for angry thunderheads. There weren't any. Less than normal puffy, white cumulus clouds lay far to the east. Skies over the Gulf were clear. "At least, it doesn't look bad."

Sean said, "That's a good omen, or sign, or whatever you want to call it."

A gentle sea breeze raised waves a foot high, certainly nothing to cause worry even in the nineteen-foot open boat in which they rode.

"Will he be in the same boat he's been renting?"

"He didn't say. He just gave me the GPS readings. It's where he has crab pots down. That's what he claims anyway." Sean looked at his smartphone and made a slight course correction. "We should see him in another five or ten minutes." Sean looked toward the shore. "We'll end up about three to four miles out and due west of Turtle Point."

It was after seven when they'd reached their destination two football fields from what Sean guessed to be a thirty-foot plus sport-fisherman. Devale peered through the binoculars and confirmed the man standing near the stern was Foreman. The two boys watched Foreman as they slowed their boat to an idle. He was pulling up stone-crab traps. Devale said, "Those traps must be damned heavy. Even Foreman's struggling to handle them." Foreman emptied them and left them stacked just inside the large white cruiser's transom. The boat was much larger than the previous boat he'd rented.

Devale dropped an anchor over the side in twenty plus feet of water. Sean waved his arms at Foreman, but the man either didn't see them or chose to ignore their presence. He continued to fuss with the traps.

"We may as well fish. He's making it clear he doesn't want us over there early." Sean reached for a spinning rod rigged with a spoon. "Might catch a mackerel or two."

"Are you alright with this?" Devale asked. He wanted to give his friend one last chance to back out.

"Yeah. I've thought about it a lot. They need us to show up after the two weeks. Our friends know about Heller and Foreman and that we worked for them. Those two know to keep from being accused of what they're hoping the law goes after Dupree for, they need us to show our asses. They don't want anybody blaming them for our murder. Heller is too smart for that."

"Heller is, but Heller isn't in that boat."

"He's waving something at us." Devale strained his eyes to see what Foreman held in his hands. The sun had dropped below the horizon fifteen minutes before, and dusk was waning. "That's got to be the signal to go to him."

Sean picked up the binoculars, pointed them at Foreman and screamed, "Yes! That's the envelopes. Get that anchor up while I get the motor cranked."

Within a couple minutes, Sean maneuvered his craft next to the cruiser.

"Let me get some bumpers over the side where I want you to tie up." Foreman scrambled around and quickly tied four boat fenders to cleats mounted on the cruiser's gunwales. "I ended up paying $800 last time because of some scratches and dings from docking without using bumpers and handling the crab traps without protecting the boat." Foreman pointed to black plastic sheeting that covered the boat's entire rear cockpit. He picked up the two manila envelopes from a seat and waved them. "I'll give you these after you do me one little favor. I want to get my traps back in the water. Sean, there are eight ropes down in the cabin. I need you to rig a marker on one end and a clip on the other. Everything you need is sitting there. Turn the lights on so you can see, but close the hatch so no one can see the light."

"Okay." Sean looked at the envelope. "What's the girl's name?"

"Ivy." Foreman turned and grinned at Devale, "Yours is named Doreen. Hey boys, in three hours you won't have to worry about looking at pictures, you'll have your hands or whatever all over them."

All three of them laughed. Devale started to go with Sean, but Foreman said, "Stay with me, Devale. I want to shift these traps around and want you to help. The quicker I get these traps in the water, the quicker you get to Ivy and Doreen."

"Oh, yes!" Sean said as he disappeared behind the cabin door.

"Devale, watch how I'm grabbing the trap. There are lead weights in the bottom, and they're heavier than hell. Keep your back straight and your head up." Foreman demonstrated. "Now, you try." Foreman took a step back and stood behind Devale as the boy bent over and assumed the position he'd been shown.

As Devale tightened his grip on the bottom of the trap, Foreman's hand clamped over his mouth and nose, Simultaneously, Devale felt a sharp pain in the side of his neck. It was the last thing he ever felt. Foreman thrust the bowie knife into his neck slicing through the carotids, Devale's voice box and then pulled outwards, completing the cut. For a split-second, gurgling sounds came from Devale as he became a corpse. Foreman released him allowing him to fall face first onto the crab trap.

Foreman sprung from behind Devale's body and walked to the cabin door. He held the bloody knife at his side and slightly behind him. Standing to the cabin door's side so he wouldn't block Sean's exit, Foreman knocked hard on the wood and yelled, "Sean, come quick. Devale's hurt!"

The door exploded open as Sean rushed to aid his friend. When he passed Foreman, his eyes were focused on Devale, crumpled over the crap trap. One of Foreman's arms swung around Sean's neck like a steel band while the other drove the blade into the boy's back at the precise spot where his killer knew it would pierce the heart. Sean managed to squeal, "Eeeeeeee," before he dropped onto the black plastic designed to catch the blood flowing from his body. He was dead within seconds.

Foreman didn't waste time on eulogies, regrets, or doubts. It was obvious guilt was the farthest thing from his mind. He opened all eight of the crab trap doors, confirmed the measurement of the opening and muttered, "Eighteen by twenty-four. Forty inches deep. Won't be that bad. I might get it finished before it gets dark enough to need a light."

Foreman went to the large fish cooler built into the boat's transom and removed a chainsaw. He put on rubber gloves, a butcher's apron, and began his grizzly task.

Foreman pulled away from Cayo Costa beach at one in the morning. His list was complete. Sean and Devale's bodies were disposed of in unmarked crab pots twenty-five feet under Gulf waters. The boys' boat was towed to the shore. He anchored at the water's edge in front of Turtle Point. Foreman smeared some of Sean's blood in the abandoned boat's bottom as "planted" evidence. The black plastic was removed from the floor and sides of the cruiser, folded up, placed in a Styrofoam cooler, then the cooler was put in a large cardboard box. All would be burned later. Everything in the cruiser was washed down, Cloroxed, and washed again. The clothes he'd worn when the murders occurred and during the cleaning were added to the cooler. The only thing left was to get rid of were the two manila envelopes with Devale and Sean's names written on them. He removed the two envelopes containing the cash and put them into his pants pocket. Five thousand dollars was a good bonus. The way Foreman chose to look at it, Heller was getting a freebie, though the professor wasn't aware of the boys' fate. Heller would bellow and threaten then accept the inevitable, like the ineffectual little nerd Foreman believed he was. Or would he? Heller's Mafia connections were something Foreman hadn't foreseen as a problem.

Foreman was sure when the sheriff was forced to investigate the boy's disappearance and *found blood*, Heller wouldn't like it, but he'd grudgingly accept Foreman's actions. Heller would have to agree the only potential informants, Sean and Devale, who could foil his plot, were eliminated. That would be a while. Foreman knew when he told Heller the boys were safe in a Tampa motel, screwing non-existent hookers, Heller would have unspoken doubts, but would "believe it" because he wanted that to be true.

Terrill looked at the two women's pictures. Porn stars, their downloaded photos did the job. The pictures went back into the manila envelopes. As he headed the boat through Boca Grande Pass into Charlotte Harbor, he set fire to each packet letting it burn until he could no longer hold onto the corner. Releasing the flaming paper into the air currents, the light flickered until extinguished in the warm waters the boat knifed through. His thoughts went to the next part of his plan, how he'd get into the sheriff's evidence room after the skeletons were discovered and exhumed. He shouted, "Yo, Maggie, I'm coming."

Chapter 88
Pine Island, Florida
May 2010

"You're an idiot." Harper's voice and face didn't show the rebuke her words carried. "What in the hell possessed you to go out there after the discussion we had?"

Benny remained silent, but his eyes were defiant. "The turtles. They mean something to me. I don't expect you to understand. It's an *emotional* bond. You don't have any," Benny said. He maintained eye contact with her. It was his way of rebuking Harper for what he saw as her total lack of feeling.

Harper looked at him several seconds before responding. "Oh, you're wrong. I understand feelings very well. That's why I avoid them. I can't function consistently if I let them affect me. In the past, I couldn't control mine on occasions. It's the reason I admire people that can do both." She paused, then added, "It's the reason I bother to help worthwhile people that can't."

Benny looked down like a small child that had just been scolded.

"If that friend of yours hadn't called Corrine and if she hadn't called me, we wouldn't be having this conversation. Because both have their feelings for you, we may save your stupid ass, yet." Harper pointed at Corrine, the third person in Benny Dupree's office. "She really doesn't know what's going on, but she cares enough about you to try to help. Don't you realize you'll let down all the people that *you* mean something to? The least you owe them is making an honest effort to save your skin."

All through the charged comments, Harper never showed the slightest change in her physical demeanor or tone of voice.

Corrine looked shocked. She asked, "Should I leave?" Corrine knew her boss was in serious trouble, but the conversation between Benny and Harper had life and death etched into it.

"No, this conversation is about over." Harper stood, put her hands on Benny's desk, and said, "This thing is about to boil, I'm sure of it. Keep your butt away from Cayo Costa for a month. Can you promise that?"

Benny shook his head.

"You are one stubborn Jackass." Harper sighed. "Give me one good reason you can't."

Benny spoke very slowly, "It might be the last thirty days that I have a chance to go there."

Chapter 89
Fort Myers, Florida
May 2010

"Hello, Rollie. This is Danielle. Do you read me?" She stood as close to the water's edge as she could without soaking her boots and her ranger uniform pants. Danielle looked at the boat floating peacefully in the shallow beach water. The anchor, embedded in beach sand, was ten feet behind her, the rope taut, stretched from the boat's bow to the heavy navy style hunk of cast iron.

Her intercom radio squawked back, "I hear you. What's up?"

"Rollie, there's a boat on the beach by Turtle Point. It's double anchored. The bow anchor is up the beach some. I've been here over an hour, but I don't see anyone around. I took the RTV a half mile in both directions. And, I'm not sure, but I think I see blood in the bottom of the boat. A lot of it."

"Did you find any identification in it?"

Danielle was quiet for a couple seconds before saying, "It's off the shore, so I haven't been inside of it."

"Why not?"

"I don't want to get my uniform wet."

"Oh, Geeez! Take your shoes off, roll your pants up or just get them wet. They'll dry out." Rollie Gates sounded exasperated.

Danielle said, "Okay" followed by a full minute of silence.

The next thing Rollie heard were faint splashing sounds made by his ranger parting the water with her legs. Her feet thumping on the boat's deck followed. "He asked, "See anything, like clothes or something that might have an ID in it?"

"No. There's some fishing tackle in it." An assortment of bumps and scraping noises told him that Danielle was looking in compartments and potential storage areas. "I don't see anything, but some safety equipment and two mackerel plus some left-over food items in a cooler. There's three large smears of blood. Oh, and there's a shovel lying on the floor."

Rollie thought for a few seconds. "Danielle, get out of the boat and don't touch any more than you have to."

"Oh, shit!" Danielle screeched over a thrashing and splashing.

"What's wrong? Rollie was alarmed.

"I fell and I'm all wet."

"You won't melt. Give me the boat's description and registration number's off the bow." After more splashing and few seconds of silence, Danielle said, "It's probably twenty to twenty-four feet. White. It's got a cuddy cabin." After a couple of gurgling steps, she added, "The registration number is FL 17577. The fee decal is up-to-date."

"Stay there. Let me know if anybody shows up. I'm going to call the sheriff and see if he wants to take a look." Rollie paused for a few seconds. "You say you looked around thoroughly?"

"Every place, but inside the fence on Dupree's property. The boat is anchored right in front of it."

Chapter 90
Fort Myers, Florida
May 2010

"Go over and check the boat out. If there was a crime out there, you need to get to it before the scene gets corrupted." Frog Hilliard squinted his eyes. "Take McNeal with you."

"Okay. James is checking the boat registration numbers to see who the boat belongs to. I'll leave as soon as he's finished. Any special instructions?" Maggie Stevens asked.

Hilliard thought for several seconds. "Only one, don't go into Benny Dupree's property. If you think there's something fishy out there, I'll get permission from him or get a warrant. I don't want evidence being made inadmissible."

Maggie laughed, "You don't think 'Turtles' Dupree had anything evil going out there, do you? He feels bad when he kills an insect. Besides, isn't he kind of friends with you?"

"Yes, he's a friend. That's all the more reason I want this done right."

Chapter 91
Cape Coral, Florida
May 2010

"They're back," Tom Mooney said.

"How in the hell did you find that out so quick?" Harper asked. "Did you figure out some way to track their cell phones?" She waved to the waitress in Durkin's Pancake City and pointed to her coffee cup. Elise nodded and scurried to get a freshly brewed pot.

Tom smiled. "Didn't take you long to train her."

"The magic is 25% tips." Harper leaned forward. "Back to Heller and Foreman. How did you find them?"

"No technology this time. Logic and some of those tips you just talked about. In fact, tips for tips." Mooney cut up the stack of pancakes sitting in front of him, splashed syrup over them, and loaded his fork. Before he jammed the first wad into his mouth, he said, "Heller is predictable. He's staying in the same motel chain he did in Fort Myers. I figured he would. I also figured he'd register under a fake name and stay out of the immediate area. I went to the ones that were at least thirty miles away, but less than a two-hour drive. Showed his picture and promised a hundred to the first person who spotted him. I got a call the next day from a bellhop. It was Heller. I followed him, and he met up with Foreman. They're both in North Port." Tom crammed the pancakes into his mouth.

Harper leaned back. "It won't take long. Whatever they have planned is going to happen right away, if it hasn't already."

Tom chewed his pancakes like a well-mannered cow before washing them down with a couple gulps of coffee. "What, *exactly*, are we supposed to do for Dupree? We don't know what Heller and Foreman intend to do. Expose him to the police? Kill him? Don't think we can handle protecting him, or at least *I can't*. Something entirely different? They have to do something before we can react. Harper, it's not like you to get involved in something like this. It's a lose, lose, lose, maybe win, or then again lose."

"I have my reasons, Tom. Besides, losing once-in-a-while isn't a bad thing. Keeps you humble."

Tom laughed while in the act of eating another forkful of pancakes. After choking them down, he said, "You, humble. This I got to see."

Chapter 92
Fort Myers, Florida
May 2010

Maggie Stevens entered Frog Hilliard's office and sat in a chair as the sheriff finished a phone conversation. When he hung up the phone, he asked, "What do you think, Maggie?"

"I think something happened. I'm not sure it was *the* crime scene. I'm pretty sure the stuff in the boat was staged. The blood spatter pattern is all wrong. Looks to me like somebody dribbled blood on the floor from a glass or maybe wrung it out of a towel. The anchors were set to well just to have been tossed out as you'd expect. It just wasn't right. There were tracks up to the sand path leading to the chain link fence where they stopped abruptly. Looked to me like someone was trying to lead us there. I had the boat towed into the boat ramp. I'll know more when I get it back here."

Hilliard nodded. "The registration is correct. I had Stew Crenshaw contact the man who owns the boat, according to what McNeal told me about the tag. It's his. He told Stew his son, Sean, and one of his friends named, Devale Whitaker, were using the boat to go on a camping trip. At least, that's what they told their parents. Stew is still getting info from them. I had Fuzzy Borden check with a few of their teenage friends. The two told their buddies they were going on some kind of treasure hunt on Cayo Costa. More specifically, on Dupree's property. Was any camping equipment on the boat?"

Maggie whistled. "No. This whole thing is strange. There's too much information."

"Yes, but I guess it's time I visited Benny Dupree," Frog said.

Chapter 93
Cape Coral, Florida
May 2010

Benny stood on one of his house's construction site; his attention focused on roofers installing tin sheeting. Noise from hammers, saws, drills, and roof panels clanging, disguised Sheriff Hilliard's arrival. The Sheriff tapped Benny on the shoulder, startling him. Benny spun around, ready to defend himself, but relaxed when he saw who it was. Benny, knowing the probable reason for the sheriff's visit, became apprehensive. He managed to say, "Hey Frog."

"Hey, Benny. Looks like you've got that one well on the way. Rains slowing you down much?"

The sheriff's half-smile didn't reassure Benny enough to drop his guard. He hoped his defensiveness wasn't visible. "It hasn't been too bad so far this summer. But, I bet you didn't stop out here to find out what the weather is doing to my building schedule. What's up?" Benny tried to sound "normal." He noted there was a different glint in Hilliard's familiar eyes and that bothered him.

"I need a favor from you and need to ask you a few questions. Let's go get in my cruiser. I have the AC on. No use us sweating to death." Hilliard led the way to his car. When they were seated inside, the sheriff asked, "Benny do you know these two kids?" He opened a file folder and showed Benny two pictures.

"No, I can't say I've ever seen them before," Benny answered truthfully. "Who are they?"

"They're a couple of high school boys who have

turned up missing. One's name is Sean Bender. The other is Devale Whitaker. Ever heard those names before?" The sheriff was watching intently.

"No, I haven't."

"Well, there are two reasons I'm here talking to you. First, they told their friends they were going treasure hunting...on Cayo Costa...on your land. Second, the Bender family boat was found anchored out on the beach in front of your property. There's no trace of either one of them. You can understand."

"Sure." Benny felt uncomfortable; he knew what was next.

"So, Benny, I'd like to get access to your property. I could've gotten a warrant, but I didn't believe that would be necessary. It won't be, will it?"

"What are you going to do?" Benny was stalling for time. Was it better to give them free access or buy time, however short, to contact Harper?

"We're going to be looking for the boys or evidence they been nosing around out there."

"I don't have a problem with it. Be careful up close to the fence on the beach side. The turtles build their nests right next to it at times." Benny knew it was inevitable.

"We'll do that. I promise we won't disturb any of the nests." Hilliard nodded and grinned. "I hope those turtles know how good a friend you are to them."

Benny shrugged his shoulders. "Do you just need a key or do you want me to go along?"

"All I need is your permission. Call Rollie Gates over at the park and tell him we'll be over there tomorrow to get his key."

"Sure." Benny felt he'd just approved his own death sentence.

Chapter 94
Fort Myers, Florida
May 2010

"I felt I didn't have a choice. Those two boys being missing aren't my doing, and it's not thirty years in the past." Benny was slumped forward in his chair. He stared at his desk looking for an answer that wasn't there. "If they'd said they were looking for Nadine or—" he failed to finish his sentence.

Harper Sturgis shook her head. "Dupree, you have to know what's happened. Heller and Foreman have buried the boys inside your fence, or they've made it look that way, even if they didn't. I knew they'd do something quick. I didn't think they'd kill those two, but it's so obvious now. Shit! I should have warned you. Forcing the sheriff to get a warrant would have given me some time to see what possibilities exist and given Heller and Foreman some time to panic. Maybe they'd make a mistake we could use."

"If I forced them to get a search warrant, I'd look so guilty—" Benny looked up. The hopeless expression on his face said more than any words he could have spoken.

"When is the sheriff going to go out there?"

"He said tomorrow."

Sturgis shifted in her chair. Her mind quickly separated her mental process from their conversation. After several minutes she said, "We need an observer on site, so we know what the sheriff knows, as soon as possible. Are the boy's bodies dumped or buried? That kind of thing. You're out. You show your emotions. If they find those skeletons, you're likely to get yourself into something I can't get you out of. Do you have any close friends who know the property, would act as observer, see what's happening, take pictures, and get back with us?"

"Yes, Aaron Warrington. He's a close friend. He'd do it. I don't know about him taking pictures. He may not have a camera."

"He can use his cell phone," Harper said.

"I know he doesn't have one of them" Benny mumbled.

"Doesn't have a cell phone? You are kidding? What is this guy, some kind of a hermit?"

Benny nodded. "That's exactly what he is. He lives over on the island to be away from people. Not having a phone is one of the ways he does it."

Harper stiffened in her chair. A small smile flitted across her face. "Finally, something on the plus side. This is the same man you call Goodun, correct?"

"Yes."

"Great! He has a reason for being there. That helps a lot. I have someone who can tag along with him in that case. My associate, Tom, can take pictures and he knows some of the things to look for."

"It might be better to let Goodun do it by himself. He doesn't do well with strangers," Benny said. He knew Warrington might refuse to take anyone with him. "I can ask, but don't bet that he'd agree to company."

Harper stared at Benny for several seconds before asking, "Is he sharp enough to handle this?"

"He's as smart as you or I."

"If he's as smart as you, he'll be okay." Harper's comment expressed doubt that he or Goodun was as intellectually capable as she was, but then she believed few people were her equal in that trait. "I'll see he has a good camera. Think he'd talk to me? I'd like to give him some instructions."

"Yes." Benny added, "If I go with you." He wanted to see that meeting. "Be sure to tell him you're a Marine. That will get you credibility."

A broad smile covered Harper's face, the first one Benny ever saw there. She said, "We'll do fine."

Benny sat looking at his hands. "This is getting complicated. And worse. More people are getting involved and hurt. What I did was bad enough, but now I'm going to end up getting blamed for horrible things I didn't do. Maybe I should go to Sheriff Hilliard and—"

Harper said, "Forget anything like that! I said Warrington would be okay if he was as intelligent as you. I take that back."

Chapter 95
Fort Myers, Florida
May 2010

"Nothing so far. I've got two dogs working inside of the fence and one outside. We've been working them for five hours—no hits. If those boys were here, the cadaver dogs would have found them in an hour. In fact, the human nose would smell the decomposition unless they were buried deep or something was used to keep the odor down. Maggie just got back with me. She says we need to do an orderly sweep to be sure the dogs didn't miss. I'm tellin' you they aren't here. Maggie's organizing what she wants done now." James McNeal shook his head, removed his hand from the chain-link fence, and scanned the sand and vegetation covering Dupree's Cayo Costa property. "So much for this being an easy case to solve."

Sheriff Hilliard said, "You really didn't believe we'd waltz over here and find those boys corpses with a note held in their hands saying, *Benedict Dupree murdered us.* First of all, Dupree isn't dumb enough to leave that boat anchored in front of his beach property *if* he did kill and plant them here. Would you post a sign telling everybody you just killed two people? That's what that's doing. I don't expect we'll find them here."

McNeal thought for a second. He offered an alternate theory. "What if he killed them, dumped them somewhere else, left the boat so we'd search his property, find nothing, and rule him out as a suspect." He looked like he'd just invented the light bulb.

"Why do it at all? There's nothing to connect Dupree to those boys. Leaving that boat is an attempt to make a connection. There's a reason here, but—"

"I think we found *something*," Maggie said as she approached them. She wore khaki pants and her green uniform shirt. Both were soaked in perspiration. Maggie looked bedraggled.

"Damn, Maggie, what you been doing?" Frog Hilliard grinned at his forensics specialist. "It looks like you've been working in a garden."

"Ha, ha." Stevens wasn't in the mood for humor.

Hilliard looked at McNeal whose shirt only showed a slight trace of moisture. "James looks cool as an ice cube compared to you. I thought you'd be okay if James is."

Maggie put her hands on her hips and raised one eyebrow. "If that's some reference about my ancestors being from Africa, forget it. I like my air conditioning. McNeal's fine for two reasons. The redneck in him thinks it's cool until the temperature is the same as it is in Hell. He hasn't chased the damned dogs for half the day. He's been supervising. That's sit on your ass time."

"I think you should buy Maggie's drinks at the Bourbon Barrel after work tonight," Frog pointed to the plastic bottle of cold water McNeal held. "Least you can do is to offer her that."

Maggie took two steps forward and removed the bottle from McNeal's hand. "Thank you," she said, took several swallows half emptying the bottle then poured the remainder on her neck and head. She handed the empty bottle to a chagrinned McNeal. "If you'll follow me, I'll show you what I found. It isn't those two boys, but I'd also bet it is something."

Maggie led them past some sea-grapes and cabbage palms to a spot denuded of vegetation compared to its surroundings. The sand had obviously been disturbed recently.

"The dogs showed interest here. Not enough to be a recent corpse, but they did show a positive." She waved her arm at a thirty-foot diameter bare sand patch. "I want to tape this area off. You see those markers I've stuck in the ground? That's where both dogs sat. The sand looks like someone's been digging in it recently. That's where I'll start looking."

"Anything you need?" Hilliard asked.

"Shovels, trowels, brushes, manpower, and, just in case, something to cart remains back to the park dock. I have everything else I need with me. Oh, I want plenty of big buckets to put sand in. If we find any bodies, I want to sift everything close to them for evidence. Let me have McNeal, Foster, Lawry and send Anne over with her cameras and a recorder."

Hilliard looked at Maggie and tilted his head to the side. "You've got it." Hilliard rubbed his hands together. Then he wiped his brow with his forearm. "I'm sure enough I know what you're gonna find to bet...and give you five-to-one odds."

She nodded, "A skeleton that's missing the humerus bone."

Hilliard nodded. "What about the dogs, Maggie? Do you need them inside the fence anymore or can I increase the search area?"

"Don't need them. They'd have found those boys if they were in here."

McNeal asked, "What do you want to do with the press and TV people."

Frog's head snapped around. He said, "There shouldn't be any here. I haven't released the location where we found the boat, other than to say it was found on one of the barrier islands. I didn't even tell the kids parents. Rollie Gates is not going to let anyone down here—he's closing the park and shutting the ferry down until I tell him we're done. There were a couple of reporters that trailed us to the marina, but they didn't have any way to follow us here."

"That might be, but I've seen some man with an expensive camera, sporting a telephoto lens, skulking around with that old hermit that lives over here. The guy was taking a bunch of pictures."

"You sure he was with Warrington?" Frog asked.

"Pretty damned sure. Every time I saw them, they were right together."

"When did you see them last?" Hilliard was interested *and* upset.

"Twenty minutes ago," McNeal said.

"Find out the man's name. Make him show you an ID. If he gives you an excuse, detain him. If you can't, run his ass off."

McNeal asked, "What about the old guy?"

"I'll visit him later." Hilliard shook his head with disgust. He'd hoped Dupree was an innocent caught up in the peripheral of some random event. That didn't appear to be the case.

Chapter 96
North Port, Florida
May 2010

Heller was exasperated. He'd tried to reach both Devale and Sean's cell phones without any success. They were always "unavailable." Foreman said he'd had a similar experience and said he'd go to Tampa and check on them. Arthur was angry and suspicious. He pulled up Foreman's number and called him.

"What's up?" Foreman asked when he answered.

"Did you go to Tampa?" Heller asked.

"Yep. Last night. I'm still at the motel. Before you ask, it's a different one than where the boys are. I'm leaving Tampa in a few minutes."

"How are things there?"

"Devale and Sean have no complaints. The only beef they brought up was them wanting to contact their parents. I explained again and they understand." Foreman's laugh was evil. "The girls are moaning. They said they should get more money. The boys are really keeping them busy."

Heller relaxed a little but was still suspicious. "Why haven't they answered the phones when we call?"

"Devale's network doesn't work there. Sean *says* he's been having trouble keeping his cell battery charged. And, he says his parents keep calling, and he doesn't want to make a mistake and answer them. I think he's enjoying giving us a hard time. Sean spent most of the time talking about the sex he was having."

"Did they say anything about their being on TV?"

"No, not a word. But, I don't know if there's much coverage on the Tampa TV stations. That's not local news there. That's just as good."

"Yes. You're right. Anything come up?"

Foreman chuckled. "Just them wanting to be sure they'll get the rest of their money when they're done."

"Nothing?"

"Nothing new there."

"The sheriff released the fact that the boys are missing and they've found the boat. Every reporter in Lee County has his own theory, but no leaks have occurred. Hilliard won't comment on anything past what's released because it's an active investigation. I imagine his people are working over on the island now."

"I'll find out tonight. I'm planning to see my friend inside the sheriff's department."

Chapter 97
Cayo Costa Island, Florida
May 2010

"They know we're watching them," Mooney said. He watched the old man crouching next to him who was in far better physical shape in his seventies than Tom was at forty-five. Warrington moved through the thick underbrush effortlessly, his clothes seemingly coating with mystic Teflon that allowed him to avoid the constant entanglements that confronted Mooney. Goodun Warrington nodded and effortlessly passed under a tangle of scrub oak limbs to keep the deputies insight. He looked at Mooney and frowned as the "city slicker" wallowed under the same brush.

"You're too slow," the old man said. "Give me the camera."

"You know how to operate it? I can explain how it works." Mooney held the camera in front of Goodun. "This is the shutter button, and this—"

Goodun took the camera from Mooney's hands. "Been watching you. I'm seventy, not senile." He put the strap around his neck and cautioned Mooney to, "Stay here." His tone left no doubt in Mooney's mind that it was a command, not a suggestion.

Warrington's moves were swift and decisive as he raced to flank the sheriff's deputies'. It looked like he was going to lose visual touch with the people he was supposed to observe. Mooney called to Goodun, "Don't lose sight of them."

"I know where they're going." Goodun melted through the underbrush, disappearing from sight within seconds. Mooney watched, realizing he'd just gathered a more important piece of information than if he'd been allowed to accompany the sheriff's forensic team and take notes.

Chapter 98
Cayo Costa Island, Florida
May 2010

Sheriff Hilliard and Maggie Stevens stood next to the open pit. Two skeletons, lying in it, were so close together they were entwined in places. It was obvious the bodies had been there for a significant time period. The clothing covering the bones was reduced to shredded rags.

Additional holes were dug in the small clearing, one of which had disclosed a huge sea turtle shell and skeleton. Maggie was discussing what she'd found with Hilliard as the remaining members rested their tired bodies by sitting on the sand. Maggie made sure they squatted outside the yellow tape marking the crime scene.

"No doubt this is where our mystery bone came from. The humerus is missing from the one closest to us. Everything else is there but disturbed. Someone recently did some digging and was looking for something. That was evident as we did our work."

Frog looked at the skulls and portions of the skeletons that were severely damaged. "I assume those crushed skulls and broken bones were what killed them."

"Seventy-five percent probable. These remains don't give us as much info to go on as a recent corpse. I'll have to get them back to the lab, and I have a friend at the University of Florida that I'd like to have take a look. We might find something from examining what's left of their clothes. We might even be able to ID them that way, but I doubt it.

There weren't any wallets or anything like that."

"What else you find?" The sheriff squatted down to examine the bones closely.

"One of them had a wedding ring on. No inscription. There were two knives. One in what I think was a pants pocket; the other looks like it was tossed in with the bodies." Maggie pointed to the turtle shell. "We found that turtle. Strictly a guess, but I'd say it was all buried at the same time. We did a quick and dirty search on the rest of the clearing. Nothing but a couple of soft drink cans. It's going to take a couple of days to be thorough, but I don't believe we'll find much more."

"Well, do it." The sheriff looked at gathering storm clouds moving toward them from the mainland. "You have enough tarps to protect everything?"

"Plenty. And anchor rods to keep them in place." Maggie arched backward to relieve an ache in her lumbar area.

"Did you see those reporters or whoever they were anymore?" Frog asked.

"No. After McNeal mentioned them, they disappeared. At least, we didn't notice them. We were pretty engrossed in digging up our friends." Maggie shook her shoulders then relaxed. "Did you guys find any trace of those two kids?"

"No. The dogs worked at least two miles on both sides of Turtle Point. Nothing except a couple dead raccoons. Oh. One thing. If you wander around inside this area, be very careful. Barney was searching in here and fell into some kind of trap. He sprained an ankle and got scratched up. I called, Dupree to ask about it. He said it was for pigs."

Maggie was unconvinced. "Pigs *and* people."

Chapter 99
Cabbage Key Cut, Cayo Costa Island Florida, May 2010

Mooney watched the old man start the Briggs and Stratton motor that powered Warrington's plywood boat. It was clean, but the faint smell of fish, absorbed in the wood that no amount of Clorox or scrubbing could eliminate, reached Tom's nose as the old man untied the boat. Goodun Warrington shoved it away from the mangroves, engaged the adapted packing plant transmission, and the motor chugged its way back to Goodun's dock. The noise from the motor was the closest thing to conversation Mooney had for the last two hours. He'd always thought Harper was the most uncommunicative person on earth. Compared to Goodun Warrington she was the town crier.

His attempts to start a conversation were answered with head shakes and nods, one-word answers or silence. Conversely, Mooney was astounded by how little time it took Harper to get Goodun's agreement to go on the "reconnaissance mission." She'd greeted the lean old man with "Semper Fi." That seemed to be enough. Their bond, both being Marines, instantly took effect. Mooney couldn't understand that. They did.

They were returning from successfully spying on the sheriff's investigative team. As it turned out, Mooney saw his beach trip as an impediment, not a help. Goodun took over. The man had a natural gift for photography. He brought back a pictorial story. Mooney's contribution to the trip was worthless, *except* for the one crucial piece of information he'd gleaned by accident.

Harper stood on the dock. Her posture, bearing, everything about her revealed she was still a Corps major at heart. When the boat was close enough, she motioned for them to throw a rope to her. He watched the approval on Goodun's face as Harper tied the mooring lines to the dock pilings with neat, tight clove hitches. She remained patient and quiet until they'd climbed onto the dock. "Were you able to keep watch on them?" she asked. Mooney marveled at that. Tom would have been shooting questions when the boat was a hundred feet from the pier.

"Yep."

"They find anything?'

"Yep."

"What?"

"Two skeletons."

"The boys' bodies?"

Warrington shook his head. If Harper was surprised, she didn't show it. She thought for several seconds and asked, "Two skeletons, not three?"

He nodded then added, "You can't find what ain't there."

Harper crossed her arms and stared at Goodun. Their eyes stayed locked in a staring contest. Finally, Harper said, "Guess we need to talk."

"Depends."

"On what?"

"You gonna be Benny's lawyer, no matter what?"

Harper tilted her head to the side, nodded and said, "Come Hell or hurricane." Goodun motioned toward his cabin, and the two Marines disappeared inside, leaving Mooney standing on the dock. He realized even his one piece of information was going to be superfluous.

Chapter 100
Pine Island, Florida
May 2010

Things were moving too fast and were too fluid for Corrine. Her whole world had been rocked. Stability and routine were what she enjoyed, and her employment with Benny Dupree's construction firm offered that. That was until the last few days. Instead of feeling like her life was firm and anchored, it bobbed, teetered, and weaved like a tiny boat in a storm. The hurricane engulfing her boss was more frightening because she didn't understand what was going on. Whispered conversations between Harper Sturgis and Benny led her to believe he was in horrible trouble, but what it might be was a complete mystery. Then she perceived there was a link between the disappearance of two high school boys and the conversations. Could it be possible, that one of the kindest, gentlest people she knew was a murderer?

She jerked in her seat as she did each time the phone rang. Corrine listened to the phone ring twice before reluctantly answering. "Dupree Construction, how can I help you?"

"Is he there?" It was Harper Sturgis' demanding voice.

"No Ms. Sturgis. I thought he was with you."

A muffled curse was barely audible. Harper's tone was urgent when she spoke. "Corrine, if he calls, have him phone me immediately on my cell. If he shows up, keep him there, and *you* call me. I don't care what you have to do, don't let him leave."

"I'll try. Could you please tell me what's going

on? I'm concerned about Mr. Dupree. I'm scared. I feel so helpless."

"You'll help him most if you do exactly as I told you," Harper said something to someone. Corrine couldn't decipher the lawyer's inaudible words. "If Dupree calls, try to find out where he is," Sturgis added.

Corrine said, "He told me he was taking you to Cayo Costa."

"He did. Then he left without telling us."

Corrine's voice became shrill, "Is he in danger?"

"I don't know."

"Should I call the sheriff for help?"

"No! Lock the office after you get off the phone. Don't let anyone in, but Benny or me. Do you hear and understand?"

"You're really scaring me!"

Harper sounded pleased as she said, "Good. Do what I told you." Sturgis hung up before Corrine could ask more questions.

Chapter 101
Fort Myers, Florida
May 2010

"I'm buying," the man the deputies knew as Fred Wilson announced. Maggie Stevens, James McNeal, and two other officers drug their tired bodies into the Bourbon Barrel. He waved for them to join him at a large table where he was its only occupant. He examined them critically and offered his opinion. "You've all been in the sun, *all* day. Since you aren't mad dogs or Englishmen, what have you been doing?"

McNeal ignored the question and asked one of his own. "Hey, Wilson, when did you get back in town? I'm getting tired of buying my own drinks." The four bedraggled deputies found seats at "Wilson's" table and dropped into them.

"I just got in a few hours ago." Foreman, the man Maggie and her friends, knew as Wilson, shouted to the bartender, "Put a round on my tab for my buddies."

"You all want what you normally get?" Alene asked from behind the bar. She was answered with nods and a yes or two.

Foreman asked, "What have you been doing?"

"Making sand castles," Maggie said. She was tired, hot, and in no mood for Pollyannaish comments, or for fending off studs looking for a lay.

McNeal was happier to see their drink buying friend. "We've been doing what deputies do, what the sheriff doesn't want to. In this case, digging, sweating, stinking, and battling insects." He put his hand on the big black man's shoulder. "Thanks for the drinks. It's good to see you back here." There were agreement grunts from all the officers, except Maggie.

Foreman said, "Hmmmmmm, Maggie, what did I do to make you upset with me since I saw you last."

"Breathe," Maggie rethought her last comment and added, "Nothing, I'm just in a shitty mood."

"What can I do about that?" Foreman asked. His pseudonym Fred Wilson could be very charming. "I certainly hate to see such a noble and lovely member of the Green Knights in distress."

"Damn, Wilson, you a black Irishman? You sure must have French kissed the Blarney Stone." Maggie took a deep breath as the rest of her group laughed. "I just need a shower and some rest."

"Maybe a good meal would help?" Foreman offered.

Stevens looked at Foreman. "I'm not a MacDonald's type of girl."

"Oh yeah!" McNeal shouted.

"Definitely, not," Foreman said. "You're the filet mignon or prime rib variety of lady."

Maggie thought for several seconds. The man was pleasant company and certainly had the money to buy her a decent meal. "Okay. But, one thing I'm making clear. We *are not* playing pool tonight, so you can count on keeping your cue in its case. Understand?"

McNeal said, "Oh-oh-oh-oh! Torpedoed! Will the captain abandon ship?"

"Where can I pick you up?" Foreman said.

"You can't. I'll meet you at the Sunset Restaurant." Maggie looked at her watch and added two hours. "At 8:30, if you don't mind it being a real short evening. I have to be back over on a crime scene early in the morning. I got a day or maybe two more of playing in the sand."

Foreman smiled. "No problem. Might give us

something to talk about. It sounds interesting."

Alene leaned over the table and distributed their drinks, changing the topic of their conversation.

Chapter 102
Pine Island, Florida
May 2010

Harper sat on her room's balcony overlooking Pine Island Sound. She was frustrated. It wasn't because she was defending a guilty individual. Or, that there were many facts about the case of which she was uncertain. That was life for a lawyer. It was the emotional unpredictability of a client she liked, and as much as she would allow, cared for. Defending an individual who ignored advice, was indifferent to his well-being, and who chose actions that defied logic, had her as close as she got to a temper tantrum. As far as she was concerned, Benedict Dupree had a death wish.

Worse, without Dupree's penchant for self-destruction, she saw several ways to proceed to get him light punishments. From what she now knew, could prove, Dupree might even get off with some kind of manslaughter or self-defense plea. She saw the case never going to trial; plea bargain was stamped on anything with which the DA might decide to charge Benny.

First, after thirty years, finding any hard evidence to link her client to the remains was unlikely. The suggestion of guilt made by the fact that Dupree had fenced the area and kept others off the property was circumstantial. The number of years that elapsed between the murders and when the chain-link enclosure was erected argued against a direct cause and effect. It would take some doing to establish the skeletons' identity and even more to create a solid link to Dupree.

Though innocent of any foul-play that happened to the high school boys, Harper had to protect Benny from erroneous charges. Devale or Sean's disappearance could be inferred, but couldn't be proven to be connected to Dupree. Lack of any relation between the high school boys and Benny was a fact. The boat's discovery was awkward but wasn't damning. Whoever left the boat anchored at the properties edge, obviously wanted the skeletons discovered. They accomplished that. But the fact the boys weren't found, meant no crime was provable in regard to them. There was no way to guess where that situation would go. Her money was on Heller and Foreman causing their disappearance, one she guessed was permanent.

She had an excellent fallback position of self-defense that would be difficult to disprove. From Dupree's description of the melee, the damage to the bones wouldn't prove conclusively how the battle unfolded. Dupree had a scar to prove he'd sustained serious physical damage to his body. There was an element of truth in the claim. Stretching the attack to self-defense took some doing, but it was plausible enough to make her feel secure. It was much easier than presenting the fact that Benny's act of rage, no matter how justified it seemed, took two lives.

She'd felt optimistic before her conversation with Goodun Warrington. After that, Harper became supremely confident she'd win. Harper was so sure; she began fanaticizing about other possibilities the case offered. That was before Dupree disappeared. It was the worst thing for him to do at the worst time. Harper was reminded of Marine tales old timers told to her about Japanese suicides in the Pacific War. As far as Harper was concerned, Dupree had the same mentality as one of those Jap soldiers who held a grenade to their chest. Her biggest challenge was to keep Benny from pulling the pin.

The phone in her room rang, she shuffled the sliding doors aside, and rushed to answer. Harper said, "Hello."

Tom Mooney's familiar voice was on the other end. She said, "Good work, Tom. When will—" A slight smile creased her lips. "Already, that's good. I'll tell Warrington." Harper paused, and her features briefly registered surprise. "So, I won't have to tell Warrington. They both all right with that?" She took a breath. "Yes, yes, it's fine with me. Remind them; they have to be careful about their security." She nodded to the phone. "Okay. Now we have to take care of the real problem. We have to find Dupree before he finds a way to hang himself."

Chapter 103
Pine Island, Florida
May 2010

What was the right thing to do? He didn't know. Benny was in hiding and intended to stay there. Knowing what was right was so confusing. Every time he tried to make a decision he'd try to be objective, to look at the logic, at the ethics, at the legalities, at the impact on others. Each time he tried, he got farther away from an answer, not closer.

His first inclination was to turn himself into the sheriff's office. He was guilty of killing two men...that was an inescapable fact, no amount of lament or rationalizing could change that. By the same token, he wasn't guilty of taking the life of the third skeleton they'd find. The press and media were determined to link him with the two high school boys' disappearances and promulgated the lightly-veiled presumption that he'd killed them. He was *not* a mass murder, and that's what media reporters sketched into the series of crimes they pictured. If he surrendered to the law, he feared that was precisely what he would face. Benny knew the act of running and hiding made him appear more guilty, but he worried the damage had been done. He hoped for a miracle that logic told him would not appear.

Each time he struggled between his conscience and his need for survival, he was aware his behavior was becoming more like an ostrich hiding its head in the sand than a rational human being. Avoiding the decision was the coward's way out. Dupree reached the conclusion that was what he'd become. His self-loathing rose, but his distaste for being blamed for murders he didn't commit, kept him from surrender.

Hiding was something he was well equipped to do. A lifetime in the area gave him access to nooks and crannies that would shelter him. Lucky circumstances augmented his capabilities. The fact he was in his boat when he reached the decision to bolt, was one of those fortunate random events. It was harder to find and stop a boat, particularly one as common as the one he owned. However, the most fortunate coincidence was the summer season, and with it, the absence of a snowbird friend.

Benny kept watch on that friend's home. Located on a canal, it was isolated with only two other homes having access to the same waterway. Since those two homeowners were in the North for the summer, there was no one to observe his coming and going. His friend's home had an enclosed boat slip built under the house, one where he could moor his boat that was invisible to prying eyes. In addition to the key to the boathouse door, its companion on Benny's key ring was one that gave him access to his friend's house. It gave him shelter, food, and the ability to see TV and observe media coverage. He was careful not to give away his location. He removed the battery from his cell phone, never turned lights on inside the house, and he didn't leave its confines during daylight. Benny knew he'd be safe unless he did something stupid...........

Chapter 104
Fort Myers, Florida
May 2010

Maggie had changed her mind. She was glad she'd agreed to accept the man she knew as Fred Wilson's dinner invitation. He'd arranged for premier seating. Their table overlooked the Caloosahatchee River on the restaurant's mezzanine. Cuisine at the Sunset was excellent, the best available in Southwest Florida. Dollars weren't a problem; he spent them freely, ordering premium wines and an assortment of appetizers before she'd arrived. The man was handsome and had a commanding presence. She looked at the half-consumed rib eye steak. Maggie decided she'd need something much larger than a "doggie bag" for the left-overs. There was enough food on her plate for two additional meals.

The conversation was light and unobtrusive. No prying into her private life. No unwanted double-entendre hinting at a desire for sex. No inquiries into her work activities. The longer they talked, the more relaxed she became.

"I hope you saved room for dessert," Wilson said. "They tell me this place is famous for its *Baked Alaska.*

"Oh, I love Baked Alaska!" Maggie said, "but, I don't know where I'd put it." She was legitimately sorry she'd eaten so much earlier. Maybe if she'd left part of her Caesar Salad...

"I'm sure you'll be able to find a place in some deep recess in your tummy." He turned to the waiter standing next to their table. "Two Baked Alaska's."

"Yes, sir!" The waiter's grin widened as the cash register in his head calculated the increase in his tip.

Maggie shook her head. "What if I can't find that tummy spot you're talking about? Baked Alaska doesn't do well in a paper bag."

"Well, I'll have to get you a cooler and some ice."

"You don't mind wasting money. Remember, we're driving separate cars." It was a gentle reminder that her escort wasn't taking a dip in Lake Maggie that evening.

"I wouldn't think of interfering with your investigation tomorrow."

"How's that?" Maggie was puzzled.

"Maggie, whatever I do, I do right. That means I don't spare expense or time to be sure everything is very satisfactory." The predatory look on the man's face was more Foreman's Mr. Hyde than Wilson's Dr. Jekyll.

"You investing for the future?" Maggie's fur rose at his presumption. "You'd be better off spending money in the Greek stock market."

"I know better than to try to predict the future, Maggie. All I'm trying to do is to ensure your present comfort. After doing whatever you been doing all day, you need some relief from what did McNeal say, doing what the sheriff didn't want to?"

Maggie laughed. "Don't get the wrong impression about old Frog. If he had the forensics knowledge he needed, he'd be right in the bone pile." She sucked her breath in vainly hoping to recall her words.

Foreman eyed her for a few seconds. "What am I supposed to do next? Pretend I didn't hear you? Say I'm not interested? Or, ask a question, so we have something interesting to discuss. Take your choice."

The delivery of his lines was so nonchalant; Foreman disarmed her. She asked, "You know something about forensics?"

"A little. Enough to know, whatever you're doing doesn't have anything to do with the disappearance of those kids I heard about on the TV while I was dressing to come to meet you."

"You're right about that. Nothing at all." Maggie watched for a reaction but wasn't sure what she expected to see. Her date showed none.

"Want more wine?" He pointed to her empty wine glass and signaled the waiter before Maggie could answer.

"I guess I do!" She emptied the dregs in her glass and placed it in a convenient spot to be refilled. "Beings, I don't really know anything about you besides the fact you like to buy people drinks, are a good conversationalist, know how a woman wants to be treated, and you're on the make, where does your knowledge of forensics and police procedure come from? From some of the things you've said at the Bourbon Barrel, I know you've been exposed."

Foreman's face became serious. He remained very quiet. The absence of his customary humor had the wanted impact on Maggie. "I can't tell you." From what he could glean from her expression, she assumed he was some type of undercover agent— probably federal.

"FBI, CIA, XYZ?" Maggie confirmed jovially, but with serious intent.

He smiled slightly and shook his head. Foreman remained silent while the waiter refilled their wine glasses and got out of hearing. He tilted his head to one side, then nodded as he said, "Good try."

"Oh, I get it. You'll tell me in return for a trip to the sheets."

"That might do it. But, then I'd have to kill you." They both laughed, but for very different reasons. Foreman said, "So?"

"You're right and wrong. We went over to Cayo Costa figuring we'd find the boys bodies. We didn't.

There were some skeletal remains, but they've been there, well, a long time. We'll find out how long, later."

"Remains? That's plural? Two? Three? Ten?"

"Just two humans. There was a sea turtle buried near them." Maggie was beginning to relax, right before she realized her company might be connected to the news media.

The caution in her face solicited a question from Foreman. "You have a problem?"

"You might be part of the press."

"Believe me, that's the last concern you have to address. Think about it. I've been around the Bourbon Barrel a long time before those boys even disappeared." Foreman smiled and said, "I'm simply curious. Professionally, that is. Besides curiosity, what interest could I have?"

"One never knows," Maggie said. Though her words denied it, she was convinced the man was telling the truth. She didn't see any connections.

"What's the reason you looked for the boys there?" Foreman asked.

"Their boat was anchored on the beach. It was left right in front of some guy's property. That man's a little strange. He's an ecology nut, at least when it comes to protecting sea turtles. The land he owns there is all fenced and posted."

"That's an obvious place to start looking."

"Yes, a little too obvious. Sheriff Hilliard thinks that it smells of a setup. The more I find out, the more I agree with him. First off, the man that owns the property is too smart to leave the boat anchored right in front on his beach. He isn't the type to develop a death wish." Maggie shook her head. "The best I can figure is that the boat was planted there so we'd have to look inside the property and find those skeletons. I don't know if the man that owns the place is involved with them or not. The Sheriff thinks not."

"Why are you going back tomorrow?"

"We want to be sure we don't miss anything. I'm going to organize another search to look for more graves. Neither the sheriff or I believe we'll find more; we were pretty thorough today, but ... I've got the cadaver dogs and an FDLE radar unit to do a 100% fail-safe search."

Foreman interrupted, "Dogs? After a long period of time?"

"Yes. They're amazing. One time they uncovered a spot that contained a woman's bones that disappeared in the 40's." Maggie waved her hand to dismiss the dogs. "I'll sift every bit of sand within ten yards from where we found the bones. I'll be looking for evidence from the original crime, but mostly for a clue to who recently disturbed the skeletons."

"Recently?" Foreman feigned innocence and surprise. "How do you know that?"

Maggie hesitated but thought she could reveal general information. "The sand has been moved around in the last several days, and we have another reason associated with an object that came into our possession in another way."

Foreman changed the subject, "So, where do you think the two high school boys are? Run off? Dead?"

"There's a possibility of a connection between the man's property and those kids. Right now, it's just a rumor. We're investigating it."

Foreman nodded, "I saw one of the boy's parents interviewed. Something about digging up a treasure?"

"Yes. We've just started on that angle. We're interested in finding out about the college professor, and some other people the boys' friends say were involved. It's a wild tale. There supposedly was a car that the boys received as compensation for doing something involved with the so-called treasure. That and other things that should give us plenty of leads. We'd like to see what those folks know, but the rumor is they've left."

"Interesting." Foreman looked uncomfortable. "Excuse me. I have to visit the restroom. Do you know where it's at?"

"Downstairs and over by the entrance."

Maggie watched as "Wilson" walked to the stairs. As he wound through the tables on the ground floor, she noticed a gun butt outlined under his coat, located at the small of his back. It was located right above his bubble butt. As Maggie watched, Foreman disappeared across the floor. She realized that rear looked familiar. Her eyes widened when she realized from where. Maggie reacted quickly. She emptied "Wilson's" water glass into hers and carefully wrapped it in a napkin to preserve fingerprints or DNA. After she put the wrapped glass in her purse, she took her cell phone from one of its compartments, set it to take a photo, and waited. Whether the man she was eating with was part of the legal system or not, she and the sheriff would be better served if they knew with whom they were dealing.

Chapter 105
Fort Myers, Florida
May 2010

"Late today, our reporter, Loretta Langer, learned that Cayo Costa State Park has been temporarily closed as Lee County Sheriff's Department personnel continue their investigation into the disappearance of high school students Sean Bender and Devale Whitaker." Benny watched the TV in his friend's darkened living room. The report continued. A young blonde woman spoke as the TV alternated pictures of her and Cayo Costa State Park. "The sheriff's department will neither, deny or confirm their activities on the island are associated with evidence connected to the disappearance of the two Cape Coral teenagers. NBC-2 was able to gather very little information from a sheriff department spokesman. She confirmed that a crime scene investigation was in progress, that human remains were discovered, but that the boys had not been found. We were able to learn from other sources that the investigation was on the property of Benedict Dupree, prominent local contractor, and ecologist. We haven't been able to confirm reports the scene being investigated was near where a boat belonging to one of the boy's parents was found. What the sheriff has discovered remains a mystery."

Benny said a prayer. He didn't want Nadine's remains desecrated. The desire to sneak over to Turtle Point became obsessive. Knowing what was happening was worth the risk of capture.

Chapter 106
North Port, Florida
May 2010

Arthur Heller's well-ordered, well-planned world was eroding like a dam with torrents of water rushing over it. He hadn't expected Benedict Dupree to disappear. Though he tried to reach the boys via cell phone continually, he was unsuccessful. Heller's fears increased; Foreman might have made Sean and Devale disappear, forever. The more time he spent around the soldier of fortune, the more convinced he became Foreman's solution to a problem was to kill it. Sooner or later he knew he'd be one of his partner's problems. Even more ominous, Foreman had suddenly stopped answering his phone and hadn't returned messages in two days.

Foreman was supposed to be getting information from his source in the sheriff's department. It was impossible to learn the information Heller was looking for through TV and newspaper reports. Had all their maneuvering been for nothing? Worse, could it destroy his chance at retrieving the treasure that was just outside his grasp for thirty years?

Now, a final straw. One of the bellmen from the hotel lobby had knocked on his door a half-hour ago. When Heller answered, the two exchanged greetings, and the bellman promptly got to the reason for his visit. He addressed Heller using the false name Heller had registered under. "Mr. Montel, I thought you'd want to know there is some man showing your picture around and asking if anyone has seen you. He says he's looking for a man named Heller. I told him, no, but I don't know if he talked to the other hotel employees or not."

"He's got the wrong man." Heller tried not to show his shock.

"Well, you sure have a twin running around."

"Did he say what he wanted or what his name was?"

The bellman stood silently and alternated his gaze from the floor to the ceiling. "I'm not sure I can remember," he said.

Heller removed a twenty from his wallet, held it in his hand, but didn't offer it. He waited.

After a ceremonious delay, the man suddenly had a revelation. "Oh, yes. I remember. I have one of his cards. He asked me to call him if the Heller guy, or someone who looked like him, or some black guy showed up. Showed me pictures of a big black man I've never seen. I told him neither of you were around." The bellman removed a business card from his pocket but made no attempt to hand it to Heller.

Heller removed another twenty from his wallet and extended them to the uninformed young man. The man stood as still as a statue. Heller bluffed, "That's all my curiosity is worth."

The young man smiled. "Can't blame a soul for trying." He handed the card to Heller and took his forty dollars. The bellman stepped back, but before he could leave, Heller said, "If he shows up here again, contact me right away, and I'll double that. I want to talk to him."

The bellman said, "Deal," and closed the door behind him.

Heller examined the card. It read, *The Sturgis Law Firm, Inc., Thomas Mooney Associate*. The address was in Tampa. He'd called the phone number and got an answering machine which gave a standard message asking to leave information.

Heller hung up. He had a completely new cause to worry.

Chapter 107
Fort Myers, Florida
May 2010

Frog Hilliard listened to Maggie's story intently. When she finished, he said, "I don't doubt there's a direct connection, somewhere." He looked at the water glass, now in a clear plastic bag, and three, five by seven photos taken by Maggie. "Have you said *anything* to James or anyone else in the department?"

"No."

"Anyone outside the department?"

"No one."

Hilliard sat silently as he weighed different courses of action. Maggie waited impatiently. He took several minutes before he said, "This is what we're going to do. With the summer rains, we don't have an option. The Cayo Costa site has to be completed before we do anything else. That will take you, what, two days to finish?"

"No more."

"We're going to hold off on tracing your mystery man, Wilson or whoever he turns out to be." Frog raised his hand when he saw Maggie's mouth start to open. "I want *you* to work on this, no one else. I want it that way for several reasons. The contacts he's established inside make it a real possibility he'd find out we suspect his involvement."

"I don't believe any of our people would tell him," Maggie said.

Hilliard shook his head. "They wouldn't have to. All that has to happen is for one person to treat him differently. If he's sharp, and from what you said, he is, he'll know something's wrong. If McNeal knew about this, you can't tell me he wouldn't react differently to Wilson."

Maggie exhaled and nodded.

"I don't want to give it to the FDLE lab. There's enough press leaks inside there to ensure we'd be reading about it or seeing it on TV. For now, let's keep it right here." Hilliard pointed his index finger at his chest then at Maggie's. "I want you to handle everything. The DNA has to go out. I know. Send it in a dummy group. Get a half-dozen samples from our people and mix it in. Disguise its name. Do what you have to. Keep enough for a second test. Time isn't critical this instant. The boys are either dead already, or they aren't going to be, leastways, that's what I believe. And, those bones have been on the island for a long time. I'm sure this Wilson guy had nothing to do with putting them there. Why would he want us to find them if he did? He's not going anyplace. Didn't he ask you out again?"

"Yes, for tonight."

"I'm not going to ask you to go undercover on this, but I won't say no if you volunteer."

Maggie didn't hesitate, "I'm volunteering."

Hilliard narrowed his eyes, "The volunteering is limited to meeting him in public places. For example, you don't get in a car with him. Put him off a day, two if you can. It will give me time to arrange back-up for you and a story about why you require it. No one is to know about this, period!"

Maggie nodded and rose to leave.

"Maggie, there *are* two other reason's we need to keep this confidential. The Wilson guy might be legitimate. We don't want to have to explain why we're investigating some-kind of a federal agent." Frog paused. "Know what the last one is?"

Maggie shook her head and said, "No."

"You might not be the expert you think you are on identifying a man's derriere.

Chapter 108
Fort Myers, Florida
May 2010

"We have a problem." Mooney waited for Harper to respond on her cell.

"Just one? Now what?"

Mooney cleared his throat, "Somehow, I believe Heller knows we're involved. I was checking the office incoming call record when I spotted a familiar number. It's the number of the hotel Heller is staying at. It was a silent hang-up. If it was one of the folks we have keeping tabs on him, they'd have said something. They'd want to get paid."

"We have to be damn careful! I'm sure desperation is setting in on those two. If Heller knows about us, we have to assume he knows about Warrington. You need to warn him. *And,* we need to find Dupree. That idiot just had his life-expectancy halved. The pooch is screwed." Harper thought about her comment for a few seconds. "On second thought, maybe not. There might be a way to use this to our advantage."

Chapter 109
Cayo Costa Island, Florida
May 2010

Benny steered his friend's cabin cruiser into the shallow waters fronting Cayo Costa's beach. Driving the large boat created a white-knuckled grip on the steering wheel and a lot more anxiety than piloting his flat bottom fishing boat in the same waters. His Carolina Skiff could move around freely in two feet of water. The cabin cruiser Dupree was driving would be sitting on the bottom in same depth water; he realistically needed four to five feet beneath his bow to be safe. The depth finder's warning buzzer reminded him of that frequently. To make his observation of the beach less noticeable, he placed a fishing pole in the transom rod holder and trolled very slowly back and forth in front of his property.

He was disappointed and upset. Benny saw practically nothing in the two hours he'd wallowed through the clear Gulf waters. Using binoculars allowed him to catch an occasional glimpse of the sheriff's personnel as they meandered around his property. A tent was set up over the area where the bodies were buried. Believing that Nadine's body was being exhumed severely distressed him. The few breaks in the vegetation disclosed nothing, but the fact that three people were busy digging in the sand. Benny picked the afternoon because having the sun at his back made it easier to see what was transpiring on the shore and more difficult for anyone to identify him. While that worked to his advantage, the tide dropped forcing him farther from the beach and increasing the angle so that he could only see shoulders and heads by four o'clock.

The only other humans in the area were Ken and Danielle. Those park rangers drove their all-terrain vehicle, patrolling every hour, looking for anyone who attempted to peek at or disturb the officer's work. Benny hid his face when they were present.

He checked the southeast for thunderstorms and got a break. There were fewer than usual thunderheads lined up inland. Those clouds remained far-back from the coast. He'd be able to stay until dark if he wished. Within minutes, he noticed the tent disappeared, dropping behind its curtain of sea-grapes and cabbage palms. The sheriff was either done for the day or for the whole investigation. As he idled along, he saw the park's tram being loaded with containers, boxes, and equipment to be taken back to the park office and docks. He sighed, there would be little or nothing to see after their departure.

Benny decided he'd make one or two more passes along the beach. He would focus on the sea turtle nests. One of the most important things he'd done was to mark the nests and post warnings for people not to walk on or disturb the eggs beneath the sand. Benny grunted his disapproval as the view through his binoculars disclosed some areas where he suspected the nests were damaged. The warning buzzer on the depth finder kept him further away than he'd have liked. He adjusted the lenses to get the closest look possible. Benny examined the sands at the place where he normally sat when visiting Turtle Point. What he saw shook him.

The vivacious curves, long auburn hair, distinctive features of a creature that was a duplicate of Nadine sat on the knoll of sand where Benny had first seen her. That could not be. He'd seen her dead body, touched it. And, the figure in the iridescent green bikini wasn't a fifty-year-old. Benny watched her until he realized for the first time in his life, he believed he saw a ghost! The alarm screamed at him and he was forced to steer the boat out of shallowing waters. By the time he guided the boat out of danger and circled it for another trip along the shore, the apparition disappeared.

Benedict Dupree shook for many minutes, wondering at the meaning. He made two more trips parallel to the beach before realizing the specter wouldn't appear again. After much thought, Benny decided that the sheriff had discovered and disturbed Nadine's grave. She wanted him to "set things right." He headed the boat toward Boca Grande Pass, unburdened, determined, for he now knew what he must do.

Chapter 110
Fort Myers, Florida
May 2010

"Yes, I'm still volunteering. I'll meet him tonight if you give me the okay." Maggie Stevens believed in herself and her ability to master any situation.

Sheriff Hilliard waved her into his office. "Have a seat." He watched her approach his desk. Frog didn't notice her attractive face and sexy body. He saw a valuable law enforcement officer that he depended upon heavily; one he didn't wish to lose. "Before I give my blessing, we need to be sure your orders are clear—notice I said orders, not rules. You understand that I'm telling you there are limits you can't go past?"

"I get it."

"You go to the restaurant, you eat, you talk, you gather as much info out of Wilson, or whatever his name is, you give him as little as you can in return, and you go home ... alone."

"I'm not into screwing a suspect in what is likely a murder case." She smiled, realizing that her boss was playing mother hen.

"You understand that's your parameters. You are definitely not to become Lady Kick-ass or some other super-hero character." Hilliard leaned forward and maintained strong eye contact. "Let me hear you say; *I won't do anything outside my orders.*"

Maggie's face was serious as she swore, "I won't do anything outside my orders."

"Okay. I have Anne observing in the restaurant. She'll be at a table and be in contact with me personally. There are three green-and-white units that I have on call and will be within a block of the Sunset. Anne's instructions are she's to look for members of the press, let me know if they show up, and to see you get into your car and head off without anyone tailing you. I'll have one of the squad cars follow you home, see you get inside your place, and see there are no unwanted, unscheduled visits."

"Is there anything I should or shouldn't tell him?" Maggie asked.

"If he is the mystery man on our security camera tapes, he already knows that the skeletons are on Cayo Costa. You have to figure he's involved with the disappearance of those boys. He might have been the man who anchored the boat out front. Don't tell him we didn't find squat out there. Tell him you think you found a few important clues, but not to what. The big thing is, *we* want to find out what *he* wants to know."

Maggie nodded. "What if he wants to go out again?"

"Tell him probably, but you'll be tied up for a couple days." Hilliard's head jerked backward and his eyes lit up. "That might be a way we can find out more about him and keep up with his whereabouts. See if you can get him to give you his phone and cell numbers where you can contact him."

Maggie smiled, "I'll be able to handle that."

"Have you come up with anything from the glass or the pictures you took?" Hilliard asked.

"Yes and no." Maggie sounded frustrated. "I'm sure I was able to get DNA from the saliva he left on the glass. It's at FDLE, but even with a rush on it, we're looking at a week to ten days. There were fingerprints on the glass if you can call them that. He's done something to distort the ridges on them. Like bathe them in some weak acid. You can do it with lemon juice if you're patient enough. Anyway, I checked them against all the databases just in case something would show up. Got zero back. I scanned the pictures and tried matching to our state and local files. Nothing. I'll try the federal files tomorrow."

"That's about what I expected. We've said all along this guy is a pro. He's dangerous, Maggie. Treat him like you're sitting across from a cobra. Take no chances!"

Chapter 111
North Port, Florida
May 2010

Heller spread out the clues and information he'd accumulated and pondered over for a quarter of a century. It had taken him years to figure out what the information meant. He picked up the leather-bound journal, the key to its understanding, and opened it. Twenty-seven years. That's what it took to figure out the code in that innocuous little book. After he finally figured it out, he removed the first page and replaced it with a slip of paper bearing the words, *good luck*. Like any mystery, it was brilliant in its simplicity, once the key was grasped.

The first page, the one he'd removed, was that key. He took the missing page from its relocated home in a three-ring binder. There were five sentences, hand-written in Italian, on its yellowing paper. Translated, they told the general location of Fascist Italy's treasure.

The last flower is the first to plant.
Plant them in a backward row.
Grow the first of each to find beauty.
Don't be blinded by the radiance of their colors.
 Look high and low for the cross near the garden they form.

Following those cryptic statements were eight pages each with the picture of a flower attached to it. The pictures sequence in the journal was: a Pink Orchid, a Tulip, an Edelweiss, a Snap Dragon, a Sun Flower, a White Orchid, a Yellow Rose, and a Gladiolus.

At first, it meant nothing to him. The journal and the other information he'd retrieved from ransacking the Bocelli's home had no value for a couple of years. The only reason he'd kept what he considered trash, was the pain the mother and father endured before parting with the information. The collection of family portraits, newspaper articles, and magazine excerpts looked more like genealogical or historical information, not a map to untold riches. It had taken him years to figure out that much of the information regarding paintings, statues, jewelry, crowns, antiques, and numbers with the prefix *Au* in front of them were, in fact, an inventory of what Mussolini had hidden. Finally, Heller connected the periodic element chart symbol for gold, *Au* and that got his mental process started. The Italian word for bars appeared over and over and over. When Heller figured out that the denotation was for gold bars, he totaled numbers. The result was mind-boggling. He knew what made up the treasure.

Among the letters, he found one to Mary Nadine Bocelli from her Grandmother Cardone. It read,

~ ~ ~ ~ ~

Dearest Nadine,

On your tenth birthday, I gave you two items to hang around your neck and instructions never to take them off or part with them. I told you they were from my friend in the old country, Clara, and they were rich in sentiment. They are rich in other things as well. On your twenty-first birthday, you will be given this letter and other materials I have saved for you. Dear grandchild, together, they are your heritage, my gift to you. It will give you the ability to do great things. The book of flowers will help you find this gift. After the flowers tell you where to go, find the sister to the cross that you have. Enter that house, all is there.

The key you have around your neck is to a drawer and in that drawer is another key, one that fits the door to death, Enter unafraid. Use what I leave you wisely.

All good things in life for you, blood of my blood, flesh of my flesh.

Grandma Illia.

~ ~ ~ ~ ~

From this letter, Heller learned he needed two things to find Mussolini's treasure. He had to decipher the riddle in the journal. But, most importantly, he had to have what hung around Mary Nadine Bocelli's neck.

His efforts to find the girl were painstaking, prolonged, frustrating, and unsuccessful. After the murder of her parents, the world swallowed her. Her father and sister's bodies were burnt so badly by the Barrollio's, tentatively identifying them was done by connecting their family vehicle to the ashes it contained. The mother's body wasn't completely destroyed. Dental records made the identification positive. The coroner suspected foul-play, but couldn't prove it. Those suspicions were enough for Nadine's relations to make her disappear. The family rumor of hidden treasure was a whispered myth that had enough veracity to promise a possibility and a motive. Nadine Bocelli initially became Mary Moran. She lived with several of her maternal relatives, changing her name as she changed homes. Thanks to her family's efforts, Heller lost the scent like a bloodhound does when a fugitive wades in a creek. Eventually, she returned to her real identity when she became college age.

Heller had abandoned his search until he solved the riddle of the flowers. After twenty plus years of struggling with the cryptic sentences, listening to a Christmas song gave him an idea. Each letter in the word Christmas was given meaning. *C is for the Christ Child*, the song said. What if the person hiding the treasure had used the flowers in the journal in a similar way?

That gave him a start. Using the first letter from each of the flowers gave him P..T..E..S..S..W..Y..G. That meant nothing. He followed the mystic instructions, reversing the order. G..Y..W..S..S..E..T..P was as meaningless. If the first letters were the answer, he'd fulfilled the conditions in the code then he remembered the fourth clue. Heller ignored the colors in front of the flower names. Using the first letter of each flower name spelled GROSSETO. Heller's joy was boundless. He knew the treasure was in a small region of Tuscany, northeast of Rome.

Armed with this information, he resumed and redoubled his search for the girl. Heller found public records bearing her name in several areas of the country, eventually narrowing the candidates to one in the Miami area. He felt he'd found her when she disappeared again

He confirmed she'd been enrolled at the University of Miami. From conversations he had with some of her classmates, he believed she'd taken a trip to the Sanibel Island area to study sea turtles. The trail ended there. Mary Nadine Bocelli ceased to exist after that. The chain of mental deductions had taken him to Cayo Costa and specifically to Benedict

Dupree's property.

Now, a new entity entered the equation. What did this mean? Who was the Harper Sturgis Law Firm and what interest did they have in him? He'd find out. It wouldn't be difficult. Was it connected to his search for the Bocelli girl? Could it be that the Sturgis Firm was working for Dupree? Was it for something completely apart from his quest for the treasure?

His cell phone rang. Foreman's caller ID was on the screen. Heller was relieved. He'd get some information good or bad.

Chapter 112
Cayo Costa Island, Florida
May 2010

Broiling hot, the sun beat down on the Cayo Costa State Park dock. Rollie Gates and Frog Hilliard stood next to the piling where the Sheriff's Department boat was tied and stared to the southeast. Tops of thunderheads loomed over the mainland as high as 35,000 feet. The blue water under the dock was lightly tinged with tannin carried in the fresh water that the seasonal summer rains pushed into the bays and estuaries from June through September. A mixture of sailboats, cruisers, and fishing boats dotted the small bay and occupied some slips at the state park's pier. If their owners were concerned with the storms approach, they didn't show it.

"It didn't take long for folks to learn we've reopened the park," Rollie said. It had been less than three hours since he'd taken down the *Park Closed* sign and notify the ferry operator he could resume his runs.

Frog nodded. "They might have burned a bunch of gas for nothing. That storm is going to be a whopper." He pointed to the black clouds. "How long before that thing gets here?"

"As long as the sea-breeze holds, it will stay put. Of course, that's just gonna add to the severity. You don't want to be out in one like that."

"I'll call my people and get their butts back here." Hilliard reached for his phone, but Gates interrupted his movement by saying, "Don't bother. I hear the tram coming." Within seconds the park's tram emerged from the wall of vegetation that veiled the beach with a half-mile wide band of mangroves, oaks, sea-grapes, palms and assorted underbrush. A glum-looking McNeal sat next to three deputies planted amongst an assortment of boxes, crates, tools, and equipment. The tram rumbled to a stop at the pier-head. Each deputy loaded the carts that were normally used to carry tourist coolers, fishing gear, and beach paraphernalia. They hauled their loads to the boat.

"You get everything?" Frog asked McNeal.

"Five crates, four shovels, three boxes of Maggie's shit, two skeletons and a partridge in a pear tree." McNeal jerked his thumb toward his buddies and said, "That's it."

"Let's get it loaded quick. I want to get out of here before the storms hit."

"Okay." McNeal paused then asked, "Where's Stevens at? If we're going to be her mules, she at least ought to be here to see us sweat."

"She's too busy. Maggie has a heavy date tonight. She's getting her hair done." Frog grinned expecting a wise-crack from his deputy.

"Really! The whole world's gone crazy. First, you've gone certifiable. I bet if I asked to get off early for that, you'd skin me and hang my hide over my chair. Hell, I even saw that old hermit walking around with a group of people. From what you've said about him, I half-way expect the sun to rise in the west tomorrow."

"You talk to them?"

"No. They didn't get within fifty yards of us. As near as I could tell, there were four or five people with him. I only got a good look at one. Real tall. I'd say it was a woman. They were all dressed in long shirts and pants, so it was hard to tell anything at that distance."

Sheriff Hilliard turned to Rollie and said, "I hate

to ask you to do—"

"I know. Send a ranger down on the ATV and keep an eye on the place. I'll let you know if anybody is poking around."

Chapter 113
North Port, Florida
May 2010

Heller's conversation with Foreman left Heller furious and afraid at the same time. Foreman's reason for calling was to get money; he claimed to be running low. "I need a couple thou for right now. My lady in the sheriff's office is expensive," Foreman said.

"Is she the right person?" Heller asked.

"Yes! Heller, do you think I'd be screwing around with someone who I couldn't get what information we're looking for? You're a bigger dumb-ass than I thought if you do. She's the head forensics technician, and she's the one actually doing the investigation on the case."

"Are you making any progress? Will she give you access to what we need?"

"Yes. But, like she said, she's not a MacDonald's type girl. It's going to cost a few bucks."

"I'll get you the money. But," Heller whined, "I need to know what's going on."

"I just told you."

"I've be trying to reach you for a couple days. Why haven't you returned my calls?"

"Because I don't have anything new to tell you. To be honest, your bugging me gets me pissed." Foreman's words were more of a growl than conversational.

Heller persisted. He asked questions about the sheriff department's investigation that made Foreman mad. Heller switched to questions about how the boys were doing. Foreman brushed off the questions, intimating that they had less to worry about from the boys than any other part of their plan. Foreman's answer heightened Heller's concern. Finally, Heller asked, "You didn't do anything bad to those boys, did you?"

"No. As far as I know, they're up in Tampa trying to push those two whores' asses through the bed springs twenty-four a day." Foreman's anger flowed through the phone. "Let's say they weren't. Let's say I killed them, which I didn't. That's not your problem. Your problem is to find out where we can get our hands on Eldorado. Don't worry about me handling my job. You do yours."

"You get those two items we're looking for and I will," Heller shouted.

"I will, and when I do ... you'd *better* do yours."

Heller calmed down and asked the remainder of his questions as rationally as he could. Was the investigation on the island finished? Did the woman think the disappearance of the boys was linked to the skeletons? How long did Foreman think it would take to extract information from her? Foreman's universal answer was, "I don't know."

When Heller asked, "Did you know we have someone asking about the two of us?" He related the bellman's story. When Heller finished, Foreman said, "I don't know anything about some lawyer being after our ass. You know it has to be something that involves *both of us*; why ask questions about *both of us* if it didn't. I guess I'll have to go in and clean your mess, too."

Heller was close to panic when the conversation ended. It was clear Foreman would kill him as soon as Foreman lost faith in the treasure's existence or thought he could find the treasure without Heller. Not only would Foreman do it, he would enjoy it. From the tone of their discussion, Foreman had lost all respect and fear of Heller...even his mafia bluff.

If Arthur went to the authorities, he was sure to spend time in prison. His hands were dirty. In the eyes of the law, he was an accessory to the Burns woman's murder in Atlanta. If there was only one death, he might have a chance, but he firmly believed Foreman had disposed of Devale and Sean. Even cutting a deal couldn't change those facts. Three murders, even just being an accessory, would carry serious time in prison for him, time Heller doubted he'd survive.

That meant one thing to Heller. He had to kill Foreman before the man killed him. That wasn't going to be easy. Heller would lose in any form of physical confrontation, Foreman was a master weapons man, and if Heller botched the job, he'd not only be dead, he could see his end as hideously painful. Heller would have to drug the man to kill him or poison him outright. As he plotted, Heller's cell-phone rang again. His eyes widened when he read the caller ID on the screen. It said, *Harper Sturgis* and gave a number. He elected not to answer. After a few minutes, the cell phone signaled he had received a message. The female's voice message was simple—"Call me."

Chapter 114
Fort Myers, Florida
May 2010

"You look ravishing tonight!" Foreman's false identity, Wilson, wasn't lying for once.

"Thank you," Maggie said. She sat down, smiled, and found acting more difficult than she thought it would be. Playing "normal" was challenging, knowing that the man sitting across from her wasn't who he pretended to be. "Wilson" could be anything from a fed to a hardened criminal. Maggie saw naked hunger in the man's eyes she hadn't seen before and wished she'd dressed a shade less provocative. It added to her apprehension. She tried to get a conversation started. "What have you been doing today? You still investigating for that company that's interested in water rights?"

"Yep, same old boring thing." Foreman reached across the table and placed one of his huge hands over hers. Maggie wanted to shy away but forced her hand to remain under her companion's paw. She had the urge to get up and run out of the restaurant. Needing moral support, she looked at the restaurant's lower level, panicking until she found Anne sitting at a table nursing a glass of something. Anne nodded slightly, the action acknowledging her presence as Maggie's backup. It settled Maggie's jumpy nerves enough for her to function. The man asked politely, "Is Riesling okay? I have a bottle on the way. You liked that last time."

"Fine." Maggie's smile was as phony as a three-dollar bill. She hoped Wilson wouldn't notice. The dress she wore exposed a large amount of cleavage. After observing the man for several seconds, she realized the plunging "V" neck was doing its job. Wilson was mesmerized by the large, partially exposed humps on her chest. Maggie guessed correctly; his thoughts were focused on what he'd like to do to them, and her, not on behavior changes she tried to mask. The waiter arrived at their table and emancipated her hand from its place under Wilson's control.

As the waiter poured the wine in their glasses, she watched her escorts mind return from the fantasy world her body parts had taken him. He asked, "You make another visit to the island today? Or, did you finish yesterday?"

"You think I'd look like this if I spent the day making sand castles on Cayo Costa?" Maggie forced a wider smile. "I only had to be over there for a little while. Everything I wanted to do to the site, I finished doing yesterday. Sheriff Hilliard wanted me to supervise getting things packed up and back over to the lab."

"Like what?" Wilson had reverted to information gathering mode though he was having a difficult time keeping his eyes off her body.

"The evidence and the equipment we use to examine a crime scene. It's all stuff that would bore you as much as your water statistics would bore me."

"Try me."

"Like what would you like to know?" It was her time to try to get information.

"What kind of evidence did you find?"

"Skeletons and some personal effects the bodies were buried with." Maggie purposely tried to sound evasive, though she was sure he already knew what they'd found.

"Skeletons? Like I think you said three? Last

time."

Maggie sat silently letting her inquisitor think she was making decisions about what to "let slip." After a few prolonged seconds, she said, "I guess telling you a little won't hurt. I can't give you much detail. We found two sets of human remains, not three. They were completely reduced. I'm sure they've been there for years."

"They weren't those two kids then?" Foreman took a sip of wine, watching Maggie closely.

"No."

"Know who they were?"

"No."

"Were they both male?"

Maggie smiled. She'd learned an important piece of information. "Yes."

"You find out much more about them?"

"Not that I can swear to until I can examine them in the lab."

Foreman tried to ask how they died without sounding suspicious. "They die of natural causes?"

"I don't know. They had a lot of broken bones in areas of their bodies. Whether it was caused by an accident or somebody who did them in, I can't say yet."

"Did they have anything around them you can use to identify them? Were they wearing clothes? Jewelry? Something hung around their necks or in their clothes?" Foreman put particular emphasis on the last sentence.

Maggie believed she found what the center of her escort's interest was. "I can't tell you."

"Oh, come on, you can tell me."

"Maybe, after I examine it." Maggie asked innocently, "You said you've had some experience in this kind of thing. Like what would you be looking for?"

"Ummm, something distinctive." The man

squirmed a little. "Maybe a key to something you can trace or something worn that people would notice like a cross."

Maggie nodded but said nothing letting 'Wilson' stew. After several seconds, she said, "If anything like that shows up, I'll give it a good look-see." Though the conversation continued for another hour-and-a-half, through supper, Maggie found out nothing more, but she felt what she learned was important.

As she was making excuses for why she had to go home, and why she had to go home alone, her cell phone rang. The screen showed one of the Sheriff Department's numbers. Frog Hilliard's voice answered her, "Hello."

"I need you to come into the office right now," Hilliard said. "What's up?" Maggie asked.

"Just get in here. Something very unexpected has happened." The sheriff hung up without any further comment.

Maggie said, "Well Fred, you won't be able to change my mind about this evening. That was my boss. I have to get into the office right now." She enjoyed his disappointed look as she left the table and headed for her car.

Chapter 115
Fort Myers, Florida
May 2010

"How much have you told them?" Harper sat across a table from Benedict "Benny" Dupree in a sheriff's department room. Benny had expected her to be furious. She wasn't. She was composed—it was as though she'd expected what had happened. When he apologized, her unemotional comment was, "No problem, I don't have to sit in the jail cell."

Benny took a big gulp of air before he answered her. "Not as much as I was planning when I decided to turn myself in."

"That doesn't help me." Harper leaned forward and spoke in a very low voice. "Look, Dupree, I'm your lawyer, your advocate. You're making things rough on yourself *and* me. I have ... or had ... a plan that included the possibility of getting you off completely. That was before you decided to disappear. Now, I need to know exactly how much damage you and your mouth did to yourself. Tell me exactly what you did and what you told them."

Benny leaned forward, looking into Harper's eyes. They remained as expressionless as the shark's he thought of each time he saw her. He dropped his gaze to his folded hands resting on the table. He mumbled, "Sorry."

"Sorry is meanin—"

"Okay, okay, I get it," Benny said. He sighed and began. "I went out to the island today and ran up and down the beach."

"How did you get out there? Ran? Did you get out of your boat? Why didn't a deputy pick you up? I know the sheriff had your home under surveillance. How did you get to your boat? They'd have picked you up if you tried taking the ferry."

"I've been hiding at a friend's house who goes north for the summer. I have access to his boat. I took it over and trolled back and forth on the beach."

"So you never got out on the island?"

"No."

"Go on."

"I watched the sheriff's crime scene crew packing up and watched them leave. I was thinking of taking a look inside the fence, but the park rangers were patrolling. I was waiting for them to do their check and leave, so I could decide whether to risk going ashore and getting caught. Then I saw something." Dupree hesitated. "I don't know what it was, I saw. I don't know if it was something my mind created ... well ... I thought ..." He looked up into Harper's eyes. "I believe I saw a ghost. I had to turn the boat around, and when I went past again, it was gone."

"Go on." Harper wasn't interested in Benny's ghost.

"I knew what I saw was there to tell me I had to face up to what I've done. I came back to my friend's place and used his car to drive into the sheriff's office."

"When was that?"

"I got here at eight-thirty."

"Why didn't you call me first?" Harper showed a little emotion—consternation.

"I thought you'd talk me out of it."

One of Harper's eyebrows twitched slightly. "Go on."

"When I got here, it was strange. I expected them to arrest me right away. They didn't. The deputies on duty asked me to wait in a room. Nobody asked me anything. I was told the sheriff would like to talk to me and they were getting him into the office. I got really shook, just sitting there. It made me rethink what my decision was. Anyway, Sheriff Hilliard and one of his detectives came in to talk to me about two hours ago."

"Okay, what happened next?" Harper asked.

"It wasn't what I expected. Frog and I talked about football for a few—"

"Skip all that and get to why you're here."

Benny shrugged his shoulders. "The first thing they asked was where I'd been. I just said I'd been away from my place. Then they asked why. I told them I had some things I had to think through. Then Frog asked me if I knew what they'd find when he asked for permission to go on my property. I didn't know how to answer that, so I asked what they'd found. This woman said she'd uncovered two skeletons."

"Was this woman a deputy?"

"Frog introduced her as Lieutenant Margaret Stevens, in charge of their crime lab. She wasn't dressed like a cop. She had this sexy—"

Harper cut him off. "I don't need to know that. After she said two skeletons, how did you answer the question?"

Dupree looked down at the table and said, "I told them I thought it was possible they might."

"Did you confess to killing them?"

"Not exactly. I wasn't sure what two skeletons they found. I just answered their question. They asked if I knew who put them there and I said yes. The sheriff asked if I knew a man named Fred Wilson. I said I didn't. Then they asked if I knew anything about those two boys disappearance. I said I didn't. That's when I realized I made a big mistake and should have talked to you first. I asked to call you. Frog was nice. He said I was doing the right thing."

"That's all of it?" Harper asked.

"Yes, ma'am." Benny looked like a scolded child.

"You didn't do yourself any favors, but it's not as disastrous as it could be." Harper looked at him non-judgmentally. "You may have to spend a day or two in jail. They're going to hold you on suspicion of murder. I should be able to get you out on bail. Your taking off didn't help that, but you came in on your own, we should be okay there."

Benny nodded.

"Look at me," Harper commanded, "I don't want you saying a damned thing to these people without me being here to tell if you can answer or not. You agree to do that?"

Benny felt her stare. It was like a tractor beam from a sci-fi novel that arrested him and removed his will to differ. He nodded woodenly and said, "I'll keep my mouth shut about what happened."

"No, you'll keep your mouth shut, *period*. I don't care if they ask you how many sheets of toilet paper you used the last time you took a dump. *YOU DON'T ANSWER!*" Her voice rose, but her countenance remained the same plaster mask.

"Okay."

"Okay isn't enough. I want your pledge."

"I promise."

"You promise what?"

"I promise I won't answer any questions I'm asked by the sheriff."

Harper leaned away from him for a second then came back even closer. "You killed two snakes. People don't like snakes. Under the *have to* that law officers operate, they do what they have to, but they dislike snakes more than most. I believe I can plea bargain this whole thing, so most of it goes away. You haven't made it easier, but it's still possible. Hell, there are all kind of things we need to talk about that you're not aware of, however, now's not the time or place." Harper got out of her chair and stared down at him. "I'll be in tomorrow early. Keep ...your...mouth...shut."

Chapter 116
Fort Myers, Florida
May 2010

Moonlight sparkled on the Gulf of Mexico illuminating the ocean and the island's shoreline as it had for more than 1,000,000 years. A constant during all that time was the late spring and summer visitation by the sea turtles that Benny Dupree had chosen to champion. For the brief period of time Benny had been capable, he'd did his best to allow them to continue their ritual. Given the opportunity, he would again. The turtles would probably survive with or without Benny or other men's protection. Even with the human propensity to destroy those things they came in contact with, the turtles had an important fact in their favor. Unlike the rest of nature, humans posed the greatest danger to their own continued existence. As their technology advanced geometrically, the potential to annihilate their species did also.

The night welcomed a small number of the female reptiles to Cayo Costa waters, and the island's warm sands beckoned them. It was time for them to perpetuate their kind. In ones or twos; they approached the gentle surf.

A flashlight searched the sand from the gentle curl of the Gulf waters licking the island to the grass above the high tide line. Three people walked the Cayo Costa beach after midnight. Goodun Warrington said, "There's one way up ahead."

All three trotted to within fifty feet and stopped so they wouldn't disturb the large Loggerhead turtle that was emerging from the sea. Her flippers clawed at the sand leaving a distinct pattern and trail on the beach as she laboriously hauled her bulk to the place where she'd build her nest.

Goodun turned off the light so it wouldn't disturb the splendid animal. They watched the turtle pursue its instincts.

Outlined in the moonlight, one of the two individuals accompanying Warrington spoke with reverence. "It has been so long. I'd forgotten how spectacular these creatures are."

Chapter 117
Cape Coral, Florida
May 2010

Tom Mooney sat in their customary "meeting place" booth in Durkin's Pancake City waiting for Harper. He hoped he'd convince her to make an unpopular decision. Handle Foreman. Now! The soldier of fortune was a serial murderer. None of them would be safe until the man was incarcerated or, even better, dead. Now that Heller knew about him and Sturgis, Foreman would soon, if he didn't know already. Tom believed that meant they both were possible targets for the psychopath. He wasn't sure what action should be taken, but they needed to do something.

"Want your coffee warmed?" Elise stood next to the table, coffee pot in hand.

"Sure." Mooney smiled at the girl.

"Ms. Sturgis coming in this morning'?" The waitress knew the tip size would drastically increase if the lady lawyer showed.

"She'll be here. Harper must have had a late night." Tom took a sip of coffee. "Wow. That's strong stuff!"

"Ms. Sturgis likes it that way." The girl's smug expression stated she knew who the boss was. "Her being late, I reckon she'll want to get done fast. I'll watch for her and put her normal order in for Eggs Benedict, to save her time. Ask her to tell me if she wants something different." Elise smiled. "I'll bring your omelet with her order. Can I get you anything while you're waitin'?"

"I'm fine." Tom thought Elise was a better

psychologist than some that had the degree. It hadn't taken much time for the young waitress to discover what made Harper tick.

Mooney stared at the menu, passing the time as he sipped coffee. He liked the strawberry pancakes and Durkin's omelets. He never tried Harper's favorite, the Eggs Benedict. It was silly, but walking in the shadow of his 6'3" boss lady wasn't easy. He made as few conformity concessions to his "commander" as possible but kept his rebellion subtle. Mooney was especially fond of the hash browns smothered with cheese and onions. He was a devout "Yankee" and never sampled Harper's cheese grits. Though most all restaurants did the same thing, it rankled him to pay two dollars for coffee when he could get anything else on the menu for nine or less. He knew restaurants had to make a profit, but paying what they charged for colored water, pissed him off. Tom remembered Harper's response to a tirade about the charge. She listened patiently until his spleen was displayed on the table and then suggested, "Drink water."

Elise returned with coffee pot in hand. He checked his watch. It had been fifteen minutes since her last visit. "How you doing?" she asked.

"I'm alright for now. Top me off when you bring my omelet."

Elise looked at Mooney quizzically. "Are you sure she's coming here? With Mr. Dupree being in jail and her being there so late last night, is it possible she went straight to the sheriff's place?"

Tom sat bolt upright in his seat. "Aaaa ... did you say the sheriff has Dupree in custody?"

"Uh-huh. James McNeal, he's a deputy, came by early this mornin' and was tellin' me about it. He said that a tall lady lawyer was talkin' to Benny, aaaaa, Mr. Dupree, last night. I figure that's Ms. Sturgis, because I've served them meals here."

Elise's head bobbed up as she looked into the parking lot. "I'm wrong. She's parkin' outside, right now."

Harper looked extra, lean, lanky, and athletic in the jeans and tee shirt she wore. She didn't look a bit tired. No matter how much sleep she lost, physical exertion she endured, or stress the woman absorbed, it never registered on her in a visible manner. As Harper sat down, Mooney said, "Elise has an order of Eggs Benedict she's putting in for you. You're supposed to tell her if you want something different." He held up his hand as she started to respond. "Now," he said as he leaned forward, "What in the hell is going on?!"

Harper tapped her fingers, her method of registering displeasure. However, her face never changed. "You know about Dupree turning himself in?"

"Yes and no. I heard about him being in the sheriff's office last night and that you were there. I didn't know he went in on his own."

"How did you know?"

"Elise told me. One of the deputies eats here. He told her this morning, I assume."

Harper tilted her head to one side. "I'm glad you didn't hear it on TV or read it in a paper. It might give me a little time. We need to eat and get out of here as quick as we can."

"Where are we going? To see Dupree?" Mooney asked. He let his displeasure show at being left 'out-of-the-loop.'

Harper ignored his reaction. "No. Let him sweat in a holding tank, for a while. It will make him more cooperative."

Mooney nodded as he asked, "So where—"

"We're going to the island. Then, you're going to babysit Dupree, and I'm going to visit Heller. Hopefully, I'll get to him before he finds out about Dupree and I'll learn some things as a result of going to Cayo Costa. After I have the information I hope to get, it will make him *very, very* cooperative."

"Okay. Now, I want to talk about Foreman." Mooney leaned forward, but Harper nodded her head toward Elise and said, "Later, we'll have plenty of time to discuss him in the car and boat going over to see Warrington."

Chapter 118
Fort Myers, Florida
May 2010

Mooney had been in many jails. While they all looked different, they all shared some things in common. The Lee County Jail was no exception. Architecturally, it was unique. It was painted with brighter colors than most. Footsteps etched on the floor in red, green, yellow, and blue used to guide visitors to their destinations were a one of a kind. The ever-present chain-link fencing, razor, and barbed wire, barred gates and doors, and stern-faced attendants transmitted the universal atmosphere accompanying freedom's loss.

Mooney wondered if Benny Dupree had ever been inside a jail cell before. He sat waiting for Dupree to be removed from whatever cage he'd been housed in and brought to the interview facility. The phone handset he held in anticipation of their discussion smelled stale even after dousing it with deodorizing germicide. It was another universal prison trait.

One look at Harper's client answered Mooney's question about whether Dupree had been the guest of a law enforcement agency before. Benny's facial expression was the human equivalent of a rabbit's, staring down a double-barreled, twelve gauge shotgun. Equal parts fear and panic gave away to disappointment when Harper wasn't the representative from the Sturgis Law Firm waiting for him. Benny was confused and suspicious when he picked up his phone on the other side of the glass separating them.

"Good morning, Mr. Dupree. I'm Tom Mooney, Harper Sturgis' investigative assistant. I'm here to brief you on a few things."

"Where's Harper?"

"She's making a few inquiries regarding your case and is starting to work on getting you out on bail."

"Good! How long will it be?" Benny's expression pleaded for a favorable answer.

"One of the things she's setting up is a bail hearing. That's not a real big deal." Tom smiled broadly to cover all traces that he was telling a whopper. Bail for a murder suspect was not a minor detail. "Until that happens, I can't tell you." Tom read Benny's crushed spirit. "Listen, Mr. Dupree, you have the absolute best lawyer you could possibly have representing you. I've seen her do unbelievable things. She'll get you out of this as lightly as humanly possible." It was obvious Dupree understood the gravity of his predicament. Mooney continued, "There's no sugarcoating this thing. You are in serious trouble. That's true. But, believe me, Harper Sturgis is the right one to be in your foxhole."

Dupree relaxed, but only a slight amount.

"You have a lot more going for you than you know. Let me tell you what's happening. You will be surprised. Aaaaa...you'll be a lot more than surprised."

Chapter 119
North Port, Florida
May 2010

Arthur Heller picked up his hotel room phone without thinking and answered "Hello." There was a pause before a feminine voice asked, "Am I speaking to Mr. Montel or Mr. Heller?"

There was no emotion expressed by his caller to read. Heller considered hanging up, but he knew that was futile. He believed he recognized the voice from the message the lady lawyer left. Dodging the inevitable wouldn't buy him anything, nor would denial. Heller answered, "Yes. I'm Heller."

"This is Harper Sturgis. I'm a lawyer representing an individual in which you have an interest. It is to my client and your mutual interest that we meet and discuss a number of issues. When will we do that?"

The calm, confident demeanor in the lawyer's voice raised Heller's apprehension level several notches. Knowing the answer, he asked, "Who do you represent?" as his mind raced to determine how to handle the problem he faced.

"Let's not play games. You know I'm here to discuss Benedict Dupree and some information he might possess." The voice remained steady and calm.

Heller tried to stall for time. "I could get with you in a few days. When would be good for you?"

"Now."

"I'm afraid I have plans for this afternoon. I have to be somewhere in less than two hours," Heller lied.

"No problem. Let's do it in a few minutes."

"By the time you drive here—"

"I'm in the lobby, calling from a house phone. I'll give you a few minutes to think. What I want to talk about is information you have that would help my client in his current difficulties and, in turn, I might be able to provide information that would be of assistance to you in your *quest...ricerca.*"

Her use of the Italian translation for quest made Heller's heart pound and hair stand up. "Aaaa...look ... I'm naked and need a little time to put clothes on. I—" He tried to stall.

"I've seen naked men before, and it won't bother or impact me in the least. Besides, you have time to slip some trousers on while I walk to your room. Heller, time is of the essence for my client. And, whether you are aware of it or not, it is for you too. The offer I'm going to make happens now or not at all. It helps Mr. Dupree. It helps you find what you're looking for and could help you with another problem, depending what you decide. Yes or no?"

Heller tried to visualize the owner of the phone voice as he capitulated. "Okay. I'm in—"

"You're in 307. I'll give you five minutes. A suggestion; forget about calling Foreman. You don't want to compound your problem."

Chapter 120
Fort Myers, Florida
May 2010

James McNeal had a hard time staying awake. The computer was going through the monotonous process of matching the photo taken by Maggie Stevens on her "date" with Fred Wilson or whoever the man turned out to be. McNeal was tasked with identifying the man. He wasn't elated with that job. Wilson, or was, *always* had plenty of cash and was *always* ready to buy the deputies drinks at the Bourbon Barrel. So long freebies.

The flickering monitor images being compared to Maggie's photo mesmerized him and induced sleep. His mind wandered to Brenda. His wife, who wanted another baby. His wife, who felt the compulsion to be constantly engaged in the baby-making process. His wife, who awakened him at all hours of the night and demanded another injection. His wife, who he wished would occasionally get a headache. Consciousness waned and dreams replaced reality. Even in this fantasy world, Brenda continued to demand perpetual intercourse. As he struggled to meet her demands, he felt his body getting smaller, hers larger. Soon it was apparent he was in dire danger of being ingested by an orifice not designed for that purpose. As he fought being sucked inside his wife's body, a buzzer sounded the alarm.

McNeal woke, stiffening in his office chair so violently he nearly tipped over backward. A buzzer screamed at him. He came out of his stupor and realized the computer had found a match. He shook his head to clear the cobwebs slumber had stretched over his mind. The picture Maggie took had a twin with different clothes, prison clothes garnishing it.

To the right on the file photo was row after row of information on the man the FBI records identified as "Terrill Albert Foreman." McNeal began reading. His eyes spread wide as he progressed with his review. Reading deeper and deeper into the file caused him to whistle or curse softly to himself. When he finished, he printed several copies of the file. He muttered, "This is one evil piece of bullshit."

James picked up his phone and dialed Maggie. When she answered, he skipped hellos and got straight to the issue. "You have any more plans to meet that Wilson guy?" He listened to her answer and nodded in relief as she finished speaking. He said, "Good," when Maggie stopped talking he added, "Don't make any. It turns out our buddy Fred Wilson is really one bad, slimy dude named, Terrill Albert Foreman. He doesn't normally date women; he rapes them. The man has a rap sheet that is as thick as a dictionary. He's done three stretches. Most recently, he was in Africa and is accused of war crimes there." Maggie made some comments to which McNeal answered, "Not funny. Consider yourself lucky to still have all your parts where they're supposed to be. This Foreman scumbag has a history of removing souvenirs from his victims. Listen, I'll get a hold of Frog. I'm sure he'll want to go over this and get us cranked up."

Chapter 121
North Port, Florida
May 2010

When Heller answered the knock on his hotel room door, to his surprise, he found himself looking up at the woman framed in the doorway, instead of down. Harper Sturgis's black hair, facial features, and pale white skin made him think of TV and movie characters portraying beautiful victims of Dracula. The woman looked like a classic vampire. A leaner, harder looking one, but it was easy to visualize the woman standing in front of him with her teeth buried in his jugular vein. The lack of any discernable emotion emanating from the lady reinforced that impression.

"Harper Sturgis," she said as she stepped past him and entered his room without invitation. She glanced around as if she was checking for something or someone.

Heller extended his hand and said, "I'm Arthur Heller."

Harper nodded, shaking his hand in a perfunctory manner. "Can we use that table?" she said, pointing to a thirty-inch wooden square. A large briefcase dangled from her other arm. Before Heller answered, Harper pulled a chair up to the table, carefully positioning it, so she faced the entrance. She sat down and removed three file folders. The second time Harper reached into the briefcase, she grasped a Colt .45 and laid it on the table.

Alarmed, Heller said, "That's not necessary."

"Not for you," Sturgis said, "If your partner

shows up ... I want to be prepared."

Heller hesitated. This wasn't the type conference or lawyer he was expecting. Was, Heller wondered, the reason she displayed the firearm because she had legitimate fears of what Foreman might do if he appeared, or was it a ploy to intimidate him. Trying to read anything in her expression was impossible. There was nothing to read.

Harper asked, "Do you have any illusions about the man you're attached to the hip with? If you do, you're either in denial, or you're mentally disabled. I don't believe it's the latter. *I* don't have illusions about Foreman. He's a killer. If he knew why I'm here, he'd *try* to kill me. He wouldn't, but he'd try. Sooner or later, Foreman will see you as a threat or see some advantage in making you disappear. Guess what? You're dead."

Heller eased into the chair across the table from the tall woman who could have stepped out of the Amazon myth. For a female who would be unanimously judged as beautiful, the chill that hovered over her dampened any such descriptions. When she remained silent, Heller said, "I know Foreman isn't a boy scout."

Harper nodded, "He's barely human. I'll assume you hired him because you needed things done that you weren't prepared to do. I don't care whether or not you expected the baggage that comes with partnering with an individual like Foreman, that's your business. One of the things I could offer you is a possible way to sever that relationship."

"I knew his past. The things he did were done while fighting in a war. I thought he wouldn't ... I thought I could control him." Heller sounded as defeated as he was.

"And you haven't. He does what he does because he enjoys it. Look, talking about your problem isn't going to solve it. I'm here to offer you a solution to that problem and access to the items you've been looking for. I'm looking to get my client the best possible deal he can get, given his circumstance, and I want, let's call it a commission, from the treasure you're hunting if you're successful in its retrieval." Before Heller could object, Harper added," It won't cost you anything. I'll just take what you promised, Foreman. He won't be using it."

Arthur Heller was astounded. "Why are you involved?"

"Dupree hired me when he discovered someone was poking around the island and asking questions about him and his property. My investigator is very good. He uncovered what you're doing. There are some things we don't know, but for the most part, we know a lot about your history and what you're looking for." Harper waved to dismiss further conversation regarding the past. "All this talk about how everybody got to this point means nothing. I've got Dupree sitting in the Lee County Jail. I need to keep him separated from the things he *didn't* do, so I get him the best deal possible for what he is responsible. Like I said, you need the pieces that I have access to so you can find what you're looking for. I'll help you make Foreman go away. That's my offer. Yes or no?"

Heller sat silently, thinking. After a minute, he asked, "What do I have to do?"

"Is that yes?"

"Yes."

Harper nodded. "Good. You're going to provide information to me; and the sheriff that will get Foreman smoked or in a cell for the rest of his life. You're going to provide it in a manner that shifts any responsibility you may have to Foreman. And, it will absolve Dupree of responsibility at the same time. I'll see you get access to the key you've been looking for and the piece of jewelry that accompanies it.

And, I need to know more about the information you have to find what you're looking for."

Chapter 122
North Port, Florida
May 2010

Harper carefully laid out her plans. She would represent both Dupree and Heller. Before they'd trade information to the law, she'd insist on written disclosure agreements affording her clients protection and figuratively offer the sheriff Foreman's head on a platter. Heller had a myriad of questions, which Harper answered as though she anticipated each one. She'd worked the situation out, so it appeared an innocent Heller became mixed up with a truly evil man. At worst, he appeared greedy, pursuing and plotting to recover a dream treasure. At best, a victim. Harper explained they'd make it possible for law enforcement to remove a dangerous psychopath from society, in return for "latitude" in handling Dupree's separate crime and Heller's "unethical" manipulations. Harper continued to talk, assuming the boys had been killed.

"But they're not dead," Heller insisted.

Harper remained quiet while she thought for a few seconds. She asked, "So you've talked to one or both boys since they went into hiding? Or do you have Foreman's word?"

"We had trouble contacting them, so Foreman went up to visit. Other than the girls bitching about the mattress time they're spending, and the boys wanting more money, Devale and Sean are fine." Heller tried to make *her believe* that *he believed* what he told her.

"Uh-huh." Harper showed no reaction. "That's

fine if we can demonstrate that. In fact, it's golden. Better than I thought it would be."

"But, I haven't been able to contact the boys myself."

"We don't need to. We need you to call Foreman and have him tell you they're fine with the sheriff present. We're in good shape. Whether they're alive or dead, he's fried. His little trip to Marietta to visit the Burns woman will ensure that."

Heller's eyes opened wide. "You know about that?"

"Yes."

Both Heller and the lady across the table from him believed that Foreman had murdered Devale and Sean. Heller saw how the lawyer was maneuvering everything to Dupree's and his advantage. He smiled at the iron-faced lady and looked relieved. "I see where you're going." He put his hands together and asked, "When will I get to see the key and the cross?"

"After we meet with the sheriff and we know that Foreman is out of the equation. That shouldn't be long. When the sheriff tries to locate those kids, do you want to bet he finds them or any trace up in Tampa?"

Heller found the amount of information Harper Sturgis and her operative had been able to unearth staggering. She answered questions he had until he could think of no more to ask.

It was time for Harper to satisfy her curiosity on a couple of issues. "How did you identify Benedict Dupree as the person that the Bocelli girl was in contact with here?"

Heller nodded. "A lot of work and a little luck. After more than twenty years of trying to figure out where the treasure was located, I finally did it. That gave me an incentive to try finding her again. I contacted one of her roommates, Amanda Hartwell.

It had been all those years since I talked to her. I guess time mellowed her because she was more receptive to answering questions. She'd already told me the only time she been contacted by Bocelli while Bocelli was here, was to tell Amanda she wasn't coming back to Miami for the next semester. I knew that much. Then the woman suggested checking something I never heard when I'd contacted her before. She said I might try contacting a man Bocelli was dating. Bocelli wouldn't tell Amanda his name, but Amanda did remember Bocelli saying he lived on one of the islands and was a defensive back for the Gators. I checked it out. There was only one defensive back from this area on the Florida football team at the time. Once I found out Dupree's name, the fact he owned a big piece of property where Bocelli was studying the turtles, and his odd behavior, well, I guessed he might have killed the girl. I never considered—"

"I have one other thing," Harper interrupted. "You told me you had the clues that allowed you to locate Mussolini's stash, with you. Could I see them?"

"You think you'll be able to figure out where it's located?" Heller smiled.

"No. I just want to be sure they exist."

Heller went to a chest of drawers and removed a leather-bound book and several three-ring binders. He placed them in front of Harper.

She looked through the three-ring binders without any comment, but asked, "Why did you tear out the journal page and put it in one of the notebooks?" when she looked at the journal. Before Heller could invent an answer, Harper found the sheet in the binder and said, "Never mind, I see." She rapidly thumbed back and forth through the journal, while removing the torn out sheet and studying it. Harper perused the pictures, articles, and documents in the notebooks. She spent extra time examining a death certificate, and when she finished, she muttered, "Clever." Harper replaced the code key sheet back into the binder. She stacked the books up and returned them to Heller. "I think we have a good chance of finding where it was hidden. We have all the information we need to walk right to its general location. The person who came up with the plan to safeguard it was very good. The touch of quarantining it with the plague warning is genius."

Heller's mouth dropped. "How? I ..." He never finished his astonished response. The woman knew more in a few minutes than he'd learned in years.

Harper half-smiled, showing a rare expression of emotion. She explained, "Most of my time in service was in a Marine intelligence unit. I was a cryptologist."

Chapter 123
Fort Myers, Florida
May 2010

James McNeal watched Anne enter Maggie Stevens' office to answer a phone that steadfastly refused to be silent. Anne was two strides ahead, made a face, and good-naturedly stuck her tongue out at her workmate. She mashed the speaker-phone button and said, "Lee County Sheriff's Department, Crime Lab."

"Hi, who have I got?" A man's bass voice filled the office. "Anne Cook."

The man asked, "Is Maggie Stevens around?"

Anne picked up a pencil and a notepad from Maggie's desk. "She's in a meeting with Sheriff Hilliard. Give me your name and phone number, and I'll have her call you back."

"Tell her Fred Wilson called, and I'll be at the Sunset tonight at seven,"

Shock spread over Anne's face as she looked at McNeal and said, "It's that Foreman guy."

McNeal frowned, slapped his index finger in front of his mouth, and made a hushing sound. He pushed the hold button with his other hand. "Tell him you'll get her to the phone and to hold. I'll let Frog and Maggie know."

As McNeal left, he hesitated. Anne picked up the handset and took the call off hold. She said, "Hello ... Hello ... Hello ... Hello." Anne shook her head and said, "I'm sorry," as the dial tone returned and she hung up the phone.

"Oh shit!" McNeal said as he left to find Sheriff Hilliard.

Chapter 124
Fort Myers, Florida
May 2010

Tom Mooney sat in the sheriff's office lobby waiting for Harper to meet him. He read Nicholas Sparks' *Message in a Bottle* while he waited. One of Tom's favorite past-times was to read a book after seeing the movie made from it. He liked to see how and the filmmaker altered what he read. They most always did. Whether it was an improvement or a detriment. Mooney, a young, old-fashioned sort, sided with the author most times. His favorite rant was how Creighton's *Jurassic Park* was "destroyed by celluloid simpletons." A clue to understanding Tom's psyche was that he owned a DVD of the Spielberg classic and frequently played it.

A collective murmur became a commotion. Deputies and clerical personnel formed little knots, talking in excited tones. One of the groups formed around the receptionist. A universal truth of any organization is that gossip, rumors, along with the latest compromised secrets are attracted to receptionists and telephone operators like opposite poles on a magnet. Mooney closed his book and joined the congregation of deputies and other employees to eavesdrop. As he approached, he heard one clerk say, "She didn't mean to do it." Another said, "It's a major flub up. Frog's a forgiving sort, but I bet he eats her ass. He's been keeping this a secret, even within the department." One lady officer offered, "I think he'll be more upset with her for going on a crying jag, guilt trip, and telling everybody about Wilson being a war criminal. The fact she accidental spilled that we knew about him over the phone, when you're on a speaker, something like that is easy to happen."

The last thing Mooney heard as he left the group was, "You can bet old Frog will have someone tearing out every speakerphone in the office this afternoon," and the laughter that accompanied the statement.

Mooney returned to his chair, removed his cell phone, and autodialed Harper. When she answered, he said, "You on the way?" After she said yes, he told her, "That's good. Things are hitting the fan here. You aren't going to surprise the sheriff's department with the information about Foreman. They already know." Mooney listened intently to instructions from his boss. When she finished, he said, "I'll explain what you want, and I'll do my best to set up the whole thing with the sheriff. Good luck on getting Heller to come in! If he's scared enough he might. But be careful when you *try* to convince Heller to come here with you. Foreman might be around. Who knows what that lunatic will do, now that he knows he's been exposed."

Chapter 125
Fort Myers, Florida
May 2010

"I can't sign something like these without getting the DA to agree. What you've laid out is very interesting. But—" Sheriff Hilliard looked at the papers in his hands.

"You'll see that there are signing blocks for the District Attorney's representative," Harper said. She tapped her fingers on the conference table. "Sheriff Hilliard, you have a serial killer within your grasp. With the information Mr. Heller and I can provide to you, you'll either put him in prison for good or, even better, in the ground. But, every minute we lose gives him a better chance of getting away. I know Foreman's killed one for sure, probably three since he's been involved with Mr. Heller. Who knows how many before? Hundreds? Heller is doing this at great peril to himself. My client is giving up part of his legal position to help apprehend this killer. Do you want the moral responsibility for letting Foreman escape?"

Hilliard took a deep breath. "I'll agree to sign Heller's so he's clear and promise to do my best to get the DA to consider self-defense or plea bargain the charges for Dupree." He looked at Heller and said, "He's no saint, but I don't believe he's murdered, anyone." The sheriff looked down at the papers in his hand. He fought an internal battle as he spoke. "Benny Dupree, that's something else. I've known him thirty years. He doesn't hunt deer because he can't pull the trigger, for crap's sake. But ...what is, is. If you can prove the story you told, I'll look seriously at man-slaughter, maybe even at self-defense like you're asking. But you have to *prove it*! No doubts. Ms. Sturgis, I can't waive a possibly valid murder charge. This thing is so damned complicated ..."

"It's horribly complicated. But, do we want to make it more complicated *and* tragic? Any delays we make is time that lunatic has to commit more carnage. I don't want that on my conscience."

Hilliard's eyes went from Sturgis to Heller. He took a deep breath. "I'll sign it if ... if ... if you produce the witness you claim you have. I'm going to write that on these papers as a condition. If you don't produce the witness, the papers are void." He wrote several sentences under the signing blocks on each copy. Hilliard pushed them to Harper. "If what I've written is acceptable, I'll sign."

Harper nodded, signed her name, and returned the documents to Hilliard.

He said, "We both have a lot invested in these. Your client's life, my job, and both our reputations." The sheriff signed and said, "Okay, let's get this show on the road. Give me the phone numbers; I'll make arrangements to place and document the call. Do what you have to do to get ready to talk to Foreman."

Chapter 126
Fort Myers, Florida
May 2010

Heller hung up the phone. A collective sigh of relief came from the eight individuals who were involved with the elaborately staged phone call to Terrill Foreman.

Sheriff Hilliard looked at the stenographer who maintained a word for word record of the conversation. "Anything you didn't get, Wendy?"

Wendy answered, "No, I got everything." She removed her headset.

The sheriff removed his headset and motioned for Maggie to do the same. Harper took hers off as well. Heller, who was petrified with fear, sat staring into space, wondering if he'd made a terrible mistake. Hilliard tapped Heller on the arm lightly, eliciting a frightened response followed by relief. The sheriff said, "You did fine."

"Did you think he got suspicious?" Heller asked.

"No, I don't think so," Hilliard answered.

Harper asked, "Do you agree you got everything that was promised."

"Yes," Hilliard answered. He motioned to Maggie Stevens and James McNeal. "Before you two leave, I want to be sure you both have a statement in the file identifying Foreman's voice to backup Heller's identification. Then, take all the info on where he's staying and what he's driving and let's lasso the asshole. If they're still alive, let's get those boys back."

He looked at Heller then at Harper. "Foreman acknowledged that the boys participated voluntarily, that he's the last person to see Sean and Devale ... alive ... and claims they're safe and he knows where they are. That absolves you, Heller, and Benedict Dupree of anything involving the boys."

"Can Mr. Heller go?" Harper asked.

Sheriff Hilliard thought for several seconds then said, "Yes, but keep us informed on your whereabouts. Leave your cell phone here and get another one. Get the new number to us. You don't want Foreman to be able to contact you and you sure as hell don't want to meet with him. Oh, be sure to get out of your motel and go someplace different, quickly. Be careful. Once you get reestablished, I'll assign some protection for you."

"Thank you." Heller gathered his emotions and rose. He looked at Harper.

"You have my card, Arthur. Call me when you get set up, and we'll discuss what's next."

Heller said, "Okay," and left.

Harper watched Heller disappear down the hall. "Think you should assign some security for him now? I heard something I didn't like in Foreman's voice right at the end of the call when Heller kept pressing him on where he had the boys stashed. Foreman's a—"

"I have both their hotels under surveillance, now. I don't want to spook Foreman if he shows up looking for Heller, and I will if Heller arrives with of a couple green and whites in convoy. Remember he's going to another county. I don't have jurisdiction. Andy Quarlles and I work real good together. He's staking out the hotels with plain clothes. Heller should be safe."

Harper stayed quiet but raised one eyebrow.

Chapter 127
Fort Myers, Florida
May 2010

Harper Sturgis opened her car's trunk and removed an aluminum case. She thought for several seconds before pushing the steel panel down and listening to the trunk lock snap. Harper climbed back into the driver's seat and handed Tom Mooney what he recognized as one of her gun carriers. He placed it on his lap, leaned against the passenger side door, and said, "You know how I feel about carrying one of these. Besides, I'm not a very good shot. I don't have time to go to the range and practice. A handgun won't be of any more use than a broadsword, a lance, or a mace. I'll be as safe without it."

Harper looked at him for several seconds before saying, "Deathwish? Look at it this way; it's as much for my conscience, as for your protection. Don't worry about being a good shot. It's the MAC 10. You've fired it before. Just put the clip in and it's ready. Aim at his low abdomen, because remember, the gun will want to pull up as you fire it in automatic. Keep the bursts short. You'll get enough slugs in him to bring him down. Don't wait for him to threaten you. If you see him, shoot him."

Mooney shook his head, "I have no intention of doing that."

"Your choice," Harper said. "Leave the gun if you refuse to use it. I don't feel like contributing a fully automatic weapon for that slime bag's use."

Mooney looked at the case sitting on his lap for several seconds before deciding to retain it. He turned his eyes toward Harper. "Now what?"

"Not much of anything until the sheriff bags Foreman. We protect ourselves. If we can do anything to keep Heller in one piece, we do that."

"How about Dupree? I told him, you were trying to set up bail for him."

"He's safer where he is for right now. I've already gone through the preliminaries. I'll stall the bail hearing until Foreman's caught. Dupree could be one of Foreman's targets because Foreman might think Dupree knows more than he does. My guess is that Foreman will look at finding the treasure as his ticket out. Just about his *only* one. He needs enough money to go hide for the rest of his life."

"Dupree isn't going to be happy about that. He doesn't like jail."

Harper stared at her associate, icily. "Unhappy? Dead? I'll make that decision for him. He stays put."

Mooney rubbed his chin, "What about the people on the island?"

"As far as we know, Foreman doesn't have a clue they're out there." Harper hesitated as though she just thought of something. "If he does find out about them, he has to get out there, quick. The way he'd find out is for him to catch up with Heller. Heller isn't the type to stand up to the things Foreman is capable of doing. You asked about things we need to do. We need to see what we can do to help Heller hide. Damn, I wish the sheriff hadn't taken Heller's cell. We don't have any way to contact him. That means there isn't much we can do until he contacts us."

Mooney raised his eyebrows and gestured with his hands. "Sheriff Hilliard said he was getting his buddy to cover him with some units. You worried they won't be able to protect Heller?"

"You've seen how Foreman operates and how efficient he is at doing what he does. Hilliard is a good man, I'm sure his friend is, but they don't fully comprehend what they're dealing with. They have as much of a chance of keeping Foreman away from Heller, as I have of growing a large hairy pair." Harper waved her hand, indicating she wanted to change the subject. "We need to let Warrington and Dr. Barlow know what's going on in case Foreman finds out about them. They need to be able to leave or defend themselves."

Mooney frowned. "I've got a cell phone number for Dr. Barlow. Problem is that the cell phone service is bad out there."

Harper nodded, "Try. Tell them what the situation is. Don't scare them if you can help it. If you can't get a hold of them in an hour, get a boat and go over there. Take the MAC 10 with you and let Goodun have it. If it's necessary, he'll put it to good use. I'll get you something else."

"Okay. What are you going to be doing?"

"Trying to keep Heller alive."

Chapter 128
Fort Myers, Florida
May 2010

Corrine sat on the opposite side of the glass from her boss in the sheriff department's visiting room. Tears were in her eyes and rolled down her cheeks. She wished she could touch the man that had been her employer, mentor, and friend for a third of her life. They discussed the issues for which she had to get answers. The business had to be kept running. Corrine asked, "Is there anything I can do for you?"

"No. I wish there was." Noticing the tears, Benny said, "Hey, Corrine, I got myself into this. I'll have to see it through. I know you're confused, but I can't tell you anything. I'm sorry. Harper Sturgis says I can't speak to anyone about what's going on without her knowledge and say so. I'll get through this and so will you." Benny looked at his faithful secretary and smiled. "There is one thing you can do for me. See if you can find out when I'll be out on bail. Call Harper. She was working on setting it up."

"I've been trying to reach Ms. Sturgis, but she doesn't answer or return my calls. I did talk to her assistant, Mr. Mooney. He's nice, not like *her*. I can call him and see if he knows about the bail. He said everything is going good. Mooney said that a person named Dr. Barlow is supposed to be an important witness that's testifying for you."

"Dr. Barlow? Who is that? I don't know any Barlow."

"I don't know anything except, Mr. Mooney said this Dr. Barlow was your get-out-of-jail-free card. Maybe Barlow's one of those psychologists or crime scientists you see on TV. I think the Dr. is a friend of Goodun Warrington's or has some connection to him."

"Goodun? That makes no sense. Do you know where this doctor's from?"

"Wyoming."

Benny shook his head in disbelief, "I don't know anybody from Wyoming."

Chapter 129
Punta Gorda, Florida
May 2010

Foreman had everything he needed. The journal and notebooks sat next to him on the front seat of his truck. Heller had made them superfluous. Cutting off a couple of fingers was sufficient. The cliché, sing like a canary, was entirely appropriate. The professor did everything possible to ingratiate himself to Foreman. He volunteered the name of the Tuscany town where the treasure was hidden, the meaning of much of the information in the binders and journal, and the critical fact that the final two items needed to gain access to the treasure were in the possession of the old hermit who lived on Cayo Costa and his 'guest.' Foreman forced Heller to admit he'd participated in "ratting him out," that he'd cooperated with law enforcement. After additional "persuasion," he related the entire story of the phone call. Heller pleaded for his life right up to the time Foreman slit his throat.

After Heller's revelations, Foreman knew his time to escape was very, very limited. He also realized that his future was somewhere out of the United States. Thanks to money received from Heller before and taken after his death, he could flee. The lure of unlimited wealth was impossible to resist, even with the threats that closed in on him from all sides. Foreman quickly devised a plan. He already had the cruiser rented. The truck Heller had leased he'd abandoned a couple of blocks from the Punta Gorda marina where his boat was docked. He'd make the now familiar trip down Charlotte

Harbor, through Pine Island Sound, and go directly to the hermit's cabin in a cove on Cayo Costa. It wouldn't take long. Foreman decided he'd do what he needed to, take the cross and key from the old man or anybody else that stood in his way. He'd seen the hermit. Overpowering him wouldn't be a problem. He needed escape time. However, breaking more eggs wouldn't bother him to ensure unlimited wealth.

Then, he thought, it was on to Key West via the cruiser, airline tickets, and the land of lasagna. Foreman ignored moral considerations; those never entered his mind. His focus was on how to acquire the treasure and what extravagances he'd enjoy in the years to come.

Chapter 130
Pine Island, Florida
May 2010

Harper changed clothes. Her lawyer persona, the dress, blouse, and coat, lay on the bed in her hotel room. She was dressing for battle. The loose fitting khaki cargo pants she wore had plenty of places to store weapons she intended to carry. She put on a Kevlar vest and covered that with a brown hunting shirt. Two throwing knives found their way into pockets on either side of her pants. A Kabar fighting knife was in its scabbard which hung from her waist. Harper snapped an ammunition pouch on her belt. Four full clips of .45 caliber bullets were inside. She removed the Colt automatic from its holster on the opposite side from her Kabar. The safety was on and the chamber empty. She nodded her head and slipped the gun back into its holster. There was one more thing to do prior to getting Heller relocated. She picked up the phone and called Sheriff Hilliard to let him know she was going to Heller's hotel.

When she was connected to Hilliard, she said, "Hey, sheriff. This is Harper Sturgis. I wanted to let you and your people know I'm heading to Heller's hotel room. Since he needs to relocate fast, I thought I'd go help get him out of there. However, I don't want to flub up what you're doing."

The phone was quiet for a few seconds before Hilliard spoke, "Don't bother. Evidently, Foreman was *very* close to Heller's hotel when he was talking to us on the phone. He got there before Quarlles people did. The front desk said, when Heller returned, he stopped and told them he was going to pack and check out. An hour later, they got a complaint about loud music coming from Heller's room. After several tries calling Heller and when he didn't answer his phone, they sent a maid to check on him. Long story short, the room was trashed. So was Heller. I got a call from Maggie Stevens a few minutes ago. I'd sent her over there to set up a collaborative crime scene investigation. Maggie was shook, and that takes a lot. She told me it was very brutal and there was lots of evidence he was tortured. I'm sorry, Sturgis. The teams were on-site within a half-hour of our call. They were in place before Heller got back. Shit, they saw Heller go into the hotel. Never saw Foreman enter. They didn't see Foreman leave. We've searched the hotel, nothing. The bastard's gone."

Harper blinked her eyes and said, "Does your scene technician have any thoughts on how long ago he was killed?"

"I asked her. Her guess is two to three hours. I have surveillance teams at the hotel Heller told us Foreman is staying at. They checked the room. He wasn't in it and hasn't shown up there. If he comes back, we'll get him. Sturgis ... Sturgis?" The dial tone replaced Harper. She was concerned wasted seconds could cost lives.

Chapter 131
Cabbage Key Cut, Cayo Costa Island Florida,
May 2010

Mooney struggled with the dock-master's instructions and the navigation chart he had folded to a size less likely to be blown from his hand. He held the steering wheel and operated the throttle of his small rented boat. Tom looked at the soundings and contour lines on the chart. The depths looked as though he should have no problem piloting the eighteen-footer across a spot the dock-master's instructions routed him around. Tom was trying to decide if he should attempt the short-cut when the phone in his pocket began vibrating. Tom threw the engine into neutral allowing it to glide to a stop.

The screen displayed Harper's number and name. Tom touched the icon and said, "Hello." There was no answer. The screen told him he had a weak signal, varying between zero and two bars. "Hello," he repeated.

" ... ello ... To... an you ... r me?" Sturgis voice broke up, but the syllables that survived had an urgent quality in them.

"Harper, there's not much service here. Can you hear me?"

"You're br ... up. I ca ... you to te ... ... man's on ... ... the island. Be da ... ful.

He ... ... Dr. Ba ... ... knows about ... ...Heller's ... ... " The signal died completely, and the call disconnected.

Mooney tried to call back, but *no service* flashed on the screen. What was Harper trying to communicate? Something important, he was sure of that. About the only thing it could be was something to do with Foreman. Either, the killer had been apprehended, that was good, or Foreman might be on the way to the island. That was very bad. From the few words he'd heard, he guessed Foreman was coming. A scraping sound diverted his attention. The outboard motor's skeg dragged in the sand and weeds covering the shallow bar he'd drifted on. Mooney mumbled, "Dock master one, chart zero." He tilted the motor and began to slowly maneuver the boat back to the point where he could put the engine down and make the circle that he'd been told to follow.

Mooney looked across the half-mile flat in front of him. A large cruiser was racing down the channel where he'd eventually find himself running his boat. The man driving the cruiser was very large and, though Tom couldn't see well enough to recognize other details of the boat captain's appearance, within a couple of seconds he screamed, "Oh shit!" Tom knew it would take ten minutes to get to the same point the cruiser was passing now. Being ten minutes behind Foreman, for that was who Mooney suspected the cruiser's driver was, meant he'd be a deadly ten minutes late.

Chapter 132
Cabbage Key Cut, Cayo Costa Island, Florida
May 2010

Goodun watched three trout splash around in his fishing boat's live well. He and his guests would enjoy a fresh fish dinner, with hush-puppies and green beans fresh from the can. Goodun chuckled. Ken, one of the uniformed park rangers was making a routine patrol, poking the bow of his small Boston Whaler into the coves and crannies on the Pine Island Sound side of Cayo Costa Park. They waved as they passed.

As he approached his dock, a large white cruiser slowed as it eased past Ken in his labeled state park vessel. The thirty footer crossed the channel, came off a plane; it was headed for his cabin. When Goodun heard the spring zing on his screened door, he yelled, "Stay inside." There was a flurry of activity at the cabin door as his house-guests retreated. Goodun had his boat tied up in seconds. He looked for something for defense if he needed it. There wasn't even a pocket knife. His only possible weapon was his limber seven-foot fishing rod. Goodun wound the artificial bait tied to the lines end up tight to the rod's top, so it became an effective fencing foil. Stepping from his boat with his fishing rod in hand, he positioned his body between where the cruiser was being tied to the dock and his cabin.

A large muscular, black man jumped down on the dock. Goodun estimated him as being seventy pounds heavier, three inches taller, and thirty years younger. They eyed each other. Warrington's mind raced to try to think of some way to offset the odds.

The big man was the same one he'd seen trespassing on Dupree's land, the one Harper Sturgis warned him about, and the one he suspected disposed of the two teenage boys. Goodun mentally prepared himself to fight...and to win or die.

When the big man took steps toward him, Goodun warned, "This is private property. Get back in your boat and move along."

A big grin covered the man's face. Goodun noticed something grasped in the intruder's right hand and was sure it was a knife. The blade was hidden behind the man's huge forearm. He stopped fifteen feet from Goodun. "Can't do that old man. You have something I need. I'm going get it. You can give it to me and make this easy on yourself or make this very hard and painful. Just tell those people inside to bring me the key and the cross."

"Get off my dock." Goodun braced for the attack he knew must come.

The big man turned the knife he held so that the fourteen-inch blade of the Bowie knife gleamed in the sunlight. "I haven't got time to screw with you." Foreman, the big man, the big killer, moved forward, pointing the blade at the center of Goodun's body. Foreman ignored Goodun's effort to tighten his grip on the fishing rod. As Foreman lunged toward his intended victim, Goodun whipped the tip of the rod around and slapped it across Foreman's face.

The action stopped Foreman as though frozen. He screamed a loud blood curdling, "Aaaaaaaaaaaaaaa." The artificial bait's treble hooks, snug on the rod's tip, buried into Foreman's face in the most damaging place. One set sunk into the flesh at the corner of his eye, another set buried into the eyeball, and the third set dug deep into the bridge of his nose. Foremen compounded his problem by slapping his hand on the bait. Immediately, some of the treble hooks ripped into his hand's flesh. He screamed again and dropped his knife. The only thing important to him was the searing pain attacking his face.

Goodun dropped his rod, snatched up the Bowie knife, and drove it into Foreman's abdomen slicing it upward into his chest. Goodun loosened his grip on the weapon and stepped away. Foreman was silent as he dropped to his knees then fell forward on his face. Red stained the dock.

Sheriff Hilliard pulled the canvas sheet back over Foreman's body. In his long career as a law enforcement officer, he seldom succumbed to the urge to excuse a criminal act as justified. He normally maintained sympathy for the victim no matter how undeserving. Frog couldn't do it this time. Restraining a celebratory fist pump and open smile was hard.

An assortment of sheriff's department personnel, including Maggie Stevens and James McNeal, were standing on the dock. Tom Mooney and Rollie Gates were the lone outsiders. Tom had been the first to arrive at the scene and had to motor up to the ranger station to summon the authorities and contact his boss. Goodun Warrington and Harper Sturgis stood a few yards away from the knot of people, talking.

Harper left Warrington and approached Sheriff Hilliard. "Sheriff Hilliard, I want you to know that I'm going to represent Mr. Warrington. I've advised him not to discuss this event or anything related to it, with anyone, without me being present. Since Tom and I are taking them," she pointed to the cabin, "back to my room at the Tarpon Inn, I'm asking you not to question him in my absence. I'll bring everyone in to make a statement at your offices. Later."

Hilliard held his hand up. He bent over and pulled the sheet back uncovering most of Foreman's corpse. He raised the body on its side. After examining it for a half-minute, he concluded, "I doubt that will be necessary. It's obvious what's happened here. That man attacked Warrington and Warrington swatted at him with the fishing pole in self-defense. Foreman was holding his own knife," Hilliard paused and looked directly at Maggie Stevens, "and he fell on it. You agree with that as a possibility for the way this thing happened?"

Maggie remained straight-faced and didn't hesitate to say, "Definitely."

"Ms. Sturgis, I'm not charging Mr. Warrington. He's free to go with you. We have a lot of documentation to do yet. We'll secure his home when we leave. I'd like to speak to the witnesses ... *later ... if they're sure they saw the whole thing very clearly.* Otherwise..."

"I understand." Sturgis moved close to Hilliard, bent over, and whispered in his ear, "I admire a man with a big set." She backed away, said, "Thank you," and guided Goodun and Tom toward Tom's boat. Then she disappeared into Goodun's cabin.

The sheriff looked at Maggie. "Okay. Maggie, finish your evaluation, the one we discussed, and documentation. When you get done, get that pile of shit in a body bag. Let's hope we don't see another one like him in our lifetime."

Chapter 133
Fort Myers, Florida
May 2010

"Mooney, I'm glad to see you. What in the hell is going on? Where's Sturgis? The people in this place look at me like I'm some kind of space alien. They whisper among themselves. They didn't do that before. What's happened?" Benny Dupree clutched the steel bars in the holding cell. "Why am I here instead meeting you in the visitation room?"

"Okay, just calm down," Tom said.

The jailer unlocked the door and slid it open. Tom entered the cell and grasped Benny's arm. "You're here because there's a meeting to discuss your arraignment and the bail hearing that's scheduled for you."

"Am I getting out of here?" Benny had one interest.

Tom smiled. "I can't say for certain, but with a 90% confidence level, I'd say yes." Benny looked relieved and took a deep breath.

"A huge number of things have happened in the last twenty-four hours, Mr. Dupree. You don't have to worry about Foreman or Heller anymore. They're both dead."

"Dead? How? What in the hell is—"

"We don't have time now." Mooney held his palms upward and bobbed his hands up and down, emphasizing his next comments. "Things look good for your case. You'll have that arraignment hearing tomorrow. Harper is in a preliminary meeting with the sheriff and the district attorney right now. We might get called into it. They're arguing over what you'll be charged with. She's convinced them to drop murder as a possible charge. Harper is trying to get them to drop everything. She's claiming your actions were self-defense. The DA wants manslaughter. Andrews will drop that after she hears the witness Harper's dug up."

"Witness? There wasn't anyone there." Dupree frowned at Tom's terminology for finding the nonexistent person. Then his eyes opened wide. "Goodun?"

"You are in for a shock. Actually, you're in for a few of them."

A deputy cleared his throat at the cell door. "They asked me to get you fellows and bring you to the meeting." Tom grinned; Benny was shocked. The jailor added, "Make sure you have everything that's yours with you. We ain't coming back here." The deputy shook a pair of leg chains and handcuffs. "Sorry, I have to put these on you, but that's procedure when you're out walking around. You're suspected of a capital offense, so ...." The deputy snapped the handcuffs around Benny's wrists.

When the deputy ushered them from the cell, Mooney spoke to Dupree, saying, "Benny, I came down here to give you information to soften some surprises. That isn't going to happen. I can't explain in the time we have." Tom patted Benny on the shoulder. "Just hang in there, man." They walked the remaining distance in strained silence; Mooney lamented his failure to prepare his client; Dupree walked in complete confusion and fear.

The guard stopped Tom and Benny outside a large double door. He pointed at Tom and said, "You're supposed to go on in. Mr. Dupree, you'll have to wait out here until they want you inside. If you want, we can sit in one of the vacant rooms, so you don't have to be sittin' in the hall like that." The guard pointed to chains and cuffs.

"I'd prefer that," Benny said.

"Hey, everything is going to be fine." Tom opened one of the double doors. "See you soon." He went inside, closing the door behind him.

The guard guided Benny into a small meeting room, where they sat and sat and sat. Thirty minutes raced by. Benny struggled to make sense of Mooney's comments. A witness? Who? The only person ... a bolt of electricity shot through him. Goodun, that's who it had to be! If that was the answer, a myriad of questions crowded into his mind. He shook his head.

Conjecture was worthless. He just had to wait. An hour passed, his anxiety rose, and seconds lengthened. At last, a woman, the guard, called Maggie stuck her head into the room and said, "You can bring him in now. Oh. Remove the restraints, sheriff's orders."

Chapter 134
Gulf of Mexico, Cayo Costa Island, Florida
May 2010

The waters were slightly murky, but still very "dive-able." Calm winds, a cooler full of drinks, and good prospects for spearfishing had him in his boat, hunting.

Bob Franco looked at the sonar. He and his three diving partners knew the waters off the Lee County barrier islands as well as anyone. While searching for a limestone ledge that housed some large mangrove snapper, new features appeared on the sonar screen. One of his buddies said, "What in the hell is that? We've been over this spot a hundred times. There's never been anything down there before."

Bob nodded and continued to circle around, focusing on the mystery formation that sat on the previously barren bottom. It wasn't large enough to be a boat unless it was a dingy. The mass was broken apart into eight uniformly sized and shaped items. Bob checked the GPS readings. He'd been in the same spot less than a month ago, and they weren't there then. A large concentration of fish had already gathered and appeared to have taken up residence near the masses. "That's strange," he said to his buddies, "Look at all the fish drawn around them already. It's like ..." Suddenly, Bob smiled and said, "We've found us someone poaching stone crabs. That's the way fish gather around freshly baited traps. Let's go take a look. I'll write down the GPS numbers, and we can give them to Fish and Game when we get in. Let's take our spears. We might pick up a snapper or two." He tossed in an anchor.

Bob and his friends were in their tanks and masks in a few minutes and dropped backward into the Gulf's tepid waters. Within seconds, they were on the bottom in less than thirty feet of water. Bob scanned the terrain. He was right. Crab traps dotted the bottom in a small area. A logical explanation occurred to him. The crabber was afraid of discovery and jettisoned his traps to avoid being caught and possibly losing his boat. He stared at the hodge-podge. There was something wrong. He realized some of the traps were stuffed to capacity. Bob swam to them, wondering what kind of sea creatures had been unfortunate enough to get caught inside. He decided to set them free if they were still alive. Swimming close to the bottom, the water was cloudy enough that he couldn't figure out what he was looking at from a distance. It certainly wasn't a large number of crabs clinging on the sides as he supposed. It was much too dense for that. He focused on one particular feature. When Bob was within three feet of the trap, he realized what he was staring at...the eye socket of a partially decomposed human head.

Chapter 135
Fort Myers, Florida
May 2010

Benny Dupree heard the squishing sound made by the door closers. There was a clicking sound as the lockset mated. "Please join us at the table, Mr. Dupree," the sheriff said. It was the first time he could remember Frog calling him anything, but Benny. In the large room he'd entered, there was a long table with many individuals crowded around its perimeter. A projection screen was set up. A projector and a laptop sat on the table. Benny focused his attention on the people clustered around the heavy wooden structure. Half-faced him and half sat with their back to the door. Benny's eyes systematically and quickly went from individual to individual. He recognized Frog, the woman called Maggie, James McNeal, knew the District Attorney Jolynn Andrews from pictures he'd seen of her, and two other strangers sitting on the side facing him. The people sitting on the opposite side of the table turned their heads toward him as he entered. All but one person, a woman. Harper Sturgis, Tom Mooney, Goodun Warrington, and the woman whose face he couldn't see were on "his side." However, one woman who had turned to look at Benny made a statue of him, except for his mouth, that dropped open. Benny's ghost from Turtle Point had returned.

The auburn hair and features were almost exactly as he remembered. It couldn't be, but it was. Nadine sat at the table, smiling a thirty-year-old smile from her twenty-year-old face. Sheriff Hilliard snapped him back from his trip to the paranormal.

"Mr. Dupree, please take the seat next to Mr. Mooney." Benny forced his eyes away from the young female specter and on the chair next to Tom Mooney. He took the remaining half-dozen steps to Tom and slumped down. Benny wasn't sure he was in the real world. Maybe, he thought, he was dreaming.

Tom Mooney leaned toward him and said in a low voice. "You'll be getting asked questions. Answer *yes, no,* or *I don't remember.*" Tom leaned closer and spoke even lower. "Anything regarding the fight answer, *I don't remember.*" Mooney straightened back up.

Benny felt like a skunk at a cat show. The other people at the table were engaged in whisperings, looked at documents scattered in front of them, and occasionally glanced his way. Each look made him feel more conspicuous. District Attorney Andrew's looks were particularly unnerving. The man next to her starred at Benny, his face expressing clear contempt.

Sheriff Hilliard said, "Is everybody ready to resume?"

A chorus of "yes" and nods responded.

Hilliard looked at Benny and said, "Mr. Dupree, your lawyer requested this preliminary inquest due to the number of highly unusual circumstances involved in happenings on the night of June 27, 1980. We've agreed to have this investigation because of your cooperation and your lawyer's assistance in providing information on events that are indirectly associated with, but are not part of that night. We're here to listen to evidence to better understand what happened. This is an informal—"

Jolynn Andrews interrupted. "Mr. Dupree, let me caution you that information may be discovered in this," Andrews paused and became derisive, "*inquest,* can be used in your prosecution. Do you understand that?"

Benny answered unsurely, "Yes."

"Are you sure you want to continue?" The DA asked.

"Yes,"

Harper leaned forward so that Benny could see her. Her expressionless face nodded. It was a message; Benny just wasn't sure about what.

"Since this is an informal process," Harper paused, "we do all agree to that?" The "yes-s" and nods were repeated. "Then may we continue? Jolynn, you've established what you wanted and had your shot at intimidating Mr. Dupree, so pull your pants back up. We've seen enough of your ass."

The DA's face burned and everyone laughed with the exception of Harper, Jolynn and the man next to the DA. Benny guessed he was Jolynn's assistant.

Sheriff Hilliard stifled the last of his laughs. "Okay. I think we have the jousting out of the way. Look, ladies; we don't have a judge or a jury here, so save it. Hopefully, you won't need to go to court if we all agree on what happened. That's the idea of us being here. We agreed that we'd have Ms. Sturgis present what she alleges happened on the night in question and substantiate that information. We also agreed that everyone present may make inquiries as the presentation is in process. Ms. Sturgis, are you ready to begin?"

Harper looked at Mooney who nodded. She stood and answered, "Yes." Harper walked to the screen, and all heads turned toward her. Benny was glad he was no longer the center of attention. It meant he only saw the auburn hair on the back of woman ghost's head, increasing Benny's burning curiosity. Mooney typed on the laptop until an aerial photo of Turtle Point and the surrounding area appeared. A number of lines and numbers had been added.

"We've already stipulated a number of facts prior to when you joined us, Mr. Dupree. You're here to confirm those facts and provide additional details." Harper hesitated, glancing at the DA. "You're also here so both Ms. Andrews and I can ask questions. I want to emphasize the importance of your answering the questions truthfully. Do not become intimidated. I know this will be a highly emotional experience for you and others here. I ask you all to keep your emotions in check. Mr. Dupree, do you understand that though you're not under oath, you should respond as though you are?"

"Yes," Benny said. He concentrated on Mooney's instructions and silently repeated, *yes, no, I don't remember* in his mind.

"Okay." Harper picked up a three-foot long pointer. She tapped it against a portion of the image projected on the screen. "Were you in this area of the Cayo Costa beach on the evening and night of June 27th, 1980?"

"Yes."

"Were you in the company of a female who you knew as Mary Nadine Bocelli?"

"Yes."

"Is this area of the beach referred to as Turtle Point?"

"Yes."

"Was your and Miss Bocelli's interest in being there," Harper waved the pointer up and down the beach, "the study of sea turtles and their protection?"

"Yes."

"Did you have an occasion to leave Miss Bocelli alone on the beach?"

"Yes."

Andrews interjected a question. "Mr. Dupree, why did you leave Miss Bocelli?"

Benny looked panicked, but Harper came to his aid. "Make your answer as brief and accurate as possible."

Benny organized his thoughts then explained, "I went to get flashlights from my boat."

Andrews asked, "Why did you need the flashlights?"

"It was getting too dark to see."

"See what?" Andrews asked. Her voice was shrill and impatient.

"Someone had been disturbing the turtles' nests; we wanted to assess damage."

Before Andrews could ask another question, Harper seized control. "Is this where you went to retrieve the flashlights?" She pointed to the cove on the island's bay side and at the spot in the mangroves he'd tied his boat. A line marked the path between the mooring spot and Turtle Point.

"Yes."

Harper asked, "When you left Miss Bocelli, was she alone?"

"Yes."

"Were you aware of any other persons on the beach at that time?"

"No."

"How long were you gone?" Andrews asked.

Benny glanced at Harper who made a slight nod. "About forty-five minutes." Jolynn rose from her chair, walked around the table, and removed the pointer from Harper's hand. The contrast in size and appearance was startling. Harper towered over the petite buxom, pleasantly plump blond. Benny couldn't help bringing an analogy to mind; the eagle eclipsed the hawk beside her. Jolynn tapped the pointer on the line representing the trail. "That path doesn't look like it would take that much time to walk. Does it normally take you forty-five minutes?"

"No."

The DA asked, "Is that the path you took from the beach to your boat?"

Benny was confused. He looked at Harper, but got no help. *Answer honestly.* He said, "Yes and no."

"Explain, please."

"That's the path I'd normally take and tried to run when I went back that night, but I missed a turn and got lost in the mangroves."

"How much extra time did that take you?" Jolynn asked.

Benny glanced at Harper again who made the same slight nod. "About twenty minutes, maybe more."

Jolynn handed the pointer to Harper and returned to her chair. Harper resumed her questions. "You returned to the beach?"

"Yes."

"Did you make it all the way?"

"No."

The DA rolled her eyes and said, "Why don't you put a ring in Dupree's nose, counsel? It would be easier to lead him."

Harper was silent for several seconds. "I thought we had this behind us. This isn't a trial. I'm providing confirmation of the information I've given you in writing, and I'm giving you the opportunity to test. I haven't interfered with your opportunity to do that, have I?"

"No, but this is so transparent," the DA said.

"It's supposed to be. Isn't this what we agreed to?" Harper asked.

The DA grudgingly agreed, "Yes."

"Okay, so pull your pants back up." Harper returned to questioning Benny.

Chapter 136
Fort Myers, Florida
May 2010

Harper painstakingly painted a step by step picture of Benny's actions as he approached where the crime had been committed. As each question brought him closer to the portion where he knew he'd be asked if he attacked the two men, Dupree became more visibly stressed. Seeing growing panic in her client's expression, Harper asked, "What's your favorite TV program?"

Benny looked totally confused. "I ... I ... I ..." he stammered.

"If you can't answer that, what do you want to eat tonight?" Benny sat silent, his eyes spread wide.

"Let's try this. Who do you think is the sexiest movie star you've ever seen?"

Dupree shook his head.

Harper raised her eyebrows as she asked, "If those questions are too hard, just repeat the first question I asked you."

Benny shook his head angrily and said, "Damn it, I'm sorry ..."

"What is this shit?" Andrews asked.

"A demonstration. I wanted you to see Mr. Dupree's reaction when under the stress of an unexpected event." Harper pointed to the spot on the screen where the attack occurred. "Take that fact into consideration as we progress." Jolynn grimaced. She knew she'd taken the bait.

"You said you saw Miss Bocelli lying on the ground. Were you sure she was dead?"

"No."

"Were the two men preparing to bury Miss

Bocelli?"

"Yes."

The sound of sobs came from the two women at the end of the table, but their faces still weren't visible to Benny.

"You said you grabbed the ax and rushed the men. Was your intent to keep them from burying Miss Bocelli?" Harper tapped the spot on the screen.

"Yes."

"Did you have a plan when you went after them?"

"No."

Harper paused, "Now, we're actually to the *fight*. Who did you swing the ax at first?" Dupree remembered Mooney's instruction.

"I don't remember."

"Did you swing the ax straight down or from the side?"

"I don't remember." Benny didn't.

"We've acknowledged your actions resulted in two men's deaths. Could you tell us about the *fight*?" Harper emphasized the last word while looking at the DA.

"I don't remember ... I'm sorry."

"Is it true you were reacting on automatic?"

"I don't know."

"Who attacked you with the knife?"

"I don't remember."

"So you didn't understand that you'd been seriously stabbed until *after* the fight?"

"Yes."

"To shorten this process, you'll find a photo of Mr. Dupree's scar in the papers you received in advance. You also have a copy of the doctor's report from the medical facility that treated the wound. I can have Mr. Dupree disrobe *now* if you have any doubts." Harper waited for an objection. When none was registered, she said, "I'll continue. Mr. Dupree, did you try to ascertain whether Miss Bocelli was alive?"

"Yes."

"Did you do this by checking her carotid artery?"

"Yes."

"I believe this establishes our *reason* for requesting this preliminary inquest. We have already stipulated that Mr. Dupree buried the bodies and did attempt to thwart their discovery. Now we will substantiate our statement of the facts. Two witnesses can support Mr. Dupree's statements. I'll start by asking Mr. Aaron Moses Warrington to answer questions. You have the details concerning Mr. Warrington's residence, etc. Any questions regarding those established facts?"

"No," the DA muttered.

Harper examined the map image projected on the screen. She pointed to a portion of the beach a short distance from where the crime scene had previously been identified. "Mr. Warrington, were you in this area of Cayo Costa the evening and night of June 27th, 1980?"

"Yes, ma'am."

Harper suggested, "Yes or no is fine."

"Yes, ma'am."

Harper lifted one eyebrow at the gentle rebuke. "Okay. When you were there, did you see anything unusual?"

"Yes, ma'am."

"What was it?"

"I saw a few unusual things."

Jolynn smiled, and Harper allowed her face to show she was perplexed. Harper tried again. "Mr. Warrington, did you see any people on the beach?"

"Yes, ma'am."

"Who did you see?"

"I saw two men, I saw a girl, and I saw Benny."

"Did you see them all at the same time or different times?"

"Different times."

Harper shifted her position as she tried to think of a way to shorten the process. When she moved, Dupree looked at the woman who had been identified as Dr. Barlow. As Harper changed position, the woman's head turned to watch Harper. Benny saw Dr. Barlow's features clearly for the first time. Buried in the face he starred at, were the eyes and facial structure he knew. *Nadine Bocelli was sitting at the table.* The perceptive instinct humans are born with that allows them to "feel" someone watching, informed Nadine that eyes were on her. She turned her head looking for the source. When Benny's and her eyes met, she immediately covered her face with her hands. It appeared she was sobbing silently. The girl next to Nadine put her arm around her. The likeness to a thirty year younger Nadine, made Benny believe the girl probably was her daughter.

Though others at the table noticed the interplay and Nadine's reaction, Harper ignored it. She asked Goodun, "Mr. Warrington, who did you see first and what were they doing?"

"I saw Walker Cole and some foreigner dragging a dead turtle."

"Did they have anything else with them?"

"Yes, ma'am."

"What."

"An ax and some buckets."

"Did they see you?"

"No, ma'am."

"What do you think they were doing?"

"Poachin'"

"Did you follow them?"

"Yes, ma'am."

"What did you do next?"

"Watched them."

"Did they see you?"

"No, ma'am."

"What were they doing and what happened?"

Goodun remained silent as he reduced what he had to say to its fewest words. He nodded and said, "They started to butcher the turtle. I'd decided I'd go get my shotgun. I didn't have anything, but a pocket knife and that asshole Cole would kill you like he'd kill a mouse. Besides, we didn't like each other much." Goodun pointed at Harper. "You told me I wasn't gonna have to talk a bunch."

"I'll do my best to get you finished." Harper repositioned herself at the map. "When you left to go back to your cabin, is this the way you went?" She used the pointer to trace a line that zigged and zagged from the crime scene to Warrington's cabin shown on the aerial photo.

"Yes, ma'am."

"You went this way because your boat was broken down at that time?"

"Yes, ma'am."

"Did you see or hear anything else?"

"Yes, ma'am. I heard Cole arguing with Miss Nadine."

"You didn't stop, why?"

"I figured there'd be trouble. There were two of them, and I needed a weapon. I took off running."

"When you came back what did you see?"

"I saw Benny finish burying them."

"When you say Benny you're referring to Mr. Dupree?"

"Yes, ma'am."

"Who are them?"

"Cole and the other feller."

"What did he do next?"

"Cried a bunch. He picked up all the stuff that was lying around and left."

"Why didn't you announce yourself?"

"I'm not sure. I've known Benny since he was a sprout. I didn't want to get him in trouble. That's the best I can do." Goodun wished he'd never agreed to attend the inquest.

"What happened next?"

"I looked around. I was gonna pick up what he missed. Wasn't nothing. I heard groans. Dug where I heard them. It was Miss Nadine. Dug her out of the ground. I did what I was taught in the Marines to help wounded. I carried her back to my place and—"

Harper interrupted, "Mr. Warrington, for clarity purposes, is Nadine Bocelli present in this room ... the person you've referred to as Miss Nadine."

"Yes, ma'am."

"Please point to her."

Goodun pointed to the woman sitting at the tables end. Her face was still buried in her hands.

"Did you know that her name had changed to Dr. Mary Barlow?"

"Yes, ma'am."

"Have you maintained contact with her over the years?"

"Yes, ma'am. Not much, but once every few years."

Harper laid the pointer down. She said, "Thank you, Mr. Warrington, that's—"

"Wait, please. We're not done here. I have some questions for Mr. Warrington." Jolynn got out of her chair, went to the screen, and picked up the pointer. Harper bowed to the DA, motioned with one hand for her to proceed before Harper took a couple steps back. Jolynn pointed to the line on the screen that identified the route Warrington took to his cabin. She asked, "How far is this distance?"

Warrington thought for a few seconds, "Somewheres between three-quarters of a mile and a mile."

"How long did it take you to go to your cabin and return?" Jolynn moved the wooden rod from one end of the route to the other.

"More than a half hour."

"Isn't that a long time to run that distance? A path that's a mile and a half to two miles? Particularly when you're trying to intervene in what proved to be a deadly assault? You said you knew that the Cole man was dangerous and unsavory." The DA was a lion preparing to pounce.

"Well, it ain't a path. It's mostly mangroves and the tide was high. You can go try and see what you can do it in." Several people chuckled at Goodun's put down.

"No path, correct? You climbed through those mangroves? Okay. And, you want us to believe you carried Dr. Barlow that distance?"

"Yes, ma'am. You got to remember, I was thirty years younger then and there wasn't quite as much of Miss Nadine, back then." The chuckles returned.

Jolynn's face reddened. She snapped the pointer to the crime scene location. "Where were you when you saw all this?"

"Off to the right. Behind that cluster of cabbage palms."

"They couldn't see you there?"

"Nobody sees me unless I want them to."

Maggie Stevens interjected, "I can attest to that if you—"

The DA frowned at Maggie and said curtly, "That's not necessary."

"What did the men do to Dr. Barlow when they attacked her?"

Goodun shrugged his shoulders, "Don't know exactly. I know what I fixed up."

Jolynn said slyly, "Then you didn't see them?"

"Didn't say I did."

"Did you see the attack Mr. Dupree made on the

two victims?"

"Didn't say I saw that either." Goodun was thinking how much he'd like to push the DA into a nest of fire ants.

"So you really *don't know what* happened? That's all." Jolynn stepped triumphantly back to her chair.

Harper clapped. "Very good, Ms. Andrews! We'll see the academy hears about your bid for an Oscar." The pine tree and the rose bush glowered at each other for a few seconds before Sheriff Hilliard said, "I see things are getting a little tense," he nodded at Nadine, "and some might need a little composure time before we proceed." He stood. "Let's take ten minutes."

Nadine and the other woman hurried to the door. Benny rose to follow and intercept them. Tom Mooney grabbed his shirt and said, "Now's not the time." Mooney got to his feet and motioned for Benny to follow him. Benny looked around the room. Everyone had evaporated with the exception of the DA and her assistant. Mooney started to the door and said, "Come on. I'll buy you a cup of coffee."

Chapter 137
Fort Myers, Florida
May 2010

"You're done," Mooney said between sips of coffee. Benny and Tom stood in front of a bank of vending machines. Benny looked in his coffee cup as if there might be answers to the myriad of questions that paraded through his mind. They appeared like "crawls" on the bottom of a TV news program. Tom put a hand on Benny Dupree's shoulder. "Sorry, I was supposed to get down to see you this morning and get you ready for what happened in there. There wasn't enough time."

"Why didn't you tell me earlier? You had to know for days." The bitterness in Benny's voice was apparent.

Tom shrugged his shoulders. "When you work for Harper or Harper works for you, there's one way ... the Harper way. She's great at what she does. Harper wins, always, at all costs. But, she doesn't always wear a white hat and ride a white horse." He sipped coffee, said, "This is really bad stuff," and made a face.

Benny shook his head. "This is too much. I'm so damned mixed up." He looked at Tom. "Should I be mad as hell or happy? Was I saved or have I been betrayed? I don't know what to think."

"I'd like to tell you that all your surprises are over; they aren't. And, don't ask, I can't tell you." He took a couple more sips, shook his head, and deposited the remaining coffee and the cup in a waste can. "I can't handle that stuff. Tastes like battery acid."

"Mooney, you can't tell me because Sturgis told you not to?"

"Yes. But on this one, I wouldn't have told you if it were my decision."

Benny snapped at Tom, "I hope you're right about her being good. It doesn't seem smart to antagonize that DA. Harper cut down Jolynn every time she could."

"You're right, she did. That was her strategy." Tom smiled and moved close to Benny's ear. In a low voice he said, "When she has a strong case, Harper demonstrates what it's going to be like in court in front of her opponent's peers. If the opposition doesn't have a strong case, they aren't going to want the humiliation Harper Sturgis will heap on them. By now, Jolynn is looking for ways to get out of that." He took a step back. "Your case will be plea bargained. The only question is whether you get a slap on the wrist or a free pass."

"How can you be sure of that?"

"When you hear what—" There was someone whistling. Down the hall, James McNeal stood outside the conference room door and waved his arm for them to return to the meeting. Tom patted Benny on the back and said, "You're about to find out."

Chapter 138
Fort Myers, Florida
May 2010

Goodun Warrington didn't return, and the man Benny assumed was DA Andrews' assistant was missing from the table. The sheriff restarted the meeting. Hilliard asked for questions, there were none, causing Mooney to wink at Benny. Hilliard said, "We've agreed Mr. Warrington is finished. Ms. Sturgis, we'll start with Dr. Barlow." The woman squirmed in her seat as her name was mentioned.

Harper started her questions to bridge to where Warrington's testimony ended. "Dr. Barlow, for the record, are you also known as Mary Nadine Bocelli?" Harper sat at the table instead of standing by the screen.

"Yes. My maiden name is Mary Nadine Bocelli. I married years ago, and my name is now Mary Nadine Barlow. The Dr. designation is from my doctorate in archaeology from Wisconsin."

"To clarify, do you know Mr. Benedict Dupree and were you acquainted with him during the month of June 1980?" Harper asked.

"Yes, I was."

"How did the two of you become acquainted?"

"I became acquainted with Mr. Dupree when I was studying to be a marine biologist. We met on Cayo Costa where I was studying sea turtles. I intended to write a dissertation on turtle reproduction. The two of us became good friends. Mr. Dupree was my transportation to and from the island."

Harper said, "Is Mr. Dupree in this room now?"

"Yes, he's seated on the opposite end of the table on the same side as me," Nadine said. Her voice quivered slightly.

Harper looked at Jolynn as she asked, "When was the last time you saw or have been in contact with Mr. Dupree?

"On the night of June 27, 1980."

"Mrs. Barlow, earlier you heard the description Mr. Dupree furnished about the interaction you two had that night before the attack." Harper paused and emphasized her next statement. "Did his statements accurately portray what happened?"

"Yes, very accurately."

Harper got up from her chair, approached Nadine, and stood behind her. "I know this may be very difficult. I want you to describe what happened after Mr. Dupree left you until you were in Mr. Warrington's cabin."

Nadine stared straight ahead and remained silent. It appeared to Benny that she purposely was avoiding eye contact with him. She rubbed her forehead and was clearly distressed.

"Do you need more time?" Harper asked.

Nadine took a deep breath and said, "No, I'm ready." She looked at her hands, laid them flat on the table, and started. "After Mr. Dupree went to get the flashlights, I walked up the beach to see if I could find more damaged nests. Some nests were high above the tide line. I was kneeling, looking at a destroyed nest when I heard talking. I looked down the beach and saw the outline of two people dragging something. I had a suspicion what it might be, so I hid, hoping I could confirm what it was."

"Why did you hide?" The DA asked.

"I thought I recognized Walker Cole's voice and I'd been warned he was violent."

Harper nodded and said, "Go ahead, Dr. Barlow."

"I thought they were dragging a person at first then I saw it was a turtle. Before they reached me, they found a path and drug it into the island. They stopped at the spot they'd left other stuff. I followed them to see what they were doing. I stayed hidden behind some sea- grapes. They—"

"Just a second," the DA said and held her hand up in a stopping motion, "From a time standpoint, you must have been at the crime site the same time that Mr. Warrington was there. Did you see him? Did you communicate?" Jolynn left her chair, picked up the pointer and held the tip against the crime scene location on the map, waiting for Nadine's answer. Harper raised an eyebrow but remained silent.

"No. I didn't see him or know he was there. If you move the pointer to the left, that's where the sea-grapes are. Based on what Mr. Warrington said earlier, we came to the clearing from opposite directions and hid on opposite sides."

"Shall we move along?" Harper suggested, "We're verifying what happened during the assaults on Dr. Barlow and her two attackers. The question isn't whether Dr. Barlow or Mr. Warrington is the best suited to join the Seal Team 6."

"Do you want to reach an agreement on this?" Jolynn's voice became shrill. "I need to ask questions. I have to feel sure that what we're agreeing on here is legitimate."

"Fine, I'll be as quiet as a mouse," Harper said.

Mooney nudged Benny with his elbow. He leaned close to Benny's ear and whispered, "You're hearing the fat lady sing."

The DA looked at Nadine and said graciously, "You understand I have a responsibility here. Please continue."

Nadine nodded. She closed her eyes and resumed her tale. "I listened to Cole, and the other man talk about getting more eggs. They also talked about butchering the turtle. It disturbed me a lot. Cole said they needed to go kill another turtle so they could butcher both at the same time. I snapped. I got up and walked into the clearing. I told them to stop. Cole and I had a heated exchange. I don't remember the exact words. The other man moved out of the clearing, and I thought he might be running away. Finally, Cole told me I should haul ass and forget what I'd seen. I told him I'd leave and go straight to the sheriff. That was a mistake. He had been kneeling. Cole got up and came at me with a knife. He stabbed me in the upper arm. I tried to run, and as I turned, he stabbed me in the back. The other man was standing behind me with a shovel, getting ready to hit me. I ducked as he swung, so the shovel hit me on the back of the head and on my neck. I blacked out." Nadine shook and became silent.

"Do you need time, Dr. Barlow?" the sheriff asked.

She shook her head. "What do you want next?"

"Start with the next thing you remember." Harper looked at Jolynn as if soliciting agreement and the DA nodded.

"The next thing would be when I felt them burying me in the sand. I kept becoming half-conscious then falling back." Nadine took a deep breath. "I heard Cole and the other man talking about how ... how to keep people from smelling my body." She shook and took several seconds to compose her emotions. She glanced at Benny and quickly looked away. "I was half-awake and afraid to say anything because I knew they'd finish killing me. I tried moving, but couldn't and passed out. Then I woke up when I heard Benny, that's Mr. Dupree, scream then yell 'Leave her alone.' I heard them fighting, yelling, and cursing. I tried calling out, but nothing happened. I tried to move, there was pain and I passed out."

The DA asked, "I know this is difficult. Do you remember anything said during the fight?"

"Just a few snatches. Mr. Dupree yelled *murder*. I heard Cole scream *kill him*. Most were just...like animals snarling. I heard blows. Like I said, I became unconscious."

"What happened next?" Harper asked, regaining control.

"I woke again and realized I was covered with sand. I didn't want to die that way. There was no way for me to know who won. I was frightened they still might be there. I figured maybe they'd dig me up and finish the job if I made noise. I started to lose consciousness, so I tried to yell. I passed out again. The next time I gained consciousness, Mr. Warrington was carrying me. I remember him telling me I'd be okay. I remember I asked him who he was, but I passed out again before he answered. When I woke in Mr. Warrington's place I—"

Harper interrupted, "Dr. Barlow, I believe that's all you need to say. This is very painful, and I appreciate you coming and suffering through what is a horrible memory. At this point, everything we can learn about Mr. Dupree's actions on that night is clear." She looked at the DA. "Do you agree that we're finished with those who have testified?"

"I have one question and I'll be satisfied ... for now." Jolynn looked at Nadine and asked, "You said you hadn't had contact with Mr. Dupree. You're saying he had no knowledge you were still alive." She looked at Harper and held her hand up to keep her silent. "So, Mr. Dupree believed you to be buried on Cayo Costa, correct?"

"As far as I know, he did not know I was alive until today."

The DA asked, "Given the relationship between

Mr. Dupree and yourself and your knowledge of him, what part of his actions was a misguided effort to protect your body and what part was to cover-up his killing your attackers."

"I can't tell you—"

Harper stopped Nadine from making additional comments saying, "Dr. Barlow, you've answered Ms. Andrews' *one* question. At this point, I believe District Attorney Andrews, Sheriff Hilliard, and I have enough information to resolve this without the need for the rest of you to be present. Do you agree, Sheriff?"

"Yep."

"Ms. Andrews?"

"I do." Jolynn looked resigned, but said, "I'd like to reserve the right to discuss this with all those from whom we've received testimony, or whatever you'd like to call it if something comes to light that needs explanation. And, I'd like to keep them in separate areas. I share your desire to dispose of this today, Counselor Sturgis. I believe those requests will allow me to do that."

"Fine, if they all agree," Harper said.

"I'll speak for my people. That's okay with them." The sheriff asked, "Mr. Dupree?"

"Yes."

"Dr. Barlow, is that okay?" The sheriff inquired.
"Yes."

Harper said, "I'll speak for Mr. Warrington. He'll return, but there will be a delay. He's on the way back to the island. Hopefully, we can do this without him."

The sheriff said, "Okay. Maggie will you take Dr. Barlow to a room and James will you take Mr. Dupree to a different one." He addressed Benny and Nadine, "You can have your people with you."

"Mr. Dupree, you're going to be released," James McNeal said after he entered the room where Benny awaited his fate. "Your lawyer will be in here to get you in a little while."

"Do you know—"

"No. They don't share that stuff with the non-coms. Your lawyer will have all the details. I can tell you that you wouldn't be walking out of here if things hadn't gone well for you." James walked to Benny as he got up from his chair. "The lady asked me to give you this." McNeil handed a folded note to Benny. "She's already left."

Benny opened it and read.

~ ~ ~ ~ ~

Dear Benny,

I am sorry for keeping this secret from you. I will explain. Hopefully, you'll be able to forgive me. Please, give me a few days. I'll contact you and, if you're willing, we will meet. Do not blame Goodun. I swore him to secrecy. Unlike most people, that wonderful man can keep his word.

Nadine

~ ~ ~ ~ ~

Chapter 139
Fort Myers, Florida
May 2010

Harper and Tom came to get Benny after an hour, but what felt like multiple lifetimes to Dupree. Harper motioned for Benny to stay seated. Tom and Harper joined him at the table.

Harper said, "I've got good news. The DA accepted your self-defense plea. You'll be charged with some dirty-drinking-fountain offenses. Failure to report stuff, that kind of thing. Don't worry about that. It's going to be plea bargained. I'll see you don't spend time in jail. That's the good part." Harper stopped talking and fixed Benny's pupils with hers. "I want you to listen very carefully. The big problem you *still* have is all those vultures flying around with press credentials that are looking for something spectacular to broadcast or publish about this. Keep your mouth shut. Never discuss what happened that night or anything connected to it with anyone. No one. Not with friends. Nobody. Don't get sweet talked. Don't trust anyone. Don't let anybody bully or bluff you. Drink alone. We know what the DA accepted was close to what happened, but not exact. You know that old cliché about horseshoes and hand grenades. It applies. *Keep your mouth shut!*"

"I understand," Benny said.

"You'd better. Particularly, until they find out what happened to those two missing boys."

"What about Goodun and Nadine?" Benny asked.

"Warrington is one of the few people I've ever met that I'd trust with my deepest secret." Harper nodded. "He's an honorable man. It's a shame there are so damned few of them. As far as Nadine is concerned, she doesn't want to see you hurt. Keep it that way."

"I owe you my life."

"Yes and a pile of money. But, we'll discuss that with you at a later date. I'm exploring possibilities with Dr. Barlow in regard to recovering some ... let's call it inheritance ... you put in a good word, and if that is successful, the pile may be considerably smaller."

Chapter 140
Pine Island, Florida
June 2010

Benedict Dupree found out how difficult and complicated his life had become in the next few days. Anywhere he went, he drew stares, the focus of unwanted attention. Old friends tried to be normal, but strain was evident in voices, faces, and actions. Even Billy MacCardle was a bit uneasy during their first few meetings and discussions. Mac's lack of comfort centered about doing something that would disturb Benny. That quickly faded.

Dupree found it difficult to go to Durkin's for breakfast and feel comfortable. Even waitress Elise found it impossible not to sneak curious peeks at the person who had become one of the communities' controversies. The reaction was magnified at other places.

The press deluged Benny with requests for interviews. He rejected them all. Relief came when the sheriff released the news that the two high school boy's remains had been discovered stuffed in submerged crab traps. Local fishermen recognized who made the crab traps, and in turn, the man identified the person to whom he'd sold them, Foreman. A portion of the press pressure gravitated to the sheriff.

The greatest mental inferno in his life was *not* his status as an infamous person. It was awaiting the promised meeting with Nadine. Benny interpreted a few days as three or four. A week came and went. All was silent. Ten days found Benny's anticipation so distracting he found it difficult to work or consider anything except his reunion with Nadine. He considered contacting her. Benny read Nadine's failure to communicate with him as either guilt for her decision to let him believe she was dead or her feeling he had abandoned her at a critical time. Stress multiplied. Benny was virtually a prisoner in his home and office. His emotional state was at its snapping point. His true friends, Corrine and Billy MacCardle, were life preservers that permitted him to remain sane. He considered going to the island, seeing Goodun, and perhaps, staying with him. Benny wasn't sure what reception he'd receive, though he believed it would be the same. Goodun was a friend, and as Harper said, an honorable man. His doubts paralyzed him.

Benny didn't know where Nadine was staying, or if she'd remained in the area. His hope of reaching her was through Harper Sturgis. Harper contacted him to tell him when he had to appear in court and she gave him instructions on his appearing in public. Her counseling: "Don't! Not between now and your court date." When Benny talked to Sturgis, he believed Nadine would contact him so he'd remained silent. Now, his hand hovered over the phone as desire fought doubt. The phone rang as an answer.

The LED screen displayed an unfamiliar number. Benny answered, "Hello," knowing Corrine had screened the call.

"It's Harper. I've got a couple of things to go over with you. I'm getting ready to leave the country and don't have much time. You have something to write with?"

Benny answered, "Yes".

"Okay. First, I need the names of three character witnesses for the hearing. They need to swear you won't be a flight risk if you're on probation, don't regularly engage in criminal behavior, don't beat dogs, run naked through the park, that kind of thing. Putting you on probation makes having your character supported a requirement. I want to be sure I don't get surprises. You call them first and be sure they're true foxhole mates. I'll put them on the witness list, and I'll call them also, but I won't have time to look for alternates. You don't want me doing that at the rates I charge."

"I'll provide three I've contacted and I'm sure will be very positive. And, I'll have at least one alternate."

"Good. Number two. I've sent you a partial billing. It's large, but your problem is large."

"I'm not complaining."

"Tell me that after you see it. I'm going to Europe and Tom's going with me. Write down the phone number you see on your LED screen. Supposedly, it will provide coverage where I'm going. If you can't get me, leave a message with Gertie in our office. I'll get back with you."

Benny copied the number and said, "Okay, I've got it."

"Last thing. Dr. Barlow is ready to meet with you. Are you ready to see her?"

"Yes!"

"I want you to know I tried to talk her out of this, but couldn't. She wants to meet you at Mr. Warrington's cabin tomorrow, 10:00 AM. I'd suggest you *not use your boat*; the media are sure to be looking for it. Contact Mac and ask him to take you out there. Do some cloak and dagger when you meet Billy to shake anybody that's trying to follow. Also, you're not going to be alone. Warrington and Barlow's daughter will be there. Still, okay?"

"Yes."

"I hope you both get something positive from it. You *might* be rushing this, but I *might* be wrong. Good luck. Now, you need to wish me good luck. Know why?"

"No idea."

"The size of your subsequent bills depends on the luck and success I have on my trip to Italy."

Chapter 141
Cabbage Key Cut, Cayo Costa Island Florida,
June 2010

Billy "Mac" MacCardle idled his boat up to Goodun Warrington's dock. Goodun, Nadine, and the woman Harper confirmed was Nadine's daughter walked out on the pier. Only 150 feet from touching, details of the three individual's appearances were clearly visible to Benny, Nadine's for the first time.

Benny strained his eyes. Goodun's gaunt form was little changed from its outline Benny remembered as a ten-year-old, forty years before. The inscrutable features would be the same, so Benny wasted no time looking at his face.

It was hard not to spend time looking at Nadine's daughter. Pictures of the woman and Nadine at the same age would have been hard to differentiate. Genetics were definitely at work for the almost cartoonish body curves the girl possessed spurred memories he felt were inappropriate, but could not suppress. The daughter was a clone right to the smile she exhibited on the boat's approach.

Nadine stood several feet from Goodun and her daughter. It was evident her isolation was purposeful. Nadine's bright auburn hair was streaked with gray, the eyes were the same, but carried sadness not evidenced when Benny had known her. The beautiful girl was now a handsome mature woman, one easily recognizable as the finished version of the youthful person he remembered. Heavier than in her youth, she'd maintained the curves and, given her heritage, had only succumbed slightly to the middle age spread. Benny thought the years had been kind to her. Though he didn't know it, the mixture of anxiety and anticipation on her face was mirrored in his.

"Are you ready for this?" Mac asked.

"Yes. I know this won't make sense to you, but I want this, and I'm scared at the same time." Benny raised his hand and waved. The people on the dock waved back.

"It's the unknown." Mac put his hand on Benny's shoulder. "Remember, for good or bad, the *first meeting* on something like this comes, and it's over. You won't go through this again."

The boat glided the final thirty feet before Mac reversed the engine controlling the boat so deftly the touch of the gunwale against the piling was barely perceptible.

Nadine walked down the pier to a spot next to the boat's bow. She said, "Hi." Her smile was forced and unsure. "May I come aboard?" She stepped down on the front deck's fiberglass without waiting for an answer. "I'm Nadine," she said as she walked back to Mac and offered her hand.

"Billy MacCardle. Most folks call me Mac." He took her hand and shook it.

"Oh Benny," she said softly, "It's been so long." She walked up to him, hesitated then embraced him lightly.

"It has," he said as his arms circled her. Their contact reassured them both. They separated after a few seconds.

"I know I shouldn't ask favors after just making your acquaintance, Mac, but I'd like to be alone with Benny for a while. Could you take us to the walk through to Turtle Point?"

Mac looked at Benny and received his nod. "Sure," Mac said.

"I'll stay here. I know you want to be by yourselves. If any visitors show up, I'll make two blasts on my air horn." Mac nosed the boat's bow into the small area where the mangroves were kept cut back to access the path that crossed the island to Turtle Point. It hadn't changed in the thirty years since Nadine and Benny last walked the sandy path. Familiar feelings from shared memories of the trail smoothed the bristling spines the unknown thrust at them as they ducked under limbs and wound through the mangroves woods. "Careful," Benny warned.

"I will be. I tore a hole in one of Goodun's shirts when he brought us out here." Nadine moved deliberately heeding Benny's warning. They walked in silence, for the most part, neither of them possessing the starting words for the conversation that had to come. When they reached the portion of the island where mangrove gave way to cabbage palms, pines, sea-grapes, and grass clumps, Nadine said, "It's a longer hike than I remembered."

"It gets longer on each of my birthdays," Benny observed.

Nadine chuckled. She trudged ahead of Benny. Perspiration dampened her blouse and rolled down her neck. "Another thing that hasn't changed is the summer heat."

Benny answered, "You're right. Summer equals heat, bugs, and rain." It was small talk, but it was the best they could do until the moment they knew they must face. Benny followed Nadine's steps as the surf's gentle roar became louder.

They neared the beach. Benny asked, "Where do you want to go?"

"The sand dune behind Turtle Point, if that's

okay. I don't want to go anywhere near ..." She didn't finish her sentence. There was no need to.

Chapter 142
Turtle Point, Cayo Costa Island, Florida
May 2010

They sat on the sand dune as they had so often, but so long ago. The midday sun beat on them, but their discomfort, their torture emanated from within. Nadine starred at the aquamarine waters of the Gulf. She searched for a way to start. "I've missed the sea. Cody, Wyoming is so far away from any ocean. I guess once you spend a lot of time around saltwater the sodium seeps into your blood. You need it. You may not be able to do anything about it, but the need is still there. There are some of the most beautiful places in the world where I live. The Grand Tetons, Yellowstone, places like that, but it isn't the Atlantic or the Gulf. That make sense, Benny?"

"Yes, there are places, things, people that become part of us." Benny nodded but purposely looked out on the Gulf.

"There's a time when you can't put off doing what has to be done. I'm at that point." Nadine picked up a handful of sand and let it drain between her fingers like the grains in an hourglass. She used the time to organize her thoughts. "I'm sure that you can't understand why I never let you know that I survived. I'll try to explain."

"You don't have to explain anything to me. If I hadn't left you alone on the beach, the whole thing wouldn't have happened. I could—"

"No, no, no, Benny. You had no way of knowing who was there. Besides, you warned me about Cole. I wasn't smart enough to avoid confronting him. All I had to do was stay quiet. They wouldn't have been able to find and kill another turtle before you returned. And if they did, Irish and Italian tempers are hot individually. Combine them and you ... I ... do things I regret. Please, let me tell you what I have to, while I have the courage to do it. Please!"

Benny looked at her, nodded, and returned his eyes to the sea.

"You know what happened there." Nadine shivered as she pointed to the spot where she'd been buried. "Goodun carried me back to his place. Seeing it—I don't know how. I walked it with him the other day. Carrying me made it very slow going. I'd wake up and pass out. He says I tried to fight with him a couple times. I don't remember. All the time, I was losing blood. Goodun put a tourniquet on my arm. If he hadn't, I'd have bled to death. By the time we made it to his cabin, I was in very bad condition. I woke up one time when we got there. I remember pleading with him not to take me to a hospital. The next time I woke was two days later. Goodun hadn't left my side. The first thing I remember was wondering where I was. I thought I was in a bar. Goodun used whiskey to disinfect my wounds when he ran out of alcohol. The stab wound in my arm was the worst. It went through my bicep and hit an artery. The stab wound on my back was long and shallow. Cole stabbed me there as I ducked. The blade hit a rib and slid along it, not between. It looked bad, but it wasn't nearly as serious as my arm. Goodun wanted to go to the ranger station for help. I told him if he took me to a hospital and my identity was discovered, the people looking for me would locate me, and I'd be no better off than if he'd left me in the ground. He believed me, thank goodness because Heller and Borollio were close to tracking me down. In addition, I convinced him that it would be a disaster for you if the authorities found out you killed those men. If I testified for you, it would have only been a matter of time before Heller found me."

She became quiet. Nadine turned to face him. Benny turned his body ninety degrees, so he faced her. He said, "Nadine, I can understand your fear of Heller and his friends, but after you got away, went off to where ever you hid, why didn't you let me know?"

"I had another problem. One my conscience wouldn't allow me to share with you. One that another of my decisions made on impulse created. It's one that has caused me guilt-ridden sleepless nights. It added pain to what I realized you must think and be going through because of me." Nadine moved closer to Benny. She placed her hands on each of his cheeks. "I hope you and God can forgive me, for what I did."

Tears streamed down her cheeks. Nadine looked at the sand between them. In a low voice, she said, "My daughter's name is Natalie Dupree Ryan-Barlow. She's your daughter, too. I took the name of a relative I stayed with. When I married a man named Sam Barlow, he adopted her."

"Does she know abo—" Benny's face was flushed but kept control of the visible part of his emotions, emotions that were exploding inside.

"No. I almost told her when Sam died ten years ago. I decided against it. She's like me. She'd have tracked you down. Goodun and I have occasionally kept in touch. At that time, he told me you were married, and I couldn't have that happen to you. I caused enough turmoil in your life. Before you ask, I never told Goodun about Natalie." She looked up into his eyes with her water drenched pools of green. "I'm so sorry."

Benny's smile grew slowly, like a seed fighting its way through the restraining ground, until it shed earth's restraints, and emerged, fresh and prepared for its bountiful future. He stood and extended both hands to assist Nadine to her feet. She complied. As they stood toe to toe, Benny placed his arms around Nadine's shoulders, gently pulled her close to him, and kissed her forehead for a gentle prolonged minute. Nadine's arms circled his torso and she pulled tight against him.

Benny released her gently. He leaned away and said, "If you don't mind, I'd like to get to know my daughter so you and I can figure how and when to tell her."

Nadine smiled through the tracks of her tears and nodded her assent. Benny offered her his hand. She grasped it and both squeezed softly. Side-by-side, their feet made another set of prints in the sands of Turtle Point, away from the storm in their past, to the east where the sun would rise in the morning.

Epilogue
The Iron Lady

Harper Sturgis and Tom Mooney stepped off the shuttle bus in front of their hotel in Grosseto, a pretty little city in Tuscany. Tom looked at the front of the Hotel Granduca. "Looks just like the Internet picture," he said. "I hope the breakfast is good."

"We're halfway around the world, we've just ridden through a city with medieval roots, circled by a wall built by one of the Medici, and your most profound observation is about eggs, bread, or cereal?" Harper's face showed the slightest bit of disbelief, but that quickly faded. "Tom, your plebian side never ceases to amaze me."

Three uniformed men approached. One asked, "Signora Sturgis?" Harper responded, "Si."

"Benvenuti per Grosseto," he replied.

Harper answered in excellent Italian, "Grazie. Dove si trova una guida turistica?"

The bellman smiled, ordered his two assistants to take Harper and Tom's suitcases inside then answered whatever question Harper had asked. Harper was comfortable with the flood of Italian which was incomprehensible to Tom. He asked, "What did you say to him?"

"I thanked him for welcoming us and asked where we could find a tour guide."

"You understand what he said?"

"Si. That's yes in Italian and Spanish."

"What's the word for no?"

"No."

"Hell, I practically speak the language."

Harper looked at Tom critically. "There's a disk in my bags. I'd suggest you try to learn a few words.

It might be very useful if you want to do anything, or *anybody,* by yourself."

"I'll be fine for as long as we'll be here. Besides, I'm sure I'll find some locals that speak English. What's next?" Tom leered at a striking blonde that gave him a sideways glance as she went through the hotel's front door.

"Don't forget Tom Hank's advice from *A League of Their Own.* Avoid the clap," Harper remarked.

"What's next?" Tom persisted.

"Check us in. Rent us a car. See if you can find out where we can rent a truck." Harper paused for a few seconds. "I don't know how long I'll be, so you're on your own. You could check out restaurants. Try asking that blonde pastry that just went inside. Judging from the width of her *derriere* she hasn't missed many meals." Harper's marble mask didn't provide Tom a clue whether she was serious or not.

"I'll take care of the rooms, the car, and see what hauling capability is available." He winked at the boss and added, "I might check to see if that pastry is Danish."

The man sitting at the tour agency desk took the cross Harper handed him. He turned it over and examined it carefully. After several seconds of thought, he said, "I'm sorry, I don't recognize it. I'm sure there are no churches or cemeteries right in Grosseto that are marked by a cross that looks like this replica. It is unique. But, since you said it was during the war, your uncle was wounded here, and came in possession of this, I will ask Rosa. She was a child then, but might remember if it was on a structure destroyed in the war." He walked to another desk and showed the cross to a gray-haired lady. After a few minutes, he returned.

"I'm sorry, she doesn't recognize it. She says it might be atop of a gravestone. But, that doesn't make sense if he took shelter there. And, it would be strange to have a replica made of that. I have a suggestion. Go to the Grosseto Cathedral and seek out Father Paul Antonio. He is a local historian. This area has a rich past. The war, the Sienans, the Medicis, the Romans, the Etruscans, and even before them; all these have their unique points of interest. I know he is especially interested in religious artifacts. If anyone in Grosseto would know, it would be him.

I'll mark a map for you." He picked up a sheet of paper with the map of Grosseto printed on it. The guide drew some lines on the map with a marker and handed it to her. "This will get you to the cathedral and back to your hotel."

"Do I just ask for him?" Harper said.

"Yes, that would be best. Tell whoever you speak to that Guido from the travel agency sent you to find Father Paul Antonio. But, if *you* see a priest, *you* have to look up to, *way up to*, that is Father Paul Antonio."

Harper entered the iconic Romanesque structure. She was impressed by the features and artifacts that adorned the exterior and interior. The marble façade and decorative items she judged to be vintage 14th century, including Evangelists symbols outside, and the interior, which was configured like a Latin cross, with an elaborate carved baptismal font and the *Madonna delle Grazie* by Matteo di Giovanni gave the church a second ambiance as a museum.

It wasn't necessary for her to ask for Father Paul Antonio. The travel agent's description was accurate and left no doubt who she was looking for. The man was close to seven foot tall. He stood in one of the nave aisles next to an ornate cruciform pilaster. The two priests standing by him were dwarfed.

Harper examined the priest's face as she approached him. His features radiated friendliness, and his mischievous eyes twinkled. She thought the man would look more at home in an NBA uniform than in the holy man's robes he wore. All three clergymen looked at her when she was close to them, and, in a less than priestly manner. They wore what Harper called shit-eating grins. Even males in the employ of the highest deity were subject to natures laws. She said, "Good afternoon, Fathers. I hope that's the proper method to address you all."

"That's fine," one of the clerics said.

The tall priest asked, "How may we help you?"

Harper said, "If you're Father Paul Antonio, I'd like to talk to you. A local travel agent, Guido, suggested I see you in regard to this." She held the cross out to him.

His face changed completely. Serious and focused he told his brothers, "Would you be so kind as to let me speak with this lady, privately?" The two priests made hasty parting words and melted away.

"Please come with me." The priest led her to an alcove and invited her to sit down. He asked, "What would you like to ask?"

"The agent said you might be able to tell me its origin or where this came from in Grosseto." Harper told her cover story. "I had an uncle that was wounded in the war and took refuge in a place that was connected to this cross. I'm trying to find it."

"May I see the cross again?"

Harper handed it to him. He examined it carefully before saying, "I've only see a few of these." Father Paul Antonio turned it over in his hands, handling it as though it was a precious egg. "You say this came into your possession from a soldier? And, he told you it was from the city of Grosseto?"

"Yes, it came from my uncle, a soldier in 1945. I'm not sure where it came from in the town."

"You're an American? Your accent—"

"Yes." Harper acknowledged.

"I know where it came from and what it is. To most people owning one of these, they would part with their life before losing ownership of it."

"Can you tell me more about it?" Harper didn't show the surprise she felt.

"I'll have to bore you with some history." The priest folded his elongated body into the pew next to Harper. "Grosseto is an old city, ancient by new world standards. Its history precedes Etruscan and Roman civilizations. What you have doesn't date quite that far back. It does tell a story of one of history's darkest eras. You have a medal that dates back to around 1348. Grosseto was a city fought over by medieval rulers and feudal principalities. It was an agricultural and trading center that had the added economic resource of ancient salt mines near it. Thousands of families lived in it. In 1348 the era of pestilence, the plague struck the city. By 1349 disease had decimated the population to a few hundred families."

Father Paul Antonio returned the cross to her. He pointed at it. "What you have is a blessed medal given to families of plague victims. It was to protect them from further ravages of the black-death. The cross you have is from the area near a community in the mountains named Scansano. That area and its neighbor, Magliano, were internment areas for a thousand years. Magliano is famous for its tombs. When the plague struck Grosseto, and the bodies had to be disposed of, many were sent to this area and buried in tombs that were already in existence. The cross you have represents an old and abandoned church in that region, one that housed black-death victims. I'm not familiar with all of its burial ground, but I know there is an extensive number of huge tombs at the old abbey. The reason why the abbey and a few other sites were abandoned was the very real fear the disease would spread from the tombs. To combat that, salt was hauled from the mines and used to seal the entrances. Fear was so great that those burying the dead were sometimes ambushed on their return, so they couldn't infect other city dwellers. When the disease struck villagers near the tombs, they were sealed, the churches were abandoned, and they remain landscape pariahs to this day. Their only use is as settings for local ghost stories. No one visits them. It is entirely possible a wounded soldier could hide there, but I doubt if the medal came from the church."

"How did you identify the medal so quickly?" Harper asked.

"The cross is a miniature of the one that sits atop the abbey. Its name is the *Church of the Blessed Cross*. Are you planning to visit it?"

"Yes. Is it difficult to find?"

"It would be for you. I would tell you to try to get someone from Scansano to take you, but there are so many wild stories about the tombs that most villagers won't go there. The locals call the burial site, *tombe strillanti*; that means the screaming graves. I can give you instructions. The roads are twisty but aren't bad most of the way. It is mountainous, and the church and the abandoned dwellings around it can't be seen from the road. A peak hides them. The cart path going back to the abbey was blocked by the Italian Army during the war for some reason. Anyone who goes there rides in on a donkey. The road is a dead end. I've never figured out why the military had any interest. I would take you there, but my duties make it several days before I can go. The directions aren't difficult except for finding the path. It can be frightening, and there are some thugs in the area so it can be dangerous. I am reticent to tell you."

A flicker of excitement passed over Harper's face. She looked the father in his pupils and said, "Father, you've dedicated yourself to a lifetime of peace. I dedicated mine to something very different. I was in the military for twenty years. An individual who tries to do me harm would quickly regret his effort. Please give me the directions. You don't have to concern yourself regarding my safety."

Father Paul Antonio saw the steel backing the pupils he starred into. "I'll fear for those who try to harm you." He stood. "If you'll wait here, I'll write the directions down. I believe I can print a map from my computer and mark it as well." He hesitated for a moment before leaving and said, "I admire your dedication to the memory of your, was it your father?"

"No, my uncle."

"I wish you success in accomplishing whatever you are...doing. I'll be right back."

"Do you want me to go with you?" Tom Mooney asked.

Harper sipped her coffee. She looked at the bowl of fruit and bread on a plate in front of her. Sturgis acted as though she hadn't heard Tom speak. "What do you think? Is the breakfast up to your standards?"

"Coffee is very good, but I'm a bacon and eggs man."

"So order them." Harper took another sip and put her cup down. "No, you stay here. Firm up the truck."

"Remember what that priest warned you."

"Colt and I will be just fine." She motioned in the hotel parking lot's direction. "I hope that little bug I'm driving will get me there."

"Best I could do," Tom lied. "Are you comfortable with the directions?"

"An idiot could follow them up to the point I have to find the trail back to the abbey. Father Paul gave me lots of landmarks to help with that. I take Via Senese from here into Grosseto and turn east on highway SP159. That's most of it. What are you going to do?"

Tom smiled. "I have a date with the Danish pastry."

Father Paul Antonio's directions were impeccable. She rounded the mountain's steep slope, and as the priest stated, the abbey was nestled on a flat spot of land with one side flush against a cliff. The stonework was anything but the imposing quality Harper saw in the churches she passed on the trip up the mountain. Its architecture was basic and fit the capabilities dark ages artisans working on a building designed for peasants' use, would have.

Gravel crunching under her feet provided the only sound. A multitude of weed generations grew in the cart path and on the surrounding terrain, proclaiming the area was abandoned. Remnants of a half-dozen homes were perched on a ledge below the church. At their zenith, they could have been called modest at best. Now only a few walls remained. Harper could understand why no attempt to reclaim the spot had occurred. The only area level enough to garden was so covered with rocks, returning it to tillable soil would be impractical.

Even if energetic and determined families

decided to attempt the daunting task of making the ground agriculturally feasible, getting to the land was a major obstacle. When Father Paul Antonio told her the path to the abbey had been blocked by the Italian army, Harper visualized a couple loads of gravel dumped on it. Not so! Huge granite blocks filled the trail at the point it had been carved from a cliff. Nearly vertical surfaces buttressed both sides. The boulders were stacked higher than her head. Though not impassable, it required strenuous and dangerous effort to get past. The elaborate effort to deter people from entering encouraged her. It was exactly what someone who was hiding something would do to keep its existence unknown.

The exertion caused by climbing the boulders started perspiration to flow. Harper wasn't dressed for the beach. Though brisk mountain breezes helped moderate the hot summer sun, its rays heated the brown work shirt she wore like a jacket, covering her tee. Her jeans were worn in anticipation of dirty work she expected. GI boots and a fatigue hat that hid her long black hair capped both ends. The brown shirt hid a large knife that hung from her belt, a flashlight that was tucked under it, and her Colt .45 that rested in a shoulder holster.

Harper stopped to take a mental picture of the structure she was approaching. The *Church of the Blessed Cross* was a large flat rectangle with a gable that had supported a roof, non-existent for hundreds of years. Crude construction featured no front windows with the building's only decoration being a large circular carving of the Madonna and Child. Typical of the period when the building was erected, the doors were low reflecting the diminutive height of humans of its time. The wood panels that had hung in the opening were gone. Located in the center of the building's front, Harper saw the door opening as the mouth of an animal that ate those who entered. She stored the impression in her memory bank.

Mounted on the gable's crest was the cross that matched the miniature one she carried in her pocket. The ornate design of circles and flourishes was precisely copied. It was amazing to Harper that a society that provided so little to its members would create something so costly as a talisman. She reflected for a second. Faith was one of the few things the poor of the time, had.

Representing belief with something of value made sense. She resumed walking.

A wing of the abbey extended from the main church building to the mountain. The vertical cliff formed one wall. Above this portion of the church's structure stood the campanile or bell tower, its resident having been pilfered in the long ago past.

Climbing the six steps to the entrance, Harper ducked slightly to go inside. Her heart dropped. There was practically nothing inside. Even wood from the fallen roof had been scavenged for fuel by locals. A few mounds of trash dotted the sun-bleached terracotta floor. She saw what looked like helmets piled in the abbey's wing that abutted the mountain face. Disappointment flooded over her as she surveyed her surroundings. Harper didn't see anything the key in her pocket could be used to open. "Think logically," she said aloud. Tombs were what she was looking for and, logically, they'd be excavated in the mountainside. Harper walked toward the wall built against the mountain.

A small portion of the roof remained where the church attached to the cliff, bathing the area in shadow. Harper saw the area showed signs of human visitation in the current century. Half-dozen helmets like those worn by Italian soldiers in World War II were in a pile along with parts of an MG-42, a

German machine gun. All were damaged beyond use, but the fact they were still there attested to how few visitors the abbey entertained.

It was then that Harper heard it. She stopped. A muffled wail came from the wall ahead of her. It didn't sound human, but since no one was near, Harper cautiously approached the wall. The noise would disappear then start again, changing in volume and pitch. *Tombe strillanti*, the screaming graves. What inspired fear in the local inhabitants, made Harper curious.

When Harper was within ten feet of the wall, an unaccustomed smile curled her lips. One panel was of much more recent vintage than its mates. The panel to its right was ancient, had a large slot in it, and strap hinges across its width; she'd seen pictures of doors like what she was looking at in books. She read the Latin inscription above it. "Here rest the dead." That panel concealed the tomb's opening.

In the center of the "new" panel, a large square of dust encrusted canvas hung. Words were printed on its surface. Harper recognized the device as one used to provide protection for posted orders in past years military organizations. The words translated from their Italian spellings stated, *Caution – Quarantined – Lift And Read*.

Harper reached to raise the canvas. The muffled wail from behind the wall resumed at the same time a cool breeze brushed the back of her neck. It froze her for a second. She muttered, "Bull-shit," and lifted the cover despite the protest screams of "souls" from the tomb. The breeze stopped and so did the ghostly objections. Harper said, "Oh, yes." A stack of death certificates like those she'd seen in Heller's notebook hung under the canvas. Where was the drawer or cabinet that was waiting for the key to unlock its mystery?

She examined the wall around where the canvas hung. Harper found nothing. It was a solid wooden panel; no hidden doors, no removable strips, nothing to provide further access. Harper was about to scour other parts of the wall when she decided to see if there were any instructions she'd missed under the canvas. When she lifted the stack of death certificates, the door to a hidden compartment was exposed. The lock and latch built into it was the right size and the made in the right time period to be the one she sought. Harper removed Nadine's key from her jeans and was excited when it was a perfect fit.

Frustration followed. More than sixty years had "frozen" the mechanism. Twisting to the point, she was concerned that she might shear off the key, didn't work. Harper was perplexed.

She prided herself in her ability to foresee problems and prepare in advance. "You dumb bitch," she admonished herself. She shook her head. If someone said that to her, she'd break their skull. "Now what?" Harper mumbled. She placed her mouth over the keyhole and blew saliva into the opening as forcefully as she could. Harper used the butt of her knife as a hammer, tapping around the lock mechanism. Rocking the key back and forth a few times did nothing until she exerted a slight bit more pressure and the key turned. The compartment door opened.

Inside the opening was an item she immediately recognized from research she'd done. Harper saw the turnkey device in history texts. She reached in, grabbed the "J" shaped device, and pulled, maneuvering the three-foot long bar through the small opening. The slot in the adjacent wall panel accommodated the curved portion of the "J" and the long lever portion was designed to provide enough force to slide open the bar mechanism that kept the door from opening.

After a quick check for some type of booby trap, Harper inserted the turnkey in the slot, prepared for a Herculean effort, but the bar slid with little force. She was ready for the moment of truth as the shrieking from inside started again. "Shut up," she said and pulled against the turnkey. The door opened enough that she grasped its edge with her fingers. Harper braced a foot against the wall and pulled the door open.

Tom recognized Harper's number when he answered his cell phone. Before he could say hello, Harper asked, "Where have you been?"

"Entertaining Denmark. Having trouble finding the church?"

"No."

"Well? What's up?"

Harper inhaled loud enough for him to hear. "Forget the truck, Tom. We need a convoy."

"Holy shit! You found it! The son-of-a-bitching story was true!" Tom flopped down on the bed he'd been standing beside.

"Yes and then some." Harper paused. "Guess what I'm doing. I'm loading that empty suitcase I took with gold bars."

"No shit! How much is there?" Tom was giddy.

"I have no idea. The inside of the tomb is huge. After I got past the discouragers, I couldn't believe what I was seeing. There are tons and tons of bars like I'm bringing, statues, paintings, all kinds of things."

"Fantastic!" Tom thought for a second. "What do you mean discouragers?"

"There were the remains of what was left of

seven soldiers stacked at the tombs opening.

Probably, they were the detail that moved the treasure here. Dead men tell no tales, I'd guess. The person that planned to hide the treasure did a hell of a job. He came up with the idea of rigging a wing siren from an old Stuka dive bomber in a pipe, so one end opened on the surface. When the wind blows the ghosts scream. Nice touch. It's kept the locals petrified of this place. A wall of skulls had been constructed across the tomb opening. I removed enough to see if there was anything behind them. They were three deep, but once I removed enough to shine my flashlight in, it lit up enough to make me realize everything was true and that we have a hell of a problem. How are we going to remove it and get it into Switzerland? I've got things covered there."

"That's not a bad problem to have. Hey, Harper. You'll find a way. I believe you can do anything."

"Remember that the next time you bitch when I want you to do something you don't like. I've already figured how. The question is: can I assemble what I need in a reasonable period of time." Harper stopped talking for several seconds then said, "I can't carry anymore. What a shame, the suitcase isn't near full."

"What do you want me to do?" Mooney asked.

"See where you can buy several cases of black spray paint, a dozen fifty-pound bags of plaster, an acetylene torch, and an all-terrain vehicle." Harper hesitated. "Call Nadine Barlow and tell her that she's about to become very, very wealthy. Oh, and have her tell Benny Dupree he's paid in full."

"What's next?"

"Whatever we want, Tom. Whatever we want!'

About Author DL Havlin

DL Havlin is an eclectic author whose varied experiences and background provide him with a memory chest full of material for writing his novels. He graduated from the University of Cincinnati and attended pre-law at Rollins.

His life has been as varied as his novels. Havlin's occupations have included tasks from systems analyst to worldwide customer service director and from licensed boat captain to football coach. He's in demand as a speaker and seminar presenter for relationship and writing skills.

Havlin's passion for fishing, hunting, Florida's wildernesses, and its historical heritage, frequently appear in his writing and his speaking engagements. His tales are just as likely to be set in Kiev, Singapore, London, Saxonhausen or other places in the over eighty countries he's visited. Their people and customs resonate in his novels. Known for creating memorable characters, his interjection of humor, and his carefully crafted plots, reading a DL Havlin book is always a pleasurable experience.

DL Havlin

Titles by DL Havlin

Turtle Point
The Bait Man
Escaping Skeletons
A Place No One Should Go
The Hangin' Oak
Mystery/Suspense

Blue Water, Red Blood
The Cross on Cotton Creek
Historical fiction

Bully Route Home
Literary, Mainstream fiction

September on Echo Creek
Woman's mainstream

StoryTime-R
Short story collection

Made in United States
Orlando, FL
21 November 2022

24822631R00257